PENGUIN CRIME FICTION

Editor: Julian Symons

RAFFLES

Ernest William Hornung was born in Middlesbrough on 7 June 1866. He was educated at Uppingham School, and at the age of eighteen he went to Australia, where he spent two years. On his return he took up journalism, and spent the rest of his life writing. His first book, *A Bride from the Bush*, was published in 1890, *Raffles* in 1899, *Mr Justice Raffles* in 1909, and his last book, *Notes of a Camp-Follower*, in 1919. Stingaree, a character very like Raffles, but operating in Australia, appeared in 1905 in *Stingaree, A Thief in the Night*. Hornung wrote a large number of other novels, and a book of verse, *The Young Guard*. He lived at Partridge Green, in Sussex, and died on 22 March 1921.

RAFFLES

E. W. HORNUNG

PENGUIN BOOKS

Penguin Books Ltd, Harmondsworth, Middlesex, England
Penguin Books, 625 Madison Avenue, New York, New York 10022, U.S.A.
Penguin Books Australia Ltd, Ringwood, Victoria, Australia
Penguin Books Canada Ltd, 41 Steelcase Road West, Markham, Ontario, Canada
Penguin Books (N.Z.) Ltd, 182–190 Wairau Road, Auckland 10, New Zealand

—

First published 1899
Published in Penguin Books 1936
Reprinted 1948, 1950, 1952, 1960, 1976

—

Made and printed in Great Britain by
Hazell Watson & Viney Ltd,
Aylesbury, Bucks
Set in Linotype Times

CONTENTS

THE IDES OF MARCH

IT was about half-past twelve when I returned to the Albany as a last desperate resort. The scene of my disaster was much as I had left it. The baccarat-counters still strewed the table, with the empty glasses and the loaded ash-trays. A window had been opened to let the smoke out, and was letting in the fog instead. Raffles himself had merely discarded his dining-jacket for one of his innumerable blazers. Yet he arched his eyebrows as though I had dragged him from his bed.

'Forgotten something?' said he, when he saw me on the mat.

'No,' said I, pushing past him without ceremony. And I led the way into his room with an impudence amazing to myself.

'Not come back for your revenge, have you? Because I'm afraid I can't give it you single-handed. I was sorry myself that the others – – '

We were face to face by his fireside, and I cut him short.

'Raffles,' said I, 'you may well be surprised at my coming back in this way and at this hour. I hardly know you. I was never in your rooms before to-night. But I fagged for you at school, and you said you remembered me. Of course that's no excuse; but will you listen to me – for two minutes?'

In my emotion I had at first to struggle for every word; but his face reassured me as I went on, and I was not mistaken in its expression.

'Certainly, my dear fellow,' said he, 'as many minutes as you like. Have a Sullivan and sit down.' And he handed me his silver cigarette-case.

'No,' said I, finding a full voice as I shook my head; 'no, I won't smoke, and I won't sit down, thank you. Nor will you ask me to do either when you've heard what I have to say.'

'Really?' said he, lighting his own cigarette with one clear blue eye upon me. 'How do you know?'

'Because you will probably show me the door,' I cried bitterly; 'and you'll be justified in doing it! But it's no good beat-

9

ing about the bush. You know I dropped over two hundred just now?'

He nodded.

'I hadn't the money in my pocket.'

'I remember.'

'But I had my cheque-book, and I wrote each of you a cheque at that desk.'

'Well?'

'Not one of them was worth the paper it was written on, Raffles. I am overdrawn already at my bank!'

'Surely only for the moment?'

'No. I have spent everything.'

'But somebody told me you were so well off. I heard you had come in for money?'

'So I did. Three years ago. It has been my curse; now it's all gone – every penny! Yes, I've been a fool; there never was nor will be such a fool as I've been ... Isn't this enough for you? Why don't you turn me out?' He was walking up and down with a very long face instead.

'Couldn't your people do anything?' he asked at length.

'Thank God,' I cried, 'I have no people! I was an only child. I came in for everything there was. My one comfort is that they're gone, and will never know.'

I cast myself into a chair and hid my face. Raffles continued to pace the rich carpet that was of a piece with everything else in his rooms. There was no variation in his soft and even footfalls.

'You used to be a literary little cuss,' he said at length; 'didn't you edit the mag. before you left? Anyway I recollect fagging you to do my verses; and literature of sorts is the very thing nowadays; any fool can make a living at it.'

I shook my head. 'Any fool couldn't write off my debts,' said I.

'You have a flat somewhere?' he went on.

'Yes, in Mount Street.'

'Well, what about the furniture?'

I laughed aloud in my misery 'There's been a bill of sale on every stick for months!' And at that Raffles stood still, with raised eyebrows and stern eyes that I could meet the better now that he knew the worst; then, with a shrug, he resumed his walk, and for some minutes neither of us spoke. But in his handsome unmoved face I read my fate and death warrant; and with every breath I cursed my folly and my cowardice in coming to him at all. Because he had been kind to me at school, when he was captain of the eleven, and I his fag, I had dared to look for kindness from him now; because I was ruined, and he rich enough to play cricket all the summer, and do nothing for the rest of the year, I had fatuously counted on his mercy, his sympathy, his help! Yes, I had relied on him in my heart, for all my outward diffidence and humility; and I was rightly served. There was as little of mercy as of sympathy in that curling nostril, that rigid jaw, that cold blue eye which never glanced my way. I caught up my hat. I blundered to my feet. I would have gone without a word, but Raffles stood between me and the door.

'Where are you going?' said he.

'That's my business,' I replied. 'I won't trouble you any more.'

'Then how am I to help you?'

'I didn't ask your help.'

'Then why come to me?'

'Why, indeed!' I echoed. 'Will you let me pass?'

'Not until you tell me where you are going and what you mean to do.'

'Can't you guess?' I cried. And for many seconds we stood staring in each other's eyes.

'Have you got the pluck?' said he, breaking the spell in a tone so cynical that it brought my last drop of blood to the boil.

'You shall see,' said I, as I stepped back and whipped the pistol from my overcoat pocket. 'Now, will you let me pass or shall I do it here?'

The barrel touched my temple, and my thumb the trigger. Mad with excitement as I was, ruined, dishonoured, and now finally determined to make an end of my misspent life, my only surprise to this day is that I did not do so then and there. The despicable satisfaction of involving another in one's destruction added its miserable appeal to my baser egoism; and had fear or horror flown to my companion's face, I shudder to think I might have died diabolically happy with that look for my last impious consolation. It was the look that came instead which held my hand. Neither fear nor horror was in it; only wonder, admiration, and such a measure of pleased expectancy as caused me after all to pocket my revolver with an oath.

'You devil!' I said. 'I believe you wanted me to do it!'

'Not quite,' was the reply, made with a little start, and a change of colour that came too late. 'To tell you the truth, though, I half thought you meant it, and I was never more fascinated in my life. I never dreamt you had such stuff in you, Bunny! No, I'm hanged if I let you go now. And you'd better not try that game again, for you won't catch me stand and look on a second time. We must think of some way out of the mess. I had no idea you were a chap of that sort! There, let me have the gun.'

One of his hands fell kindly on my shoulder, while the other slipped into my overcoat pocket, and I suffered him to deprive me of my weapon without a murmur. Nor was this simply because Raffles had the power of making himself irresistible at will. He was beyond comparison the most masterful man whom I have ever known; yet my acquiescence was due to more than the mere subjection of the weaker nature to the stronger. The forlorn hope which had brought me to the Albany was turned as by magic into an almost staggering sense of safety. Raffles would help me after all! A. J. Raffles would be my friend! It was as though all the world had come round suddenly to my side; so far, therefore, from resisting his action, I caught and clasped his hand with a fervour as uncontrollable as the frenzy which had preceded it.

'God bless you!' I cried. 'Forgive me for everything. I will tell you the truth. I did think you might help me in my extremity, though I well knew that I had no claim upon you. Still – for the old school's sake – the sake of old times – I thought you might give me another chance. If you wouldn't, I meant to blow out my brains – and will still if you change your mind.'

In truth I fear that it was changing, with his expression, even as I spoke, and in spite of his kindly tone and kindlier use of my old school nickname. His next words showed me my mistake.

'What a boy it is for jumping to conclusions! I have my vices, Bunny, but backing and filling is not one of them. Sit down, my good fellow, and have a cigarette to soothe your nerves. I insist. Whisky? The worst thing for you; here's some coffee that I was brewing when you came in. Now listen to me. You speak of "another chance." What do you mean? Another chance at baccarat? Not if I know it! You think the luck must turn; suppose it didn't? We should only have made bad worse. No, my dear chap, you've plunged enough. Do you put yourself in my hands or do you not? Very well then, you plunge no more, and I undertake not to present my cheque. Unfortunately, there are the other men; and still more unfortunately, Bunny, I'm as hard up at this moment as you are yourself!'

It was my turn to stare at Raffles. 'You?' I vociferated. 'You hard up? How am I to sit here and believe that?'

'Did I refuse to believe it of you?' he returned, smiling. 'And, with your own experience, do you think that because a fellow has rooms in this place, and belongs to a club or two, and plays a little cricket, he must necessarily have a balance at the bank? I tell you, my dear man, that at this moment I'm as hard up as ever you were. I have nothing but my wits to live on – absolutely nothing else. It was as necessary for me to win some money this evening as it was for you. We're in the same boat, Bunny, we'd better pull together.'

'Together!' I jumped at it. 'I'll do anything in this world for you, Raffles,' I said, 'if you really mean that you won't give me away. Think of anything you like and I'll do it! I was a desperate man when I came here, and I'm just as desperate now. I don't mind what I do if only I can get out of this without a scandal.'

Again I see him, leaning back in one of the luxurious chairs with which his room was furnished. I see his indolent, athletic figure; his pale, sharp, clean-shaven features; his curly black hair; his strong unscrupulous mouth. And again I feel the clear beam of his wonderful eye, cold and luminous as a star, shining into my brain – sifting the very secrets of my heart.

'I wonder if you mean all that!' he said at length. 'You do in your present mood; but who can back his mood to last? Still, there's hope when a chap takes that tone. Now I think of it, too,

13

you were a plucky little devil at school; you once did me rather a good turn, I recollect. Remember it, Bunny? Well, wait a bit, and perhaps I'll be able to do you a better one. Give me time to think.'

He got up, lit a fresh cigarette, and fell to pacing the room once more, but with a slower and more thoughtful step, and for a much longer period than before. Twice he stopped at my chair as though on the point of speaking, but each time he checked himself and resumed his stride in silence. Once he threw up the window, which he had shut some time since, and stood for some moments leaning out into the fog which filled the Albany courtyard. Meanwhile a clock on the chimney-piece struck one, and one again for the half-hour, without a word between us.

Yet I not only kept my chair with patience, but I acquired an incongruous equanimity in that half-hour. Insensibly I had shifted my burden to the broad shoulders of this splendid friend, and my thoughts wandered with my eyes as the minutes passed. The room was the good-sized, square one, with the folding doors, the marble mantelpiece, and the gloomy, old-fashioned distinction peculiar to the Albany. It was charmingly furnished and arranged with the right amount of negligence and the right amount of taste. What struck me most, however, was the absence of the usual insignia of a cricketer's den. Instead of the conventional rack of war-worn bats, a carved oak bookcase, with every shelf in a litter, filled the better part of one wall; and where I looked for cricketing groups, I found reproductions of such words as 'Love and Death' and 'The Blessed Damozel,' in dusty frames and different parallels. The man might have been a minor poet instead of an athlete of the first water. But there had always been a fine streak of æstheticism in his complex composition; some of these very pictures I had myself dusted in his study at school; and they set me thinking of yet another of his many sides – and of the little incident to which he had just referred.

Everybody knows how largely the tone of a public school depends on that of the eleven, and on the character of the captain of cricket in particular; and I have never heard it denied that in A. J. Raffles's time our tone was good, or that such influence as he troubled to exert was on the side of the angels. Yet it was whispered in the school that he was in the habit of parading the town at night in loud checks and a false beard. It was whispered, and disbelieved. I alone knew it for a fact; for night after night had I pulled the rope up after him when the rest of the dormitory was asleep, and kept awake by the hour to let it down again on a given signal. Well, one night he was over-bold, and within an ace of ignominious expulsion in the hey-day of his fame. Consummate daring and extraordinary nerve on his part, aided, doubtless, by some little presence of mind on mine, averted that untoward result; and no more need be said of a discreditable incident. But I cannot pretend to have forgotten it in throwing myself on this man's mercy in my desperation. And I was wondering how much of his leniency was owing to the fact that Raffles had not forgotten it either, when he stopped and stood over my chair once more.

'I've been thinking of that night we had the narrow squeak,' he began. 'Why do you start?'

'I was thinking of it too.'

He smiled, as though he had read my thoughts.

'Well, you were the right sort of little beggar then, Bunny; you didn't talk and you didn't flinch. You asked no questions and you told no tales. I wonder if you're like that now?'

'I don't know,' said I, slightly puzzled by his tone. 'I've made such a mess of my own affairs that I trust myself about as little as I'm likely to be trusted by anybody else. Yet I never in my life went back on a friend. I will say that; otherwise perhaps I mightn't be in such a hole to-night.'

'Exactly,' said Raffles, nodding to himself, as though in assent to some hidden train of thought; 'exactly what I remember of you, and I'll bet it's as true now as it was ten years ago. We don't alter, Bunny. We only develop. I suppose neither you nor I are really altered since you used to let down that rope and I used to come up it hand over hand. You would stick at nothing for a pal – what?'

'At nothing in this world,' I was pleased to cry.

'Not even at a crime?' said Raffles, smiling.

I stopped to think, for his tone had changed, and I felt sure he was chaffing me. Yet his eye seemed as much in earnest as

15

ever, and for my part I was in no mood for reservations.

'No, not even at that,' I declared; 'name your crime, and I'm your man.'

He looked at me one moment in wonder, and another moment in doubt; then turned the matter off with a shake of his head, and the little cynical laugh that was all his own.

'You're a nice chap, Bunny! A real desperate character – what? Suicide one moment, and any crime I like the next! What you want is a drag, my boy, and you did well to come to a decent law-abiding citizen with a reputation to lose. None the less we must have that money to-night – by hook or crook.'

'To-night, Raffles?'

'The sooner the better. Every hour after ten o'clock to-morrow morning is an hour of risk. Let one of those cheques get round to your own bank, and you and it are dishonoured together. No, we must raise the wind to-night and re-open your account first thing to-morrow. And I rather think I know where the wind can be raised.'

'At two o'clock in the morning?'

'Yes.'

'But how – but where – at such an hour?'

'From a friend of mine here in Bond Street.'

'He must be a very intimate friend.'

'Intimate's not the word. I have the run of his place and a latchkey all to myself.'

'You would knock him up at this hour of the night?'

'If he's in bed.'

'And it's essential that I should go with you?'

'Absolutely.'

'Then I must; but I'm bound to say I don't like the idea, Raffles.'

'Do you prefer the alternative?' asked my companion, with a sneer. 'No, hang it, that's unfair!' he cried apologetically in the same breath. 'I quite understand. It's a beastly ordeal. But it would never do for you to stay outside. I tell you what, you shall have a peg before we start – just one. There's the whisky, there's the siphon, and I'll be putting on an overcoat while you help yourself.'

Well, I dare say I did so with some freedom, for this plan of

16

his was not the less distasteful to me from its apparent inevitability. I must own, however, that it possessed fewer terrors before my glass was empty. Meanwhile Raffles rejoined me, with a covert coat over his blazer, and a soft felt hat set carelessly on the curly head he shook with a smile as I passed him the decanter.

'When we come back,' said he. 'Work first, play afterwards. Do you see what day it is?' he added, tearing a leaflet from a Shakespearean calendar as I drained my glass. 'March 15th. "The Ides of March, the Ides of March, remember." Eh, Bunny, my boy? You won't forget them, will you?'

And, with a laugh, he threw some coals on the fire before turning down the gas like a careful householder. So we went out together as the clock on the chimney-piece was striking two.

II

Piccadilly was a trench of raw white fog, rimmed with blurred street-lamps, and lined with a thin coating of adhesive mud. We met no other wayfarers on the deserted flagstones, and were ourselves favoured with a very hard stare from the constable of the beat, who, however, touched his helmet on recognising my companion.

'You see, I'm known to the police,' laughed Raffles as we passed on. 'Poor devils, they've got to keep their weather eye open on a night like this! A fog may be a bore to you and me, Bunny, but it's a perfect godsend to the criminal classes, especially so late in their season. Here we are, though – and I'm hanged if the beggar isn't in bed and asleep after all!'

We had turned into Bond Street, and had halted on the kerb a few yards down on the right. Raffles was gazing up at some windows across the road, windows barely discernible through the mist, and without the glimmer of a light to throw them out. They were over a jeweller's shop, as I could see by the peephole in the shop door, and the bright light burning within. But the entire 'upper part', with the private street door next to the shop, was black and blank as the sky itself.

'Better give it up for to-night,' I urged. 'Surely the morning will be time enough!'

'Not a bit of it,' said Raffles. 'I have his key. We'll surprise him. Come along.'

And seizing my right arm, he hurried me across the road, opened the door with his latchkey, and in another moment had shut it swiftly but softly behind us. We stood together in the dark. Outside, a measured step was approaching; we had heard it through the fog as we crossed the street; now, as it drew nearer, my companion's fingers tightened on my arm.

'It may be the chap himself,' he whispered. 'He's the devil of a night-bird. Not a sound, Bunny! We'll startle the life out of him. Ah!'

The measured step had passed without a pause. Raffles drew a deep breath, and his singular grip of me slowly relaxed.

'But still, not a sound,' he continued in the same whisper; 'we'll take a rise out of him, wherever he is! Slip off your shoes and follow me.'

Well, you may wonder at my doing so, but you can never have met A. J. Raffles. Half his power lay in a conciliating trick of sinking the commander in the leader. And it was impossible not to follow one who led with such a zest. You might question, but you followed first. So now, when I heard him kick off his own shoes, I did the same, and was on the stairs at his heels before I realised what an extraordinary way was this of approaching a stranger for money in the dead of night. But obviously Raffles and he were on exceptional terms of intimacy, and I could not but infer that they were in the habit of playing practical jokes on each other.

We groped our way so slowly upstairs that I had time to make more than one note before we reached the top. The stair was uncarpeted. The spread fingers of my right hand encountered nothing on the damp wall: those of my left trailed through a dust that could be felt on the banisters. An eerie sensation had been upon me since we entered the house. It increased with every step we climbed. What hermit were we going to startle in his cell?

We came to a landing. The banisters led us to the left, and to the left again. Four steps more, and we were on another and a longer landing, and suddenly a match blazed from the back. I never heard it struck. Its flash was blinding. When my eyes became accustomed to the light, there was Raffles holding up the match with one hand, and shading it with the other, between bare boards, stripped walls, and the open doors of empty rooms.

'Where have you brought me?' I cried. 'The house is unoccupied?'

'Hush! Wait!' he whispered, and he led the way into one of the empty rooms. His match went out as we crossed the threshold, and he struck another without the slightest noise. Then he stood with his back to me, fumbling with something that I could not see. But, when he threw the second match away, there was some other light in its stead, and a slight smell of oil. I stepped forward to look over his shoulder, but before I could do so he had turned and flashed a tiny lantern in my face.

'What's this?' I gasped. 'What rotten trick are you going to play?'

'It's played,' he answered, with his quiet laugh.

'On me?'

'I'm afraid so, Bunny.'

'Is there no one in the house, then?'

'No one but ourselves.'

'So it was mere chaff about your friend in Bond Street who could let us have that money?'

'Not altogether. It's quite true that Danby is a friend of mine.'

'Danby?'

'The jeweller underneath.'

'What do you mean?' I whispered, trembling like a leaf as his meaning dawned upon me. 'Are you going to get the money from the jeweller?'

'Well, not exactly.'

'What then?'

'The equivalent – from his shop.'

There was no need for another question. I understood everything but my own density. He had given me a dozen hints, and I had taken none. And there I stood staring at him, in that empty room; and there he stood with his dark lantern laughing at me.

'A burglar!' I gasped. 'You – you!'

'I told you I lived by my wits.'

'Why couldn't you tell me what you were going to do? Why couldn't you trust me? Why must you lie?' I demanded, piqued to the quick for all my horror.

'I wanted to tell you,' said he. 'I was on the point of telling you more than once. You may remember how I sounded you about crime, though you have probably forgotten what you said yourself. I didn't think you meant it at the time, but I thought I'd put you to the test. Now I see you didn't, and I don't blame you. I only am to blame. Get out of it, my dear boy, as quick as you can; leave it to me. You won't give me away, whatever else you do!'

Oh, his cleverness! His fiendish cleverness! Had he fallen back on threats, coercion, sneers, all might have been different even then. But he set me free to leave him in the lurch. He would not blame me. He did not even bind me to secrecy; he trusted me. He knew my weakness and my strength, and was playing on both with his master's touch.

'Not so fast,' said I. 'Did I put this into your head, or were you going to do it in any case?'

'Not in any case,' said Raffles. 'It's true I've had the key for days, but when I won to-night I thought of chucking it; for, as a matter of fact, it's not a one-man job.'

'That settles it. I'm your man.'

'You mean it?'

'Yes – for to-night.'

'Good old Bunny,' he murmured, holding the lantern for one moment to my face; the next he was explaining his plans, and I was nodding, as though we had been fellow-cracksmen all our days.

'I know the shop,' he whispered, 'because I've got a few things there. I know this upper part too; it's been to let for a month, and I got an order to view, and took a cast of the key before using it. The one thing I don't know is how to make a connection between the two; at present there's none. We may make it up here, though I rather fancy the basement myself. If you wait a minute I'll tell you.'

He set his lantern on the floor, and crept to a back window, and opened it with scarcely a sound; only to return shaking his head, after shutting the window with the same care.

'That was our one chance,' said he, 'a back window above a back window; but it's too dark to see anything, and we daren't show an outside light. Come down after me to the basement; and remember, though there's not a soul on the premises, you can't make too little noise. There – there – listen to that!'

It was the measured tread that we had heard before on the flagstones outside. Raffles darkened his lantern, and again we stood motionless till it had passed

'Either a policeman,' he muttered, 'or a watchman that all these jewellers run between them. The watchman's the man for us to watch; he's simply paid to spot this kind of thing.'

We crept very gingerly down the stairs, which creaked a bit in spite of us, and we picked up our shoes in the passage; then down some narrow stone steps, at the foot of which Raffles showed his light, and put on his shoes once more, bidding me do the same in rather a louder tone than he had permitted himself to employ overhead. We were now considerably below the level of the street, in a small space with as many doors as it had sides. Three were ajar, and we saw through them into empty cellars; but in the fourth a key was turned and a bolt drawn; and this one presently let us out into the bottom of a deep square well of fog. A similar door faced it across this area, and Raffles had the lantern close against it, and was hiding the light with his body, when a short and sudden crash made my heart stand still. Next moment I saw the door wide open, and Raffles standing within and beckoning me with a jemmy.

'Door number one,' he whispered. 'Deuce knows how many more there'll be, but I know of two at least. We won't have to make much noise over them, either; down here there's less risk.'

We were now at the bottom of the exact fellow to the narrow stone stair which we had just descended; the yard, or well, being the one part common to both the private and the business premises. But this flight led to no open passage; instead, a singularly solid mahogany door confronted us at the top.

'I thought so,' muttered Raffles, handing me the lantern, and pocketing a bunch of skeleton keys, after tampering for a few minutes with the lock. 'It'll be an hour's work to get through that!'

'Can't you pick it?'

'No. I know these locks. It's no use trying. We must cut it out, and it'll take us an hour.'

It took us forty-seven minutes by my watch; or rather it took Raffles, and never in my life have I seen anything more deliberately done. My part was simply to stand by with the dark lantern in one hand, and a small bottle of rock-oil in the other. Raffles had produced a pretty embroidered case, intended obviously for his razors, but filled instead with the tools of his secret trade, including the rock-oil. From this case he selected a bit, capable of drilling a hole an inch in diameter, and fitted it to a small but very strong steel brace. Then he took off his covert coat and his blazer, spread them neatly on the top step – knelt on them – turned up his shirt-cuffs – and went to work with brace-and-bit near the keyhole. But first he oiled the bit to minimise the noise, and this he did invariably before beginning a fresh hole, and often in the middle of one. It took thirty-two separate borings to cut round that lock.

I noticed that through the first circular orifice Raffles thrust a forefinger; then, as the circle became an ever-lengthening oval, he got his hand through up to the thumb, and I heard him swear softly to himself.

'I was afraid so!'

'What is it?'

'An iron gate on the other side!'

'How on earth are we to get through that?' I asked in dismay.

'Pick the lock. But there may be two. In that case they'll be top and bottom, and we shall have two fresh holes to make, as the door opens inwards. It won't open two inches as it is.'

I confess I did not feel sanguine about the lock-picking, seeing that one lock had baffled us already; and my disappointment and impatience must have been a revelation to me had I stopped to think. The truth is that I was entering into our nefarious undertaking with an involuntary zeal of which I was myself quite unconscious at the time. The romance and the peril of the whole proceeding held me spellbound and entranced. My moral sense and my sense of fear were stricken

22

by a common paralysis. And there I stood, shining my light and holding my phial with a keener interest than I had ever brought to any honest avocation. And there knelt A. J. Raffles, with his black hair tumbled, and the same watchful, quiet, determined half-smile with which I have seen him send down over after over in a county match!

At last the chain of holes was complete, the lock wrenched out bodily, and a splendid bare arm plunged up to the shoulder through the aperture, and through the bars of the iron gate beyond.

'Now,' whispered Raffles, 'if there's only one lock it'll be in the middle. Joy! Here it is! Only let me pick it, and we're through at last.'

He withdrew his arm, a skeleton key was selected from the bunch, and then back went his arm to the shoulder. It was a breathless moment. I heard the heart throbbing in my body, the very watch ticking in my pocket, and ever and anon the tinkle-tinkle of the skeleton key. Then – at last – there came a single unmistakable click. In another minute the mahogany door and the iron gate yawned behind us, and Raffles was sitting on an office table, wiping his face, with the lantern throwing a steady beam by his side.

We were now in a bare and roomy lobby behind the shop, but separated therefrom by an iron curtain, the very sight of which filled me with despair. Raffles, however, did not appear in the least depressed, but hung up his coat and hat on some pegs in the lobby before examining this curtain with his lantern.

'That's nothing,' said he, after a minute's inspection; 'we'll be through that in no time, but there's a door on the other side which may give us trouble.'

'Another door!' I groaned. 'And how do you mean to tackle this thing?'

'Prise it up with the jointed jemmy. The weak point of these iron curtains is the leverage you can get from below. But it makes a noise, and this is where you're coming in, Bunny; this is where I couldn't do without you. I must have you overhead to knock through when the street's clear. I'll come with you and show a light.'

Well, you may imagine how little I liked the prospect of this lonely vigil; and yet there was something very stimulating in the vital responsibility which it involved. Hitherto I had been a mere spectator. Now I was to take part in the game. And the fresh excitement made me more than ever insensible to those considerations of conscience and of safety which were already as dead nerves in my breast.

So I took my post without a murmur in the front room above the shop. The fixtures had been left for the refusal of the in-coming tenant, and fortunately for us they included Venetian blinds, which were already down. It was the simplest matter in the world to stand peeping through the laths into the street, to beat twice with my foot when anybody was approaching, and once when all was clear again. The noises that even I could hear below, with the exception of one metallic crash at the beginning, were indeed incredibly slight; but they ceased alto-gether at each double rap from my toe, and a policeman passed quite half a dozen times beneath my eyes, and the man whom I took to be the jeweller's watchman oftener still, during the better part of an hour that I spent at the window. Once, indeed, my heart was in my mouth, but only once. It was when the watchman stopped and peered through the peep-hole into the lighted shop. I waited for his whistle. I waited for the gallows or the gaol! But my signals had been studiously obeyed, and the man passed on in undisturbed serenity. In the end I had a sig-nal in my turn, and retraced my steps with lighted matches down the broad stairs, down the narrow ones, across the area, and up into the lobby where Raffles awaited me with an out-stretched hand.

'Well done, my boy!' said he. 'You're the same good man in a pinch, and you shall have your reward. I've got a thousand pounds' worth if I've got a penn'orth. It's all in my pockets. And here's something else I found in this locker; very decent port and some cigars, meant for poor dear Danby's business friends. Take a pull, and you shall light up presently. I've found a lavatory, too, and we must have a wash-and-brush-up before we go, for I'm as black as your boot.'

The iron curtain was down, but he insisted on raising it until I could peep through the glass door on the other side and see his handiwork in the shop beyond. Here two electric lights were

24

left burning all night long, and in their cold white rays I could at first see nothing amiss. I looked along an orderly lane, an empty glass counter on my left, glass cupboards of untouched silver on my right, and facing me the filmy black-eye of the peep-hole that shone like a stage moon on the street. The counter had not been emptied by Raffles; its contents were in the Chubb's safe, which he had given up at a glance; nor had he looked at the silver, except to choose a cigarette-case for me. He had confined himself entirely to the shop window. This was in three compartments, each secured for the night by removable panels with separate locks. Raffles had removed them a few hours before their time, and the electric light shone on a corrugated shutter bare as the ribs of an empty carcase. Every article of value was gone from the one place which was invisible from the little window in the door; elsewhere all was as it had been left overnight. And but for a train of mangled doors behind the iron curtain, a bottle of wine and a cigar-box with which liberties had been taken, a rather black towel in the lavatory, a burnt match here and there, and our finger-marks on the dusty banisters, not a trace of our visit did we leave.

'Had it in my head for long?' said Raffles, as we strolled through the streets towards dawn, for all the world as though we were returning from a dance. 'No, Bunny, I never thought of it till I saw that upper part empty about a month ago, and bought a few things in the shop to get the lie of the land. That reminds me that I never paid for them; but, by Jove, I will tomorrow, and if that isn't poetic justice, what is? One visit showed me the possibilities of the place, but a second convinced me of its impossibilities without a pal. So I had practically given up the idea, when you came along on the very night and in the very plight for it! But here we are at the Albany, and I hope there's some fire left; for I don't know how you feel, Bunny, but for my part I'm as cold as Keats' owl.'

He could think of Keats on his way from a felony! He could hanker for his fireside like another. Flood-gates were loosened within me, and the plain English of our adventure rushed over me as cold as ice. Raffles was a burglar. I had helped to commit one burglary, therefore I was a burglar too. Yet I could stand and warm myself by his fire and watch him empty his pockets, as though we had done nothing wonderful or wicked!

My blood froze. My heart sickened. My brain whirled. How I had liked this villain! How I had admired him! Now my liking and admiration must turn to loathing disgust. I waited for the change. I longed to feel it in my heart. But – I longed and waited in vain!

I saw he was emptying his pockets; the table sparkled with their hoard. Rings by the dozen, diamonds by the score; bracelets, pendants, aigrettes, necklaces; pearls, rubies, amethysts, sapphires; and diamonds always, diamonds in everything, flashing bayonets of light, dazzling me – blinding me – making me disbelieve because I could no longer forget. Last of all came no gem, indeed, but my own revolver from an inner pocket. And that struck a chord. I suppose I said something – my hand flew out. I can see Raffles now, as he looked at me once more with a high arch over each clear eye. I can see him pick out the cartridges with his quiet cynical smile, before he would give me my pistol back again.

'You mayn't believe it, Bunny,' said he, 'but I never carried a loaded one before. On the whole I think it gives one confidence. Yet it would be very awkward if anything went wrong; one might use it, and that's not the game at all, though I have often thought that the murderer who has just done the trick must have great sensations before things get too hot for him. Don't look so distressed, my dear chap. I've never had those sensations, and I don't suppose I ever shall.'

'But this much you have done before?' said I hoarsely.

'Before? My dear Bunny, you offend me! Did it look like a first attempt? Of course I have done it before.'

'Often?'

'Well – no. Not often enough to destroy the charm, at all events; never, as a matter of fact, unless I'm cursedly hard up. Did you hear about the Thimbleby diamonds? Well, that was the last time – and a poor lot of paste they were. Then there was the little business of the Dormer house-boat at Henley last year. That was mine also – such as it was. I've never brought off a really big *coup* yet; when I do I shall chuck it up.'

Yes, I remember both cases very well. To think that he was

their author! It was incredible, outrageous, inconceivable. Then my eyes would fall upon the table, twinkling and glittering in a hundred places, and incredulity was at an end.

'How came you to begin? I asked, as curiosity overcame mere wonder, and a fascination for his career gradually wove itself into my fascination for the man.

'Ah! that's a long story, said Raffles. 'It was in the Colonies, when I was out there playing cricket. It's too long a story to tell you now, but I was in much the same fix that you were in to-night, and it was my only way out. I never meant it for anything more; but I'd tasted blood, and it was all over with me. Why should I work when I could steal? Why settle down to some humdrum uncongenial billet, when excitement, romance, danger, and a decent living were all going begging together? Of course, it's very wrong, but we can't all be moralists, and the distribution of wealth is very wrong to begin with. Besides, you're not at it all the time. I'm sick of quoting Gilbert's lines to myself, but they're profoundly true. I only wonder if you'll like the life as much as I do!'

'Like it?' I cried. 'Not I! It's no life for me. Once is enough!'

'You wouldn't give me a hand another time?'

'Don't ask me, Raffles. Don't ask me, for God's sake!'

'Yet you said you would do anything for me! You asked me to name my crime! But I knew at the time you didn't mean it; you didn't go back on me to-night, and that ought to satisfy me, goodness knows! I suppose I'm ungrateful, and unreasonable, and all that. I ought to let it end at this. But you're the very man for me, Bunny, the – very – man! Just think how we got through to-night. Not a scratch – not a hitch! There's nothing very terrible in it, you see; there never would be, while we worked together.'

He was standing in front of me with a hand on either shoulder; he was smiling as he knew so well how to smile. I turned on my heel, planted my elbows on the chimney-piece, and my burning head between my hands. Next instant a still heartier hand had fallen on my back.

'All right, my boy! You are quite right and I'm worse than wrong. I'll never ask it again. Go, if you want to, and come again about midday for the cash. There was no bargain; but, of course, I'll get you out of your scrape – especially after the way you've stood by me to-night.'

I was round again with my blood on fire.

'I'll do it again,' I said through my teeth.

He shook his head. 'Not you,' he said, smiling quite good-humouredly at my insane enthusiasm.

'I will,' I cried with an oath. 'I'll lend you a hand as often as you like! What does it matter now? I've been in it once. I'll be in it again. I've gone to the devil anyhow. I can't go back, and wouldn't if I could. Nothing matters another rap! When you want me I'm your man.'

And that is how Raffles and I joined felonious forces on the Ides of March.

A COSTUME PIECE

LONDON was just then talking of one whose name is already a name and nothing more. Reuben Rosenthall had made his millions on the diamond fields of South Africa, and had come home to enjoy them according to his lights; how he went to work will scarcely be forgotten by any reader of the halfpenny evening papers, which revelled in endless anecdotes of his original indigence and present prodigality, varied with interesting particulars of the extraordinary establishment which the millionaire set up in St John's Wood. Here he kept a retinue of Kaffirs, who were literally his slaves; and hence he would sally with enormous diamonds in his shirt and on his finger, in the convoy of a prize-fighter of heinous repute, who was not, however, by any means the worst element in the Rosenthall *ménage*. So said common gossip; but the fact was sufficiently established by the interference of the police on at least one occasion, followed by certain magisterial proceedings which were reported with justifiable gusto and huge headlines in the newspapers aforesaid. And this was all one knew of Reuben Rosenthall up to the time when the Old Bohemian Club, having fallen on evil days, found it worth its while to organise a great dinner in honour of so wealthy an exponent of the club's principles. I was not at the banquet myself, but a member took Raffles, who told me all about it that very night.

'Most extraordinary show I ever went to in my life,' said he. 'As for the man himself – well, I was prepared for something grotesque, but the fellow fairly took my breath away. To begin with, he's the most astounding brute to look at, well over six feet, with a chest like a barrel and a great hook-nose, and the reddest hair and whiskers you ever saw. Drank like a fire-engine, but only got drunk enough to make us a speech that I wouldn't have missed for ten pounds. I'm only sorry you weren't there too, Bunny, old chap.'

I began to be sorry myself, for Raffles was anything but an excitable person, and never had I seen him so excited before.

Had he been following Rosenthall's example? His coming to
my rooms at midnight, merely to tell me about his dinner, was
in itself enough to excuse a suspicion which was certainly at
variance with my knowledge of A. J. Raffles.

'What did he say?' I inquired mechanically, divining some
subtler explanation of this visit, and wondering what on earth
it could be.

'Say?' cried Raffles. 'What did he not say? He boasted of
his race, he bragged of his riches, and he blackguarded society
for taking him up for his money and dropping him out of sheer
pique and jealousy because he had so much. He mentioned
names, too, with the most charming freedom, and swore he
was as good a man as the Old Country had to show – *pace* the
Old Bohemians. To prove it he pointed to a great diamond in
the middle of his shirt-front with a little finger loaded with
another just like it; which of our bloated princes could show
a pair like that? As a matter of fact, they seemed quite wonderful stones, with a curious purple gleam to them that must mean
a pot of money. But old Rosenthall swore he wouldn't take
fifty thousand pounds for the two, and wanted to know where
the other man was who went about with twenty-five thousand
in his shirt-front, and the other twenty-five on his little finger.
He didn't exist. If he did, he wouldn't have the pluck to wear
them. But he had – he'd tell us why. And before you could say
Jack Robinson he had whipped out a whacking great revolver!'

'Not at the table?'

'At the table! In the middle of his speech! But it was nothing to what he wanted to do. He actually wanted us to let him
write his name in bullets on the opposite wall to show us why
he wasn't afraid to go about in all his diamonds! That brute
Purvis, the prize-fighter who is his paid bully, had to bully his
master before he could be persuaded out of it. There was quite
a panic for the moment; one fellow was saying his prayers
under the table, and the waiters bolted to a man.'

'What a grotesque scene!'

'Grotesque enough, but I rather wish they had let him go the
whole hog and blaze away. He was as keen as knives to show
us how he could take care of his purple diamonds; and, do you
know, Bunny, I was as keen as knives to see.'

And Raffles leant towards me with a sly, slow smile that made the hidden meaning of his visit only too plain to me at last.

'So you think of having a try for his diamonds yourself?'

He shrugged his shoulders.

'It is horribly obvious, I admit. But – yes, I have set my heart upon them! To be quite frank, I have had them on my conscience for some time; one couldn't hear so much of the man, and his prize-fighter, and his diamonds, without feeling it a kind of duty to have a go for them; but when it comes to brandishing a revolver and practically challenging the world, the thing becomes inevitable. It is simply thrust upon one. I was fated to hear that challenge, Bunny, and I, for one, must take it up. I was only sorry I couldn't get on my hind legs and say so then and there.'

'Well,' I said, 'I don't see the necessity as things are with us; but, of course, I'm your man.'

My tone may have been half-hearted. I did my best to make it otherwise. But it was barely a month since our Bond Street exploit, and we certainly could have afforded to behave ourselves for some time to come. We had been getting along so nicely; by his advice I had scribbled a thing or two; inspired by Raffles, I had even done an article on our own jewel robbery; and for the moment I was quite satisfied with this sort of adventure. I thought we ought to know when we were well off and could see no point in our running fresh risks before we were obliged. On the other hand, I was anxious not to show the least disposition to break the pledge that I had given a month ago. But it was not on my manifest disinclination that Raffles fastened.

'Necessity, my dear Bunny? Does the writer only write when the wolf is at the door? Does the painter paint for bread alone? Must you and I be driven to crime like Tom of Bow and Dick of Whitechapel? You pain me, my dear chap; you needn't laugh, because you do. Art for art's sake is a vile catchword, but I confess it appeals to me. In this case my motives are absolutely pure, for I doubt if we shall ever be able to dispose of such peculiar stones. But if I don't have a try for them – after to-night, I shall never be able to hold up my head again.'

His eye twinkled, but it glittered too.

'We shall have our work cut out,' was all I said.

'And do you suppose I should be keen on it if we hadn't?' cried Raffles. 'My dear fellow, I would rob St Paul's Cathedral if I could, but I could no more scoop a till when the shop-walker wasn't looking than I could bag apples out of an old woman's basket. Even that little business last month was a sordid affair, but it was necessary, and I think its strategy re-deemed it to some extent. Now there's some credit, and more sport, in going where they boast they're on their guard against you. The Bank of England, for example, is the ideal crib; but that would need half a dozen of us with years to give to the job; and meanwhile Reuben Rosenthall is high enough game for you and me. We know he's armed. We know how Billy Purvis can fight. It'll be no soft thing, I grant you. But what of that, my good Bunny – what of that? A man's reach must exceed his grasp, dear boy, or what the dickens is a heaven for?'

'I would rather we didn't exceed ours just yet,' I answered, laughing, for his spirit was irresistible, and the plan was grow-ing upon me, despite my qualms.

'Trust me for that,' was his reply; 'I'll see you through. After all, I expect to find that the difficulties are nearly all on the surface. These fellows both drink like the devil, and that should simplify matters considerably. But we shall see, and we must take our time. There will probably turn out to be a dozen different ways in which the thing might be done, and we shall have to choose between them. It will mean watching the house for at least a week in any case; it may mean lots of other things that will take much longer; but give me a week, and I will tell you more. That's to say if you're really on?'

'Of course I am,' I replied indignantly. 'But why should I give you a week? Why shouldn't we watch the house together?'

'Because two eyes are as good as four, and take up less room. Never hunt in couples unless you're obliged. But don't look offended, Bunny; there'll be plenty for you to do when the time comes, that I promise you. You shall have your share of the fun, never fear, and a purple diamond all to yourself – if we're lucky.'

On the whole, however, this conversation left me less than lukewarm, and I still remember the depression which came over me when Raffles was gone. I saw the folly of the enterprise to which I had committed myself – the sheer, gratuitous, unnecessary folly of it. And the paradoxes in which Raffles revelled, and the frivolous casuistry which was nevertheless half sincere, and which his mere personality rendered wholly plausible at the moment of utterance, appealed very little to me when recalled in cold blood. I admired the spirit of pure mischief in which he seemed prepared to risk his liberty and his life, but I did not find it an infectious spirit on calm reflection. Yet the thought of withdrawal was not to be entertained for a moment. On the contrary, I was impatient of the delay ordained by Raffles; and, perhaps, no small part of my secret disaffection came of his galling determination to do without me until the last moment.

It made it no better that this was characteristic of the man and of his attitude towards me. For a month we had been, I suppose, the thickest thieves in all London, and yet our intimacy was curiously incomplete. With all his charming frankness, there was in Raffles a vein of capricious reserve which was perceptible enough to be very irritating. He had the instinctive secretiveness of the inveterate criminal. He would make mysteries of matters of common concern; for example, I never knew how or where he disposed of the Bond Street jewels, on the proceeds of which we were both still leading the outward lives of hundreds of other young fellows about town. He was consistently mysterious about that and other details, of which it seemed to me that I had already earned the right to know everything. I could not but remember how he had led me into my first felony, by means of a trick, while yet uncertain whether he could trust me or not. That I could no longer afford to resent, but I did resent his want of confidence in me now. I said nothing about it, but it rankled every day, and never more than in the week that succeeded the Rosenthall dinner. When I met Raffles at the club he would tell me nothing; when I went to his rooms he was out, or pretended to be. One day he told me he was getting on well, but slowly; it was a more ticklish game that he had thought; but when I began to ask questions he would say no more. Then and there, in my annoyance, I took my own decision. Since he would tell me nothing of the result of his vigils, I determined to keep one on my own account, and that very evening found my way to the millionaire's front gates.

The house he was occupying is, I believe, quite the largest in the St John's Wood district. It stands in the angle formed by two broad thoroughfares, neither of which, as it happens, is a bus route, and I doubt if many quieter spots exist within the four-mile radius. Quiet also was the great square house, in its garden of grass-plots and shrubs; the lights were low, the millionaire and his friends obviously spending their evening elsewhere. The garden walls were only a few feet high. In one there was a side door opening into a glass passage; in the other two five-barred grained-and-varnished gates, one at either end of the little semi-circular drive, and both wide open. So still was the place that I had a great mind to walk boldly in and learn something of the premises; in fact, I was on the point of doing so, when I heard a quick, shuffling step on the pavement behind me. I turned round and faced the dark scowl and the dirty clenched fists of a dilapidated tramp.

'You fool!' said he. 'You utter idiot!'

'Raffles!'

'That's it,' he whispered savagely; 'tell all the neighbourhood – give me away at the top of your voice!'

With that he turned his back upon me, and shambled down the road, shrugging his shoulders, and muttering to himself as though I had refused him alms. A few moments I stood astounded, indignant, at a loss; then I followed him. His feet trailed, his knees gave, his back was bowed, his head kept nodding; it was the gait of a man eighty years of age. Presently he waited for me midway between two lamp-posts. As I came up he was lighting rank tobacco, in a cutty pipe, with an evil-smelling match, and the flame showed me the suspicion of a smile.

'You must forgive my heat, Bunny, but it really was very foolish of you. Here am I trying every dodge – begging at the door one night – hiding in the shrubs the next – doing every mortal thing but stand and stare at the house as you went and

34

did. It's a costume piece, and in you rush in your ordinary
clothes. I tell you they're on the look-out for us night and day.
It's the toughest nut I ever tackled!'

'Well,' said I, 'if you had told me so before I shouldn't have
come. You told me nothing.'

He looked hard at me from under the broken rim of a
battered billycock.

'You're right,' he said at length. 'I've been too close. It's become second nature with me, when I've anything on. But there's
an end of it, Bunny, so far as you're concerned. I'm going home
now, and I want you to follow me; but for Heaven's sake keep
your distance, and don't speak to me again till I speak to you.
There – give me a start.' And he was off again, a decrepit vaga-
bond, with his hands in his pockets, his elbows squared, and
frayed coat-tails swinging raggedly from side to side.

I followed him to the Finchley Road. There he took an
omnibus, and I sat some rows behind him on the top, but not
far enough to escape the pest of his vile tobacco. That he could
carry his character-sketch to such a pitch – he would only
smoke one brand of cigarettes! It was the last, least touch of
the insatiable artist, and it charmed away what mortification
there still remained in me. Once more I felt the fascination of
a comrade who was for ever dazzling one with a fresh and unsuspected facet of his character.

As we neared Piccadilly I wondered what he would do. Surely he was not going into the Albany like that? No, he took
another omnibus to Sloane Street, I sitting behind him as before. At Sloane Street we changed again, and were presently in
the long lean artery of the King's Road. I was now all agog to
know our destination, nor was I kept many more minutes in
doubt. Raffles got down. I followed. He crossed the road and
disappeared up a dark turning. I pressed after him, and was in
time to see his coat-tails as he plunged into a still darker flagged
alley to the right. He was holding himself up and stepping out
like a young man once more; also, in some subtle way, he
already looked less disreputable. But I alone was there to see
him, the alley was absolutely deserted, and desperately dark. At
the farther end he opened a door with a latchkey, and it was
darker yet within.

Instinctively I drew back and heard him chuckle. We could no longer see each other.

'All right, Bunny! There's no hanky-panky this time. These are studios, my friend, and I'm one of the lawful tenants.'

Indeed, in another minute we were in a lofty room with sky-light, easels, dressing-cupboard, platform, and every other adjunct save the signs of actual labour. The first thing I saw, as Raffles lit the gas, was its reflection in his silk hat on the pegs beside the rest of his normal garments.

'Looking for the works of art?' continued Raffles, lighting a cigarette and beginning to divest himself of his rags. 'I'm afraid you won't find any, but there's the canvas I'm always going to make a start upon. I tell them I'm looking high and low for my ideal model. I have the stove lit on principle twice a week, and look in and leave a newspaper and a smell of Sulli-vans – how good they are after shag! Meanwhile I pay my rent and am a good tenant in every way; and it's a very useful little *pied-à-terre* – there's no saying how useful it might be at a pinch. As it is, the billycock comes in and the topper goes out, and nobody takes the slightest notice of either; at this time of night the chances are that there's not a soul in the building except ourselves.'

'You never told me you went in for disguises,' said I, watching him as he cleansed the grime from his face and hands.

'No, Bunny, I've treated you very shabbily all round. There was really no reason why I shouldn't have shown you this place a month ago, and yet there was no point in my doing so, and circumstances are just conceivable in which it would have suited us both for you to be in genuine ignorance of my where-abouts. I have something to sleep on, as you perceive, in case of need, and, of course, my name is not Raffles in the King's Road. So you will see that one might bolt farther and fare worse.'

'Meanwhile you use the place as a dressing-room?'

'It's my private pavilion,' said Raffles. 'Disguises? In some cases they're half the battle, and it's always pleasant to feel that, if the worst comes to the worst, you needn't necessarily be convicted under your own name. Then they're indispensable in dealing with the fences. I drive all my bargains in the tongue and raiment of Shoreditch. If I didn't there'd be the very devil to pay in blackmail. Now, this cupboard's full of all sorts of toggery. I tell the woman who cleans the room that it's for my models when I find 'em. By the way, I only hope I've got something that'll fit you, for you'll want a rig for to-morrow night.'

'To-morrow night!' I exclaimed. 'Why, what do you mean to do?'

'The trick,' said Raffles. 'I intended writing to you as soon as I got back to my rooms, to ask you to look me up to-morrow afternoon; then I was going to unfold my plan of campaign, and take you straight into action then and there. There's nothing like putting the nervous players in first; it's the sitting with their pads on that upsets their apple cart; that was another of my reasons for being so confoundedly close. You must try to forgive me. I couldn't help remembering how well you played up last trip, without any time to weaken on it beforehand. All I want is for you to be as cool and smart to-morrow night as you were then; though, by Jove, there's no comparison between the two cases!'

'I thought you would find it so.'

'You were right. I have. Mind you, I don't say this will be the tougher job all round; we shall probably get in without any difficulty at all; it's the getting out again that may flummux us. That's the worst of an irregular household!' cried Raffles, with quite a burst of virtuous indignation. 'I assure you, Bunny, I spent the whole of Monday night in the shrubbery of the garden next door looking over the wall, and, if you'll believe me, somebody was about all night long! I don't mean the Kaffirs. I don't believe they ever get to bed at all, poor devils! No, I mean Rosenthall himself, and that pasty-faced beast Purvis. They were up and drinking from midnight when they came in, to broad daylight, when I cleared out. Even then I left them sober enough to slang each other. By the way, they very nearly came to blows in the garden, within a few yards of me, and I heard something that might come in useful and make Rosenthall shoot crooked at a critical moment. You know what an I.D.B. is?'

'Illicit Diamond Buyer?'

'Exactly. Well, it seems that Rosenthall was one. He must

have let it out to Purvis in his cups. Anyhow, I heard Purvis taunting him with it, and threatening him with the breakwater at Cape Town; and I begin to think our friends are friend and foe. But about to-morrow night: there's nothing subtle in my plan. It's simply to get in while these fellows are out on the loose, and to lie low till they come back, and longer. If possible we must doctor the whisky. That would simplify the whole thing, though it's not a very sporting game to play; still, we must remember Rosenthall's revolver; we don't want him to sign his name on us. With all those Kaffirs about, however, it's ten to one on the whisky, and a hundred to one against us if we go looking for it. A brush with the heathen would spoil everything, if it did no more. Besides, there are the ladies – –'

'The deuce there are!'

'Ladies with an "i", and the very voices for raising Cain. I fear, I fear the clamour! It would be fatal to us. *Au contraire,* if we can manage to stow ourselves away unbeknownst, half the battle will be won. If Rosenthall turns in drunk, it's a purple diamond apiece. If he sits up sober, it may be a bullet instead. We will hope not, Bunny; and all the firing wouldn't be on one side; but it's on the knees of the gods.'

And so we left it when we shook hands in Piccadilly – not by any means as much later as I could have wished. Raffles would not ask me to his rooms that night. He said he made it a rule to have a long night before playing cricket and – other games. His final word to me was framed on the same principle.

'Mind, only one drink to-night, Bunny. Two at the outside – as you value your life – and mine!'

I remember my abject obedience, and the endless, sleepless night it gave me; and the roofs of the houses opposite standing out at last against the blue-grey London dawn. I wondered whether I should ever see another, and was very hard on myself for that little expedition which I had made on my own wilful account.

It was between eight and nine o'clock in the evening when we took up our position in the garden adjoining that of Reuben Rosenthall; the house itself was shut up, thanks to the outrageous libertine next door, who, by driving away the neighbours, had gone far towards delivering himself into our hands.

Practically secure from surprise on that side, we could watch our house under cover of a wall just high enough to see over, while a fair margin of shrubs in either garden afforded us additional protection. Thus entrenched we had stood an hour, watching a pair of lighted bow-windows with vague shadows flitting continually across the blinds, and listening to the drawing of corks, the clink of glasses, and a gradual crescendo of coarse voices within. Our luck seemed to have deserted us; the owner of the purple diamonds was dining at home and dining at undue length. I thought it was a dinner-party. Raffles differed; in the end he proved right. Wheels grated in the drive, a carriage and pair stood at the steps; there was a stampede from the dining-room, and the loud voices died away, to burst forth presently from the porch.

Let me make our position perfectly clear. We were over the wall, at the side of the house, but a few feet from the dining-room windows. On our right, one angle of the building cut the back lawn in two, diagonally; on our left, another angle just permitted us to see the jutting steps and the waiting carriage. We saw Rosenthall come out – saw the glimmer of his diamonds before anything. Then came the pugilist; then a lady with a head of hair like a bath sponge; then another, and the party was complete.

Raffles ducked and pulled me down in great excitement.

'The ladies are going with them,' he whispered. 'This is great!'

'That's better still.'

'The Gardenia!' the millionaire had bawled.

'And that's best of all,' said Raffles, standing upright as hoofs and wheels crunched through the gates and rattled off at a fine speed.

'Now what?' I whispered, trembling with excitement.

'They'll be clearing away. Yes, here come their shadows. The drawing-room windows open on the lawn. Bunny, it's the psychological moment. Where's that mask?'

I produced it with a hand whose trembling I tried in vain to still, and could have died for Raffles when he made no comment on what he could not fail to notice. His own hands were firm and cool as he adjusted my mask for me, and then his own.

'By Jove, old boy,' he whispered cheerily, 'you look about the greatest ruffian I ever saw! These masks alone will down a nigger, if we meet one. But I'm glad I remembered to tell you not to shave. You'll pass for Whitechapel if the worst comes to the worst and you don't forget to talk the lingo. Better sulk like a mule if you're not sure of it, and leave the dialogue to me; but, please our stars, there will be no need. Now, are you ready?'

'Quite.'

'Got your gag?'

'Yes.'

'Shooter?'

'Yes.'

'Then follow me.'

In an instant we were over the wall, in another on the lawn behind the house. There was no moon. The very stars in their courses had veiled themselves for our benefit. I crept at my leader's heels to some french windows opening upon a shallow verandah. He pushed. They yielded.

'Luck again,' he whispered; 'nothing but luck! Now for a light.'

And the light came!

A good score of electric burners glowed red for the fraction of a second, then rained merciless white beams into our blinded eyes. When we found our sight, four revolvers covered us, and between two of them the colossal frame of Reuben Rosenthall shook with a wheezy laughter from head to foot.

'Good evening, boys,' he hiccoughed. 'Glad to see ye at last! Shift foot or finger, you on the left, though, and you're a dead boy. I mean you, you greaser!' he roared out at Raffles. 'I know you. I've been waitin' for you. I've been watching you all this week! Plucky smart you thought yerself, didn't you? One day beggin', next time shammin' tight, and next one o' them old pals from Kimberley who never come when I'm in. But you left the same tracks every day, you buggins, an' the same tracks every night, all round the blessed premises.'

'All right, guv'nor,' drawled Raffles; 'don't excite. It's a fair cop. We don't sweat to know 'ow you brung it orf. On'y don't you go for to shoot, 'cos we ain't awmed, s'help me Gord!'

'Ah, you're a knowin' one,' said Rosenthall, fingering his triggers. 'But you've struck a knowin'er.'

'Ho, yuss, we know all abaht thet! Set a thief to catch a thief – ho, yuss.'

My eyes had torn themselves from the round black muzzles, from the accursed diamonds that had been our snare, the pasty pig-face of the over-fed pugilist, and the flaming cheeks and hook-nose of Rosenthall himself. I was looking beyond them at the doorway filled with quivering silk and plush, black faces, white eyeballs, woolly pates. But a sudden silence recalled my attention to the millionaire. And only his nose retained its colour.

'What d'ye mean?' he whispered with a hoarse oath. 'Spit it out, or, by Christmas, I'll drill you!'

'Whort price thet brikewater?' drawled Raffles coolly.

'Eh?'

Rosenthall's revolvers were describing widening orbits.

'What price thet brikewater – old I.D.B.?'

'Where in hell did you get hold o' that?' asked Rosenthall, with a rattle in his thick neck meant for mirth.

'You may well arst,' says Raffles. 'It's all over the plice w'ere I come from.'

'Who can have spread such rot?'

'I dunno,' says Raffles; 'arst the gen'leman on yer left; p'raps 'e knows.'

The gentleman on his left had turned livid with emotion. Guilty conscience never declared itself in plainer terms. For a moment his small eyes bulged like currants in the suet of his face; the next, he had pocketed his pistols on a professional instinct, and was upon us with his fists.

'Out o' the light – out o' the light!' yelled Rosenthall in a frenzy.

He was too late. No sooner had the burly pugilist obstructed his fire than Raffles was through the window at a bound; while I, for standing still and saying nothing, was scientifically felled to the floor.

I cannot have been many moments without my senses. When I recovered them there was a great to-do in the garden, but I had the drawing-room to myself. I sat up. Rosenthall and

41

Purvis were rushing about outside, cursing the Kaffirs and nagging at each other.

'Over that wall, I tell yer!'

'I tell you it was this one. Can't you whistle for the police?'

'Police be damned! I've had enough of the blessed police.'

'Then we'd better get back and make sure of the other rotter.'

'Oh, make sure o' yer skin. That's what you'd better do. Jala, you black hog, if I catch you skulkin' ...'

I never heard the threat. I was creeping from the drawing-room on my hands and knees, my own revolver swinging by its steel ring from my teeth.

For an instant I thought that the hall also was deserted. I was wrong, and I crept upon a Kaffir on all-fours. Poor devil, I could not bring myself to deal him a base blow, but I threatened him most hideously with my revolver, and left the white teeth chattering in his black head as I took the stairs three at a time. Why I went upstairs in that decisive fashion, as though it were my only course, I cannot explain. But garden and ground floor seemed alive with men, and I might have done worse.

I turned into the first room I came to. It was a bedroom – empty, though lit up; and never shall I forget how I started as I entered, on encountering the awful villain that was myself at full length in a pier-glass! Masked, armed, and ragged, I was indeed fit carrion for a bullet or the hangman, and to one or the other I made up my mind. Nevertheless, I hid myself in the wardrobe behind the mirror, and there I stood shivering and cursing my fate, my folly, and Raffles most of all – Raffles first and last – for I dare say half an hour. Then the wardrobe door was flung suddenly open; they had stolen into the room without a sound; and I was hauled downstairs, an ignominious captive.

Gross scenes followed in the hall. The ladies were now upon the stage, and at sight of the desperate criminal they screamed with one accord. In truth I must have given them fair cause, though my mask was now torn away and hid nothing but my left ear. Rosenthall answered their shrieks with a roar for silence; the woman with the bath-sponge hair swore at him shrilly in return; the place became a Babel impossible to describe. I remember wondering how long it would be before the police appeared. Purvis and the ladies were for calling them in and giving me in charge without delay. Rosenthall would not hear of it. He swore that he would shoot man or woman who left his sight. He had had enough of the police. He was not going to have them coming there to spoil sport; he was going to deal with me in his own way. With that he dragged me from all other hands, flung me against a door, and sent a bullet crashing through the wood within an inch of my ear.

'You drunken fool! It'll be murder!' shouted Purvis, getting in the way a second time.

'Wha' do I care? He's armed, isn't he? I shot him in self-defence. It'll be a warning to others. Will you stand aside, or d'ye want it yourself?'

'You're drunk,' said Purvis, still between us. 'I saw you take a neat tumblerful since you came in, and it's made you drunk as a fool. Pull yourself together, old man. You ain't a-going to do what you'll be sorry for.'

'Then I won't shoot at him, I'll only shoot roun' an' roun' the beggar. You're quite right, ole feller. Wouldn't hurt him. Great mishtake. Roun' an' roun'. There – like that!'

His freckled paw shot up over Purvis's shoulder, mauve lightning came from his ring, a red flash from his revolver, and shrieks from the women as the reverberations died away. Some splinters lodged in my hair.

Next instant the prize-fighter disarmed him; and I was safe from the devil, but finally doomed to the deep sea. A policeman was in our midst. He had entered through the drawing-room window; he was an officer of few words and creditable promptitude. In a twinkling he had the handcuffs on my wrists, while the pugilist explained the situation, and his patron reviled the force and its representative with impotent malignity. A fine watch they kept; a lot of good they did; coming in when all was over and the whole household might have been murdered in their sleep. The officer only deigned to notice him as he marched me off.

'We know all about you, sir,' said he contemptuously, and he refused the sovereign Purvis proffered. 'You will be seeing me again, sir, at Marylebone.'

'Shall I come now?'

'As you please, sir. I rather think the other gentleman requires you more, and I don't fancy this young man means to give much trouble.'

'Oh, I'm coming quietly,' I said.

And I went.

In silence we traversed perhaps a hundred yards. It must have been midnight. We did not meet a soul. At last I whispered:

'How on earth did you manage it?'

'Purely by luck,' said Raffles. 'I had the luck to get clear away through knowing every brick of those back-garden walls, and the double luck to have these togs with the rest over at Chelsea. The helmet is one of a collection I made up at Oxford; here it goes over this wall, and we'd better carry the coat and belt before we meet a real officer. I got them once for a fancy ball – ostensibly – and thereby hangs a yarn. I always thought they might come in useful a second time. My chief crux to-night was getting rid of the cab that brought me back. I sent him off to Scotland Yard with ten bob and a special message to good old Mackenzie. The whole detective department will be at Rosenthall's in about half an hour. Of course I speculated on our gentleman's hatred of the police – another huge slice of luck. If you'd got away, well and good; if not, I felt he was the man to play with his mouse as long as possible. Yes, Bunny, it's been more of a costume piece than I intended, and we've come out of it with a good deal less credit. But, by Jove, we're jolly lucky to have come out of it at all!'

GENTLEMEN AND PLAYERS

OLD Raffles may or may not have been an exceptional criminal, but as a cricketer I dare swear he was unique. Himself a dangerous bat, a brilliant field, and perhaps the very finest slow bowler of his decade, he took incredibly little interest in the game at large. He never went up to Lord's without his cricket-bag, or showed the slightest interest in the result of a match in which he was not himself engaged. Nor was this mere hateful egotism on his part. He professed to have lost all enthusiasm for the game, and to keep it up only from the very lowest motives.

'Cricket,' said Raffles, 'like everything else, is good enough sport until you discover a better. As a source of excitement it isn't in it with other things you wot of, Bunny, and the involuntary comparison becomes a bore. What's the satisfaction of taking a man's wicket when you want his spoons? Still, if you can bowl a bit your low cunning won't get rusty, and always looking for the weak spot's just the kind of mental exercise one wants. Yes, perhaps there's some affinity between the two things after all. But I'd chuck up cricket to-morrow, Bunny, if it wasn't for the glorious protection it affords a person of my proclivities.'

'How so?' said I. 'It brings you before the public, I should have thought, far more than is either safe or wise.'

'My dear Bunny, that's exactly where you make a mistake. To follow crime with reasonable impunity you simply must have a parallel ostensible career – the more public the better. The principle is obvious. Mr Peace, of pious memory, disarmed suspicion by acquiring a local reputation for playing the fiddle and taming animals, and it's my profound conviction that Jack the Ripper was a really eminent public man, whose speeches were very likely reported alongside his atrocities. Fill the bill in some prominent part, and you'll never be suspected of doubling it with another of equal prominence. That's why I want you to cultivate journalism, my boy, and sign all you can. And it's the one and only reason why I don't burn my bats for firewood.'

Nevertheless, when he did play there was no keener performer on the field, nor one more anxious to do well for his side. I remember how he went to the nets, before the first match of the season, with his pocket full of sovereigns which he put on the stumps instead of bails. It was a sight to see the professionals bowling like demons for the hard cash, for whenever a stump was hit a pound was tossed to the bowler and another balanced in its stead, while one man took £3 with a ball that spread-eagled the wicket. Raffles's practice cost him either eight or nine sovereigns; he had absolutely first-class bowling all the time, and he made fifty-seven runs next day.

It became my pleasure to accompany him to all his matches, to watch every ball he bowled, or played, or fielded, and to sit chatting with him in the pavilion when he was doing none of these three things. You might have seen us there, side by side, during the greater part of the Gentlemen's first innings against the Players (who had lost the toss) on the second Monday in July. We were to be seen, but not heard, for Raffles had failed to score, and was uncommonly cross for a player who cared so little for the game. Merely taciturn with me, he was positively rude to more than one member who wanted to know how it had happened, or who ventured to commiserate him on his luck; there he sat, with a straw hat tilted over his nose and a cigarette stuck between lips that curled disagreeably at every advance. I was, therefore, much surprised when a young fellow of the exquisite type came and squeezed himself in between us, and met with a perfectly civil reception despite the liberty. I did not know the boy by sight, nor did Raffles introduce us; but their conversation proclaimed at once the slightness of acquaintanceship and a licence on the lad's part which combined to puzzle me. Mystification reached its height when Raffles was informed that the other's father was anxious to meet him, and he instantly consented to gratify that whim.

'He's in the Ladies' Enclosure. Will you come round now?'

'With pleasure,' said Raffles. 'Keep a place for me, Bunny.' And they were gone.

'Young Crowley,' said some voice farther back. 'Last year's Harrow Eleven.'

'I remember him. Worst man in the team.'

'Keen cricketer, however. Stopped till he was twenty to get his colours. Governor made him. Keen breed. Oh, pretty, sir! Very pretty!'

The game was boring me. I only came to see old Raffles perform. Soon I was looking wistfully for his return, and at length I saw him beckoning me from the palings to the right.

'Want to introduce you to old Amersteth,' he whispered, when I joined him. 'They've a cricket week next month, when this boy Crowley comes of age, and we've both got to go down and play.'

'Both!' I echoed. 'But I'm no cricketer!'

'Shut up,' says Raffles. 'Leave that to me. I've been lying for all I'm worth,' he added sepulchrally, as we reached the bottom of the steps. 'I trust to you not to give the show away.'

There was the gleam in his eye that I knew well enough elsewhere, but was unprepared for in those healthy, sane surroundings; and it was with very definite misgivings and surmises that I followed the Zingari blazer through the vast flower-bed of hats that bloomed beneath the ladies' awning.

Lord Amersteth was a fine-looking man with a short moustache and a double chin. He received me with much dry courtesy, through which, however, it was not difficult to read a less flattering tale. I was accepted as the inevitable appendage of the invaluable Raffles, with whom I felt deeply incensed as I made my bow.

'I have been bold enough,' said Lord Amersteth, 'to ask one of the Gentlemen of England to come down and play some rustic cricket for us next month. He is kind enough to say that he would have liked nothing better, but for this little fishing expedition of yours, Mr –, Mr –,' and Lord Amersteth succeeded in remembering my name.

It was, of course, the first I had ever heard of that fishing expedition, but I made haste to say that it could easily, and should certainly, be put off. Raffles gleamed approval through his eyelashes. Lord Amersteth bowed and shrugged.

'You're very good, I'm sure,' said he. 'But I understand you're a cricketer yourself?'

'He was one at school,' said Raffles, with infamous readiness.

'Not a real cricketer,' I was stammering meanwhile.

'In the eleven?' said Lord Amersteth.

'I'm afraid not,' said I.

'But only just out of it,' declared Raffles, to my horror.

'Well, well, we can't all play for the Gentlemen,' said Lord Amersteth slyly. 'My son Crowley only just scraped into the eleven at Harrow, and he's going to play. I may even come in myself at a pinch; so you won't be the only duffer, if you are one, and I shall be very glad if you will come down and help us too. You shall flog a stream before breakfast and after dinner, if you like.'

'I should be very proud,' I was beginning, as the mere prelude to resolute excuses; but the eye of Raffles opened wide upon me; and I hesitated weakly, to be duly lost.

'Then that's settled,' said Lord Amersteth, with the slightest suspicion of grimness. 'It's to be a little week, you know, when my son comes of age. We play the Free Foresters, the Dorsetshire Gentlemen, and probably some local lot as well. But Mr Raffles will tell you all about it, and Crowley shall write. Another wicket! By Jove, they're all out! Then I rely on you both.' And, with a little nod, Lord Amersteth rose and sidled to the gangway.

Raffles rose also, but I caught the sleeve of his blazer.

'What are you thinking of?' I whispered savagely. 'I was nowhere near the eleven. I'm no sort of cricketer. I shall have to get out of this!'

'Not you,' he whispered back. 'You needn't play, but come you must. If you wait for me after half-past six, I'll tell you why.'

But I could guess the reason; and I am ashamed to say that it revolted me much less than did the notion of making a public fool of myself on a cricket-field. My gorge rose at this as it no longer rose at crime, and it was in no tranquil humour that I strolled about the ground while Raffles disappeared in the pavilion. Nor was my annoyance lessened by a little meeting I witnessed between young Crowley and his father, who shrugged as he stopped and stooped to convey some information which made the young man look a little blank. It may have been pure self-consciousness on my part, but I could have sworn that the trouble was their inability to secure the great Raffles without his insignificant friend.

Then the bell rang, and I climbed to the top of the pavilion to watch Raffles bowl. No subtleties are lost up there; and if ever a bowler was full of them, it was A. J. Raffles on this day, as, indeed, all the cricket world remembers. One had not to be a cricketer oneself to appreciate his perfect command of pitch and break, his beautifully easy action, which never varied with the varying pace, his great ball on the leg-stump – his dropping head-ball – in a word, the infinite ingenuity of that versatile attack. It was no mere exhibition of athletic prowess, it was an intellectual treat, and one with a special significance in my eyes. I saw the 'affinity between the two things,' saw it in that afternoon's tireless warfare against the flower of professional cricket. It was not that Raffles took many wickets for a few runs; he was too fine a bowler to mind being hit; and time was short, and the wicket good. What I admired, and what I remember, was the combination of resource and cunning, of patience and precision, of hard work and handiwork, which made every over an artistic whole. It was all so characteristic of that other Raffles whom I alone knew!

'I felt like bowling this afternoon,' he told me later – in the cab. 'With a pitch to help me, I'd have done something big; as it is, three for forty-one, out of the four that fell, isn't bad for a slow bowler on a plumb wicket against those fellows. But I felt venomous! Nothing riles me more than being asked about for my cricket as though I were a pro myself.'

'Then why on earth go?'

'To punish them, and – because we shall be jolly hard up, Bunny, before the season's over!'

'Ah!' said I. 'I thought it was that.'

'Of course it was! It seems they're going to have the very devil of a week of it – balls – dinner-parties – swagger house-party – general junketings – and, obviously, a houseful of diamonds as well. Diamonds galore! As a general rule nothing would induce me to abuse my position as a guest. I've never done it, Bunny. But in this case we're engaged like the waiters and the band, and by heaven we'll take our toll! Let's have a quiet dinner somewhere and talk it over.'

'It seems rather a vulgar sort of theft,' I could not help saying; and to this, my single protest, Raffles instantly assented.

'It is a vulgar sort,' said he; 'but I can't help that. We're getting vulgarly hard up again, and there's an end on't. Besides, these people deserve it and can afford it. And don't you run away with the idea that all will be plain sailing; nothing will be easier than getting some stuff, and nothing harder than avoiding all suspicion, as, of course, we must. We may come away with no more than a good working plan of the premises. Who knows? In any case, there's weeks of thinking in it for you and me.'

But with those weeks I will not weary you further than by remarking that the 'thinking' was done entirely by Raffles, who did not always trouble to communicate his thoughts to me. His reticence, however, was no longer an irritant. I began to accept it as a necessary convention of these little enterprises. And, after our last adventure of the kind, more especially after its *dénouement,* my trust in Raffles was much too solid to be shaken by a want of trust in me, which I still believe to have been more the instinct of the criminal than the judgment of the man.

It was on Monday, August 10, that we were due at Milchester Abbey, Dorset; and the beginning of the month found us cruising about that very county, with fly-rods actually in our hands. The idea was that we should acquire at once a local reputation as decent fishermen, and some knowledge of the countryside, with a view to further and more deliberate operations in the event of an unprofitable week. There was another idea which Raffles kept to himself until he had got me down there. Then one day he produced a cricket-ball in a meadow we were crossing, and threw me catches for an hour together. More hours he spent in bowling to me on the nearest green; and, if I was never a cricketer, at least I came nearer to being one, by the end of that week, than ever before or since.

Incident began early on the Monday. We had sallied forth from a desolate little junction within quite a few miles of Milchester, had been caught in a shower, had run for shelter to a wayside inn. A florid, overdressed man was drinking in the parlour, and I could have sworn it was at the sight of him that

Raffles recoiled on the threshold, and afterwards insisted on returning to the station through the rain. He assured me, however, that the odour of stale ale had almost knocked him down. And I had to make what I could of his speculative, downcast eyes and knitted brows.

Milchester Abbey is a grey, quadrangular pile, deep-set in rich woody country, and twinkling with triple rows of quaint windows, every one of which seemed alight as we drove up just in time to dress for dinner. The carriage had whirled us under I know not how many triumphal arches in process of construction, and past the tents and flag-poles of a juicy-looking cricket-field, on which Raffles undertook to bowl up to his reputation. But the chief signs of festival were within, where we found an enormous house-party assembled, including more persons of pomp, majesty, and dominion than I had ever encountered in one room before. I confess I felt overpowered. Our errand and my own pretences combined to rob me of an address upon which I had sometimes plumed myself; and I have a grim recollection of my nervous relief when dinner was at last announced. I little knew what an ordeal it was to prove.

I had taken in a much less formidable young lady than might have fallen to my lot. Indeed, I began by blessing my good fortune in this respect. Miss Melhuish was merely the rector's daughter, and she had only been asked to make an even number. She informed me of both facts before the soup reached us, and her subsequent conversation was characterised by the same engaging candour. It exposed what was little short of a mania for imparting information. I had simply to listen, to nod, and be thankful. When I confessed to knowing very few of those present, even by sight, my entertaining companion proceeded to tell me who everybody was, beginning on my left and working conscientiously round to her right. This lasted quite a long time, and really interested me; but a great deal that followed did not: and, obviously to recapture my unworthy attention, Miss Melhuish suddenly asked me, in a sensational whisper, whether I could keep a secret.

I said I thought I might, whereupon another question followed, in still lower and more thrilling accents:

'Are you afraid of burglars?'

Burglars! I was roused at last. The word stabbed me. I repeated it in horrified query.

'So I've found something to interest you at last!' said Miss Melhuish in naïve triumph. 'Yes – burglars! But don't speak so loud. It's supposed to be kept a great secret. I really oughtn't to tell you at all!'

'But what is there to tell?' I whispered, with satisfactory impatience.

'You promise not to speak of it?'

'Of course!'

'Well, then, there are burglars in the neighbourhood.'

'Have they committed any robberies?'

'Not yet.'

'Then how do you know?'

'They've been seen. In the district. Two well-known London thieves!'

Two! I looked at Raffles. I had done so often during the evening, envying him his high spirits, his iron nerve, his buoyant wit, his perfect ease, and his self-possession. But now I pitied him; through all my own terror and consternation I pitied him as he sat eating and drinking, and laughing, and talking, without a cloud of fear or of embarrassment on his handsome, taking, dare-devil face. I caught up my champagne and emptied the glass.

'Who has seen them?' I then asked calmly.

'A detective. They were traced down from town a few days ago. They are believed to have designs on the Abbey!'

'But why aren't they run in?'

'Exactly what I asked papa on the way here this evening; he says there is no warrant out against the men at present, and all that can be done is to watch their movements.'

'Oh! so they are being watched?'

'Yes, by a detective who is down here on purpose. And I heard Lord Amersteth tell papa that they had been seen this afternoon at Warbeck Junction.'

The very place where Raffles and I had been caught in the rain! Our stampede from the inn was now explained; on the other hand, I was no longer to be taken by surprise by anything that my companion might have to tell me; and I succeeded in looking her in the face with a smile.

'This is really quite exciting, Miss Melhuish,' said I. 'May I ask how you come to know so much about it?'

'It's papa,' was the confidential reply. 'Lord Amersteth consulted him, and he consulted me. But for goodness' sake don't let it get about! I can't think what tempted me to tell you!'

'You may trust me, Miss Melhuish. But – aren't you frightened?'

Miss Melhuish giggled.

'Not a bit! They won't come to the rectory. There's nothing for them there. But look round the table; look at the diamonds. Look at old Lady Melrose's necklace alone!'

The Dowager Marchioness of Melrose was one of the few persons whom it had been unnecessary to point out to me. She sat on Lord Amersteth's right, flourishing her ear-trumpet, and drinking champagne with her usual notorious freedom, as dissipated and kindly a dame as the world has ever seen. It was a necklace of diamonds and sapphires that rose and fell about her ample neck.

'They say it's worth five thousand pounds at least,' continued my companion. 'Lady Margaret told me so this morning (that's Lady Margaret next your Mr Raffles, you know); and the old dear will wear them every night. Think what a haul they would be! No; we don't feel in immediate danger at the rectory.'

When the ladies rose, Miss Melhuish bound me to fresh vows of secrecy; and left me, I should think, with some remorse for her indiscretion, but more satisfaction at the importance which it had undoubtedly given her in my eyes. The opinion may smack of vanity, though, in reality, the very springs of conversation reside in that same human universal itch to thrill the auditor. The peculiarity of Miss Melhuish was that she must be thrilling at all costs. And thrilling she had surely been.

I spare you my feelings of the next two hours. I tried hard to get a word with Raffles, but again and again I failed. In the dining-room he and Crowley lit their cigarettes with the same match, and had their heads together all the time. In the drawing-room I had the mortification of hearing him talk interminable nonsense into the ear-trumpet of Lady Melrose, whom he knew in town. Lastly, in the billiard-room, they had a great and lengthy pool, while I sat aloof and chafed more than ever in the company of a very serious Scotsman, who had arrived since dinner, and who would talk of nothing but the recent improvements in instantaneous photography. He had not come to play in the matches (he told me), but to obtain for Lord Amersteth such a series of cricket photographs as had never been taken before; whether as an amateur or a professional photographer I was unable to determine. I remember, however, seeking distraction in little bursts of resolute attention to the conversation of this bore. And so at last the long ordeal ended: glasses were emptied, men said good night, and I followed Raffles to his room.

'It's all up!' I gasped, as he turned up the gas and I shut the door. 'We're being watched. We've been followed down from town. There's a detective here on the spot!'

'How do you know?' asked Raffles, turning upon me quite sharply, but without the least dismay. And I told him how I knew.

'Of course,' I added, 'it was the fellow we saw in the inn this afternoon.'

'The detective?' said Raffles. 'Do you mean to say you don't know a detective when you see one, Bunny?'

'If that wasn't the fellow, which is?'

Raffles shook his head.

'To think that you've been talking to him for the last hour in the billiard-room, and couldn't spot what he was!'

'The Scotch photographer – '

I paused aghast.

'Scotch he is,' said Raffles, 'and photographer he may be. He is also Inspector Mackenzie of Scotland Yard – the very man I sent the message to that night last April. And you couldn't spot who he was in a whole hour! Oh, Bunny, Bunny, you were never built for crime!'

'But,' said I, 'if that was Mackenzie, who was the fellow you bolted from at Warbeck?'

'The man he's watching.'

'But he's watching us!'

Raffles looked at me with a pitying eye, and shook his head again before handing me his open cigarette-case.

'I don't know whether smoking's forbidden in one's bedroom, but you'd better take one of these and stand tight, Bunny, because I'm going to say something offensive.'

I helped myself with a laugh.

'Say what you like, my dear fellow, if it really isn't you and me that Mackenzie's after.'

'Well, then, it isn't, and it couldn't be, and nobody but a born Bunny would suppose for a moment that it was! Do you seriously think he would sit there and knowingly watch his man playing pool under his nose? Well, he might; he's a cool hand, Mackenzie; but I'm not cool enough to win a pool under such conditions. At least, I don't think I am; it would be interesting to see. The situation wasn't free from strain as it was, though I knew he wasn't thinking of us. Crowley told me all about it after dinner, you see, and then I'd seen one of the men for myself this afternoon. You thought it was a detective who made me turn tail at that inn. I really don't know why I didn't tell you at the time, but it was just the opposite. That loud, red-faced brute is one of the cleverest thieves in London, and I once had a drink with him and our mutual fence. I was an Eastender from tongue to toe at the moment, but you will understand that I don't run unnecessary risks of recognition by a brute like that.'

'He's not alone, I hear.'

'By no means; there's at least one other man with him; and it's suggested that there may be an accomplice here in the house.'

'Did Lord Crowley tell you so?'

'Crowley and the champagne between them. In confidence, of course, just as your girl told you; but even in confidence he never let on about Mackenzie. He told me there was a detective in the background, but that was all. Putting him up as a guest is evidently their big secret, to be kept from the other guests because it might offend them, but more particularly from the servants whom he's here to watch. That's my reading of the situation. Bunny, and you will agree with me that it's infinitely more interesting than we could have imagined it would prove.

'But infinitely more difficult for us,' said I, with a sigh of pusillanimous relief. 'Our hands are tied for this week, at all events.'

'Not necessarily, my dear Bunny, though I admit that the chances are against us. Yet I'm not so sure of that either. There are all sorts of possibilities in these three-cornered combinations. Set A to watch B, and he won't have an eye left for C. That's the obvious theory, but then Mackenzie's a very big A. I should be sorry to have any boodle about me with that man in the house. Yet it would be great to nip in between A and B and score off them both at once! It would be worth a risk, Bunny, to do that; it would be worth risking something merely to take on old hands like B and his men at their old game! Eh, Bunny? That would be something like a match. Gentlemen and Players at single wicket, by Jove!'

His eyes were brighter than I had known them for many a day. They shone with the perverted enthusiasm which was roused in him only by the contemplation of some new audacity. He kicked off his shoes and began pacing his room with noiseless rapidity; not since the night of the Old Bohemian dinner to Reuben Rosenthall had Raffles exhibited such excitement in my presence; and I was not sorry at the moment to be reminded of the fiasco to which that banquet had been the prelude.

'My dear A. J.,' said I in his very own tone, 'you're far too fond of the uphill game; you will eventually fall a victim to the sporting spirit and nothing else. Take a lesson from our last escape, and fly lower as you value our skins. Study the house as much as you like but do – not – go and shove your head into Mackenzie's mouth!'

My wealth of metaphor brought him to a standstill, with his cigarette between his fingers and a grin beneath his shining eyes.

'You're quite right, Bunny. I won't. I really won't. Yet – you saw old Lady Melrose's necklace? I've been wanting it for years! But I'm not going to play the fool, honour bright, I'm not; yet – by Jove! – to get to windward of the professors and Mackenzie too! It would be a great game, Bunny, it would be a great game!'

'Well, you mustn't play it this week.'

'No, no, I won't. But I wonder how the professors think of going to work? That's what one wants to know. I wonder if they've really got an accomplice in the house? How I wish I knew their game! But it's all right, Bunny; don't you be jealous; it shall be as you wish."

And with that assurance I went off to my own room and so to bed with an incredibly light heart. I had still enough of the honest man in me to welcome the postponement of our actual felonies, to dread their performance, and to deplore their necessity; which is merely another way of stating the too patent fact that I was an incomparably weaker man than Raffles, while every whit as wicked. I had, however, one rather strong point. I possessed the gift of dismissing unpleasant considerations, not intimately connected with the passing moment, entirely from my mind. Through the exercise of this faculty I had lately been living my frivolous life in town with as much ignoble enjoyment as I had derived from it the year before; and similarly, here at Milchester, in the long-dreaded cricket-week, I had after all a quite excellent time.

It is true that there were other factors in this pleasing disappointment. In the first place, *mirabile dictu,* there were one or two even greater duffers than I on the Abbey cricket-field. Indeed, quite early in the week, when it was of most value to me, I gained considerable kudos for a lucky catch; a ball, of which I had merely heard the hum, stuck fast in my hand, which Lord Amersteth himself grasped in public congratulation. This happy accident was not to be undone even by me, and, as nothing succeeds like success, and the constant encouragement of the one great cricketer on the field was in itself an immense stimulus, I actually made a run or two in my very next innings. Miss Melhuish said pretty things to me that night at the great ball in honour of Viscount Crowley's majority; she also told me that was the night on which the robbers would assuredly make their raid, and was full of arch tremors when we sat out in the garden, though the entire premises were illuminated all night long. Meanwhile, the quiet Scotsman took countless photographs by day, which he developed by night in a dark room admirably situated in the servants' part of the house; and it is my firm belief that only two of his fellow-guests knew Mr

Clephane of Dundee for Inspector Mackenzie of Scotland Yard.

The week was to end with a trumpery match on the Saturday, which two or three of us intended abandoning early in order to return to town that night. The match, however, was never played. In the small hours of the Saturday morning a tragedy took place at Milchester Abbey

Let me tell of the thing as I saw and heard it. My room opened upon the central gallery, and was not even on the same floor as that on which Raffles – and I think all the other men – were quartered. I had been put, in fact, into the dressing-room of one of the grand suites, and my two near neighbours were old Lady Melrose and my host and hostess. Now, by the Friday evening the actual festivities were at an end, and, for the first time that week, I must have been sound asleep since midnight, when all at once I found myself sitting up breathless. A heavy thud had come against my door, and now I heard hard breathing and the dull stamp of muffled feet.

'I've got ye,' muttered a voice. 'It's no use struggling.'

It was the Scotch detective, and a new fear turned me cold. There was no reply, but the hard breathing grew harder still, and the muffled feet beat the floor to a quicker measure. In sudden panic I sprang out of bed and flung open my door. A light burnt low on the landing, and by it I could see Mackenzie swaying and staggering in a silent tussle with some powerful adversary.

'Hold this man!' he cried, as I appeared. 'Hold the rascal!'

But I stood like a fool until the pair of them backed into me, when, with a deep breath, I flung myself on the fellow, whose face I had seen at last. He was one of the footmen who waited at table; and no sooner had I pinned him than the detective loosed his hold.

'Hang on to him,' he cried. 'There's more of 'em below.'

And he went leaping down the stairs, as other doors opened, and Lord Amersteth and his son appeared simultaneously in their pyjamas. At that my man ceased struggling, but I was still holding him when Crowley turned up the gas.

'What the devil's all this?' asked Lord Amersteth, blinking. 'Who was that ran downstairs?'

'Clephane!' said I hastily.

'Aha!' said he, turning to the footman. 'So you're the scoundrel, are you? Well done! Well done! Where was he caught?'

I had no idea.

'Here's Lady Melrose's door open,' said Crowley. 'Lady Melrose! Lady Melrose!'

'You forget she is deaf,' said Lord Amersteth. 'Ah! that'll be her maid.'

An inner door had opened; next instant there was a little shriek, and a white figure gesticulated on the threshold.

'Où donc est l'écrin de Madame la Marquise? La fenêtre est ouverte. Il a disparu!'

'Window open and jewel-case gone, by Jove!' exclaimed Lord Amersteth. 'Mais comment est Madame la Marquise? Est-elle bien?'

'Oui, milord. Elle dort.'

'Sleeps through it all,' said my lord. 'She's the only one, then!'

'What made Mackenzie – Clephane – bolt?' young Crowley asked me.

'Said there were more of them below.'

'Why the devil couldn't you tell us so before?' he cried, and went leaping downstairs in his turn.

He was followed by nearly all the cricketers, who now burst upon the scene in a body, only to desert it for the chase. Raffles was one of them, and I would gladly have been another, had not the footman chosen this moment to hurl me from him, and to make a dash in the direction from which they had come. Lord Amersteth had him in an instant; but the fellow fought desperately, and it took the two of us to drag him downstairs, amid a terrified chorus from half-open doors. Eventually we handed him over to two other footmen who appeared with their night-shirts tucked into their trousers, and my host was good enough to compliment me as he led the way outside.

'I thought I heard a shot,' he added. 'Didn't you?'

'I thought I heard three.'

And out we dashed into the darkness.

I remember how the gravel pricked my feet, how the wet grass numbed them as we made for the sound of voices on an outlying lawn. So dark was the night that we were in the cricketers' midst before we saw the shimmer of their pyjamas, and then Lord Amersteth almost trod on Mackenzie as he lay prostrate in the dew.

'Who's this?' he cried. 'What on earth's happened?'

'It's Clephane,' said a man who knelt over him. 'He's got a bullet in him somewhere.'

'Is he alive?'

'Barely.'

'Good God! Where's Crowley?'

'Here I am,' called a breathless voice. 'It's no good, you fellows. There's nothing to show which way they've gone. Here's Raffles; he's chucked it, too.' And they ran up panting.

'Well, we've got one of them, at all events,' muttered Lord Amersteth. 'The next thing is to get this poor fellow indoors. Take his shoulders, somebody. Now his middle. Join hands under him. Altogether, now; that's the way. Poor fellow! Poor fellow! His name isn't Clephane at all. He's a Scotland Yard detective, down here for these very villains!'

Raffles was the first to express surprise; but he had also been the first to raise the wounded man. Nor had any of them a stronger or more tender hand in the slow procession to the house. In a little we had the senseless man stretched on a sofa in the library. And there, with ice on his wound and brandy in his throat, his eyes opened and his lips moved.

Lord Amersteth bent down to catch the words.

'Yes, yes,' said he, 'we've got one of them safe and sound. The brute you collared upstairs.' Lord Amersteth bent lower. 'By Jove! Lowered the jewel-case out of the window, did he? And they've got clean away with it! Well, well! I only hope we'll be able to pull this good fellow through. He's off again.'

An hour passed; the sun was rising.

It found a dozen young fellows on the settees in the billiard-room, drinking whisky and soda-water in their overcoats and pyjamas, and still talking excitedly in one breath. A time-table was being passed from hand to hand: the doctor was still in the library. At last the door opened, and Lord Amersteth put in his head.

'It isn't hopeless,' said he, 'but it's bad enough. There'll be no cricket to-day.'

Another hour, and most of us were on our way to catch the early train; between us we filled a compartment almost to suffocation. And still we talked all together of the night's event; and still I was a little hero in my way, for having kept my hold of the one ruffian who had been taken; and my gratification was subtle and intense. Raffles watched me under lowered lids. Not a word had we had together; not a word did we have until we had left the others at Paddington, and were swimming through the streets in a hansom with noiseless tyres and a tinkling bell.

'Well, Bunny,' said Raffles, 'so the professors have it, eh?'

'Yes,' said I. 'And I'm jolly glad!'

'That poor Mackenzie has a ball in his chest?'

'That you and I have been on the decent side for once.'

He shrugged his shoulders.

'You're hopeless, Bunny, quite hopeless! I take it you wouldn't have refused your share if the boodle had fallen to us? Yet you positively enjoy coming off second best – for the second time running! I confess, however, that the professors' methods were full of interest to me. I, for one, have probably gained as much in experience as I have lost in other things. That lowering the jewel-case out of the window was a very simple and effective expedient; two of them had been waiting below for it for hours.'

'How did you know?' I asked.

'I saw them from my own window, which was just above the dear old lady's. I was fretting for that necklace in particular, when I went up to turn in for our last night – and I happened to look out of the window. In point of fact, I wanted to see whether the one below was open, and whether there was the slightest chance of working the oracle with my sheet for a rope. Of course, I took the precaution of turning my light off first, and it was a lucky thing I did. I saw the pros right down below, and they never saw me. I saw a little tiny luminous disc just for an instant, and then again for an instant a few minutes later. Of course, I knew what it was, for I have my own watch-dial daubed with luminous paint; it makes a lantern of sorts when you can get no better. But these fellows were not using theirs as a lantern. They were under the old lady's window. They were watching the time. The whole thing was arranged with their accomplice inside. Set a thief to catch a thief; in a minute I had guessed what the whole thing proved to be.'

'And you did nothing!' I exclaimed.

'On the contrary, I went downstairs and straight into Lady Melrose's room – –'

'You did?'

'Without a moment's hesitation. To save her jewels. And I was prepared to yell as much into her ear-trumpet for all the house to hear. But the dear lady is too deaf and too fond of her dinner to wake easily.'

'Well?'

'She didn't stir.'

'And yet you allowed the professors, as you call them, to take her jewels, case and all!'

'All but this,' said Raffles, thrusting his fist into my lap. 'I would have shown it you before, but really, old fellow, your face all day has been worth a fortune to the firm!'

And he opened his fist, to shut it next instant on the bunch of diamonds and of sapphires that I had last seen encircling the neck of Lady Melrose.

LE PREMIER PAS

THAT night he told me the story of his earliest crime. Not since the fateful morning of the Ides of March, when he had just mentioned it as an unreported incident of a certain cricket tour, had I succeeded in getting a word out of Raffles on the subject. It was not for want of trying; he would shake his head, and watch his cigarette smoke thoughtfully; a subtle look in his eyes, half cynical, half wistful, as though the decent honest days that were no more had had their merits after all. Raffles would plan a fresh enormity, or glory in the last, with the unmitigated enthusiasm of the artist. It was impossible to imagine one throb or twitter of compunction beneath those frankly egoistic and infectious transports. And yet the ghost of a dead remorse seemed still to visit him with the memory of his first felony, so that I had given the story up long before the night of our return from Milchester. Cricket, however, was in the air, and Raffles's cricket-bag back where he sometimes kept it, in the fender, with the remains of an old Orient label still adhering to the leather. My eyes had been on this label for some time, and I suppose his eyes had been on mine, for all at once he asked me if I still burned to hear that yarn.

'It's no use,' I replied. 'You won't spin it. I must imagine it for myself.'

'How can you?'

'Oh, I begin to know your methods.'

'You take it I went with my eyes open, as I do now, eh?'

'I can't imagine your doing otherwise.'

'My dear Bunny, it was the most unpremeditated thing I ever did in my life!'

His chair wheeled back into the books as he sprang up with sudden energy. There was quite an indignant glitter in his eyes.

'I can't believe that,' said I craftily. 'I can't pay you such a poor compliment.'

'Then you must be a fool – –'

He broke off, stared hard at me, and in a trice stood smiling in his own despite.

'Or a better knave than I thought you, Bunny, and by Jove, it's the knave! Well – I suppose I'm fairly drawn; I give you best, as they say out here. As a matter of fact, I've been thinking of the thing myself; last night's racket reminds me of it in one or two respects. I tell you what, though, this is an occasion in any case, and I'm going to celebrate it by breaking the one good rule of my life. I'm going to have a second drink!'

The whisky tinkled, the siphon fizzed, and ice plopped home; and seated there in his pyjamas, with the inevitable cigarette, Raffles told me the story that I had given up hoping to hear. The windows were wide open; the sounds of Piccadilly floated in at first. Long before he finished, the last wheels had rattled, the last brawler was removed, we alone broke the quiet of the summer night.

'... No, they do you very well indeed. You pay for nothing but drinks, so to speak, but I'm afraid mine were of a comprehensive character. I had started in a hole, I ought really to have refused the invitation; then we all went to the Melbourne Cup, and I had the certain winner that didn't win, and that's not the only way you can play the fool in Melbourne. I wasn't the steady old stager I am now, Bunny; my analysis was a confession in itself. But the others didn't know how hard up I was, and I swore they shouldn't. I tried the Jews, but they're extra fly out there. Then I thought of a kinsman of sorts, a second cousin of my father's whom none of us knew anything about, except that he was supposed to be in one or other of the Colonies. If he were a rich man, well and good, I would work him; if not there would be no harm done. I tried to get on his tracks, and, as luck would have it, I succeeded (or thought I had) at the very moment when I happened to have a few days to myself. I was cut on the hand, just before the big Christmas match, and couldn't have bowled a ball if they had played me.

'The surgeon who fixed me up happened to ask me if I was any relation of Raffles of the National Bank, and the pure luck of it almost took my breath away. A relation who was a high official in one of the banks, who would finance me on my mere name – could anything be better? I made up my mind that this Raffles was the man I wanted, and was awfully sold to find next moment that he wasn't a high official at all. Nor had the doctor so much as met him, but had merely read of him in connection with a small sensation at the suburban branch which my namesake managed; an armed robber had been rather pluckily beaten off, with a bullet in him, by this Raffles; and the sort of thing was so common out there that this was the first I had heard of it! A suburban branch – my financier had faded into some excellent fellow with a billet to lose if he called his soul his own. Still a manager was a manager, and I said I would soon see whether this was the relative I was looking for, if he would be good enough to give me the name of that branch.

‘ "I'll do more," said the doctor. "I'll give you the name of the branch he's been promoted to, for I think I heard they'd moved him up one already." And the next day he brought me the name of the township of Yea, some fifty miles north of Melbourne; but, with the vagueness which characterised all his information, he was unable to say whether I should find my relative there or not.

‘ "He's a single man, and his initials are W. F.," said the doctor, who was certain enough of the immaterial points. "He left his old post several days ago, but it appears he's not due at the new one till the New Year. No doubt he'll go before then to take things over and settle in. You might find him up there and you might not. If I were you I should write."

‘ "That'll lose two days," said I, "and more if he isn't there," for I'd grown quite keen on this up-country manager, and I felt that if I could get at him while the holidays were still on, a little conviviality might help matters considerably.

‘ "Then," said the doctor, "I should get a quiet horse and ride. You needn't use that hand."

‘ "Can't I go by train?"

‘ "You can and you can't. You would still have to ride. I suppose you're a horseman?"

‘ "Yes."

‘ "Then I should certainly ride all the way. It's a delightful road, through Whittlesea and over the Plenty Ranges. It'll give you some idea of the bush, Mr Raffles, and you'll see the sources of the water-supply of this city, sir. You'll see where every drop of it comes from, the pure Yan Yean! I wish I had time to ride with you."

' "But where can I get a horse?"

'The doctor thought a moment.

' "I've a mare of my own that's as fat as butter for want of work," said he. "It would be a charity to me to sit on her back for a hundred miles or so, and then I should know you'd have no temptation to use that hand."

' "You're far too good," I protested.

' "You're A. J. Raffles," he said.

'And if ever there was a prettier compliment or a finer instance of even Colonial hospitality, I can only say, Bunny, that I never heard of either.'

He sipped his whisky, threw away the stump of his cigarette, and lit another before continuing.

'Well, I managed to write a line to W. F. with my own hand, which, as you will gather, was not very badly wounded; it was simply this third finger that was split and in splints; the next morning the doctor packed me off on a bovine beast that would have done for an ambulance. Half the team came up to see me start; the rest were rather sick with me for not stopping to see the match out, as if I could help them to win by watching them. They little knew the game I'd got on myself, but still less did I know the game I was going to play.

'It was an interesting ride enough, especially after passing the place called Whittlesea, a real wild township on the lower slopes of the ranges, where I recollect having a deadly meal of hot mutton and tea with the thermometer at three figures in the shade. The first thirty miles or so was a good metal road, too good to go half round the world to ride on, but after Whittlesea it was a mere track over the ranges, a track I often couldn't see and left entirely to the mare. Now it dipped into a gully and ran through a creek, and all the time the local colour was inches thick : gum trees galore and parrots all colours of the rainbow. In one place a whole forest of gums had been ringbarked, and were just as though they had been painted white, without a leaf or a living thing for miles. And the first living thing I did meet was the sort to give you the creeps; it was a riderless horse coming full tilt through the bush, with the saddle twisted round and the stirrup-irons ringing. Without thinking, I had a shot at heading him with the doctor's mare, and blocked him just enough to allow a man who came galloping after to do the rest.

' "Thank ye, mister," growled the man, a huge chap in a red checked shirt, with a beard like W. G. Grace, but the very devil of an expression.

' "Been an accident?" said I, reining up.

' "Yes," said he, scowling as though he defied me to ask any more.

' "And a nasty one," I said, "if that's blood on the saddle!"

'Well, Bunny, I may be a blackguard myself, but I don't think I ever looked at a fellow as that chap looked at me. But I stared him out, and forced him to admit that it was blood on the twisted saddle, and after that he became quite tame. He told me exactly what had happened. A mate of his had been dragged under a branch, and had his nose smashed, but that was all; had sat tight after it till he dropped from loss of blood, another mate was with him back in the bush.

'As I've said already, Bunny, I wasn't the old stager that I am now – in any respect – and we parted good enough friends. He asked me which way I was going, and when I told him, he said I should save seven miles, and get a good hour earlier to Yea, by striking off the track and making for a peak that we could see through the trees and following a creek that I should see from the peak. Don't smile, Bunny! I began by saying I was a child in those days. Of course, the short cut was the long way round; and it was nearly dark when that unlucky mare and I saw the single street of Yea.

'I was looking for the bank when a fellow in a white suit ran down from the verandah.

' "Mr Raffles?" said he.

' "Mr Raffles!" said I, laughing, as I shook his hand.

' "You're late."

' "I was misdirected."

' "That all? I'm relieved," he said. "Do you know what they

are saying? There are some brand-new bushrangers on the road between Whittlesea and this – a second Kelly gang! They'd have caught a Tartar in you, eh?"

' "They would in you," I retorted, and my *tu quoque* shut him up and seemed to puzzle him. Yet there was much more sense in it than in his compliment to me, which was absolutely pointless.

' "I'm afraid you'll find things pretty rough," he resumed, when he had unstrapped my valise, and handed my reins to his man. "It's lucky you're a bachelor like myself."

'I could not quite see the point of this remark either, since, had I been married, I should hardly have sprung my wife upon him in this free-and-easy fashion. I muttered the conventional sort of thing, and then he said I should find it all right when I settled, as though I had come to graze upon him for weeks! "Well," thought I, "these Colonials do take the cake for hospitality!" And, still marvelling, I let him lead me into the private part of the bank.

' "Dinner will be ready in a quarter of an hour," said he, as we entered. "I thought you might like a tub first, and you'll find all ready in the room at the end of the passage. Sing out if there's anything you want. Your luggage hasn't turned up yet, by the way, but here's a letter that came this morning."

' "Not for me?"

' "Yes; didn't you expect one?"

' "I certainly did not!"

' "Well, here it is."

'And, as he lit me to my room, I read my own superscription of the previous day – to W. F. Raffles!

'Bunny, you've had your wind bagged at footer, I dare say; you know what that's like? All I can say is that my moral wind was bagged by that letter as I hope, old chap, I have never yet bagged yours. I couldn't speak. I could only stand with my own letter in my hands until he had the good taste to leave me by myself.

'W. F. Raffles! We had mistaken each other for W. F. Raffles – for the new manager who had not yet arrived! Small wonder we had conversed at cross-purposes; the only wonder was that we had not discovered our mutual mistake. How the other man would have laughed! But I – I could not laugh. By Jove, no, it was no laughing matter for me! I saw the whole thing in a flash, without a tremor, but with the direct depression from my own single point of view. Call it callous if you like, Bunny, but remember that I was in much the same hole as you've since been in yourself, and that I had counted on W. F. Raffles even as you counted on A. J. I thought of the man with the W. G. beard – the riderless horse with the bloody saddle – the deliberate misdirection that had put me off the track and out of the way – and now the missing manager and the report of bushrangers at this end. But I simply don't pretend to have felt any personal pity for a man whom I had never seen; that kind of pity's usually cant; and besides, all mine was needed for myself.

'I was in as big a hole as ever. What the devil was I to do? I doubt if I have sufficiently impressed upon you the absolute necessity of my returning to Melbourne in funds. As a matter of fact, it was less the necessity than my own determination which I can truthfully describe as absolute.

'Money I would have – but how – but how? Would this stranger be open to persuasion – if I told him the truth? No; that would set us all scouring the country for the rest of the night. Why should I tell him? Suppose I left him to find out his mistake ... would anything be gained? Bunny, I give you my word that I went to dinner without a definite intention in my head, or one premeditated lie upon my lips. I might do the decent, natural thing, and explain matters without loss of time; on the other hand, there was no hurry. I had not opened the letter, and could always pretend I had not noticed the initials; meanwhile something might turn up. I could wait a little and see. Tempted I already was, but as yet the temptation was vague, and its very vagueness made me tremble.

' "Bad news, I'm afraid," said the manager, when at last I sat down at his table.

' "A mere annoyance," I answered – I do assure you – on the spur of the moment and nothing else. But my lie was told; my position was taken; from that moment onward there was no retreat. By implication, without realising what I was doing, I had already declared myself W. F. Raffles. Therefore, W. F.

Raffles I would be, in that bank, for that night. And the devil teach me how to use my lie!'

Again he raised his glass to his lips – I had forgotten mine. His cigarette-case caught the gaslight as he handed it to me. I shook my head without taking my eyes from his.

'The devil played up,' continued Raffles, with a laugh. 'Before I tasted my soup I had decided what to do. I had determined to rob that bank instead of going to bed, and be back in Melbourne for breakfast if the doctor's mare could do it. I would tell the old fellow that I had missed my way and been bushed for hours, as I easily might have been, and had never got to Yea at all. At Yea, on the other hand, the personation and robbery would ever after be attributed to a member of the gang that had waylaid and murdered the new manager with that very object. You are acquiring some experience in such matters, Bunny. I ask you, was there ever a better get-out? Last night's was something like it, only never such a certainty. And I saw it from the beginning – saw to the end before I had finished my soup!

'To increase my chances, the cashier, who also lived in the bank, was away over the holidays, had actually gone down to Melbourne to see us play; and the man who had taken my horse also waited at table; for he and his wife were the only servants, and they slept in a separate building. You may depend I ascertained this before we had finished dinner. Indeed, I was by way of asking too many questions (the most oblique and delicate was that which elicited my host's name, Ewbank) nor was I careful enough to conceal their drift.

' "Do you know," said this fellow Ewbank, who was one of the downright sort, "if it wasn't you, I should say you were in a funk of robbers? Have you lost your nerve?"

' "I hope not," said I, turning jolly hot, I can tell you; "but – well, it's not a pleasant thing to have to put a bullet through a fellow!"

' "No?" said he coolly. "I should enjoy nothing better myself; besides, yours didn't go through."

' "I wish it had!" I was smart enough to cry.

' "Amen!" said he.

'And I emptied my glass: actually I did not know whether

my wounded bank-robber was in prison, dead, or at large!

'But now that I had had more than enough of it, Ewbank would come back to the subject. He admitted that the staff was small; but as for himself, he had a loaded revolver under his pillow all night, under the counter all day, and he was only waiting for his chance.

' "Under the counter, eh?" I was ass enough to say.

' "Yes; so had you!"

'He was looking at me in surprise, and something told me that to say "of course – I had forgotten!" would have been quite fatal, considering what I was supposed to have done. So I looked down my nose and shook my head.

' "But the papers said you had!" he cried.

' "Not under the counter," said I.

' " But it's the regulation!"

'For the moment, Bunny, I felt stumped, though I trust I only looked more superior than before, and I think I justified my look.

' "The regulation!" I said at length, in the most offensive tone at my command. "Yes, the regulation would have us all dead men! My dear sir, do you expect your bank-robber to let you reach for your gun in the place where he knows it's kept? I had mine in my pocket, and I got my chance by retreating from the counter with all visible reluctance."

'Ewbank stared at me with open eyes and a five-barred forehead, then down came his fist on the table.

' "By God, that was smart! Still," he added, like a man who would not be in the wrong, "the papers said the other thing, you know!"

' "Of course," I replied, "because they said what I told them. You wouldn't have had me advertise the fact that I improved upon the bank's regulations, would you?"

'So that cloud rolled over, and by Jove it was a cloud with a golden lining! Not silver – real good Australian gold! For old Ewbank hadn't quite appreciated me till then; he was a hard nut, a much older man than myself, and I felt pretty sure he thought me young for the place, and my supposed feat a fluke. But I never saw a man change his mind more openly. He got out his best brandy, he made me throw away the cigar I was smoking, and opened a fresh box. He was a convivial-looking party, with a red moustache, and a very humorous face (not unlike Tom Emmett's), and from that moment I laid myself out to attack him on his convivial flank. But he wasn't a Rosenthall, Bunny; he had a treble-seamed, hand-sewn head, and could have drunk me under the table ten times over.

' "All right," I thought, "you may go to bed sober, but you'll sleep like a timber yard!" And I threw half he gave me through the open window when he wasn't looking.

'But he was a good chap, Ewbank, and don't you imagine he was at all intemperate. Convivial I called him, and I only wish he had been something more. He did, however, become more and more genial as the evening advanced, and I had not much difficulty in getting him to show me round the bank at what was really an unearthly hour for such a proceeding. It was when he went to fetch the revolver before turning in. I kept him out of his bed another twenty minutes, and I knew every inch of the business premises before I shook hands with Ewbank in my room.

'You won't guess what I did with myself for the next hour. I undressed and went to bed. The incessant strain involved in even the most deliberate impersonation is the most wearing thing I know; then how much more so when the impersonation is impromptu! There's no getting your eye in; the next word may bowl you out; it's batting in a bad light all through. I haven't told you half the tight places I was in during the conversation that ran into hours and became dangerously intimate towards the end, you can imagine them for yourself, and then picture me spread out on my bed, getting my second wind for the big deed of the night.

'Once more I was in luck, for I had not been lying there long before I heard my dear Ewbank snoring like a harmonium, and the music never ceased for a moment; it was as loud as ever when I crept out and closed my door behind me, as regular as ever when I stopped to listen at his. And I have still to hear the concert that I shall enjoy much more. The good fellow snored me out of the bank, and was still snoring when I again stood and listened under his open window.

'Why did I leave the bank first? To catch and saddle the mare and tether her in a clump of trees close by: to have the means of escape nice and handy before I went to work. I have often wondered at the instinctive wisdom of the precaution; unconsciously I was acting on what has been one of my guiding principles ever since. Pains and patience were required; I had to get my saddle without waking the man, and I was not used to catching horses in a horse-paddock. Then I distrusted the poor mare, and I went back to the stables for a hatful of oats, which I left with her in the clump, hat and all. There was a dog, too, to reckon with (our very worst enemy, Bunny); but I had been cute enough to make immense friends with him during the evening; and he wagged his tail, not only when I came downstairs, but when I reappeared at the back door.

'As the *soi-disant* new manager, I had been able, in the most ordinary course, to pump poor Ewbank about anything and everything connected with the working of the bank, especially in those twenty last invaluable minutes before turning in. And I had made a very natural point of asking him where he kept, and would recommend me to keep, the keys at night. Of course, I thought he would take them with him to his room; but no such thing; he had a dodge worth two of that. What it was doesn't much matter, but no outsider would have found those keys in a month of Sundays.

'I, of course, had them in a few seconds, and in a few more I was in the strong-room itself. I forgot to say that the moon had risen and was letting quite a lot of light into the bank. I had, however, brought a bit of candle with me from my room; and in the strong-room, which was down some narrow stairs behind the counter in the banking chamber, I had no hesitation in lighting it. There was no window down there, and though I could no longer hear old Ewbank snoring, I had not the slightest reason to anticipate disturbance from that quarter. I did think of locking myself in while I was at work, but, thank goodness, the iron door had no keyhole on the inside.

'Well, there was heaps of gold in the safe, but I only took what I needed and could comfortably carry, not much more

73

than a couple of hundred altogether. Not a note would I touch, and my native caution came out also in the way I divided the sovereigns between all my pockets, and packed them up so that I shouldn't be like the old woman of Banbury Cross. Well, you think me too cautious still, but I was insanely cautious then. And so it was that, just as I was ready to go, whereas I might have been gone ten minutes, there came a violent knocking at the outer door.

'Bunny, it was the outer door of the banking chamber! My candle must have been seen! And there I stood, with the grease running hot over my fingers, in that brick grave of a strongroom!

'There was only one thing to be done. I must trust to the sound sleeping of Ewbank upstairs, open the door myself, knock the visitor down, or shoot him with the revolver I had been new chum enough to buy before leaving Melbourne, and make a dash for that clump of trees and the doctor's mare. My mind was made up in an instant, and I was at the top of the strong-room stairs, the knocking still continuing, when a second sound drove me back. It was the sound of bare feet coming along a corridor.

'My narrow stair was stone. I tumbled down it with little noise, and had only to push open the iron door, for I had left the keys in the safe. As I did so I heard a handle turn overhead, and thanked my gods that I had shut every single door behind me. You see, old chap, one's caution doesn't always let one in!

' "Who's that knocking?" said Ewbank, up above.

'I could not make out the answer, but it sounded to me like the irrelevant supplication of a spent man. What I did hear plainly, was the cocking of the bank revolver before the bolts were shot back. Then, a tottering step, a hard, short, shallow breathing, and Ewbank's voice in horror:

' "Good Lord! What's happened to you? You're bleeding like a pig!'

' "Not now," came a grateful sort of sigh.

' "But you have been! What's done it?"

' "Bushrangers."

' "Down the road?"

' "This and Whittlesea – tied to tree – pot-shots – left me – bleed to death. ..."'

'The weak voice failed, and the bare feet bolted. Now was my time – if the poor devil had fainted. But I could not be sure, and there I crouched down below in the dark, at the half-shut iron door, not less spell-bound than imprisoned. It was just as well, for Ewbank wasn't gone a minute.

' "Drink this," I heard him say, and when the other spoke again his voice was stronger.

' "Now I begin to feel alive."

' "Don't talk!"

' "It does me good. You don't know what it was, all those miles alone, one an hour at the outside! I never thought I should come through. You must let me tell you – in case I don't!"

' "Well, have another sip."

' "Thank you. ... I said bushrangers; of course there are no such things nowadays."

' "What were they, then?"

' "Bank thieves; the one that had the pot-shots was the very brute I drove out of the bank at Coburg, with a bullet in him!" '

'I knew it!'

'Of course you did, Bunny; so did I, down in that strong-room; but old Ewbank didn't, and I thought he was never going to speak again.

' "You're delirious," he said at last. "Who in blazes do you think you are?"

' "The new manager."

' "The new manager's in bed and asleep upstairs!"

' "When did he arrive?"

' "This evening."

' "Call himself Raffles?"

' "Yes."

' "Well, I'm damned!" whispered the real man. "I thought it was just revenge, but now I see what it was. My dear sir, the man upstairs is an impostor – if he's upstairs still! He must be one of the gang. He's going to rob the bank – if he hasn't done so already!"

' "If he hasn't done so already," muttered Ewbank after him; "if he's upstairs still! By God, if he is I'm sorry for him!"

'His tone was quiet enough, but about the nastiest I ever heard. I tell you, Bunny, I was glad I'd brought that revolver. It looked as though it must be mine against his, muzzle to muzzle.

' "Better have a look down here, first," said the new manager.

' "While he gets through his window? No, no, he's not down here."

' "It's easy to have a look."

'Bunny, if you ask me what was the most thrilling moment of my infamous career, I say it was that moment. There I stood at the bottom of those narrow stone stairs, inside the strong-room, with the door a good foot open, and I didn't know whether it would creak or not. The light was coming nearer – and I didn't know! I had to chance it. And it didn't creak a bit; it was far too solid and well-hung; and I couldn't have banged it if I'd tried. It was too heavy; and it fitted so close that I felt and heard the air squeeze out in my face. Every shred of light went out, except the streak underneath, and it brightened. How I blessed that door!

' "No, he's not down there," I heard, as though through cotton-wool; then the streak went out too, and in a few seconds I ventured to open once more, and was in time to hear them creeping to my room.

'Well, now, there was not a fifth of a second to be lost; but I'm proud to say I came up those stairs on my toes and fingers, and out of that bank (they'd gone and left the door open) just as gingerly as though my time had been my own. I didn't even forget to put on the hat that the doctor's mare was eating her oats out of, as well as she could with a bit, or it alone would have landed me. I didn't even gallop away, but just jogged off quietly in the thick dust at the side of the road (though I own my heart was galloping), and thanked my stars the bank was at the end of the township, in which I really hadn't set foot. The very last thing I heard was the two managers raising Cain and the coachman. And now, Bunny – –'

He stood up and stretched himself, with a smile that ended in a yawn. The black windows had faded through every shade of indigo; they now framed their opposite neighbours, stark and livid in the dawn; and the gas seemed turned to nothing in the globes.

'But that's not all?' I cried.

'I'm sorry to say it is,' said Raffles apologetically. 'The thing should have ended with an exciting chase, I know, but somehow it didn't. I suppose they thought I had got no end of a start; then they had made up their minds that I belonged to the gang, which was not so many miles away; and one of them had got as much as he could carry from that gang as it was. But I wasn't to know all that, and I'm bound to say that there was plenty of excitement left for me. Lord, how I made that poor brute travel when I got among the trees! Though we must have been well over fifty miles from Melbourne, we had done it at a snail's pace; and those stolen oats had brisked the old girl up to such a pitch that she fairly bolted when she felt her nose turned south. By Jove, it was no joke, in and out among those trees, and under branches with your face in the mane! I told you about the forest of dead gums? It looked perfectly ghostly in the moonlight. And I found it as still as I had left it – so still that I pulled up there, my first halt, and lay with my ear to the ground for two or three minutes. But I heard nothing – not a thing but the mare's bellows and my own heart. I'm sorry, Bunny; but if ever you write my memoirs, you won't have any difficulty in working up that chase. Play those dead gum trees for all they're worth, and let the bullets fly like hail. I'll turn round in my saddle to see Ewbank coming up hell-for-leather in his white suit, and I'll duly paint it red. Do it in the third person, and they won't know how it's going to end.'

'But I don't know myself,' I complained. 'Did the mare carry you all the way back to Melbourne?'

'Every rod, pole, or perch! I had her well seen to at our hotel, and returned her to the doctor in the evening. He was tremendously tickled to hear I had been bushed; next morning he brought me the paper to show me what I had escaped at Yea!'

'Without suspecting anything?'

'Ah!' said Raffles, as he put out the gas; 'that's a point on which I've never made up my mind. The mare and her colour was a coincidence – luckily she was only a bay – and I fancy the condition of the beast must have told a tale. The doctor's manner was certainly different. I'm inclined to think he suspected something, though not the right thing. I wasn't expecting him, and I fear my appearance may have increased his suspicions.'

I asked him why.

'I used to have rather a heavy moustache,' said Raffles, 'but I lost it the day after I lost my innocence.'

WILFUL MURDER

OF the various robberies in which we were both concerned, it is but the few, I find, that will bear telling at any length. Not that the others contained details which even I would hesitate to recount; it is, rather, the very absence of untoward incident which renders them useless for my present purpose. In point of fact, our plans were so craftily laid (by Raffles) that the chances of a hitch were invariably reduced to a minimum before we went to work. We might be disappointed in the market value of our haul; but it was quite the exception for us to find ourselves confronted by unforeseen impediments, or involved in a really dramatic dilemma. There was a sameness, even in our spoil; for, of course, only the most precious stones are worth the trouble we took and the risks we ran. In short, our most successful escapades would prove the greatest weariness of all in narrative form; and none more so than the dull affair of the Ardagh emeralds, some eight or nine weeks after the Milchester cricket week. The former, however, had a sequel that I would rather forget than all our burglaries put together.

It was the evening after our return from Ireland, and I was waiting at my rooms for Raffles, who had gone off as usual to dispose of the plunder. Raffles had his own method of conducting this very vital branch of our business, which I was well content to leave entirely in his hands. He drove the bargains, I believe, in a thin but subtle disguise of the flashy-seedy order, and always in the Cockney dialect, of which he had made himself a master. Moreover, he invariably employed the same 'fence', who was ostensibly a money-lender in a small (but yet notorious) way, and in reality a rascal as remarkable as Raffles himself. Only lately I also had been to the man, but in my proper person. We had needed capital for the getting of these very emeralds, and I had raised a hundred pounds, on the terms you would expect from a soft-spoken greybeard with an ingratiating smile, an incessant bow, and the shiftiest old eyes that ever flew from rim to rim of a pair of spectacles. So the original sinews and the final spoils of war came in this case from the self-same source – a circumstance which appealed to us both.

But these same final spoils I was still to see, and I waited and waited with an impatience that grew upon me with the growing dusk. At my open window I had played Sister Ann until the faces in the street below were no longer distinguishable. And now I was tearing to and fro in the grip of horrible hypothesis – a grip that tightened when at last the lift-gates opened with a clatter outside – that held me breathless until a well-known tattoo followed on my door.

'In the dark!' said Raffles, as I dragged him in. 'Why, Bunny, what's wrong?'

'Nothing – now you've come,' said I, shutting the door behind him in a fever of relief and anxiety. 'Well? Well? What did they fetch?'

'Five hundred.'

'Down?'

'Got it in my pocket.'

'Good man!' I cried. 'You don't know what a stew I've been in. I'll switch on the light. I've been thinking of you and nothing else for the last hour. I – I was ass enough to think something had gone wrong!'

Raffles was smiling when the white light filled the room, but for the moment I did not perceive the peculiarity of his smile. I was fatuously full of my own late tremors and present relief, and my first idiotic act was to spill some whisky and squirt the soda-water all over in my anxiety to do justice to the occasion.

'So you thought something had happened?' said Raffles, leaning back in my chair as he lit a cigarette, and looking much amused. 'What should you say if something had? Sit tight, my dear chap! It was nothing of the slightest consequence, and it's all over now. A stern chase and a long one, Bunny, but I think I'm well to windward this time.'

And suddenly I saw that his collar was limp, his hair matted, his boots thick with dust.

'The police?' I whispered, aghast.

'Oh dear, no; only old Baird.'

'Baird! But wasn't it Baird who took the emeralds?'

'It was.'

'Then how came he to chase you?'

'My dear fellow, I'll tell you if you give me a chance, it's really nothing to get in the least excited about. Old Baird has at last spotted that I'm not quite the common cracksman I would have him think me. So he's been doing his best to run me to my burrow.'

'And you call that nothing!'

'It would be something if he had succeeded; but he has still to do that. I admit, however, that he made me sit up for the time being. It all comes of going on the job so far from home. There was the old brute with the whole thing in his morning paper. He knew it must have been done by some fellow who could pass himself off for a gentleman, and I saw his eyebrows go up the moment I told him I was the man, with the same old twang that you could cut with a paper knife. I did my best to get out of it – swore I had a pal who was a real swell – but I saw very plainly that I had given myself away. He gave up haggling. He paid my price as though he enjoyed doing it. But I felt him following me when I made tracks – though, of course, I didn't turn round to see.'

'Why not?'

'My dear Bunny, it's the very worst thing you can do. As long as you look unsuspecting they'll keep their distance, and so long as they keep their distance you stand a chance. Once show that you know you're being followed, and it's flight or fight for all you're worth. I never even looked round; and mind you never do in the same hole. I just hurried up to Blackfriars and booked for High Street, Kensington, at the top of my voice; and as the train was leaving Sloane Square out I hopped, and up all those stairs like a lamp-lighter, and round to the studio by the back streets. Well, to be on the safe side, I lay low there all the afternoon, hearing nothing in the least suspicious, and only wishing I had a window to look through instead of that beastly skylight. However, the coast seemed clear enough, and thus far it was my mere idea that he would follow me; there was nothing to show he had. So at last I marched out in my proper rig – almost straight into old Baird's arms!'

'What on earth did you do?'

'Walked past him as though I had never set eyes on him in my life, and didn't then; took a cab in the King's Road, and drove like the deuce to Clapham Junction; rushed on to the nearest platform, without a ticket, jumped into the first train I saw, got out at Twickenham, walked full tilt back to Richmond, took the District to Charing Cross, and here I am! Ready for a tub and a change, and the best dinner the club can give us. I came to you first, because I thought you might be getting anxious. Come round with me, and I won't keep you long.'

'You're certain you've given him the slip?' I said, as we put on our hats.

'Certain enough; but we can make assurance doubly sure,' said Raffles, and went to my window, where he stood for a minute or two looking down into the street.

'All right?' I asked him.

'All right,' said he; and we went downstairs forthwith, and so to the Albany arm-in-arm.

But we were both rather silent on the way. I, for my part, was wondering what Raffles would do about the studio in Chelsea, whither, at all events, he had been successfully dogged. To me the point seemed one of immediate importance, but when I mentioned it he said there was time enough to think about that. His other remark was made after we had nodded (in Bond Street) to a young blood of our acquaintance who happened to be getting himself a bad name.

'Poor Jack Rutter!' said Raffles, with a sigh. 'Nothing's sadder than to see a fellow going to the bad like that. He's about mad with drink and debt; did you see his eye? Odd that we should have met him to-night, by the way; it's old Baird who's said to have skinned him. I've a jolly good mind to skin old Baird!'

And his tone took a sudden low fury, made the more noticeable by another long silence, which lasted, indeed, throughout an admirable dinner at the club, and for some time after we had settled down in a quiet corner of the smoking-room with our coffee and cigars. Then at last I saw Raffles looking at me with his lazy smile, and I knew that the morose fit was at an end.

'I dare say you wonder what I've been thinking about all this time?' said he. 'I've been thinking what rot it is to go doing things by halves!'

'Well,' said I, returning his smile, 'that's not a charge that you can bring against yourself, is it?'

'I'm not so sure,' said Raffles, blowing a meditative puff; 'as a matter of fact, I was thinking less of myself than of that poor devil of a Jack Rutter. There's a fellow who does things by halves; he's only half gone to the bad; and look at the difference between him and us! He's under the thumb of a villainous money-lender; we are solvent citizens. He's taken to drink; we're as sober as we are solvent. His pals are beginning to cut him; our difficulty is to keep the pal from the door. *Enfin,* he begs or borrows, which is stealing by halves; and we steal outright and are done with it. Obviously, ours is the more honest course. Yet I'm not sure, Bunny, but we're doing the thing by halves ourselves!'

'Why? What more could we do?' I exclaimed in soft derision, looking round, however, to make sure that we were not overheard.

'What more?' said Raffles. 'Well, murder – for one thing.'

'Rot!'

'A matter of opinion, my dear Bunny; I don't mean it for rot. I've told you before that the biggest man alive is the man who's committed a murder, and not yet been found out; at least he ought to be, but he so very seldom has the soul to appreciate himself. Just think of it! Think of coming here and talking to the men, very likely about the murder itself; and knowing you've done it; and wondering how they'd look if they knew! Oh, it would be great, simply great! But, besides all that, when you were caught, there'd be a merciful and dramatic end of you. You'd fill the bill for a few weeks and then snuff out with a flourish of extra-specials; you wouldn't rust with a vile repose for seven or fourteen years.'

'Good old Raffles!' I chuckled. 'I begin to forgive you for being in bad form at dinner.'

'But I was never more earnest in my life.'

'Go on!'

'I mean it.'

'You know very well that you wouldn't commit a murder, whatever else you might do.'

'I know very well I'm going to commit one to-night!'

He had been leaning back in the saddle-bag chair, watching me with keen eyes sheathed by languid lids; now he started forward, and his eyes leapt to mine like cold steel from the scabbard. They struck home to my slow wits; their meaning was no longer in doubt. I, who knew the man, read murder in his clenched hands, and murder in his locked lips, but a hundred murders in those hard blue eyes.

'Baird?' I faltered, moistening my lips with my tongue.

'Of course.'

'But you said it didn't matter about the room in Chelsea?'

'I told a lie.'

'Anyway, you gave him the slip afterwards!'

'That was another. I didn't. I thought I had when I came up to you this evening; but when I looked out of your window – you remember? – to make assurance doubly sure – there he was on the opposite pavement down below.'

'And you never said a word about it!'

'I wasn't going to spoil your dinner, Bunny, and I wasn't going to let you spoil mine. But there he was as large as life, and, of course, he followed us to the Albany. A fine game for him to play, a game after his mean old heart; blackmail for me, bribes from the police, the one bidding against the other; but he shan't play it with me, he shan't live to, and the world will have an extortioner the less. Waiter! Two Scotch whiskies and sodas. I'm off at eleven, Bunny; it's the only thing to be done.'

'You know where he lives, then?'

'Yes, out Willesden way, and alone; the fellow's a miser among other things. I long ago found out all about him.'

Again I looked around the room; it was a young man's club, and young men were laughing, chatting, smoking, drinking, on every hand. One nodded to me through the smoke. Like a machine I nodded to him, and turned back to Raffles with a groan.

'Surely you will give him a chance!' I urged. 'The very sight of your pistol should bring him to terms.'

'It wouldn't make him keep them.'

'But you might try the effect?'

'I probably shall. Here's a drink for you, Bunny. Wish me luck.'

'I'm coming too.'

'I don't want you.'

'But I must come!'

An ugly gleam shot from the steel-blue eyes.

'To interfere?' said Raffles.

'Not I.'

'You give me your word?'

'I do.'

'Bunny, if you break it – –'

'You may shoot me too!'

'I most certainly should,' said Raffles solemnly. 'So you come at your own peril, my dear man; but if you are coming – well, the sooner the better, for I must stop at my rooms on the way.'

Five minutes later I was waiting for him at the Piccadilly entrance to the Albany. I had a reason for remaining outside. It was the feeling – half hope, half fear – that Angus Baird might still be on our trail – that some more immediate and less cold-blooded way of dealing with him might result from a sudden encounter between the money-lender and myself. I would not warn him of his danger; but I would avert tragedy at all costs. And when no such encounter had taken place, and Raffles and I were fairly on our way to Willesden, that, I think, was still my honest resolve. I would not break my word if I could help it, but it was a comfort to feel that I could break it if I liked, on an understood penalty. Alas! I fear my good intentions were tainted with a devouring curiosity, and overlaid by the fascination which goes hand in hand with horror.

I have a poignant recollection of the hour it took us to reach the house. We walked across St James's Park (I can see the lights now, bright on the bridge and blurred on the water), and we had some minutes to wait for the last train to Willesden. It left at 11.21, I remember, and Raffles was put out to find it did not go on to Kensal Rise. We had to get out at Willesden Junction and walk on through the streets into fairly open country that happened to be quite new to me. I could never find the house again. I remember, however, that we were on a dark footpath between the woods and fields when the clocks began striking twelve.

'Surely,' said I, 'we shall find him in bed and asleep?'

'I hope we do,' said Raffles grimly.

'Then you mean to break in?'

'What else did you think?'

I had not thought about it at all; the ultimate crime had monopolised my mind. Beside it burglary was a bagatelle, but one to deprecate none the less. I saw obvious objections; the man was *au fait* with cracksmen and their ways, he would certainly have firearms, and might be the first to use them.

'I could wish nothing better,' said Raffles. 'Then it will be man to man, and devil take the worst shot. You don't suppose I prefer foul play to fair, do you? But die he must by one or the other, or it's a long stretch for you and me."

'Better that than this!'

'Then stay where you are, my good fellow. I told you I didn't want you; and this is the house. So good-night.'

I could see no house at all, only the angle of a high wall rising solitary in the night, with the starlight glittering on battlements of broken glass and in the wall a tall green gate, bristling with spikes, and showing a front for battering-rams in the feeble rays of an outlying lamp-post cast across the new-made road. It seemed to me a road of building sites, with but this one house built, all by itself, at one end; but the night was too dark for more than a mere impression.

Raffles, however, had seen the place by daylight, and had come prepared for the special obstacles; already he was reaching up and putting champagne corks on the spikes, and in another moment he had his folded covert coat across the corks. I stepped back as he raised himself, and saw a little pyramid of slates snip the sky above the gate; as he squirmed over I ran forward, and had my own weight on the spikes and corks and covert coat when he gave the latter a tug.

'Coming after all?'

'Rather!'

'Take care, then; the place is all bell-wires and springs. It's no soft spring this! There – stand still while I take off the corks.'

The garden was very small and new, with a grass-plot still in separate sods, but a quantity of full-grown laurels stuck into the raw clay beds. 'Bells in themselves,' Raffles whispered; 'there's nothing else rustles so – cunning old beast!' And we gave them a wide berth as we crept across the grass.

'He's gone to bed!'

'I don't think so, Bunny. I believe he's seen us.'

'Why?'

'I saw a light.'

'Where?'

'Downstairs, for an instant, when I – –'

His whisper died away; he had seen the light again, and so had I.

It lay like a golden rod under the front door – and vanished. It reappeared like a gold thread under the lintel – and vanished for good. We heard the stairs creak, creak, and cease, also for good. We neither saw nor heard any more, though we stood waiting on the grass till our feet were soaked with the dew.

'I'm going in,' said Raffles at last. 'I don't believe he saw us at all. I wish he had. This way.'

We trod gingerly on the path, but the gravel stuck to our wet soles, and grated horribly in a little tiled verandah with a glass door leading within. It was through this glass that Raffles had first seen the light; and he now proceeded to take out a pane, with the diamond, the pot of treacle, and the sheet of brown paper which were seldom omitted from his impedimenta. Nor did he dispense with my own assistance, though he may have accepted it as instinctively as it was proffered. In any case it was these fingers that helped to spread the treacle on the brown paper, and pressed the latter to the glass until the diamond had completed its circuit and the pane fell gently back into our hands.

Raffles now inserted his hand, turned the key in the lock, and, by making a long arm, succeeded in drawing the bolt at the bottom of the door; it proved to be the only one, and the door opened, though not very wide.

'What's that?' said Raffles, as something crunched beneath his feet on the very theshold.

'A pair of spectacles,' I whispered, picking them up. I was still fingering the broken lenses and the bent rims when Raffles tripped and almost fell, with a gasping cry that he made no effort to restrain.

'Hush, man, hush!' I entreated under my breath. 'He'll hear you!'

For answer his teeth chattered – even his – and I heard him fumbling with his matches.

'No, Bunny; he won't hear us,' whispered Raffles presently, and he rose from his knees and lit a gas as the match burnt down.

Angus Baird was lying on his own floor, dead, with his grey hairs glued together by his blood; near him a poker with the black end glistening; in the corner his desk, ransacked, littered. A clock ticked noisily on the chimney-piece; for perhaps a hundred seconds there was no other sound.

Raffles stood very still, staring down at the dead, as a man might stare into an abyss after striding blindly to its brink. His breath came audibly through wide nostrils; he made no other sign, and his lips seemed sealed.

'That light!' said I hoarsely; 'the light we saw under the door!'

With a start he turned to me.

'It's true. I had forgotten it. It was in here I saw it first!'

'He must be upstairs still!'

'If he is we'll soon rout him out. Come on!'

Instead I laid a hand upon his arm, imploring him to reflect – that his enemy was dead now – that we should certainly be involved – that now or never was our own time to escape. He shook me off in a sudden fury of impatience, a reckless contempt in his eyes, and, bidding me save my own skin if I liked, he once more turned his back upon me, and this time left me half resolved to take him at his word. Had he forgotten on what errand he himself was here? Was he determined that this night should end in black disaster? As I asked myself these questions his match flared in the hall; in another moment the stairs were creaking under his feet, even as they had creaked

under those of the murderer; and the humane instinct that inspired him in defiance of his risk was borne in also upon my
slower sensibilities. Could we let the murderer go? My answer
was to bound up the creaking stairs and to overhaul Raffles on
the landing.

But three doors presented themselves; the first opened into
a bedroom with the bed turned down but undisturbed; the
second room was empty in every sense; the third door was
locked.

Raffles lit the landing gas.

'He's in there,' said he, cocking his revolver. 'Do you remember how we used to break into the studies at school? Here
goes!'

His flat foot crashed over the keyhole, the lock gave, the
door flew open, and in the sudden draught the landing gas
heeled over like a coble in a squall; as the flame righted itself
I saw a fixed bath, two bath-towels knotted together – an
open window – a cowering figure – and Raffles struck aghast
on the threshold.

'Jack – Rutter?'

The words came thick and slow with horror, and in horror
I heard myself repeating them, while the cowering figure by
the bath-room window rose gradually erect.

'It's you!' he whispered, in amazement no less than our own;
'it's you two! What's it mean, Raffles? I saw you get over the
gate; a bell rang, the place is full of them. Then you broke in!
What's it all mean?'

'We may tell you that, when you tell us what in God's name
you've done, Rutter!'

'Done? What have I done?' The unhappy wretch came out
into the light with bloodshot, blinking eyes, and a bloody
shirt-front. 'You know – you've seen – but I'll tell you if you
like. I've killed a robber; that's all. I've killed a robber, a
usurer, a jackal, a blackmailer, the cleverest and the cruellest
villain unhung. I'm ready to hang for him. I'd kill him again!'

And he looked us fiercely in the face, a fine defiance in his
dissipated eyes; his breast heaving, his jaw like a rock.

'Shall I tell you how it happened?' he went on passionately.
'He's made my life a hell these weeks and months past. You

may know that. A perfect hell. Well, to-night I met him in Bond Street. Do you remember when I met you fellows? He wasn't twenty yards behind you; he was on your tracks, Raffles; he saw me nod to you, and stopped me and asked me who you were. He seemed as keen as knives to know. I couldn't think why, and didn't care either, for I saw my chance. I said I'd tell him all about you if he'd give me a private interview. He said he wouldn't. I said he should, and held him by the coat; by the time I let him go you were out of sight, and I waited where I was till he came back in despair. I had the whip-hand of him then. I could dictate where the interview should be, and I made him take me home with him, still swearing to tell him all about you when we'd had our talk. Well, when we got here I made him give me something to eat, putting him off and off; and about ten o'clock I heard the gate shut. I waited a bit, and then asked him if he lived alone.

' " Not at all," says he; "did you not see the servant?"

'I said I'd seen her, but I thought I heard her go; if I was mistaken, no doubt she would come when she was called; and I yelled three times at the top of my voice. Of course there was no servant to come. I knew that, because I came to see him one night last week, and he interviewed me himself through the gate, but wouldn't open it. Well, when I had done yelling, and not a soul had come near us, he was as white as that ceiling. Then I told him we could have our chat at last; and I picked the poker out of the fender, and told him how he'd robbed me, but by God he shouldn't rob me any more. I gave him three minutes to write and sign a settlement of all his iniquitous claims against me, or have his brains beaten out over his own carpet. He thought a minute and then went to his desk for pen and paper. In two seconds he was round like lightning with a revolver, and I went for him bald-headed. He fired two or three times and missed – you can find the holes if you like; but I hit him every time – by God! I was like a savage till the thing was done. And then I didn't care. I went through his desk looking for my own bills, and was coming away when you turned up. I said I didn't care, nor do I; but I was going to give myself up to-night, and shall still; so you see I shan't give you fellows much trouble!'

He was done; and there we stood on the landing of the lonely house, the low, thick, eager voice still racing and ringing through our ears; the dead man below, and in front of us his impenitent slayer. I knew to whom the impenitence would appeal when he had heard the story, and I was not mistaken.

'That's all rot,' said Raffles, speaking after a pause; 'we shan't let you give yourself up.'

'You shan't stop me! What would be the good? The woman saw me; it would only be a question of time; and I can't face waiting to be taken. Think of it : waiting for them to touch you on the shoulder! No, no, no; I'll give myself up and get it over.'

His speech was changed; he faltered, floundered. It was as though a clearer perception of his position had come with the bare idea of escape from it.

'But listen to me,' urged Raffles. 'We're here at our peril ourselves. We broke in like thieves to enforce redress for a grievance like your own. But don't you see? We took out a pane — did the thing like regular burglars. We shall get the credit of all the rest!'

'You mean that I shan't be suspected?'

'I do.'

'But I don't want to get off scot-free,' cried Rutter hysterically. 'I've killed him. I know that. But it was in self-defence; it wasn't murder. I must own up and take the consequences. I shall go mad if I don't.'

His hands twitched; his lips quivered; the tears were in his eyes. Raffles took him roughly by the shoulder.

'Look here, you fool! If the three of us are caught here now, do you know what the consequences would be? We should swing in a row in six weeks' time! You talk as though we were sitting in a club; don't you know it's one o'clock in the morning, and the lights on, and a dead man down below? For God's sake pull yourself together, and do what I tell you, or you're a dead man yourself.'

'I wish I was one!' Rutter sobbed. 'I wish I had his revolver, I'd blow my own brains out. It's somewhere under him! O my God, my God!'

His knees knocked together; the frenzy of reaction was at its height. We had to take him downstairs between us, and so through the front door out into the open air.

All was still outside – all but the smothered weeping of the unstrung wretch upon our hands. Raffles returned for a moment to the house; then all was dark as well. The gate opened from within; we closed it carefully behind us; and so left the starlight shining on broken glass and polished spikes, one and all as we had found them.

We escaped; no need to dwell on our escape. Our murderer seemed set upon the scaffold: drunk with his deed, he was more trouble than six men drunk with wine. Again and again we threatened to leave him to his fate, to wash our hands of him. But incredible and unmerited luck was with the three of us. Not a soul did we meet between that and Willesden; and of those who saw us later, did one think of the two young men with crooked white ties, supporting a third in a seemingly unmistakable condition, when the evening papers apprised the town of a terrible tragedy at Kensal Rise?

We walked to Maida Vale, and thence drove openly to my rooms. But I alone went upstairs; the other two proceeded to the Albany, and I saw no more of Raffles for forty-eight hours. He was not at his rooms when I called in the morning, he had left no word. When he reappeared the papers were full of the murder; and the man who had committed it was on the wide Atlantic, a steerage passenger from Liverpool to New York.

'There was no arguing with him,' so Raffles told me; 'either he must make a clean breast of it or flee the country. So I rigged him up at the studio, and we took the first train to Liverpool. Nothing would induce him to sit tight and enjoy the situation as I should have endeavoured to do in his place; and it's just as well! I went to his diggings to destroy some papers, and what do you think I found? The police in possession; there's a warrant out against him already! The idiots think that window wasn't genuine, and the warrant's out. It won't be my fault if it's ever served!'

Nor, after all these years, can I think it will be mine.

NINE POINTS OF THE LAW

'WELL,' said Raffles, 'what do you make of it?'

I read the advertisement once more before replying. It was in the last column of the *Daily Telegraph*, and it ran:

'TWO THOUSAND POUNDS REWARD. – The above sum may be earned by any one qualified to undertake delicate mission and prepared to run certain risk. – Apply by telegram, Security, London.'

'I think,' said I, 'it's the most extraordinary advertisement that ever got into print!'

Raffles smiled.

'Not quite all that, Bunny; still, extraordinary enough, I grant you.'

'Look at the figure.'

'It is certainly large.'

'And the mission – and the risk!'

'Yes, the combination is frank, to say the least of it. But the really original point is requiring applications by telegram to a telegraphic address! There's something in the fellow who thought of that, and something in his game; with one word he chokes off the million who answer an advertisement every day – when they can raise the stamp. My answer cost me five bob; but then I prepaid another.'

'You don't mean to say that you've applied?'

'Rather,' said Raffles. 'I want two thousand pounds as much as any man.'

'Put your own name?'

'Well – no, Bunny, I didn't. In point of fact, I smell something interesting and illegal, and you know what a cautious chap I am. I signed myself Glasspool, care of Hickey, 38 Conduit Street; that's my tailor, and after sending the wire I went round and told him what to expect. He promised to send the reply along the moment it came. I shouldn't be surprised if that's it!'

And he was gone before a double knock on the outer door had done ringing through the rooms, to return next minute with an open telegram and a face full of news.

'What do you think?' said he. 'Security's that fellow Addenbrooke, the police court lawyer, and he wants to see me *instanter*!'

'Do you know him, then?'

'Merely by repute. I only hope he doesn't know me. He's the chap who got six weeks for sailing too close to the wind in the Sutton-Wilmer case; everybody wondered why he wasn't struck off the rolls. Instead of that he's got a first-rate practice on the seamy side, and every blackguard with half a case takes it straight to Bennett Addenbrooke. He's probably the one man who would have the cheek to put in an advertisement like that, and the one man who could do it without exciting suspicion. It's simply in his line; but you may be sure there's something shady at the bottom of it. The odd thing is that I have long made up my mind to go to Addenbrooke myself if accidents should happen.'

'And you're going to him now?'

'This minute,' said Raffles, brushing his hat; 'and so are you.'

'But I came in to drag you out to lunch.'

'You shall lunch with me when we've seen this fellow. Come on, Bunny, and we'll choose your name on the way. Mine's Glasspool, and don't you forget it.'

Mr Bennett Addenbrooke occupied substantial offices in Wellington Street, Strand, and was out when we arrived; but he had only just gone 'over the way to the court'; and five minutes sufficed to produce a brisk, fresh-coloured, resolute-looking man, with a very confident, rather festive air, and black eyes that opened wide at the sight of Raffles.

'Mr – Glasspool?' exclaimed the lawyer.

'My name,' said Raffles, with dry effrontery.

'Not up at Lord's, however!' said the other slyly. 'My dear sir, I have seen you take far too many wickets to make any mistake.'

For a single moment Raffles looked venomous; then he shrugged and smiled, and the smile grew into a little cynical chuckle.

'So you have bowled me out in my turn?' said he. 'Well, I don't think there's anything to explain. I am harder up than I wished to admit under my own name, that's all, and I want that thousand pounds reward.'

'Two thousand,' said the solicitor. 'And the man who is not above an alias happens to be just the sort of man I want; so don't let that worry you, my dear sir. The matter, however, is of a strictly private and confidential character," and he looked very hard at me.

'Quite so,' said Raffles. 'But there was something about a risk?'

'A certain risk is involved.'

'Then surely three heads will be better than two. I said I wanted that thousand pounds; my friend here wants the other. We are both cursedly hard up, and we go into this thing together or not at all. Must you have his name too? I should give him my real one, Bunny.'

Mr Addenbrooke raised his eyebrows over the card I found for him; then he drummed upon it with his finger-nail, and his embarrassment expressed itself in a puzzled smile.

'The fact is, I find myself in a difficulty,' he confessed at last. 'Yours is the first reply I have received; people who can afford to send long telegrams don't rush to the advertisements in the *Daily Telegraph*; but on the other hand, I was not quite prepared to hear from men like yourselves. Candidly, and on consideration, I am not sure that you are the stamp of men for me – men who belong to good clubs! I rather intended to appeal to the – er – adventurous classes.'

'We are adventurers,' said Raffles gravely.

'But you respect the law?'

The black eyes gleamed shrewdly.

'We are not professional rogues, if that's what you mean,' said Raffles, smiling. 'But on our beam-ends we are; we would do a good deal for a thousand pounds apiece, eh, Bunny?'

'Anything,' I murmured.

The solicitor rapped his desk.

'I'll tell you what I want you to do. You can but refuse. It's illegal, but it's illegality in a good cause; that's the risk, and my client is prepared to pay for it. He will pay for the attempt, in case of failure; the money is as good as yours once you consent to run the risk. My client is Sir Bernhard Debenham, of Broom Hall, Esher.'

'I know his son,' I remarked.

Raffles knew him too, but said nothing, and his eye drooped disapproval in my direction. Bennett Addenbrooke turned to me.

'Then,' said he, 'you have the privilege of knowing one of the most complete young blackguards about town, and the *fons et origo* of the whole trouble. As you know the son, you may know the father too, at all events by reputation; and in that case I needn't tell you that he is a very peculiar man. He lives alone in a storehouse of treasures which no eye but his ever beheld. He is said to have the finest collection of pictures in the south of England, though nobody ever sees them to judge; pictures, fiddles, and furniture are his hobby, and he is undoubtedly very eccentric. Nor can one deny that there has been considerable eccentricity in his treatment of his son. For years Sir Bernard paid his debts, and the other day, without the slightest warning, not only refused to do so any more, but absolutely stopped the lad's allowance. Well, I'll tell you what has happened; but first of all you must know, or you may remember, that I appeared for young Debenham in a little scrape he got into a year or two ago. I got him off all right, and Sir Bernard paid me handsomely on the nail. And no more did I hear or see of either of them until one day last week.'

The lawyer drew his chair nearer ours, and leant forward with a hand on either knee.

'On Tuesday of last week I had a telegram from Sir Bernard; I was to go to him at once. I found him waiting for me in the drive; without a word he led me to the picture-gallery, which was locked and darkened, drew up a blind, and stood simply pointing to an empty picture-frame. It was a long time before I could get a word out of him. Then at last he told me that that frame had contained one of the rarest and most valuable pictures in England – in the world – an original Velasquez. I have checked this,' said the lawyer, 'and it seems literally true; the picture was a portrait of the Infanta Maria Teresa, said to be one of the artist's greatest works, second only to another portrait of one of the Popes of Rome – so they told me at the National Gallery, where they had its history by heart. They say there that the picture is practically priceless. And young Debenham has sold it for five thousand pounds!'

'The deuce he has,' said Raffles.

I inquired who had bought it.

'A Queensland legislator of the name of Craggs – the Hon. John Montague Craggs, M.L.C., to give him his full title. Not that we knew anything about him on Tuesday last; we didn't even know for certain that young Debenham had stolen the picture. But he had gone down for money on the Monday evening, had been refused, and it was plain enough that he had helped himself in this way; he had threatened revenge, and this was it. Indeed, when I hunted him up in town on the Tuesday night, he confessed as much in the most brazen manner imaginable. But he wouldn't tell me who was the purchaser, and finding out took the rest of the week; but I did find out, and a nice time I've had of it ever since! Backwards and forwards between Esher and the Metropole, where the Queenslander is staying, sometimes twice a day; threats, offers, prayers, entreaties, not one of them a bit of good!'

'But,' said Raffles, 'surely it's a clear case? The sale was illegal; you can pay him back his money and force him to give the picture up.'

'Exactly; but not without an action and a public scandal, and that my client declines to face. He would rather lose even his picture than have the whole thing get into the papers; he has disowned his son, but he will not disgrace him; yet his picture he must have by hook or crook, and there's the rub! I am to get it back by fair means or foul. He gives me *carte blanche* in the matter, and, I verily believe, would throw in a blank cheque if asked. He offered one to the Queenslander, but Craggs simply tore it in two; the one old boy is as much a character as the other, and between the two of them I'm at my wits' end.'

'So you put that advertisement in the paper?' said Raffles, in the dry tones he had adopted throughout the interview.

'As a last resort, I did.'

'And you wish us to steal this picture?'

It was magnificently said; the lawyer flushed from his hair to his collar.

'I knew you were not the men!' he groaned. 'I never thought of men of your stamp! But it's not stealing,' he exclaimed heatedly; 'it's recovering stolen property. Besides, Sir Bernard will pay him his five thousand as soon as he has the picture; and, you'll see, old Craggs will be just as loath to let it come out as Sir Bernard himself. No, no – it's an enterprise, and adventure, if you like – but not stealing.'

'You yourself mentioned the law,' murmured Raffles.

'And the risk,' I added.

'We pay for that,' he said once more.

'But not enough,' said Raffles, shaking his head. 'My good sir, consider what it means to us. You spoke of those clubs; we should not only get kicked out of them but put in prison like common burglars! It's true we're hard up, but it simply isn't worth it at the price. Double your stakes, and I for one am your man.'

Addenbrooke wavered.

'Do you think you could bring it off?'

'We could try.'

'But you have no – –'

'Experience? Well, hardly!'

'And you would really run the risk for four thousand pounds?'

Raffles looked at me. I nodded.

'We would,' said he, 'and blow the odds!'

'It's more than I can ask my client to pay,' said Addenbrooke, growing firm.

'Then it's more than you can expect us to risk.'

'You are in earnest?'

'Yes!'

'Say three thousand if you succeed!'

'Four is our figure, Mr Addenbrooke.'

'Then I think it should be nothing if you fail.'

'Double or quits?' cried Raffles. 'Well, that's sporting. Done!'

Addenbrooke opened his lips, half rose, then sat back in his chair, and looked long and shrewdly at Raffles – never once at me.

'I know your bowling,' said he reflectively. 'I go up to Lord's whenever I want an hour's real rest, and I've seen you bowl again and again – yes, and take the best wickets in England on a plumb pitch. I don't forget the last Gentlemen and Players; I was there. You're up to every trick – every one ... I'm inclined to think that if anybody could bowl out this old Australian ... Damme, I believe you're my very man!'

The bargain was clenched at the Café Royal, where Bennett Addenbrooke insisted on playing host at an extravagant luncheon. I remember that he took his whack of champagne with the nervous freedom of a man at high pressure, and have no doubt I kept him in countenance by an equal indulgence; but Raffles, ever an exemplar in such matters, was more abstemious even than his wont, and very poor company to boot. I can see him now, his eyes on his plate – thinking – thinking. I can see the solicitor glancing from him to me in an apprehension of which I did my best to disabuse him by reassuring looks. At the close Raffles apologised for his preoccupation, called for an A.B.C. time-table, and announced his intention of catching the 3.2 to Esher.

'You must excuse me, Mr Addenbrooke,' said he, 'but I have my own idea, and, for the moment I would much prefer to keep it to myself. It may end in fizzle, so I would rather not speak about it to either of you just yet. But speak to Sir Bernard I must, so will you write me one line to him on your card? Of course, if you wish you must come down with me and hear what I say; but I really don't see much point in it.'

And as usual Raffles had his way, though Bennett Addenbrooke showed some temper when he was gone, and I myself shared his annoyance to no small extent. I could only tell him that it was in the nature of Raffles to be self-willed and secretive, but that no man of my acquaintance had half his audacity and determination; that I for my part would trust him through and through and let him gang his own gait every time. More I dared not say, even to remove those chill misgivings with which I knew that the lawyer went his way.

That day I saw no more of Raffles, but a telegram reached me when I was dressing for dinner:

'Be in your rooms to-morrow from noon and keep rest of day clear. – RAFFLES.'

It had been sent from Waterloo at 6.42.

So Raffles was back in town; at an earlier stage of our relations I should have hunted him up then and there, but now I knew better. His telegram meant that he had no desire for my society that night or the following forenoon; that when he wanted me I should see him soon enough.

And see him I did, towards one o'clock next day. I was watching for him from my window in Mount Street, when he drove up furiously in a cab, and jumped out without a word to the man. I met him next minute at the lift gates, and he fairly pushed me back into my rooms.

'Five minutes, Bunny!' he cried. 'Not a moment more.'

And he tore off his coat, flinging himself into the nearest chair.

'I'm fairly on the rush,' he panted; 'having the very devil of a time! Not a word till I've told you all I've done. I settled my plan of campaign yesterday at lunch. The first thing was to get in with this man Craggs; you can't break into a place like the Metropole, it's got to be done from the inside. Problem one, how to get at the fellow. Only one sort of pretext would do – it must be something to do with this blessed picture, so that I might see where he'd got it and all that. Well, I couldn't go and ask to see it out of curiosity, and I couldn't go as a second representative of the old chap, and it was thinking how I could go that made me such a bear at lunch. But I saw my way before we got up. If I could only lay hold of a copy of the picture I might ask leave to go and compare it with the original. So down I went to Esher to find out if there was a copy in existence, and was at Broom Hall for one hour and a half yesterday afternoon. There was no copy there, but they must exist, for Sir Bernard himself (there's "copy" there!) has allowed a couple to be made since the picture has been in his possession. He hunted up the painters' addresses, and the rest of the evening I spent in hunting up the painters themselves; but their work had been done on commission; one copy had gone out of the country, and I'm still on the track of the other.'

'Then you haven't seen Craggs yet?'

'Seen him and made friends with him, and if possible he's the funnier old cuss of the two; but you should study 'em both. I took the bull by the horns this morning, went in and lied like Ananias, and it was just as well I did – the old ruffian sails for Australia by to-morrow's boat. I told him a man wanted to sell me a copy of the celebrated Infanta Maria Teresa of Velasquez, that I'd been down to the supposed owner of the picture, only to find that he had just sold it to him. You should have seen his face when I told him that! He grinned all round his wicked old head. "Did old Debenham admit the sale?" says he; and when I said he had, he chuckled to himself for about five minutes. He was so pleased that he did just what I hoped he would do; he showed me the great picture – luckily it isn't by any means a large one – also the case he's got it in. It's an iron map-case in which he brought over the plans of his land in Brisbane; he wants to know who would suspect it of containing an Old Master too? But he's had it fitted with a new Chubb's lock, and I managed to take an interest in the key while he was gloating over the canvas. I had the wax in the palm of my hand, and I shall make my duplicate this afternoon.'

Raffles looked at his watch and jumped up, saying he had given me a minute too much.

'By the way,' he added, 'you've got to dine with him at the Metropole to-night!'

'I?'

'Yes; don't look so scared. Both of us are invited – I swore you were dining with me. I accepted for us both; but I shan't be there.'

His clear eye was upon me, bright with meaning and with mischief. I implored him to tell me what his meaning was.

'You will dine in his private sitting-room,' said Raffles; 'it adjoins his bedroom. You must keep him sitting as long as possible, Bunny, and talking all the time!'

In a flash I saw his plan.

'You're going for the picture while we're at dinner?'

'I am.'

'If he hears you!'

'He shan't.'

'But if he does!'

And I fairly trembled at the thought.

'If he does,' said Raffles, 'there will be a collision, that's all. Revolvers would be out of place in the Metropole, but I shall certainly take a life-preserver.'

'But it's ghastly!' I cried. 'To sit and talk to an utter stranger and to know that you're at work in the next room!'

'Two thousand apiece,' said Raffles quietly.

'Upon my soul I believe I shall give it away!'

'Not you, Bunny. I know you better than you know yourself.' He put on his coat and his hat.

'What time have I to be there?' I asked him, with a groan.

'Quarter to eight. There will be a telegram from me saying I can't turn up. He's a terror to talk, you'll have no difficulty to keep the ball rolling; but head him off his picture for all you're worth. If he offers to show it you, say you must go. He locked up the case elaborately this afternoon, and there's no earthly reason why he should unlock it again in this hemisphere.'

'Where shall I find you when I get away?'

'I shall be down at Esher. I hope to catch the 9.55.'

'But surely I can see you again this afternoon?' I cried in a ferment, for his hand was on the door. 'I'm not half-coached up yet! I know I shall make a mess of it!'

'Not you,' he said again, 'but I shall if I waste any more time. I've got a deuce of a lot of rushing about to do yet. You won't find me at my rooms. Why not come down to Esher yourself by the last train? That's it – down you come with the latest news! I'll tell old Debenham to expect you: he shall give us both a bed. By Jove! he won't be able to do us too well if he's got his picture.'

'If!' I groaned as he nodded his adieu; and he left me limp with apprehension, sick with fear, in a perfectly pitiable condition of pure stage-fright.

For, after all, I had only to act my part; unless Raffles failed where he never did fail, unless Raffles the neat and noiseless was for once clumsy and inept, all I had to do was indeed to 'smile and smile and be a villain.' I practised that smile half the afternoon. I rehearsed putative parts in hypothetical conversations. I got up stories. I dipped in a book on Queensland at the club. And at last it was 7.45, and I was making my bow to a somewhat elderly man with a small bald head and a retreating brow.

'So you're Mr Raffles's friend?' said he, overhauling me rather rudely with his light small eyes. 'Seen anything of him? Expected him early to show me something, but he's never come.'

No more, evidently, had his telegram, and my troubles were beginning early. I said I had not seen Raffles since one o'clock, telling the truth with unction while I could; even as we spoke there came a knock at the door; it was the telegram at last, and, after reading it himself, the Queenslander handed it to me.

'Called out of town!' he grumbled. 'Sudden illness of near relative! What near relatives has he got?'

I knew of none, and for an instant I quailed before the perils of invention; then I replied that I had never met any of his people, and again felt fortified by my veracity.

'Thought you were bosom pals?' said he, with (as I imagined) a gleam of suspicion in his crafty little eyes.

'Only in town,' said I. 'I've never been to his place.'

'Well,' he growled, 'I suppose it can't be helped. Don't know why he couldn't come and have his dinner first. Like to see the deathbed I'd go to without my dinner; it's a full-skin billet, if you ask me. Well, must just dine without him, and he'll have to buy his pig in a poke after all. Mind touching that bell? Suppose you know what he came to see me about. Sorry I shan't see him again, for his own sake. I like Raffles – took to him amazingly. He's a cynic. Like cynics. One myself. Rank bad form of his mother, or his aunt, and I hope she will kick the bucket.'

I connect these specimens of his conversation, though they were doubtless detached at the time, and interspersed with remarks of mine here and there. They filled the intervals until dinner was served, and they gave me an impression of the man which his every subsequent utterance confirmed. It was an impression which did away with all remorse for my treacherous presence at his table. He was that terrible type, the Silly Cynic, his aim a caustic commentary on all things and all men, his achievement mere vulgar irreverence, and unintelligent scorn. Ill-bred and ill-informed, he had (on his own showing) fluked into fortune on a rise in land; yet cunning he possessed, as well as malice, and he chuckled till he choked over the misfortunes of less astute speculators in the same boom. Even now I cannot feel much compunction for my behaviour to the Hon. J. M. Craggs, M.L.C.

But never shall I forget the private agonies of the situation, the listening to my host with one ear and for Raffles with the other! Once I heard him – though the rooms were not divided by the old-fashioned folding-doors, and though the door that did divide them was not only shut but richly curtained, I could have sworn I heard him once. I spilt my wine and laughed at the top of my voice at some coarse sally of my host's. And I heard nothing more, though my ears were on the strain. But later, to my horror, when the waiter had finally withdrawn, Craggs himself sprang up and rushed to his bedroom without a word. I sat like stone till he returned.

'Thought I heard a door go,' he said. 'Must have been mistaken ... imagination ... gave me quite a turn. Raffles tell you of the priceless treasure I've got in there?'

It was the picture at last; up to this point I had kept him to Queensland and the making of his pile. I tried to get him back there now, but in vain. He was reminded of his great ill-gotten possession. I said that Raffles had just mentioned it, and that set him off. With the confidential garrulity of a man who has dined too well, he plunged into his darling topic, and I looked past him at the clock. It was only a quarter to ten.

In common decency I could not go yet. So there I sat (we were still at port) and learnt what had originally fired my host's ambition to possess what he was pleased to call 'a real, genuine, twin-screw, double-funnelled, copper-bottomed Old Master'; it was to 'go one better' than some rival legislator of pictorial proclivities. But even an epitome of his monologue would be so much weariness; suffice it that it ended inevitably in the invitation I had dreaded all the evening.

'But you must see it. Next room. This way.'

'Isn't it packed up?' I inquired hastily.

'Lock and key. That's all.'

'Pray don't trouble,' I urged.

'Trouble be hanged!' said he. 'Come along.'

And all at once I saw that to resist him further would be to heap suspicion upon myself against the moment of impending discovery. I therefore followed him into his bedroom without further protest, and suffered him first to show me the iron map-case which stood in one corner; he took a crafty pride in this receptacle, and I thought he would never cease descanting on its innocent appearance and its Chubb's lock. It seemed an interminable age before the key was in the latter. Then the ward clicked, and my pulse stood still.

'By Jove!' I cried the next instant.

The canvas was in its place among the maps!

'Thought it would knock you,' said Craggs, drawing it out and unfolding it for my benefit. 'Grand thing, ain't it? Wouldn't think it had been painted two hundred and thirty years? It has, though, my word! Old Johnson's face will be a treat when he sees it; won't go bragging about his pictures much more. Why, this one's worth all the pictures in Colony o' Queensland put together. Worth fifty thousand pounds, my boy – and I got it for five!'

He dug me in the ribs, and seemed in the mood for further confidences. My appearance checked him, and he rubbed his hands.

'If you take it like that,' he chuckled, 'how will old Johnson take it? Go out and hang himself to his own picture-rods, I hope!'

Heaven knows what I contrived to say at last. Struck speechless first by my relief, I continued silent from a very different cause. A new tangle of emotions tied my tongue. Raffles had failed – could I not succeed? Was it too late? Was there no way?

'So long,' he said, taking a last look at the canvas before he rolled it up – 'so long till we get to Brisbane.'

The flutter I was in as he closed the case!

'For the last time,' he went on, as his keys jingled back into his pocket. 'It goes straight into the strong-room on board.'

For the last time! If I could but send him out to Australia with only its legitimate contents in his precious map-case! I could but succeed where Raffles had failed!

We returned to the other room. I have no notion how long he talked, or what about. Whisky and soda-water became the order of the hour. I scarcely touched it, but he drank copiously, and before eleven I left him incoherent. And the last train for Esher was the 11.50 out of Waterloo.

I took a cab to my rooms. I was back at the hotel in thirteen minutes. I walked upstairs. The corridor was empty; I stood an instant on the sitting-room threshold, heard a snore within, and admitted myself softly with my gentleman's own key, which it had been a very simple matter to take away with me.

Craggs never moved; he was stretched on the sofa fast asleep. But not fast enough for me. I saturated my handkerchief with the chloroform I had brought, and I laid it gently over his mouth. Two or three stertorous breaths, and the man was a log.

I removed the handkerchief; I extracted the keys from his pocket. In less than five minutes I put them back, after winding the picture about my body beneath my Inverness cape. I took some whisky and soda-water before I went.

The train was easily caught – so easily that I trembled for ten minutes in my first-class smoking carriage, in terror of every footstep on the platform – in unreasonable terror till the end. Then at last I sat back and lit a cigarette, and the lights of Waterloo reeled out behind.

Some men were returning from the theatre. I can recall their conversation even now. They were disappointed with the piece they had seen. It was one of the later Savoy operas, and they spoke wistfully of the days of *Pinafore* and *Patience*. One of them hummed a stave, and there was an argument as to whether the air was out of *Patience* or the *Mikado*. They all got out at Surbiton, and I was alone with my triumph for a few intoxicating minutes. To think that I had succeeded where Raffles had failed! Of all our adventures this was the first in which I had played a commanding part; and, of them all, this was infinitely the least discreditable. It left me without a conscientious qualm; I had but robbed a robber, when all was said.

And I had done it myself, single-handed – *ipse egomet!*

I pictured Raffles, his surprise, his delight. He would think a little more of me in future. And that future, it should be different. We had two thousand pounds apiece – surely enough to start afresh as honest men – and all through me.

In a glow I sprang out at Esher, and took the one belated cab that was waiting under the bridge. In a perfect fever I beheld Broom Hall, with the lower story still lit up, and saw the, front door open as I climbed the steps.

'Thought it was you,' said Raffles cheerily. 'It's all right. There's a bed for you. Sir Bernard's sitting up to shake your hand.'

His good spirits disappointed me. But I knew the man; he was one of those who wear their brightest smile in the blackest hour. I knew him too well by this time to be deceived.

'I've got it!' I cried in his ear. 'I've got it!'

'Got what?' he asked, stepping back.

'The picture!'

'What?'

'The picture. He showed it me. You had to go without it; I saw that. So I determined to have it. And here it is.'

'Let's see,' said Raffles grimly.

I threw off my cape and unwound the canvas from about my body. While I was doing so an untidy old gentleman made his appearance in the hall, and stood looking on with raised eyebrows.

'Looks pretty fresh for an Old Master, doesn't she?' said Raffles.

His tone was strange. I could only suppose that he was jealous of my success.

'So Craggs said. I hardly looked at it myself.'

'Well, look now – look closely. By Jove, I must have faked her better than I thought!'

'It's a copy!' I cried.

'It's the copy,' he answered. 'It's the copy I've been tearing all over the country to procure. It's the copy I faked back and front, so that, on your own showing, it imposed upon Craggs, and might have made him happy for life. And you go and rob him of that!'

I could not speak.

'How did you manage it?' inquired Sir Bernard Debenham.

'Have you killed him?' asked Raffles sardonically.

I did not look at him: I turned to Sir Bernard Debenham, and to him I told my story, hoarsely, excitedly, for it was all that I could do to keep from breaking down. But as I spoke I became calmer, and I finished in mere bitterness, with the remark that another time Raffles might tell me what he meant to do.

'Another time!' he cried instantly. 'My dear Bunny, you speak as though we were going to turn burglars for a living!'

'I trust you won't,' said Sir Bernard, smiling, 'for you are certainly two very daring young men. Let us hope our friend from Queensland will do as he said, and not open his map-case till he gets back there. He will find my cheque awaiting him, and I shall be very much surprised if he troubles any of us again.'

Raffles and I did not speak till I was in the room which had been prepared for me. Nor was I anxious to do so then. But he followed me and took my hand.

'Bunny,' said he, 'don't you be hard on a fellow! I was in the deuce of a hurry, and didn't know that I should get what I wanted in time, and that's a fact. But it serves me right that you should have gone and undone one of the best things I ever did. As for your handiwork, old chap, you won't mind my saying that I didn't think you had it in you. In future – '

'Don't talk to me about the future!' I cried. 'I hate the whole thing! I'm going to chuck it up!'

'So am I,' said Raffles, 'when I've made my pile.'

THE RETURN MATCH

I HAD turned into Piccadilly, one thick evening in the following November, when my guilty heart stood still at the sudden grip of a hand upon my arm. I thought – I was always thinking – that my inevitable hour was come at last. It was only Raffles, however, who stood smiling at me through the fog.

'Well met!' said he; 'I've been looking for you at the club.'

'I was just on my way there,' I returned, with an attempt to hide my tremors. It was an ineffectual attempt, as I saw from his broader smile, and by the indulgent shake of his head.

'Come up to my place instead,' said he. 'I've something amusing to tell you.'

I made excuses, for his tone foretold the kind of amusement, and it was a kind against which I had successfully set my face for months. I have stated before, however, and I can but reiterate, that to me, at all events, there was never anybody in the world so irresistible as Raffles when his mind was made up. That we had both been independent of crime since our little service to Sir Bernard Debenham – that there had been no occasion for that masterful mind to be made up in any such direction for many a day – was the undeniable basis of a longer spell of honesty than I had hitherto enjoyed during the term of our mutual intimacy. Be sure I would deny it if I could; the very thing I am to tell you would discredit such a boast. I made my excuses, as I have said. But his arm slid through mine, with his little laugh of light-hearted mastery. And even while I argued we were on his staircase in the Albany.

His fire had fallen low. He poked and replenished it after turning on the lights. As for me, I stood by sullenly in my overcoat until he dragged it off my back.

'What a chap you are!' said Raffles playfully. 'One would really think I had proposed to crack another crib, this blessed night! Well, it isn't that, Bunny; so get into that chair and take one of these Sullivans, and sit tight.'

He held the match to my cigarette; he brought me a whisky and soda. Then he went out in the lobby, and, just as I was beginning to feel happy, I heard the bolt shot home. It cost me an effort to remain in that chair; next moment he was straddling another and gloating over my discomfiture across his folded arms.

'You remember Milchester, Bunny, old boy?'

His tone was as bland as mine was grim when I answered that I did.

'We had a little match there that wasn't down on the card. Gentlemen and Players, if you recollect?'

'I don't forget it.'

'Seeing that you never got an innings, so to speak, I thought you might. Well, the Gentlemen scored pretty freely, but the Players were all caught – '

'Poor devils!'

'Don't be too sure. You remember the fellow we saw in the inn? The florid, over-dressed chap who I told you was one of the cleverest thieves in town?'

'I remember him. Crawshay his name turned out to be.'

'Well, it was certainly the name he was convicted under, so Crawshay let it be. You needn't waste any pity on him, old chap; he escaped from Dartmoor yesterday afternoon.'

'Well done!'

Raffles smiled, but his eyebrows had gone up and his shoulders followed suit.

'You are perfectly right; it was very well done indeed. I wonder you didn't see it in the paper. In a dense fog on the moor yesterday good old Crawshay made a bolt for it, and got away without a scratch under heavy fire. All honour to him, I agree; a fellow with that much grit deserves his liberty. But Crawshay has a good deal more. They hunted him all night long; couldn't find him for nuts; and that was all you missed in the morning papers.'

He unfolded a *Pall Mall*, which he had brought in with him.

'But listen to this; here's an account of the escape, with just the addition which puts the thing on a higher level. "The fugitive has been traced to Totnes, where he appears to have committed a peculiarly daring outrage in the early hours of this

110

morning. He is reported to have entered the lodgings of the Rev. A. H. Ellingworth, curate of the parish, who missed his clothes on rising at the usual hour; later in the morning those of the convict were discovered neatly folded at the bottom of a drawer. Meanwhile Crawshay had made good his second escape, though it is believed that so distinctive a guise will lead to his recapture during the day." What do you think of that, Bunny?'

'He is certainly a sportsman,' said I, reaching for the paper.

'He's more,' said Raffles; 'he's an artist, and I envy him. The curate, of all men! Beautiful – beautiful! But that's not all. I saw just now on the board at the club that there's been an outrage on the line near Dawlish. Parson found insensible in the six-foot way. Our friend again. The telegram doesn't say so, but it's obvious; he's simply knocked some other fellow out, changed clothes again, and come on gaily to town. Isn't it great? I do believe it's the best thing of the kind that's ever been done!'

'But why should he come to town?'

In an instant the enthusiasm faded from Raffles's face. Clearly I had reminded him of some prime anxiety, forgotten in his impersonal joy over the exploit of a fellow-criminal. He looked over his shoulder towards the lobby before replying.

'I believe,' said he, 'that the beggar's on my tracks!'

And as he spoke he was himself again – quietly amused – cynically unperturbed – characteristically enjoying the situation and my surprise.

'But look here, what do you mean?' said I. 'What does Crawshay know about you?'

'Not much; but he suspects.'

'Why should he?'

'Because, in his way, he's very nearly as good a man as I am; because, my dear Bunny, with eyes in his head and brains behind them, he couldn't help suspecting. He saw me once in town with old Baird. He must have seen me that day in the pub, on the way to Milchester, as well as afterwards on the cricket-field. As a matter of fact, I know he did, for he wrote and told me so before his trial.'

'He wrote to you! And you never told me!'

The old shrug answered the old grievance.

'What was the good, my dear fellow? It would only have worried you.'

'Well, what did he say?'

'That he was sorry he had been run in before getting back to town, as he had proposed doing himself the honour of paying me a call; however, he trusted it was only a pleasure deferred, and he begged me not to go and get lagged myself before he came out. Of course he knew the Melrose necklace was gone, though he hadn't got it; and he said that the man who could take that and leave the rest was a man after his own heart. And so on, with certain little proposals for the far future, which I fear may be the very near future indeed! I'm only surprised he hasn't turned up yet.'

He looked again towards the lobby, which he had left in darkness, with the inner door shut as carefully as the outer one. I asked him what he meant to do.

'Let him knock – if he gets so far. The porter is to say I'm out of town; it will be true, too, in another hour or so.'

'You're going off to-night?'

'By the 7.15 from Liverpool Street. I don't say much about my people, Bunny, but I have the best of sisters married to a country parson in the eastern counties. They always make me welcome, and let me read the lessons for the sake of getting me to church. I'm sorry you won't be there to hear me on Sunday, Bunny. I've figured out some of my best schemes in that parish, and I know of no better port in a storm. But I must pack. I thought I'd just let you know where I was going, and why, in case you cared to follow my example.'

He flung the stump of his cigarette into the fire, stretched himself as he rose, and remained so long in the inelegant attitude that my eyes mounted from his body to his face; a second later they had followed his eyes across the room, and I also was on my legs. On the threshold of the folding doors that divided bedroom and sitting-room, a well-built man stood in ill-fitting broadcloth, and bowed to us until his bullet head presented an unbroken disc of short red hair.

Brief as was my survey of this astounding apparition, the interval was long enough for Raffles to recover his composure;

his hands were in his pockets, and a smile upon his face, when my eyes flew back to him.

'Let me introduce you, Bunny,' said he, 'to our distinguished colleague, Mr Reginald Crawshay.'

The bullet head bobbed up, and there was a wrinkled brow above the coarse, shaven face, crimson, also I remember, from the grip of a collar several sizes too small. But I noted nothing consciously at the time. I had jumped to my own conclusion, and I turned on Raffles with an oath.

'It's a trick!' I cried. 'It's another of your cursed tricks. You got him here, and then you got me. You want me to join you, I suppose? I'll see you damned!'

So cold was the stare which met this outburst that I became ashamed of my words while they were yet upon my lips.

'Really, Bunny!' said Raffles, and turned his shoulder with a shrug.

'Lord love yer,' cried Crawshay, ' 'e knew nothin'. 'E didn't expect me; 'e's all right. And you're the cool canary, you are,' he went on to Raffles. 'I knoo you were, but, do me proud, you're one after my own kidney.' And he thrust out a shaggy hand.

'After that,' said Raffles, taking it, 'what am I to say? But you must have heard my opinion of you. I am proud to make your acquaintance. How the deuce did you get in?'

'Never you mind,' said Crawshay, loosening his collar; 'let's talk about how I'm to get out. Lord love yer, but that's better!' There was a livid ring round his bull-neck, that he fingered tenderly. 'Didn't know how much longer I might have to play the gent,' he explained, 'didn't know who you'd bring in.'

'Drink whisky and soda?' inquired Raffles, when the convict was in the chair from which I had leapt.

'No, I drink it neat,' replied Crawshay, 'but I talk business first. You don't get over me like that, Lor' love yer!'

'Well, then, what can I do for you?'

'You know without me tellin' you.'

'Give it a name.'

'Clean heels, then; that's what I want to show, and I leaves the way to you. We're brothers in arms, though I ain't armed this time. It ain't necessary. You've too much sense. But brothers we are, and you'll see a brother through. Let's put it at that. You'll see me through in your own way. I leaves it all to you.'

His tone was rich with conciliation and concession; he bent over and tore a pair of button boots from his bare feet, which he stretched towards the fire, painfully uncurling his toes.

'I hope you take a larger size than them,' said he. 'I'd have had a see if you'd given me time. I wasn't in long afore you.'

'And you won't tell me how you got in?'

'Wot's the use? I can't teach you nothin'. Besides, I want out. I want out of London, an' England, an' bloomin' Europe too. That's all I want of you, mister. I don't arst how you got on the job. You know w'ere I come from, 'cos I heard you say; you know w'ere I want to 'ead for, 'cos I've just told yer; the details I leaves entirely to you.'

'Well,' said Raffles, 'we must see what can be done.'

'We must,' said Mr Crawshay, and leaned back comfortably, and began twirling his stubby thumbs.

Raffles turned to me with a twinkle in his eye; but his fore-head was scored with thought, and resolve mingled with resignation in the lines of his mouth. And he spoke exactly as though he and I were alone in the room.

'You seize the situation, Bunny? If our friend here is "copped," to speak his language, he means to "blow the gaff" on you and me. He is considerate enough not to say so in so many words, but it's plain enough, and natural enough for that matter. I would do the same in his place. We had the bulge before; he has it now; it's perfectly fair. We must take on this job; we aren't in a position to refuse it; even if we were, I should take it on. Our friend is a great sportsman; he has got clear away from Dartmoor; it would be a thousand pities to let him go back. Nor shall he; not if I can think of a way of getting him abroad.'

'Any way you like,' murmured Crawshay, with his eyes shut. 'I leaves the 'ole thing to you.'

'But you'll have to wake up and tell us things.'

'All right, mister; but I'm fair on the rocks for a sleep!'

And he stood up blinking.

'Think you were traced to town?'

'Must have been.'

'And here?'

'Not in this fog – not with any luck.'

Raffles went into the bedroom, lit the gas there, and returned next minute.

'So you got in by the window?'

'That's about it.'

'It was devilish smart of you to know which one; it beats me how you brought it off in daylight, fog or no fog! But let that pass. Don't you think you were seen?'

'I don't think it, sir.'

'Well, let's hope you are right. I shall reconnoitre and soon find out. And you'd better come too, Bunny, and have something to eat and talk it over.'

As Raffles looked at me, I looked at Crawshay, anticipating trouble; and trouble brewed in his blank, fierce face, in the glitter of his startled eyes, in the sudden closing of his fists.

'And what's to become of me?' he cried out with an oath.

'You wait here.'

'No, you don't,' he roared, and at a bound had his back to the door. 'You don't get round me like that, you cuckoos!'

Raffles turned to me with a twitch of the shoulders.

'That's the worst of these professors,' said he; 'they never will use their heads. They see the pegs, and they mean to hit 'em; but that's all they do see and mean, and they think we're the same. No wonder we licked them last time!'

'Don't talk through yer neck,' snarled the convict. 'Talk out straight, curse you!'

'Right,' said Raffles. 'I'll talk as straight as you like. You say you put yourself in my hands – you leave it all to me – yet you don't trust me an inch! I know what's to happen if I fail. I accept the risk. I take this thing on. Yet you think I'm going straight out to give you away and make you give me away in my turn. You're a fool, Mr Crawshay, though you have broken Dartmoor; you've got to listen to a better man, and obey him. I see you through in my own way, or not at all. I come and go as I like, and with whom I like, without your interference; you stay here and lie just as low as you know how, be as wise as your word, and leave the whole thing to me. If you won't – if you're fool enough not to trust me – there's the door. Go out and say what you like, and be damned to you!'

Crawshay slapped his thigh.

'That's talking!' said he. 'Lord love yer, I know where I am when you talk like that. I'll trust yer. I know a man when he gets his tongue between his teeth; you're all right. I don't say so much about this other gent, though I saw him along with you on the job that time in the provinces; but if he's a pal of yours, Mr Raffles, he'll be all right too. I only hope you gents ain't too stony – –'

And he touched his pockets with a rueful face.

'I only went for their togs,' said he. 'You never struck two such stony-broke cusses in yer life.'

'That's all right,' said Raffles. 'We'll see you through properly. Leave it to us, and you sit tight.'

'Rightum!' said Crawshay. 'And I'll have a sleep time you're gone. But no sperrits – no thank'ee – not yet! Once let me loose on lush, and, Lord love yer, I'm a gone coon!'

Raffles got his overcoat, a long, light driving coat, I remember, and even as he put it on our fugitive was dozing in the chair; we left him murmuring incoherently, with the lights out, and his bare feet toasting.

'Not such a bad chap, that professor,' said Raffles on the stairs; 'a real genius in his way, too, though his methods are a little elementary for my taste. But technique isn't everything; to get out of Dartmoor and into the Albany in the same twenty-four hours is the whole that justifies its parts. Good Lord!'

We had passed a man in the foggy courtyard, and Raffles had nipped my arm.

'Who was it?'

'The last man we want to see! I hope to Heaven he didn't hear me! Our old friend Mackenzie, from the Yard!'

I stood still with horror.

'Do you think he's on Crawshay's track?'

'I don't know. I'll find out.'

And before I could remonstrate he had wheeled me round; when I found my voice he merely laughed, and whispered that the bold course was the safe one every time.

'But it's madness – –'

'Not it. Shut up! Is that you, Mr Mackenzie?'

The detective turned about and scrutinised us keenly; and through the gaslit mist I noticed that his hair was grizzled at the temples, and his face still cadaverous from the wound that had nearly been his death.

'Ye have the advantage o' me, sirs,' said he.

'I hope you're fit again,' said my companion. 'My name is Raffles, and we met at Milchester last year.'

'Is that a fact?' cried the Scotsman, with quite a start. 'Yes, now I remember your face, and yours too, sir, Ay, yon was a bad business, but it ended vera well, an' that's the main thing.'

His native caution had returned to him. Raffles pinched my arm.

'Yes, it ended splendidly, but for you,' said he. 'But what about this escape of the leader of the gang, that fellow Crawshay? What do you think of that, eh?'

'I havena the parteeculars,' replied the Scot.

'Good!' cried Raffles. 'I was only afraid you might be on his tracks once more!'

Mackenzie shook his head with a dry smile, and wished us good evening, as an invisible window was thrown up and a whistle blown softly through the fog.

'We must see this out,' whispered Raffles. 'Nothing more natural than a little curiosity on our part. After him, quick!'

And he followed the detective into another entrance on the same side as that from which we had emerged, the left-hand side on one's way to Piccadilly; quite openly we followed him, and at the foot of the stairs met one of the porters of the place. Raffles asked him what was wrong.

'Nothing, sir,' said the fellow glibly.

'Rot!' said Raffles. 'That was Mackenzie, the detective. I've just been speaking to him. What's he here for? Come on, my good fellow; we won't give you away, if you've instructions not to tell.'

The man looked quaintly wistful, the temptation of an audience hot upon him; a door shut upstairs, and he fell.

'It's like this,' he whispered. 'This afternoon a gen'leman comes arfter rooms, and I sent him to the orfice; one of the

117

clurks,' 'e goes round with 'im an' shows 'im the empties, an' the gen'leman's partic'ly struck on the set the coppers is up in now. So he sends the clurk to fetch the manager, as there was one or two things he wished to speak about; an' when they come back, blowed if the gent isn't gone! Beg your pardon, sir, but he's clean disappeared off the face of the premises!' And the porter looked at us with shining eyes.

'Well?' said Raffles.

'Well, sir, they looked about, an' at larst they give him up for a bad job; thought he'd changed his mind an' didn't want to tip the clurk; so they shut up the place and come away. An' that's all till about 'alf an hour ago, when I takes the manager his extry-speshul *Star*; in about ten minutes he comes running out with a note an' sends me with it to Scotland Yard in a hansom. An' that's all I know, sir – straight. The coppers is up there now, and the tec and the manager, and they think their gent is about the place somewhere still. Least, I reckon that's their idea; but who he is, or what they want him for, I dunno.'

'Jolly interesting!' said Raffles. 'I'm going up to inquire. Come on, Bunny; there should be some fun.'

'Beg yer pardon, Mr Raffles, but you won't say nothing about me?'

'Not I; you're a good fellow. I won't forget it if this leads to sport. Sport!' he whispered, as we reached the landing. 'It looks like precious poor sport for you and me, Bunny!'

'What are you going to do?'

'I don't know. There's no time to think. This, to start with.'

And he thundered on the shut door; a policeman opened it. Raffles strode past him with the air of a chief commissioner, and I followed before the man had recovered from his astonishment. The bare boards rang under us; in the bedroom we found a knot of officers stooping over the window-ledge with a constable's lantern. Mackenzie was the first to stand upright, and he greeted us with a glare.

'May I ask what you gentlemen want?' said he.

'We want to lend a hand,' said Raffles briskly. 'We lent one once before, and it was my friend here who took over from you the fellow who split on all the rest and held him tight. Surely that entitles him, at all events, to see any fun that's going? As for myself, well, it's true I only helped to carry you to the house; but for old acquaintance I do hope, my dear Mr Mackenzie, that you will permit us to share such sport as there may be. I myself can only stop a few minutes, in any case.'

'Then ye'll not see much,' growled the detective, 'for he's not up here. Constable, go you and stand at the foot o' the stairs, and let no other body come up on any consideration; these gentlemen may be able to help us after all.'

'That's kind of you, Mackenzie!' cried Raffles warmly. 'But what is it all? I questioned a porter I met coming down, but could get nothing out of him, except that somebody had been to see these rooms and not since been seen himself.'

'He's a man we want,' said Mackenzie. 'He's concealed himself somewhere about these premises, or I'm vera much mistaken. D'ye reside in the Albany, Mr Raffles?'

'I do.'

'Will your rooms be near these?'

'On the next staircase but one.'

'Ye'll just have left them?'

'Just.'

'Been in all the afternoon, likely?'

'Not all.'

'Then I may have to search your rooms, sir. I am prepared to search every room in the Albany! Our man seems to have gone for the leads; but unless he's left more marks outside than in, or we find him up there, I shall have the entire building to ransack.'

'I will leave you my key,' said Raffles at once. 'I am dining out, but I'll leave it with the officer down below.'

I caught my breath in mute amazement. What was the meaning of this insane promise? It was wilful, gratuitous, suicidal; it made me catch at his sleeve in open horror and disgust; but, with a word of thanks, Mackenzie had returned to his window-sill, and we sauntered unwatched through the folding doors in the adjoining room. Here the window looked down into the courtyard; it was still open; and as we gazed out in apparent idleness, Raffles reassured me.

'It's all right, Bunny; you do what I tell you and leave the

119

rest to me. It's a tight corner, but I don't despair. What you've got to do is to stick to these chaps, especially if they search my rooms; they mustn't poke about more than necessary, and they won't if you're there.'

'But where will you be? You're never going to leave me to be landed alone?'

'If I do, it will be to turn up trumps at the right moment. Besides, there are such things as windows, and Crawshay's the man to take his risks. You must trust me, Bunny; you've known me long enough.'

'And you're going now?'

'There's no time to lose. Stick to them, old chap, don't let them suspect you, whatever else you do.' His hand lay an instant on my shoulder; then he left me at the window, and recrossed the room.

'I've got to go now,' I heard him say; 'but my friend will stay and see this through, and I'll leave the light on in my rooms – and my key with the constable downstairs. Good luck, Mackenzie; only wish I could stay.'

'Good-bye, sir,' came in a preoccupied voice, 'and many thanks.'

Mackenzie was still busy at his window, and I remained at mine, a prey to mingled fear and wrath, for all my knowledge of Raffles and of his infinite resource. By this time I felt that I knew more or less what he would do in any given emergency; at least I could conjecture a characteristic course of equal cunning and audacity. He would return to his rooms, put Crawshay on his guard, and – stow him away? No – there were such things as windows. Then why was Raffles going to desert us all? I thought of many things – lastly of a cab. These bedroom windows looked into a narrow side-street; they were not very high; from them a man might drop on to the roof of a cab – even as it passed – and be driven away – even under the noses of the police! I pictured Raffles driving that cab, unrecognisable in the foggy night; the vision came to me as he passed under the window, tucking up the collar of his great driving-coat on the way to his rooms; it was still with me when he passed again on his way back, and stopped to hand the constable his key.

'We're on his track,' said a voice behind me. 'He's got up on the leads, sure enough, though how he managed it from yon window is a myst'ry to me. We're going to lock up here and try what it is like from the attics. So you'd better come with us if you've a mind.'

The top floor at the Albany, as elsewhere, is devoted to the servants – a congeries of little kitchens and cubicles, used by many as lumber-rooms – by Raffles among the many. The annexe in this case was, of course, empty as the rooms below; and that was lucky, for we filled it, what with the manager, who now joined us, and another tenant whom he brought with him, to Mackenzie's undisguised annoyance.

'Better let in all Piccadilly at a crown a head,' said he. 'Here, my man, out you go on to the roof to make one less, and have your truncheon handy.'

We crowded to the little window, which Mackenzie took care to fill; and a minute yielded no sound but the crunch and slither of constabulary boots upon sooty slates. Then came a shout.

'What now?' cried Mackenzie.

'A rope,' we heard, 'hanging from the spout by a hook!'

'Sirs,' purred Mackenzie, 'yon's how he got up from below! He would do it with one o' they telescope sticks, an' I never thocht o't! How long a rope, my lad?'

'Quite short. I've got it.'

'Did it hang over a window? Ask him that!' cried the manager. 'He can see by leaning over the parapet.'

The question was repeated by Mackenzie; a pause then, 'Yes, it did.'

'Ask him how many windows along!' shouted the manager in high excitement.

'Six, he says,' said Mackenzie the next minute; and he drew in his head and shoulders. 'I should just like to see those rooms, six windows along.'

'Mr Raffles's,' announced the manager after a mental calculation.

'Is that a fact?' cried Mackenzie. 'Then we shall have no difficulty at all. He's left me his key down below.'

The words had a dry, speculative intonation, which even

then I found time to dislike; it was as though the coincidence had already struck the Scotsman as something more.

'Where is Mr. Raffles?' asked the manager, as we all filed downstairs.

'He's gone out to his dinner,' said Mackenzie.

'Are you sure?'

'I saw him go,' said I. My heart was beating horribly. I would not trust myself to speak again. But I wormed my way to a front place in the little procession, and was, in fact, the second man to cross the threshold that had been the Rubicon of my life. As I did so I uttered a cry of pain, for Mackenzie had trod back heavily on my toes; in another second I saw the reason, and saw it with another and a louder cry.

A man was lying at full length before the fire, on his back, with a little wound in the white forehead, and the blood draining into his eyes. And the man was Raffles himself!

'Suicide,' said Mackenzie calmly. 'No – here's the poker – looks more like murder.' He went on his knees and shook his head quite cheerfully. 'An' it's not even murder,' said he, with a shade of disgust in his matter-of-fact voice; 'yon's no more than a flesh-wound, and I have my doubts whether it felled him; but, sirs, he just stinks o' chloryform!'

He got up and fixed his keen grey eyes upon me; my own were full of tears, but they faced him unashamed.

'I understood ye to say ye saw him go out?' said he sternly.

'I saw that long driving-coat; of course I thought he was inside it.'

'And I could ha' sworn it was the same gent when he gave me the key!'

It was the disconsolate voice of the constable in the background; on him turned Mackenzie, white to the lips.

'You'd think anything, some of you damned policemen,' said he. 'What's your number, you rotter? P 34? You'll be hearing more of this, Mr P 34! If that gentleman were dead – instead of coming to himself while I'm talking – do you know what you'd be? Guilty of his manslaughter, you stuck pig in buttons! Do you know who you've let slip, butter-fingers? Crawshay – no less – him that broke Dartmoor yesterday. By the God that made ye, P 34, if I lose him I'll hound ye from the forrce!'

Working face – shaking fist – a calm man on fire. It was a new side of Mackenzie, and one to mark and to digest. Next moment he had flounced from our midst.

'Difficult thing to break your own head,' said Raffles later; 'infinitely easier to cut your own throat. Chloroform's another matter; when you've used it on others, you know the dose to a nicety. So you thought I was really gone? Poor old Bunny! But I hope Mackenzie saw your face?'

'He did,' said I. I would not tell him all Mackenzie must have seen, however.

'That's all right. I wouldn't have had him miss it for worlds; and you mustn't think me a brute, old boy, for I fear that man; and, you know, we sink or swim together.'

'And now we sink or swim with Crawshay too,' said I dolefully.

'Not we!' cried Raffles with conviction. 'Old Crawshay's a true sportsman, and he'll do by us as we've done by him; besides, this makes us quits; and I don't think, Bunny, that we'll take on the professors again!'

THE GIFT OF THE EMPEROR

I

WHEN the King of the Cannibal Islands made faces at Queen Victoria, and a European monarch set the cables tingling with his compliments on the exploit, the indignation in England was not less than the surprise, for the thing was not so common as it has since become. But when it transpired that a gift of peculiar significance was to follow the congratulations, to give them weight, the inference prevailed that the white potentate and the black had taken simultaneous leave of their fourteen senses. For the gift was a pearl of price unparalleled, picked aforetime by British cutlasses from a Polynesian setting, and presented by British royalty to the sovereign who seized this opportunity of restoring it to its orginal possessor.

The incident would have been a godsend to the Press a few weeks later. Even in June there were leaders, letters, large headlines, leaded type; the *Daily Chronicle* devoted half its literary page to a charming drawing of the island capital which the new *Pall Mall*, in a leading article headed by a pun, advised the Government to blow to flinders. I was myself driving a poor but not dishonest quill at the time, and the topic of the hour goaded me into satiric verse which obtained a better place than anything I had yet turned out. I had let my flat in town, and taken inexpensive quarters at Thames Ditton, on a plea of a disinterested passion for the river.

'First-rate, old boy,' said Raffles (who must needs come and see me there), lying back in the boat while I sculled and steered. 'I suppose they pay you pretty well for these, eh?'

'Not a penny.'

'Nonsense, Bunny! I thought they paid so well? Give them time, and you'll get your cheque.'

'Oh no, I shan't,' said I gloomily. 'I've got to be content with the honour of getting in; the editor wrote to say so, in so many words,' I added. But I gave the gentleman his distinguished name.

'You don't mean to say you've written for payment already?'

No; it was the last thing I had intended to admit. But I had done it. The murder was out; there was no sense in further concealment. I had written for my money because I really needed it; if he must know, I was cursedly hard up. Raffles nodded as though he knew already. I warmed to my woes. It was no easy matter to keep your end up as a raw free-lance of letters; for my part, I was afraid I wrote neither well enough nor ill enough for success. I suffered from a persistent ineffectual feeling after style. Verse I could manage; but it did not pay. To personal paragraphs or to baser journalism I could not and I would not stoop.

Raffles nodded again, this time with a smile that stayed in his eyes as he leant back watching me. I knew that he was thinking of other things I had stooped to, and I thought I knew what he was going to say. He had said it before so often; he was sure to say it again. I had my answer ready, but evidently he was tired of asking the same question. His lids fell, he took up the paper he had dropped, and I sculled the length of the old red wall of Hampton Court before he spoke again.

'And they gave you nothing for these! My dear Bunny, they're capital, not only *qua* verses, but for crystallising your subject and putting it in a nutshell. Certainly you've taught me more about it than I knew before. But is it really worth fifty thousand pounds – a single pearl?'

'A hundred, I believe; but that wouldn't scan.'

'A hundred thousand pounds!' said Raffles, with his eyes shut. And again I made certain what was coming, but again I was mistaken. 'If it's worth all that,' he cried at last, 'there would be no getting rid of it at all; it's not like a diamond that you can sub-divide. But I beg your pardon, Bunny. I was forgetting!'

And we said no more about the emperor's gift; for pride thrives on an empty pocket, and no privation would have drawn from me the proposal which I had expected Raffles to make. My expectation had been half a hope, though I only knew it now. But neither did we touch again on what Raffles professed to have forgotten – my 'apostasy,' 'my lapse into virtue,' as he had been pleased to call it. We were both a little silent, a little constrained, each preoccupied with his own thoughts. It was months since we had met, and, as I saw him off towards eleven o'clock that Sunday night, I fancied it was for more months that we were saying good-bye.

But as we waited for the train I saw those clear eyes peering at me under the station lamps, and when I met their glance Raffles shook his head.

'You don't look well on it, Bunny,' said he. 'I never did believe in this Thames Valley. You want a change of air.'

I wished I might get it.

'What you really want is a sea voyage.'

'And a winter at St. Moritz, or do you recommend Cannes or Cairo? It's all very well, A. J., but you forget what I told you about my funds."

'I forget nothing. I merely don't want to hurt your feelings. But, look here, a sea voyage you shall have. I want a change myself, and you shall come with me as my guest. We'll spend July in the Mediterranean.'

'But you're playing cricket – –'

'Hang the cricket!'

'Well, if I thought you meant it – –'

'Of course I mean it. Will you come?'

'Like a shot – if you go.'

And I shook his hand, and waved mine in farewell with the perfectly good-humoured conviction that I should hear no more of the matter. It was a passing thought, no more, no less. I soon wished it were more; that week found me wishing myself out of England for good and all. I was making nothing. I could but subsist on the difference between the rent I paid for my flat and the rent at which I had sublet it, furnished, for the season. And the season was near its end, and creditors awaited me in town. Was it possible to be entirely honest? I had run no bills when I had money in my pocket, and the more downright dishonesty seemed to me the less ignoble.

But from Raffles, of course, I heard nothing more; a week went by, and half another week; then, late on the second Wednesday night, I found a telegram from him at my lodgings, after seeking him vainly in town, and dining with desperation at the solitary club to which I still belonged.

'Arranged to leave Waterloo by North German Lloyd special,' he wired, '9.25 a.m. Monday next, will meet you Southampton aboard *Uhlan* with tickets, am writing.'

And write he did, a light-hearted letter enough, but full of serious solicitude for me and for my health and prospects; a letter almost touching in the light of our past relations, in the twilight of their complete rupture. He said that he had booked two berths to Naples, that we were bound for Capri, which was clearly the Island of the Lotos-eaters, that we would bask there together, 'and for a while forget'. It was a charming letter. I had never seen Italy; the privilege of initiation should be his. No mistake was greater than to deem it an impossible country for the summer. The Bay of Naples was never so divine, and he wrote of 'faery lands forlorn', as though the poetry sprang unbidden to his pen. To come back to earth and prose, I might think it unpatriotic of him to choose a German boat, but on no other line did you receive such attention and accommodation for your money. There was a hint of better reasons. Raffles wrote, as he had telegraphed, from Bremen; and I gathered that the personal use of some little influence with the authorities there had resulted in a material reduction in our fares.

Imagine my excitement and delight! I managed to pay what I owed at Thames Ditton, to squeeze a small editor for a very small cheque, and my tailors for one more flannel suit. I remember that I broke my last sovereign to get a box of Sullivan's cigarettes for Raffles to smoke on the voyage. But my heart was as light as my purse on the Monday morning, the fairest morning of an unfair summer, when the special whirled me through the sunshine to the sea.

A tender awaited us at Southampton. Raffles was not on board, nor did I really look for him till we reached the liner's side. And then I looked in vain. His face was not among the many that fringed the rail; his hand was not one of the few that waved to friends. I climbed aboard in a sudden heaviness. I had no ticket, nor the money to pay for one. I did not even know the number of my room. My heart was in my mouth as I waylaid a steward and asked if a Mr. Raffles was on board. Thank Heaven – he was! But where? The man did not know;

he was plainly on some other errand, and a-hunting I must go. But there was no sign of him on the promenade deck, and none below in the saloon; the smoking-room was empty but for a little German with a red moustache twisted into his eyes; nor was Raffles in his own cabin, whither I inquired my way in desperation, but where the sight of his own name on the baggage was certainly a further reassurance. Why he kept himself in the background, however, I could not conceive, and only sinister reasons would suggest themselves in explanation.

'So there you are! I've been looking for you all over the ship!'

Despite the graven prohibition, I had tried the bridge as a last resort; and there, indeed, was A. J. Raffles, seated on a skylight, and leaning over one of the officers' long chairs, in which reclined a girl in a white drill coat and skirt – a slip of a girl with a pale skin, dark hair, and rather remarkable eyes. So much I noted as he rose and quickly turned; thereupon I could think of nothing but the swift grimace which preceded a start of well-feigned astonishment.

'Why – Bunny?' cried Raffles. 'Where have you sprung from?'

I stammered something as he pinched my hand.

'And you are coming in this ship? And to Naples too? Well, upon my word! Miss Werner, may I introduce my friend?'

And he did so without a blush, describing me as an old schoolfellow whom he had not seen for months, with wilful circumstance and gratuitous detail that filled me at once with confusion, suspicion, and revolt. I felt myself blushing for us both, and I did not care. My address utterly deserted me, and I made no effort to recover it, to carry the thing off. All I would do was to mumble such words as Raffles actually put into my mouth, and that I doubt not with a thoroughly evil grace.

'So you saw my name in the list of passengers, and came in search of me? Good old Bunny! I say, though, I wish you'd share my cabin! I've got a beauty on the promenade deck, but they wouldn't promise to keep me by myself. We ought to see about it before they shove in some alien. In any case we shall have to get out of this.'

For a quartermaster had entered the wheel-house, and even

while we had been speaking, the pilot had taken possession of the bridge; as we descended, the tender left us with flying handkerchiefs and shrill good-byes; and as we bowed to Miss Werner on the promenade deck there came a deep, slow throbbing underfoot, and our voyage had begun.

It did not begin pleasantly between Raffles and me. On deck he had overborne my stubborn perplexity by dint of a forced though forceful joviality; in his cabin the gloves were off.

'You idiot,' he snarled, 'you've given me away again!'

'How have I given you away?'

I ignored the separate insult in his last word.

'How? I should have thought any clod could see that I meant us to meet by chance!'

'After taking both tickets yourself?'

'They know nothing about that on board; besides, I hadn't decided when I took the tickets.'

'Then you should have let me know when you did decide. You lay your plans and never say a word, and expect me to tumble to them by the light of nature. How was I to know you had anything on?'

I had turned the tables with some effect. Raffles almost hung his head.

'The fact is, Bunny, I didn't mean you to know. You – you've grown such a pious rabbit in your old age!'

My nickname and his tone went far to mollify me; other things went further, but I had to forgive him still.

'If you were afraid of writing,' I pursued, 'it was your business to give me the tip the moment I set foot on board. I would have taken it all right. I am not so virtuous as all that.'

Was it my imagination, or did Raffles look slightly ashamed? If so, it was the first and last time in all the years I knew him; nor can I swear to it even now.

'That,' said he, 'was the very thing I meant to do – to lie in wait in my room and get you as you passed, but – –'

'You were better engaged?'

'Say otherwise.'

'The charming Miss Werner?'

'She is quite charming.'

'Most Australian girls are,' said I.

'How did you know she was one?' he cried.

'I heard her speak.'

'Brute!' said Raffles, laughing; 'she has no more twang than you have. Her people are German, she has been to school in Dresden, and is on her way out alone.'

'Money?' I inquired.

'Confound you!' he said, and, though he was laughing, I thought it was a point at which the subject might be changed.

'Well,' I said, 'it wasn't for Miss Werner you wanted us to play strangers, was it? You have some deeper game than that, eh?'

'I suppose I have.'

'Then hadn't you better tell me what it is?'

Raffles treated me to the old cautious scrutiny that I knew so well; the familiarity of it, after all these months, set me smiling in a way that might have reassured him; for dimly already I divined his enterprise.

'It won't send you off in the pilot's boat, Bunny?'

'Not quite.'

'Then – you remember the pearl you wrote the – –'

I did not wait for him to finish his sentence.

'You've got it!' I cried, my face on fire, for I caught sight of it that moment in the state-room mirror.

Raffles seemed taken aback.

'Not yet,' said he; 'but I mean to have it before we get to Naples.'

'Is it on board?'

'Yes.'

'But how – where – who's got it?'

'A little German officer, a whipper-snapper with perpendicular moustaches.'

'I saw him in the smoke-room.'

'That's the chap; he's always there. Herr Captain Wilhelm von Heumann, if you look in the list. Well, he's the special envoy of the emperor, and he's taking the pearl out with him.'

'You found this out in Bremen?'

'No, in Berlin, from a newspaper man I know there. I'm ashamed to tell you, Bunny, that I went there on purpose!'

I burst out laughing.

'You needn't be ashamed. You are doing the very thing I was rather hoping you were going to propose the other day on the river.'

'You were hoping it?' said Raffles, with his eyes wide open. Indeed, it was his turn to show surprise, and mine to be much more ashamed than I felt.

'Yes,' I answered, 'I was quite keen on the idea; but I wasn't going to propose it.'

'Yet you would have listened to me the other day?'

Certainly I would, and I told him so without reserve; not brazenly, you understand; not even now with the gusto of a man who savours such an adventure for its own sake, but doggedly, defiantly, through my teeth, as one who had tried to live honestly and had failed. And, while I was about it, I told him much more. Eloquently enough, I dare say, I gave him chapter and verse of my hopeless struggle, my inevitable defeat; for hopeless and inevitable they were to a man with my record, even though that record was written only in one's own soul. It was the old story of the thief trying to turn honest man; the thing was against nature, and there was an end of it.

Raffles entirely disagreed with me. He shook his head over my conventional view. Human nature was a board of chequers; why not reconcile one's self to alternate black and white? Why desire to be all one thing or all the other, like our forefathers on the stage or in the old-fashioned fiction? For his part, he enjoyed himself on all squares of the board, and liked the light the better for the shade. My conclusion he considered absurd.

'But you err in good company, Bunny, for all the cheap moralists who preach the same twaddle; old Virgil was the first and worst offender of you all. I back myself to climb out of Avernus any day I like, and sooner or later I shall climb out for good. I suppose I can't very well turn myself into a Limited Liability Company. But I could retire and settle down and live blamelessly ever after. I'm not sure that it couldn't be done on this pearl alone!'

'Then you don't still think it too remarkable to sell?'

'We might take a fishery and haul it up with smaller fry. It would come after months of ill-luck, just as we were going to sell the schooner; by Jove, it would be the talk of the Pacific!'

'Well, we've got to get it first. Is this von What's-his-name a formidable cuss?'

'More so than he looks; and he has the cheek of the devil!'

As he spoke, a white drill skirt fluttered past the open state-room door, and I caught a glimpse of an upturned moustache beyond. 'But is he the chap we have to deal with? Won't the pearl be in the purser's keeping?'

Raffles stood at the door, frowning out upon the Solent, but for an instant he turned to me with a sniff.

'My good fellow, do you suppose the whole ship's company knows there's a gem like that aboard? You said that it was worth a hundred thousand pounds; in Berlin they say it's price-less. I doubt if the skipper himself knows that von Heumann has it on him.'

'And he has?'

'Must have.'

'Then we have only him to deal with?'

He answered me without a word. Something white was flut-tering past once more, and Raffles, stepping forth, made the promenaders three.

II

I do not ask to set foot aboard a finer steamship than the *Uhlan* of the Norddeutscher Lloyd, to meet a kindlier man than her then commander or better fellows than his officers. This much at least let me have the grace to admit. I hated the voyage. It was no fault of anybody connected with the ship; it was no fault of the weather, which was monotonously ideal. Not even in my own heart did the reason reside; conscience and I were divorced at last, and the decree made absolute. With my scruples had fled all fear, and I was ready to revel between bright skies and sparkling sea with the light-hearted detach-ment of Raffles himself. It was Raffles himself who prevented me, but not Raffles alone. It was Raffles and that Colonial minx on her way home from school.

What he could see in her – but that begs the question. Of course he saw no more than I did, but to annoy me, or per-

THE GIFT OF THE EMPEROR

haps to punish me for my long defection, he must turn his back
on me and devote himself to this chit from Southampton to
the Mediterranean. They were always together. It was too
absurd. After breakfast they would begin, and go on until
eleven or twelve at night; there was no intervening hour at
which you might not hear her nasal laugh, or his quiet voice
talking soft nonsense into her ear. Of course it was nonsense!
Is it conceivable that a man like Raffles, with his knowledge of
the world, and his experience of women (a side of his character upon which I have purposely never touched, for it deserves
another volume); is it credible, I ask, that such a man could
find anything but nonsense to talk by the day together to a
giddy young schoolgirl? I would not be unfair for the world.
I think I have admitted that the young person had points. Her
eyes, I suppose, were really fine, and certainly the shape of the
little brown face was charming, so far as mere contour can
charm. I admit also more audacity than I cared about, with
enviable health, mettle, and vitality. I may not have occasion
to report any of this young lady's speeches (they would scarcely
bear it), and am therefore the more anxious to describe her
without injustice. I confess to some little prejudice against her.
I resented her success with Raffles of whom, in consequence, I
saw less and less each day. It is a mean thing to have to confess,
but there must have been something not unlike jealousy rank-
ling within me.

Jealousy there was in another quarter – crude, rampant, un-
dignified jealousy. Captain von Heumann would twirl his
moustaches into twin spires, shoot his white cuffs over his
rings, and stare at me insolently through his rimless eye-
glasses; we ought to have consoled each other, but we never
exchanged a syllable. The captain had a murderous scar across
one of his cheeks, a present from Heidelberg, and I used to
think how he must long to have Raffles there to serve the same.
It was not as though von Heumann never had his innings.
Raffles let him go in several times a day, for the malicious pleasure of bowling him out as he was 'getting set'; those were his
words when I taxed him disingenuously with obnoxious conduct towards a German on a German boat.

'You'll make yourself disliked on board!'

133

'By von Heumann merely.'

'But is that wise when he's the man we've got to diddle?'

'The wisest thing I ever did. To have chummed up with him would have been fatal – the common dodge.'

I was consoled, encouraged, almost content. I had feared Raffles was neglecting things, and I told him so in a burst. Here we were near Gibraltar, and not a word since the Solent. He shook his head with a smile.

'Plenty of time, Bunny, plenty of time. We can do nothing before we get to Genoa, and that won't be till Sunday night. The voyage is still young, and so are we; let's make the most of things while we can.'

It was after dinner on the promenade deck, and as Raffles spoke he glanced sharply fore and aft, leaving me next moment with a step full of purpose. I retired to the smoking-room, to smoke and read in a corner, and to watch von Heumann, who very soon came to drink beer and to sulk in another.

Few travellers tempt the Red Sea at midsummer; the *Uhlan* was very empty indeed. She had, however, but a limited supply of cabins on the promenade deck, and there was just that excuse for my sharing Raffles's room. I could have had one to myself downstairs, but I must be up above. Raffles had insisted that I should insist on that point. So we were together, I think, without suspicion, though also without any object that I could see.

On the Sunday afternoon I was asleep in my berth, the lower one, when the curtains were shaken by Raffles, who was in his shirt-sleeves on the settee.

'Achilles sulking in his bunk!'

'What else is there to do?' I asked him as I stretched and yawned. I noted, however, the good-humour of his tone, and did my best to catch it.

'I have found something else, Bunny.'

'I dare say!'

'You understand me. The whipper-snapper's making his century this afternoon. I've had other fish to fry.'

I swung my legs over the side of my berth and sat forward, as he was sitting, all attention. The inner door, a grating, was shut and bolted, and curtained like the open port-hole.

'We shall be at Genoa before sunset,' continued Raffles. 'It's the place where the deed's got to be done.'

'So you still mean to do it!'

'Did I ever say I didn't?'

'You have said so little either way.'

'Advisedly so, my dear Bunny; why spoil a pleasure trip by talking unnecessary shop? But now the time has come. It must be done at Genoa or not at all.'

'On land?'

'No, on board, to-morrow night. To-night would do, but to-morrow is better, in case of mishap. If we were forced to use violence we could get away by the earliest train, and nothing be known till the ship was sailing and von Heumann found dead or drugged − −'

'Not dead!' I exclaimed.

'Of course not,' assented Raffles, 'or there would be no need for us to bolt; but if we should have to bolt, Tuesday morning is our time when the ship has got to sail, whatever happens. But I don't anticipate any violence. Violence is a confession of terrible incompetence. In all these years how many blows have you known me strike? Not one, I believe; but I have been quite ready to kill my man every time, if the worst came to the worst.'

I asked him how he proposed to enter von Heumann's stateroom unobserved, and even through the curtained gloom of ours his face lighted up.

'Climb into my bunk, Bunny, and you shall see.'

I did so, but could see nothing. Raffles reached across me and tapped the ventilator, a sort of trap-door in the wall above his bed, some eighteen inches long and half that height. It opened outwards into the ventilating shaft.

'That,' said he, 'is our door to fortune. Open it if you like; you won't see much, because it doesn't open far; but loosening a couple of screws will set that all right. The shaft, as you may see, is more or less bottomless; you pass under it whenever you go to your bath, and the top is a skylight on the bridge. That's why this thing has to be done while we're at Genoa, because they keep no watch on the bridge in port. The ventilator opposite ours is von Heumann's. It again will only mean a couple of screws and there's a beam to stand on while you work.'

'But if anybody should look from below?'

'It's extremely unlikely that anybody will be astir below, so unlikely that we can afford to chance it. No, I can't have you there to make sure. The great point is that neither of us should be seen from the time we turn in. A couple of ship's boys do sentry-go on these decks; and they shall be our witnesses; by Jove, it'll be the biggest mystery that ever was made!'

'If von Heumann doesn't resist.'

'Resist! He won't get the chance. He drinks too much beer to sleep light, and nothing is so easy as to chloroform a heavy sleeper; you've even done it yourself on an occasion of which it's perhaps unfair to remind you. Von Heumann will be past sensation almost as soon as I get my hand through his ventilator. I shall crawl in over his body, Bunny, my boy!'

'And I?'

'You will hand me what I want, and hold the fort in case of accidents, and generally lend me the moral support you've made me require. It's a luxury, Bunny, but I found it devilish difficult to do without it after you turned pi!'

He said that von Heumann was certain to sleep with a bolted door, which he, of course, would leave unbolted, and spoke of other ways of laying a false scent while rifling the cabin. Not that Raffles anticipated a tiresome search. The pearl would be about von Heumann's person; in fact, Raffles knew exactly where and in what he kept it. Naturally, I asked how he could have come by such knowledge, and his answer led up to a momentary unpleasantness.

'It's a very old story, Bunny. I really forget in what book it comes; I'm only sure of the Testament. But Samson was the unlucky hero, and one Delilah the heroine.'

And he looked so knowing that I could not be in a moment's doubt as to his meaning.

'So the fair Australian has been playing Delilah?' said I.

'In a very harmless, innocent sort of way.'

'She got his mission out of him?'

'Yes; I've forced him to score all the points he could, and that was his great stroke, as I hoped it would be. He has even shown Amy the pearl.'

'Amy, eh! and she promptly told you?'

'Nothing of the kind. What makes you think so? I had the greatest trouble in getting it out of her.'

His tone should have been a sufficient warning to me. I had not the tact to take it as such. At last I knew the meaning of his furious flirtation, and stood wagging my head and shaking my finger, blinded to his frowns by my own enlightenment.

'Wily worm!' said I. 'Now I see through it all; how dense I've been!'

'Sure you're not still?'

'No; now I understand what has beaten me all the week. I simply couldn't fathom what you saw in that little girl. I never dreamt it was part of the game.'

'So you think it was that and nothing more?'

'You deep old dog – of course I do!'

'You didn't know she was the daughter of a wealthy squatter?'

'There are wealthy women by the dozen who would marry you to-morrow.'

'It doesn't occur to you that I might like to draw stumps, start clean, and live happily ever after – in the bush?'

'With that voice? It certainly does not!'

'Bunny!' he cried so fiercely that I braced myself for a blow. But no more followed.

'Do you think you would live happily?' I made bold to ask him.

'God knows!' he answered. And with that he left me, to marvel at his look and tone, and, more than ever, at the insufficiently exciting cause.

III

Of all the mere feats of cracksmanship which I have seen Raffles perform, at once the most delicate and most difficult was that which he accomplished between one and two o'clock on the Tuesday morning, aboard the North German steamer *Uhlan*, lying at anchor in Genoa harbour.

Not a hitch occurred. Everything had been foreseen; everything happened as I had been assured everything must. Nobody was about below, only the ship's boys on deck, and nobody on the bridge. It was twenty-five minutes past one when Raffles, without a stitch of clothing on his body, but with a glass phial, corked with cotton-wool, between his teeth, and a tiny screwdriver behind his ear, squirmed feet first through the ventilator over his berth; and it was nineteen minutes to two when he returned, head first, with the phial still between his teeth, and the cotton-wool rammed home to still the rattling of that which lay like a great grey bean within. He had taken screws out and put them in again; he had unfastened von Heumann's ventilator and had left it fast as he had found it – fast as he instantly proceeded to make his own. As for von Heumann, it had been enough to place the drenched wad first on his moustache, and then to hold it between his gaping lips; thereafter the intruder had climbed both ways across his shins without eliciting a groan. And here was the prize – this pearl as large as a filbert – with a pale pink tinge like a lady's finger-nail – this spoil of the filibustering age – this gift from a European emperor to a South Sea chief. We gloated over it when all was snug. We toasted it in whisky and soda-water, laid in overnight in view of the great moment. But the moment was greater, more triumphant, than our most sanguine dreams. All we had now to do was to secrete the gem (which Raffles had prised from its setting, replacing the latter), so that we could stand the strictest search and yet take it ashore with us at Naples; and this Raffles was doing when I turned in. I myself would have landed incontinently, that night, at Genoa, and bolted with the spoil; he would not hear of it, for a dozen good reasons which will be obvious.

On the whole I do not think that anything was discovered or suspected before we weighed anchor; but I cannot be sure. It is difficult to believe that a man could be chloroformed in his sleep and feel no tell-tale effects, sniff no suspicious odour, in the morning. Nevertheless, von Heumann reappeared as though nothing had happened to him, his German cap over his eyes and his moustaches brushing the peak. And by ten o'clock we were quit of Genoa; the last lean, blue-chinned official had left our decks; the last fruitseller had been beaten off with bucketsful of water and left cursing us from his boat; the last passenger had come aboard at the last moment – a fussy greybeard who kept the big ship waiting while he haggled with his boatman over half a lira. But at length we were off, the tug was shed, the lighthouse passed, and Raffles and I leaned together over the rail, watching our shadows on the pale green, liquid, veined marble that again washed the vessel's side.

Von Heumann was having his innings once more; it was part of the design that he should remain in all day, and so postpone the inevitable hour; and, though the lady looked bored, and was for ever glancing in our direction, he seemed only too willing to avail himself of his opportunities. But Raffles was moody and ill at ease. He had not the air of a successful man. I could but opine that the impending parting at Naples sat heavily on his spirit. He would neither talk to me, nor would he let me go.

'Stop where you are, Bunny. I've things to tell you. Can you swim?'

'A bit.'

'Ten miles?'

'Ten?' I burst out laughing. 'Not one! Why do you ask?'

'We shall be within a ten miles' swim of the shore most of the day.'

'What on earth are you driving at, Raffles?'

'Nothing; only I shall swim for it if the worst comes to the worst. I suppose you can't swim under water at all?'

I did not answer his question. I scarcely heard it; cold beads were bursting through my skin.

'Why should the worst come to the worst?' I whispered. 'We aren't found out, are we?'

'No.'

'Then why speak as though we were?'

'We may be; an old enemy of ours is on board.'

'An old enemy?'

'Mackenzie.'

'Never.'

'The man with the beard who came aboard last.'

'Are you sure?'

'Sure! I was only sorry to see you didn't recognise him too.'

I took my handkerchief to my face; now that I thought of it,

139

there had been something familiar in the old man's gait, as well as something rather youthful for his apparent years; his very beard seemed unconvincing, now that I recalled it in the light of this horrible revelation. I looked up and down the deck, but the old man was nowhere to be seen.

'That's the worst of it,' said Raffles. 'I saw him go into the captain's cabin twenty minutes ago.'

'But what can have brought him?' I cried miserably. 'Can it be a coincidence – is it somebody else he's after?'

Raffles shook his head.

'Hardly, this time.'

'Then you think he's after you?'

'I've been afraid of it for some weeks.'

'Yet there you stand!'

'What am I to do? I don't want to swim for it before I must. I begin to wish I'd taken your advice, Bunny, and left the ship at Genoa. But I've not the smallest doubt that Mac was watching both ship and station till the last moment. That's why he ran it so fine.'

He took a cigarette and handed me the case, but I shook my head impatiently.

'I still don't understand,' said I. 'Why should he be after you? He couldn't come all this way about a jewel which was perfectly safe for all he knew. What's your own theory?'

'Simply that he's been on my track for some time, probably ever since friend Crawshay slipped clean through his fingers last November. There have been other indications. I am really not unprepared for this. But it can only be pure suspicion. I'll defy him to bring anything home, and I'll defy him to find the pearl! Theory, my dear Bunny! I know how he's got here as well as though I'd been inside that Scotsman's skin, and I know what he'll do next. He found out I'd gone abroad, and looked for a motive; he found out about von Heumann and his mission, and here was his motive cut and dried. Great chance – to nab me on a new job altogether. But he won't do it, Bunny; mark my words, he'll search the ship and search us all, when the loss is known; but he'll search in vain. And there's skipper beckoning the whipper-snapper to his cabin; the fat will be in the fire in five minutes!'

Yet there was no conflagration, no fuss, no searching of the passengers, no whisper of what had happened in the air; instead of a stir there was portentous peace; and it was clear to me that Raffles was not a little disturbed at the falsification of all his predictions. There was something sinister in silence under such a loss, and the silence was sustained for hours, during which Mackenzie never reappeared. But he was abroad during the luncheon-hour – he was in our cabin! I had left my book in Raffles's berth, and in taking it after lunch I touched the quilt. It was warm from the recent pressure of flesh and blood, and on an instinct I sprang to the ventilator; as I opened it the ventilator opposite was closed with a snap.

I waylaid Raffles. 'All right. Let him find the pearl.'

'Have you dumped it overboard?'

'That's a question I shan't condescend to answer.'

He turned on his heel, and at subsequent intervals I saw him making the most of his last afternoon with the inevitable Miss Werner. I remember that she looked both cool and smart in quite a simple affair of brown holland, which toned well with her complexion, and was cleverly relieved with touches of scarlet. I quite admired her that afternoon, for her eyes were really very good, and so were her teeth, yet I had never admired her more directly in my own despite. For I passed them again and again in order to get a word with Raffles, to tell him I knew there was danger in the wind; but he would not so much as catch my eye. So at last I gave it up. And I saw him next in the captain's cabin.

They had summoned him first; he had gone in smiling; and smiling I found him when they summoned me. The stateroom was spacious, as befitted that of a commander. Mackenzie sat on the settee, his beard in front of him on the polished table; but a revolver lay in front of the captain; and, when I had entered, the chief officer, who had summoned me, shut the door and put his back to it. Von Heumann completed the party, his fingers busy with his moustache.

Raffles greeted me.

'This is a great joke!' he cried. 'You remember the pearl you were so keen about, Bunny, the emperor's pearl, the pearl money wouldn't buy? It seems it was entrusted to our little friend here, to take out to Canoodle Dum, and the poor little chap's gone and lost it; *ergo*, as we're Britishers, they think we've got it!'

'But I know ye have,' put in Mackenzie, nodding to his beard.

'You will recognise that loyal and patriotic voice,' said Raffles. 'Mon, 'tis our auld acquaintance Mackenzie, o' Scoteland Yarrd an' Scoteland itsel'!'

'Dat is enought,' cried the captain. 'Have you submid to be searge, or do I vorce you?'

'What you will,' said Raffles, 'but it will do you no harm to give us fair play first. You accuse us of breaking into Captain von Heumann's stateroom during the small hours of this morning, and abstracting from it this confounded pearl. Well, I can prove that I was in my own room all night long, and I have no doubt my friend can prove the same.'

'Most certainly I can,' said I indignantly. 'The ship's boys can bear witness to that.'

Mackenzie laughed, and shook his head at his reflection in the polished mahogany.

'That was vera clever,' said he, 'and like enough it would ha' served ye had I not stepped aboard. But I've just had a look at they ventilators, and I think I know how ye worrked it. Anyway, captain, it makes no matter. I'll just be clappin' the darbies on these young sparks, an' then – –'

'By what right?' roared Raffles in a ringing voice, and I never saw his face in such a blaze. 'Search us if you like; search every scrap and stitch we possess; but you dare to lay a finger on us without a warrant!'

'I wouldna dare,' said Mackenzie gravely, as he fumbled in his breast-pocket, and Raffles dived his hand into his own. 'Haud his wrist!' shouted the Scotsman; and the huge Colt that had been with us many a night, but had never been fired in my hearing, clattered on the table and was raked in by the captain.

'All right,' said Raffles savagely to the mate. 'You can let go now. I won't try it again. Now, Mackenzie, let's see your warrant!'

'Ye'll no mishandle it?'

'What good would that do me? Let me see it,' said Raffles

peremptorily, and the detective obeyed. Raffles raised his eyebrows as he perused the document; his mouth hardened, but suddenly relaxed; and it was with a smile and a shrug that he returned the paper.

'Wull that do for ye?' inquired Mackenzie.

'It may. I congratulate you, Mackenzie; it's a strong hand, at any rate. Two burglaries and the Melrose necklace, Bunny!' And he turned to me with a rueful smile.

'An' all easy to prove,' said the Scotsman, pocketing the warrant. 'I've one o' these for you,' he added, nodding to me, 'only not such a long one.'

'To thingk,' said the captain reproachfully, 'that my shib should be made a den of thiefs! It shall be a very disagreeable madder. I have been obliged to pud you both in irons until we ged to Nables.'

'Surely not!' exclaimed Raffles. 'Mackenzie, intercede with him; don't give your countrymen away before all hands! Captain, we can't escape; surely you could hush it up for the night? Look here, here's everything I have in my pockets; you empty yours too, Bunny, and they shall strip us stark if they suspect we've weapons up our sleeves. All I ask is that we are allowed to get out of this without gyves upon our wrists!'

'Webbons you may not have,' said the captain, 'bud wad about der bearl dat you were sdealing?'

'You shall have it!' cried Raffles. 'You shall have it this minute if you guarantee no public indignity on board!'

'That I'll see to,' said Mackenzie, 'as long as you behave yourselves. There now, where is't?'

'On the table under your nose.'

My eyes fell with the rest, but no pearl was there; only the contents of our pockets – our watches, pocket-books, pencils, penknives, cigarette-cases – lay on the shiny table along with the revolvers already mentioned.

'Ye're humbuggin' us,' said Mackenzie. 'What's the use?'

'I'm doing nothing of the sort,' laughed Raffles. 'I'm testing you. Where's the harm?'

'It's here, joke apart?'

'On that table, by all my gods.'

Mackenzie opened the cigarette-case and shook each particular cigarette. Thereupon Raffles prayed to be allowed to smoke one, and, when his prayer was heard, observed that the pearl had been on the table much longer than the cigarettes. Mackenzie promptly caught up the Colt and opened the chamber in the butt.

'Not there, not there,' said Raffles; 'but you're getting hot. Try the cartridges.'

Mackenzie emptied them into his palm, and shook each one at his ear without result.

'Oh, give them to me!'

And, in an instant, Raffles had found the right one, had bitten out the bullet, and placed the emperor's pearl with a flourish in the centre of the table.

'After that you will perhaps show me such little consideration as is in your power. Captain, I have been a bit of a villain, as you see, and as such I am ready and willing to lie in irons all night if you deem it requisite for the safety of the ship. All I ask is that you do me one favour first.'

'That shall debend on wad der vafour has been.'

'Captain, I've done a worse thing aboard your ship than any of you know. I have become engaged to be married, and I want to say good-bye!'

I suppose we were all equally amazed; but the only one to express his amazement was von Heumann, whose deep-chested German oath was almost his first contribution to the proceedings. He was not slow to follow it, however, with a vigorous protest against the proposed farewell; but he was overruled, and the masterful prisoner had his way. He was to have five minutes with the girl, while the captain and Mackenzie stood within range (but not earshot), with their revolvers behind their backs. As we were moving from the cabin in a body, he stopped and gripped my hand.

'So I've let you in at last, Bunny – at last and after all! If you knew how sorry I am ... But you won't get much – I don't see why you should get anything at all. Can you forgive me? This may be for years, and it may be for ever, you know! You were a good pal always when it came to the scratch; some day or other you mayn't be so sorry to remember you were a good pal at the last!'

There was a meaning in his eye that I understood; and my teeth were set, and my nerves strung ready, as I wrung that strong and cunning hand for the last time in my life.

How that last scene stays with me, and will stay to my death! How I see every detail, every shadow on the sunlit deck! We were among the islands that dot the course from Genoa to Naples; that was Elba falling back on our starboard quarter, that purple patch with the hot sun setting over it. The captain's cabin opened to starboard, and the starboard promenade deck, sheeted with sunshine and scored with shadow, was deserted but for the group of which I was one, and for the pale, slim, brown figure farther aft with Raffles. Engaged? I could not believe it, cannot to this day. Yet there they stood together, and we did not hear a word; there they stood out against the sunset, and the long, dazzling highway of sunlit sea that sparkled from Elba to the *Uhlan's* plates; and their shadows reached almost to our feet.

Suddenly – an instant – and the thing was done – a thing I have never known whether to admire or to detest. He caught her – he kissed her before us all – then flung her from him so that she almost fell. It was that action which foretold the next. The mate sprang after him, and I sprang after the mate.

Raffles was on the rail, but only just.

'Hold him, Bunny!' he cried. 'Hold him tight!'

And, as I obeyed that last behest with all my might, without a thought of what I was doing, save that he bade me do it, I saw his hands shoot up and his head bob down, and his lithe, spare body cut the sunset as cleanly and precisely as though he had plunged at his leisure from a diver's board!

.   .   .

Of what followed on deck I can tell you nothing, for I was not there. Nor can my final punishment, my long imprisonment, my everlasting disgrace, concern or profit you, beyond the interest and advantage to be gleaned from the knowledge that I at least had my deserts. But one thing I must set down, believe it who will – one more thing only and I am done.

It was into a second-class cabin, on the starboard side, that I was promptly thrust in irons, and the door locked upon me as though I were another Raffles. Meanwhile, a boat was lowered, and the seas scoured to no purpose, as is doubtless on record elsewhere. But either the setting sun, flashing over the waves, must have blinded all eyes, or else mine were victims of a strange illusion.

For the boat was back, the screw throbbing, and the prisoner peering through his port-hole across the sunlit waters that he believed had closed for ever over his comrade's head. Suddenly the sun sank behind the Island of Elba, the lane of dancing sunlight was instantaneously quenched and swallowed in the trackless waste, and in the middle distance, already miles astern, either my sight deceived me or a black speck bobbed amid the grey. The bugle had blown for dinner; it may well be that all save myself had ceased to strain an eye. And now I lost what I had found, now it rose, now sank, and now I gave it up utterly. Yet anon it would rise again, a mere mote dancing in the dim grey distance, drifting towards a purple island, beneath a fading western sky, streaked with dead gold and cerise. And night fell before I knew whether it was a human head or not.

NO SINECURE

I

I AM still uncertain which surprised me more, the telegram calling my attention to the advertisement or the advertisement itself. The telegram is before me as I write. It would appear to have been handed in at Vere Street at eight o'clock in the morning of May 11, 1897, and received before half-past at Holloway B.O. And in that drab region it duly found me unwashed but at work before the day grew hot and my attic insupportable.

'See Mr Maturin's advertisement *Daily Mail* might suit you earnestly beg try will speak if necessary ... '

I transcribe the thing as I see it before me, all in one breath that took away mine; but I leave out the initials at the end, which completed the surprise. They stood very obviously for the knighted specialist whose consulting-room is within a cab-whistle of Vere Street, and who once called me kinsman for his sins. More recently he had called me other names. I was a disgrace, qualified by an adjective which seemed to me another. I had made my bed, and I could go and lie and die in it. If I ever again had the insolence to show my nose in that house, I should go out quicker than I came in. All this, and more, my least distant relative could tell a poor devil to his face; could ring for his man, and give him his brutal instructions on the spot; and then relent to the tune of this telegram! I have no phrase for my amazement. I literally could not believe my eyes. Yet their evidence was more and more conclusive; a very epistle could not have been more characteristic of its sender. Meanly elliptical, ludicrously precise, saving half-pence at the expense of sense, yet paying like a man for 'Mr' Maturin, that was my distinguished relative from his bald patch to his corns. Nor was all the rest unlike him, upon second thoughts. He had a reputation

147

for charity; he was going to live up to it after all. Either that, or it was the sudden impulse of which the most calculating are capable at times; the morning papers with the early cup of tea, this advertisement seen by chance, and the rest upon the spur of a guilty conscience.

Well, I must see it for myself, and the sooner the better, though work pressed. I was writing a series of articles upon prison life, and had my nib into the whole system; a literary and philanthropic daily was parading my 'charges', the graver ones with the more gusto; and the terms, if unhandsome for creative work, were temporary wealth to me. It so happened that my first cheque had just arrived by the eight o'clock post; and my position should be appreciated when I say that I had to cash it to obtain a *Daily Mail*.

Of the advertisement itself, what is to be said? It should speak for itself if I could find it, but I cannot, and only remember that it was a 'male nurse and constant attendant' that was 'wanted for an elderly gentleman in feeble health'. A male nurse! An absurd tag was appended, offering 'liberal salary to University or public-school man'; and of a sudden I saw that I should get this thing if I applied for it. What other 'University or public-school man' would dream of doing so? Was any other in such straits as I? And then my relenting relative; he not only promised to speak for me, but was the very man to do so. Could any recommendation compete with his in the matter of a male nurse? And need the duties of such be necessarily loathsome and repellent? Certainly the surroundings would be better than those of my common lodging-house and own particular garret; and the food; and every other condition of life that I could think of on my way back to that unsavoury asylum. So I dived into a pawnbroker's shop, where I was a stranger only upon my present errand, and within the hour was airing a decent if antiquated suit, but little corrupted by the pawnbroker's moth, and a new straw hat, on the top of a tram.

The address given in the advertisement was that of a flat at Earls Court, which cost me a cross-country journey, finishing with the District Railway and a seven minutes' walk. It was now past midday, and the tarry wood-pavement was good to smell as I strode up the Earls Court Road. It was great to walk the civilised world again. Here were men with coats on their backs, and ladies in gloves. My only fear was lest I might run up against one or other whom I had known of old. But it was my lucky day. I felt it in my bones. I was going to get this berth; and sometimes I should be able to smell the wood-pavement on the old boy's errands; perhaps he would insist on skimming over it in his bath-chair with me behind.

I felt quite nervous when I reached the flats. They were a small pile in a side-street, and I pitied the doctor whose plate I saw upon the palings before the ground-floor windows; he must be in a very small way, I thought. I rather pitied myself as well. I had indulged in visions of better flats than these. There were no balconies. The porter was out of livery. There was no lift, and my invalid on the third floor! I trudged up, wishing I had never lived in Mount Street, and brushed against a dejected individual coming down. A full-blooded young fellow in a frock-coat flung the right door open at my summons.

'Does Mr Maturin live here?' I inquired.

'That's right,' said the full-blooded young man, grinning all over a convivial countenance.

'I – I've come about his advertisement in the *Daily Mail*.'

'You're the thirty-ninth,' cried the blood; 'that was the thirty-eighth you met upon the stairs, and the day's still young. Excuse my staring at you. Yes, you pass your prelim., and can come inside; you're one of the few. We had most just after breakfast, but now the porter's heading off the worst cases, and that last chap was the first for twenty minutes. Come in here.'

And I was ushered into an empty room with a good bay-window, which enabled my full-blooded friend to inspect me yet more critically in a good light; this he did without the least false delicacy; then his questions began.

' 'Varsity man?'

'No.'

'Public School?'

'Yes.'

'Which one?'

I told him, and he sighed relief.

'At last! You're the very first I've not had to argue with as to what is and what is not a public school. Expelled?'

'No,' I said, after a moment's hesitation; 'no, I was not expelled. And I hope you won't expel me if I ask a question in my turn?'

'Certainly not.'

'Are you Mr Maturin's son?'

'No, my name's Theobald. You may have seen it down below.'

'The doctor?' I said.

'His doctor,' said Theobald, with a satisfied eye. 'Mr Maturin's doctor. He is having a male nurse and attendant if he can get one. I rather think he'll see you, though he's only seen two or three all day. There are certain questions which he prefers to ask himself, and it's no good going over the same ground twice. So perhaps I had better tell him about you before we get any further.'

And he withdrew to a room still nearer the entrance, as I could hear, for it was a very small flat indeed. But now two doors were shut between us, and I had to rest content with murmurs through the wall until the doctor returned to summon me.

'I have persuaded my patient to see you,' he whispered, 'but I confess I am not sanguine of the result. He is very difficult to please. You must prepare yourself for a querulous invalid, and for no sinecure if you get the billet.'

'May I ask what's the matter with him?'

'By all means – when you've got the billet.'

Dr Theobald then led the way, his professional dignity so thoroughly intact that I could not but smile as I followed his swinging coat-tails to the sick-room. I carried no smile across the threshold of a darkened chamber which reeked of drugs and twinkled with medicine bottles, and in the middle of which a gaunt figure lay abed in the half-light.

'Take him to the window, take him to the window,' a thin voice snapped, 'and let's have a look at him. Open the blind a bit. Not as much as that, damn you, not as much as that!'

The doctor took the oath as though it had been a fee. I no longer pitied him. It was now very clear to me that he had one patient who was a little practice in himself. I determined there and then that he should prove a little profession to me, if we could but keep him alive between us. Mr Maturin, however, had the whitest face that I have ever seen, and his teeth gleamed out through the dusk as though the withered lips no longer met about them; nor did they except in speech; and anything ghastlier than the perpetual grin of his repose I defy you to imagine. It was with this grin that he lay regarding me while the doctor held the blind.

'So you think you could look after me, do you?'

'I'm certain I could, sir.'

'Single-handed, mind! I don't keep another soul. You would have to cook your own grub and my slops. Do you think you could do all that?'

'Yes, sir, I think so.'

'Why do you? Have you any experience of the kind?'

'No, sir, none.'

'Then why do you pretend you have?'

'I only meant that I would do my best.'

'Only meant, only meant! Have you done your best at everything else, then?'

I hung my head. This was a facer. And there was something in my invalid which thrust the unspoken lie down my throat.

'No, sir, I have not,' I told him plainly.

'He, he, he!' the old wretch tittered; 'and you do well to own it; you do well, sir, very well indeed. If you hadn't owned up, out you would have gone, out neck and crop! You've saved your bacon. You may do more. So you are a public-school boy, and a very good school yours is, but you weren't at either University. Is that correct?'

'Absolutely.'

'What did you do when you left school?'

'I came in for money.'

'And then?'

'I spent my money.'

'And since then?'

I stood like a mule.

'And since then, I say!'

'A relative of mine will tell you if you ask him. He is an

eminent man, and he has promised to speak for me. I would rather say no more myself.'

'But you shall, sir, but you shall! Do you suppose that I suppose a public-school boy would apply for a berth like this if something or other hadn't happened? What I want is a gentleman of sorts, and I don't much care what sort; but you've got to tell me what did happen, if you don't tell anybody else. Dr Theobald, sir, you can go to the devil if you won't take a hint. This man may do or he may not. You have no more to say to it till I send him down to tell you one thing or the other. Clear out, sir, clear out; and if you think you've anything to complain of, you stick it down in the bill!'

In the mild excitement of our interview the thin voice had gathered strength, and the last shrill insult was screamed after the devoted medico, as he retired in such order that I felt certain he was going to take this trying patient at his word. The bedroom door closed, then the outer one, and the doctor's heels went drumming down the common stair. I was alone in the flat with this highly singular and rather terrible old man.

'And a damned good riddance!' croaked the invalid, raising himself on one elbow without delay. 'I may not have much body left to boast about, but at least I've got a lost old soul to call my own. That's why I want a gentleman of sorts about me. I've been too dependent on that chap. He won't even let me smoke, and he's been in the flat all day to see I didn't. You'll find the cigarettes behind the *Madonna of the Chair*.'

It was a steel engraving of the great Raffaele, and the frame was tilted from the wall; at a touch a packet of cigarettes tumbled down from behind.

'Thanks; and now a light.'

I struck the match and held it, while the invalid inhaled with normal lips; and suddenly I sighed. I was irresistibly reminded of my poor dear old Raffles. A smoke-ring worthy of the great A. J. was floating upward from the sick man's lips.

'And now take one yourself. I have smoked more poisonous cigarettes. But even these are not Sullivans!'

I cannot repeat what I said. I have no idea what I did. I only know – I only knew – that it was A. J. Raffles in the flesh.

II

'Yes, Bunny, it was the very devil of a swim; but I defy you to sink in the Mediterranean. That sunset saved me. The sea was on fire. I hardly swam under water at all, but went all I knew for the sun itself; when it set I must have been a mile away; until it did I was the invisible man. I figured on that, and only hope it wasn't set down as a case of suicide. I shall get outed quite soon enough, Bunny, but I'd rather be dropped by the hangman than throw my own wicket away.'

'Oh, my dear old chap, to think of having you by the hand again! I feel as though we were both aboard that German liner, and all that's happened since a nightmare. I thought that time was the last!'

'It looked rather like it, Bunny. It was taking all the risks, and hitting at everything. But the game came off, and some day I'll tell you how.'

'Oh, I'm in no hurry to hear. It's enough for me to see you lying there. I don't want to know how you came here, or why, though I fear you must be pretty bad. I must have a good look at you before I let you speak another word!'

I raised one of the blinds, I sat upon the bed, and I had that look. It left me all unable to conjecture his true state of health, but quite certain in my own mind that my dear Raffles was not and never would be the man that he had been. He had aged twenty years; he looked fifty at the very least. His hair was white; there was no trick about that; and his face was another white. The lines about the corners of the eyes and mouth were both many and deep. On the other hand, the eyes themselves were alight and alert as ever; they were still keen and grey and gleaming like finely tempered steel. Even the mouth, with a cigarette to close it, was the mouth of Raffles and no other: strong and unscrupulous as the man himself. It was only the physical strength which appeared to have departed; but that was quite sufficient to make my heart bleed for the dear rascal who had cost me every tie I valued but the tie between us two.

'Think I look much older?' he asked at length.

'A bit,' I admitted. 'But it is chiefly your hair.'

'Whereby hangs a tale for when we've talked ourselves out, though I have often thought it was that long swim that started it. Still, the Island of Elba is a rummy show, I can assure you. And Naples is a rummier.'

'You went there after all?'

'Rather! It's the European paradise for such as our noble selves. But there's no place that's a patch on little London as a non-conductor of heat; it never need get too hot for a fellow here; if it does it's his own fault. It's the kind of wicket you don't get out on, unless you get yourself out. So here I am again, and have been for the last six weeks. And I mean to have another knock.'

'But surely, old fellow, you're not awfully fit, are you?'

'Fit? My dear Bunny, I'm dead – I'm at the bottom of the sea – and don't you forget it for a minute.'

'But are you all right, or are you not?'

'No; I'm half poisoned by Theobald's prescriptions and putrid cigarettes, and as weak as a cat from lying in bed.'

'Then why on earth lie in bed, Raffles?'

'Because it's better than lying in gaol, as I am afraid *you* know, my poor dear fellow. I tell you I am dead; and my one terror is of coming to life again by accident. Can't you see? I simply dare not show my nose out of doors – by day. You have no idea of the number of perfectly innocent things a dead man daren't do. I can't even smoke Sullivans, because no one man was ever so partial to them as I was in my lifetime, and you never know when you may start a clue.'

'What brought you to these mansions?'

'I fancied a flat, and a man recommended these on the boat; such a good chap, Bunny; he was my reference when it came to signing the lease. You see, I landed on a stretcher – most pathetic case – old Australian without a friend in old country – ordered Engadine as last chance – no gō – not an earthly – sentimental wish to die in London – that's the history of Mr. Maturin. If it doesn't hit you hard, Bunny, you're the first. But it hit friend Theobald hardest of all. I'm an income to him. I believe he's going to marry on me.'

'Does he guess there's nothing wrong?'

'Knows, bless you! But he doesn't know I know he knows, and there isn't a disease in the dictionary that he hasn't treated me for since he's had me in hand. To do him justice, I believe he thinks me a hypochondriac of the first water; but that young man will go far if he keeps on the wicket. He has spent half his nights up here, at guineas apiece.'

'Guineas must be plentiful, old chap!'

'They have been, Bunny. I can't say more. But I don't see why they should be again.'

I was not going to inquire where the guineas came from. As if I cared! But I did ask old Raffles how in the world he had got upon my tracks; and thereby drew the sort of smile with which old gentlemen rub their hands, and old ladies nod their noses. Raffles merely produced a perfect oval of blue smoke before replying.

'I was waiting for you to ask that, Bunny; it's a long time since I did anything upon which I plume myself more. Of course, in the first place, I spotted you at once by these prison articles; they were not signed, but the fist was the fist of my sitting rabbit!'

'But who gave you my address?'

'I wheedled it out of your excellent editor; called on him at dead of night, when I occasionally go afield like other ghosts, and wept it out of him in five minutes. I was your only relative; your name was not your own name; if he insisted I would give him mine. He didn't insist, Bunny, and I danced down his stairs with your address in my pocket.'

'Last night?'

'No, last week.'

'And so the advertisement was yours, as well as the telegram!'

I had, of course, forgotten both in the high excitement of the hour, or I should scarcely have announced my belated discovery with such an air. As it was, I made Raffles look at me as I had known him look before, and the droop of his eyelids began to sting.

'Why all this subtlety?' I petulantly exclaimed. 'Why couldn't you come straight away to me in a cab?'

He did not inform me that I was hopeless as ever. He did

not address me as his good rabbit. He was silent for a time, and then spoke in a tone which made me ashamed of mine.

'You see, there are two or three of me now, Bunny: one's at the bottom of the Mediterranean, and one's an old Australian desirous of dying in the old country, but in no immediate danger of dying anywhere. The old Australian doesn't know a soul in town; he's got to be consistent, or he's done. This sitter Theobald is his only friend, and has seen rather too much of him; ordinary dust won't do for his eyes. Begin to see? To pick you out of a crowd, that was the game; to let old Theobald help to pick you, better still! To start with, he was dead against my having anybody at all; wanted me all to himself, naturally; but anything rather than kill the goose! So he is to have a fiver a week, while he keeps me alive, and he's going to be married next month. That's a pity in some ways, but a good thing in others; he will want more money than he foresees, and he may always be of use to us at a pinch. Meanwhile he eats out of my hand.'

I complimented Raffles on the mere composition of his telegram, with half the characteristics of my distinguished kinsman squeezed into a dozen odd words; and let him know how the old ruffian had really treated me. Raffles was not surprised; we had dined together at my relative's in the old days and filed for reference a professional valuation of his household goods. I now learnt that the telegram had been posted, with the hour marked for its dispatch, at the pillar nearest Vere Street, on the night before the advertisement was due to appear in the *Daily Mail*. This also had been carefully pre-arranged; and Raffles's only fear had been lest it might be held over despite his explicit instructions, and so drive me to the doctor for an explanation of his telegram. But the adverse chances had been weeded out, and weeded out to the irreducible minimum of risk.

His greatest risk, according to Raffles, lay nearest home: bedridden invalid that he was supposed to be, his nightly terror was of running into Theobald's arms in the immediate neighbourhood of the flat. But Raffles had characteristic methods of minimising even that danger, of which something anon; meanwhile he recounted more than one of his nocturnal adventures, all, however, of a singularly innocent type; and one thing I noticed while he talked. His room was the first as you entered the flat. The long inner wall divided the room not merely from the passage but from the outer landing as well. Thus every step upon the bare stone stairs could be heard by Raffles where he lay; and he would never speak while one was ascending, until it had passed his door. The afternoon brought more than one applicant for the post that it was my duty to tell them I had already obtained. Between three and four, however, Raffles suddenly looking at his watch, packed me off in a hurry to the other end of London for my things.

'I'm afraid you must be famishing, Bunny. It's a fact that I eat very little, and that at odd hours, but I ought not to have forgotten you. Get yourself a snack outside, but not a square meal if you can resist one. We've got to celebrate this day this night!'

'To-night?' I cried.

'To-night at eleven, and Kellner's the place. You may well open your eyes, but we didn't go there much, if you remember, and the staff seems changed. Anyway, we'll risk it for once. I was in last night, talking like a stage American, and supper's ordered for eleven sharp.'

'You made as sure of me as all that!'

'There was no harm in ordering supper. We shall have it in a private room, but you may as well dress if you've got the duds.'

'They're at my only forgiving relative's.'

'How much will get them out, and square you up, and bring you back bag and baggage in good time?'

I had to calculate.

'A tenner, easily.'

'I had one ready for you. Here it is, and I wouldn't lose any time if I were you. On the way you might look up Theobald, tell him you've got it and how long you'll be gone, and that I can't be left alone all the time. And, by Jove, yes! You get me a stall for the Lyceum at the nearest agent's; there are two or three in High Street; and say it was given you when you come in. That young man shall be out of the way to-night.'

I found our doctor in a minute consulting-room and in his shirt-sleeves, a tall tumbler at his elbow; at least, I caught sight of the tumbler on entering; thereafter he stood in front of it, with a futility which had my sympathy.

'So you've got the billet,' said Dr. Theobald. 'Well, as I told you before, and as you have since probably discovered for yourself, you won't find it exactly a sinecure. My own part of the business is by no means that; indeed, there are those who would throw up the case, after the kind of treatment that you have seen for yourself. But professional considerations are not the only ones, and one cannot make too many allowances in such a case.'

'But what is the case?' I asked him. 'You said you would tell me if I were successful.'

Dr. Theobald's shrug was worthy of the profession he seemed destined to adorn; it was not incompatible with any construction which one chose to put upon it. Next moment he had stiffened. I suppose I still spoke more or less like a gentleman. Yet, after all, I was only a male nurse. He seemed to remember this suddenly, and he took occasion to remind me of the fact.

'Ah,' said he, 'that was before I knew you were altogether without experience; and I must say that I was surprised even at Mr. Maturin's engaging you after that; but it will depend upon yourself how long I allow him to persist in so curious an experiment. As for what is the matter with him, my good fellow, it is no use my giving you an answer which would be double Dutch to you; moreover, I have still to test your discretionary powers. I may say, however, that that poor gentleman presents at once the most complex and most troublesome case, which is responsibility enough without certain features which make it all but insupportable. Beyond this I must refuse to discuss my patient for the present; but I shall certainly go up if I can find time.'

He went up within five minutes. I found him there on my return at dusk. But he did not refuse my stall for the Lyceum, which Raffles would not allow me to use myself, and presented to him off-hand without my leave.

'And don't you bother any more about me till to-morrow,'

snapped the high thin voice as he was off. 'I can send for you now when I want you, and I'm hoping to have a decent night for once.'

III

It was half-past ten when we left the flat, in an interval of silence on the noisy stairs. The silence was unbroken by our wary feet. Yet for me a surprise was in store upon the very landing. Instead of going downstairs, Raffles led me up two flights, and so out upon a perfectly flat roof.

'There are two entrances to these mansions,' he explained between stars and chimney-stacks: 'one to our staircase, and another round the corner. But there's only one porter, and he lives in the basement underneath us, and affects the door nearest home. We miss him by using the wrong stairs, and we run less risk of old Theobald. I got the tip from the postmen, who come up one way and down the other. Now follow me, and look out!'

There was indeed some necessity for caution, for each half of the building had its L-shaped well dropping sheer to the base, the parapets so low that one might easily have tripped over them into eternity. However, we were soon upon the second staircase, which opened on the roof like the first. And twenty minutes of the next twenty-five we spent in an admirable hansom, skimming east.

'Not much change in the old hole, Bunny. More of these magic-lantern advertisements ... and absolutely the worst bit of taste in town, though it's saying something, is that equestrian statue with the gilt stirrups and fixings: why don't they black the buffer's boots and his horse's hoofs while they are about it? ... More bicyclists, of course. That was just beginning, if you remember. It might have been useful to us ... And there's the old club, getting put into a crate for the Jubilee; by Jove, Bunny, we ought to be there. I wouldn't lean forward in Piccadilly, old chap. If you're seen I'm thought of, and we shall have to be jolly careful at Kellner's ... Ah, there it is! Did I tell you I was a low-down stage Yankee at Kellner's? You'd better be another, while the waiter's in the room.'

We had the little room upstairs; and on the very threshold I, even I, who knew my Raffles of old, was taken horribly aback. The table was laid for three. I called his attention to it in a whisper.

'Why, yep!' came through his nose. 'Say, boy, the lady, she's not com'n', but you leave that tackle where 'tis. If I'm liable to pay, I guess I'll have all there is to it.'

I have never been in America, and the American public is the last on earth that I desire to insult; but idiom and intonation alike would have imposed upon my inexperience. I had to look at Raffles to make sure that it was he who spoke, and I had my own reasons for looking hard.

'Who on earth was the lady?' I inquired, aghast, at the first opportunity.

'She isn't on earth. They don't like wasting this room on two, that's all. Bunny – my Bunny – here's to us both!'

And we clinked glasses swimming with the liquid gold of Steinberg, 1868; but of the rare delights of that supper I can scarcely trust myself to write. It was no mere meal, it was no coarse orgy, but a little feast for the fastidious gods, not unworthy of Lucullus at his worst. And I who had bolted my skilly at Wormwood Scrubs, and tightened my belt in a Holloway attic, it was I who sat down to this ineffable repast! Where the courses were few, but each a triumph of its kind, it would be invidious to single out any one dish; but the *jambon de Westphalie au champagne* tempts me sorely. And then the champagne that we drank, not the quantity but the quality! Well, it was Pol Roger, '84, and quite good enough for me; but even so it was not more dry, nor did it sparkle more, than the merry rascal who had dragged me thus far to the devil, but should lead me dancing the rest of the way. I was beginning to tell him so. I had done my honest best since my reappearance in the world; but the world had done its worst by me. A further antithesis and my final intention were both upon my tongue when the waiter with the Château Margaux cut me short; for he was the bearer of more than that great wine; bringing also a card upon a silver tray.

'Show him up,' said Raffles laconically.

'And who is this?' I cried, when the man was gone. Raffles

reached across the table and gripped my arm in his vice. His eyes were steel points fixed on mine.

'Bunny, stand by me,' said he in the old irresistible voice, a voice both stern and winning. 'Stand by me, Bunny – if there's a row!'

And there was time for nothing more, the door flying open, and a dapper person entering with a bow; a frock-coat on his back, gold *pincé-nez* on his nose; a shiny hat in one hand, and a black bag in the other.

'Good-evening, gentlemen,' said he, at home and smiling.

'Sit down,' drawled Raffles in casual response. 'Say, let me introduce you to Mr Ezra B. Martin, of Shicawgo. Mr Martin is my future brother-in-law. This is Mr Robinson, Ezra, manager to Sparks and Company, the celebrated joolers on Regent Street.'

I pricked up my ears, but contented myself with a nod. I altogether distrusted my ability to live up to my new name and address.

'I figured on Miss Martin bein' right here, too,' continued Raffles, 'but I regret to say she's not feelin' so good. We light out for Parrus on the 9 a.m. train to-morrer mornin', and she guessed she'd be too dead. Sorry to disappoint you, Mr Robinson; but you'll see I'm advertisin' your wares.'

Raffles held his right hand under the electric light, and a diamond ring flashed upon his little finger. I could have sworn it was not there five minutes before.

The tradesman had a disappointed face, but for a moment it brightened as he expatiated on the value of the ring and on the price his people had accepted for it. I was invited to guess the figure, but I shook a discreet head. I have seldom been more taciturn in my life.

'Forty-five pounds,' cried the jeweller; 'and it would be cheap at fifty guineas.'

'That's right,' assented Raffles. 'That'd be dead cheap, I allow. But then, my boy, you gotten ready cash, and don't you forget it.'

I do not dwell upon my own mystification in all this. I merely pause to state that I was keenly enjoying that very element. Nothing could have been more typical of Raffles and the past. It was only my own attitude that was changed.

It appeared that the mythical lady, my sister, had just become engaged to Raffles, who seemed all anxiety to pin her down with gifts of price. I could not quite gather whose gift to whom was the diamond ring; but it had evidently been paid for; and I voyaged to the moon, wondering when and how. I was recalled to this planet by a deluge of gems from the jeweller's bag. They lay alight in their cases like the electric lamps above. We all three put our heads together over them, myself without the slightest clue as to what was coming, but not unprepared for violent crime. One does not do eighteen months for nothing.

'Right away,' Raffles was saying. 'We'll choose for her, and you'll change anything she don't like. Is that the idea?'

'That was my suggestion, sir.'

'Then come on, Ezra. I guess you know Sadie's taste. You help me choose.'

And we chose – Lord! What did we not choose? There was her ring, a diamond half-hoop. It cost £95, and there was no attempt to get it for £90. Then there was a diamond necklet – two hundred guineas, but pounds accepted. That was to be the gift of the bridegroom. The wedding was evidently imminent. It behoved me to play a brotherly part. I therefore rose to the occasion; calculated she would like a diamond star (£116), but reckoned it was more than I could afford; and sustained a vicious kick under the table for either verb. I was afraid to open my mouth on finally obtaining the star for the round hundred. And then the fat fell in the fire; for pay we could not; though a remittance (said Raffles) was 'overdoo from Noo York.'

'But I don't know you, gentlemen,' the jeweller exclaimed. 'I haven't even the name of your hotel!'

'I told you we was stoppin' with friends,' said Raffles, who was not angry, though thwarted and crushed. 'But that's right, sir! Oh, that's dead right, and I'm the last man to ask you to take Quixotic risks. I'm tryin' to figure a way out. Yes, *sir*, that's what I'm tryin' to do.'

'I wish you could, sir,' the jeweller said, with feeling. 'It isn't as if we hadn't seen the colour of your money. But certain rules I am sworn to observe; it isn't as if I were in business for myself; and – you say you start for Paris in the morning!'

'On the 9 a.m. train,' mused Raffles; 'and I've heard no-end yarns about the joolers' stores in Parrus. But that ain't fair; don't you take no notice o' that. I'm tryin' to figure a way out. Yes, *sir!*"

He was smoking cigarettes out of a twenty-five box; the tradesman and I had cigars. Raffles sat frowning with a pregnant eye, and it was only too clear to me that his plans had miscarried. I could not help thinking, however, that they deserved to do so, if he had counted upon buying credit for all but £400 by a single payment of some 10 per cent. That again seemed unworthy of Raffles, and I, for my part, still sat prepared to spring any moment at our visitor's throat.

'We could mail you the money from Parrus,' drawled Raffles at length. 'But how should we know you'd hold up your end of the string, and mail us the same articles we've selected tonight?'

The visitor stiffened in his chair. The name of his firm should be sufficient guarantee for that.

'I guess I'm no better acquainted with their name than they are with mine,' remarked Raffles, laughing. 'See here, though! I got a scheme. You pack 'em in this!'

He turned the cigarettes out of the tin box, while the jeweller and I joined wondering eyes.

'Pack 'em in this,' repeated Raffles, 'the three things we want, and never mind the boxes; you can pack 'em in cotton-wool. Then we'll ring for string and sealing-wax, seal up the lot right here, and you can take 'em away in your grip. Within three days we'll have our remittance, and mail you the money, and you'll mail us this darned box with my seal unbroken! It's no use you lookin' so sick, Mr Jooler; you won't trust us any, and yet we're goin' to trust you some. Ring the bell, Ezra, and we'll see if they've gotten any sealing-wax and string.'

They had; and the thing was done. The tradesman did not like it; the precaution was absolutely unnecessary; but since he was taking all his goods away with him, the sold with the unsold, his sentimental objections soon fell to the ground. He packed necklet, ring, and star, with his own hands, in cotton-wool; and the cigarette-box held them so easily that at the last moment, when the box was closed, and the string ready, Raffles very nearly added a diamond bee-brooch at £51 10*s*. This temptation, however, he ultimately overcame, to the other's chagrin. The cigarette-box was tied up, and the string sealed, oddly enough, with the diamond of the ring that had been bought and paid for.

'I'll chance your having another ring in the store the dead spit of mine,' laughed Raffles, as he relinquished the box, and it disappeared into the tradesman's bag. 'And now, Mr Robinson, I hope you'll appreciate my true hospitality in not offering you anything to drink while business was in progress. That's Château Margaux, sir, and I should judge it's what you'd call an eighteen-carat article.'

In the cab which we took to the vicinity of the flat, I was instantly snubbed for asking questions which the driver might easily overhear, and I took the repulse just a little to heart. I could make neither head nor tail of Raffles's dealings with the man from Regent Street, and was naturally inquisitive as to the meaning of it all. But I held my tongue until we had re-gained the flat in the cautious manner of our exit, and even there until Raffles rallied me with a hand on either shoulder and the old smile upon his face.

'You rabbit!' said he. 'Why couldn't you wait till we got home?'

'Why couldn't you tell me what you were going to do?' I retorted as of yore.

'Because your dear old phiz is still worth its weight in inno-cence, and because you never could act for nuts! You looked as puzzled as the other poor devil; but you wouldn't if you had known what my game really was.'

'And pray what was it?'

'That,' said Raffles, and he smacked the cigarette-box down upon the mantelpiece. It was not tied. It was not sealed. It flew open from the force of the impact. And the diamond ring that cost £95, the necklet for £200, and my flaming star at another £100, all three lay safe and snug in the jeweller's own cotton-wool!

'Duplicate boxes!' I cried.

'Duplicate boxes, my brainy Bunny. One was already packed, and weighted, and in my pocket. I don't know whether you noticed me weighing the three things together in my hand? I know that neither of you saw me change the boxes, for I did it when I was nearest buying the bee-brooch at the end, and you were too puzzled, and the other Johnny too keen. It was the cheapest shot in the game; the dear ones were sending old Theobald to Southampton on a fool's errand yesterday afternoon, and showing one's own nose down Regent Street in broad daylight while he was gone; but some things are worth paying for and certain risks one must always take. Nice boxes, aren't they? I only wished they contained a better cigarette; but a notorious brand was essential; a box of Sullivans would have brought me to life to-morrow.'

'But they oughtn't to open it to-morrow.'

'Nor will they, as a matter of fact. Meanwhile, Bunny, I may call upon you to dispose of the boodle.'

'I'm on for any mortal thing!'

My voice rang true, I swear, but it was the way of Raffles to take the evidence of as many senses as possible. I felt the cold steel of his eye through mine and through my brain. But what he saw seemed to satisfy him no less than what he heard, for his hand found my hand, and pressed it with a fervour foreign to the man.

'I know you are, and I knew you would be. Only remember, Bunny, it's my turn to pay the shot!'

You shall hear how he paid it when the time came.

A JUBILEE PRESENT

THE room of gold, in the British Museum, is probably well enough known to the inquiring alien and the travelled American. A true Londoner, however, I myself had never heard of it until Raffles casually proposed a raid.

'Is the Room of Gold a roomful of sovereigns?'

Raffles laughed softly at my scorn.

'No, Bunny, it's principally in the shape of archaic ornaments, whose value, I admit, is largely extrinsic. But gold is gold, from Phœnicia to Klondike, and if we cleared the room we should eventually do very well.'

'How?'

'I should melt it down into a nugget, and bring it home from the U.S.A. to-morrow.'

'And then?'

'Make them pay up in hard cash across the counter of the Bank of England. And you *can* make them.'

That I knew, and so said nothing for a time, remaining a hostile though a silent critic, while we paced the cool black leads with our bare feet, softly as cats.

'And how do you propose to get enough away,' at length I asked, 'to make it worth while?'

'Ah, there you have it,' said Raffles. 'I only propose to reconnoitre the ground, to see what we can see. We might find some hiding-place for a night; that, I am afraid, would be our only chance.'

'Have you ever been there before?'

'Not since they got the one good, portable piece which I believe that they exhibit now. It's a long time since I read of it – I can't remember where – but I know they have got a gold cup of sorts worth several thousands. A number of the immorally rich clubbed together and presented it to the nation; and two of the richly immoral intend to snaffle it for themselves. At any rate, we might go and have a look at it, Bunny, don't you think?'

Think! I seized his arm.

'When? When? When?' I asked, like a quick-firing gun.

'The sooner the better.'

'Well, then, when — when?' I began to repeat.

'To-morrow, if you like.'

'Only to look?'

The limitation was my one regret.

'We must do so, Bunny, before we leap.'

'Very well,' I sighed. 'But to-morrow it is!'

And the morrow it really was.

I saw the porter that night, and, I still think. bought his absolute allegiance for the second coin of the realm. My story, however, invented by Raffles, was sufficiently specious in it-self. Would the porter help me in so innocent and meritorious an intrigue? The man hesitated. I produced my half-sovereign. The man was lost. And at half-past eight next morning — be-fore the heat of the day — Raffles and I drove to Kew Gardens in a hired landau which was to call for us at midday and wait until we came. The porter had assisted me to carry my invalid downstairs, in a carrying-chair hired (like the landau) from Harrod's Stores for the occasion.

It was little after nine when we crawled together into the gardens; by half-past my invalid had had enough, and out he tottered on my arm; a cab, a message to our coachman, a timely train to Baker Street, another cab, and we were at the British Museum — brisk pedestrians now — not very many minutes after the opening hour of 10 a.m.

It was one of those glowing days which will not be for-gotten by many who were in town at the time. The Diamond Jubilee was upon us, and Queen's weather had already set in. Raffles, indeed, declared it was hot as Italy and Australia put together; and certainly the short summer nights gave the channels of wood and asphalt and the continents of brick and mortar but little time to cool. At the British Museum the pigeons were crooning among the shadows of the grimy colon-nade, and the stalwart janitors looked less stalwart than usual, as though their medals were too heavy for them. I recognised some habitual readers going to their labour underneath the dome; of mere visitors we seemed among the first.

'That's the room,' said Raffles, who had bought the two-penny guide, as we studied it openly on the nearest bench; 'Number 43, upstairs and sharp round to the right. Come on, Bunny!'

And he led the way in silence, but with a long methodical stride which I could not understand until we came to the corridor leading to the Room of Gold, when he turned to me for a moment.

'A hundred and thirty-nine yards from this to the open street,' said Raffles, 'not counting the stairs. I suppose we *could* do it in twenty seconds, but if we did we should have to jump the gates. No, you must remember to loaf out at slow march, Bunny, whether you like it or not.'

'But you talked about a hiding-place for a night?'

'Quite so – for all night. We should have to get back, go on lying low, and saunter out with the crowd next day – after doing the whole show thoroughly.'

'What! With gold in our pockets – –'

'And gold in our boots, and gold up the sleeves and legs of our suits! You leave that to me, Bunny, and wait till you've tried two pair of trousers sewn together at the foot! This is only a preliminary reconnoitre. And here we are.'

It is none of my business to describe the so-called Room of Gold, with which I, for one, was not a little disappointed. The glass cases, which both fill and line it, may contain unique examples of the goldsmith's art in times and places of which one heard quite enough in the course of one's classical education; but, from a professional point of view, I would as lief have the ransacking of a single window in the West End as the pick of all those spoils of Etruria and of Ancient Greece. The gold may not be so soft as it appears, but it certainly looks as though you could bite off the business ends of the spoons, and stop your own teeth in doing so. Nor should I care to be seen wearing one of the rings; but the greatest fraud of all (from the aforesaid standpoint) is assuredly that very cup of which Raffles had spoken. Moreover, he felt this himself.

'Why, it's as thin as paper,' said he, 'and enamelled like a middle-aged lady of quality! But, by Jove, it's one of the most

beautiful things I ever saw in my life, Bunny. I should like to
have it for its own sake, by all my gods!'

The thing had a little square case of plate-glass all to itself
at one end of the room. It may have been the thing of beauty
that Raffles affected to consider it, but I for my part was in no
mood to look at it in that light. Underneath were the names of
the plutocrats who had subscribed for this national gewgaw,
and I fell to wondering where their £8,000 came in, while
Raffles devoured his twopenny guide-book as greedily as a
schoolgirl with a zeal for culture.

'Those are scenes from the martyrdom of St Agnes,' said
he ... ' "translucent on relief ... one of the finest specimens of its
kind." I should think it was! Bunny, you Philistine, why can't
you admire the thing for its own sake? It would be worth
having only to live up to! There never was such rich enamel-
ling on such thin gold; and what a good scheme to hang the
lid up over it, so that you can see how thin it is. I wonder if
we could lift it, Bunny, by hook or crook?'

'You'd better try, sir,' said a dry voice at his elbow.

The madman seemed to think we had the room to ourselves.
I knew better, but like another madman, had let him ramble
on unchecked. And here was a stolid constable confronting
us, in the short tunic that they wear in summer, his whistle on
its chain, but no truncheon at his side. Heavens! how I see him
now; a man of medium size, with a broad, good-humoured,
perspiring face, and a limp moustache. He looked sternly at
Raffles, and Raffles looked merrily at him.

'Going to run me in, officer?' said he. 'That *would* be a joke
– my hat!'

'I didn't say as I was, sir,' replied the policeman. 'But that's
queer talk for a gentleman like you, sir, in the British
Museum!' And he wagged his helmet at my invalid, who had
taken his airing in coat-frock and top-hat, the more readily to
assume his present part.

'What!' cried Raffles, 'simply saying to my friend that I'd
like to lift the gold cup? Why, so I should, officer, so I should!
I don't mind who hears me say so. It's one of the most beautiful things I ever saw in all my life.'

The constable's face had already relaxed, and now a grin

peeped under the limp moustache. 'I dare say there's many as feels like that, sir,' said he.

'Exactly; and I say what I feel, that's all,' said Raffles airily. 'But, seriously, officer, is a valuable thing like this quite safe in a case like that?'

'Safe enough as long as I'm here,' replied the other between grim jest and stout earnest. Raffles studied his face; he was still watching Raffles; and I kept an eye on them both without putting in my word.

'You appear to be single-handed,' observed Raffles. 'Is that wise?'

The note of anxiety was capitally caught; it was at once personal and public-spirited, that of the enthusiastic savant, afraid for a national treasure which few appreciated as he did himself. And, to be sure, the three of us now had this treasury to ourselves; one or two others had been there when we entered; but now they were gone.

'I'm not single-handed,' said the officer comfortably. 'See that seat by the door? One of the attendants sits there all day long.'

'Then where is he now?'

'Talking to another attendant just outside. If you listen you'll hear them for yourself.'

We listened, and we did hear them, but not just outside. In my own mind I even questioned whether they were in the corridor through which we had come; to me it sounded as though they were just outside the corridor.

'You mean the fellow with the billiard-cue who was here when we came in?' pursued Raffles.

'That wasn't a billiard-cue! It was a pointer,' the intelligent officer explained.

'It ought to be a javelin,' said Raffles nervously. 'It ought to be a pole-axe! The public treasure ought to be better guarded than this. I shall write to *The Times* about it – you see if I don't!'

All at once, yet somehow not so suddenly as to excite suspicion, Raffles had become the elderly busybody with nerves; why, I could not for the life of me imagine; and the policeman seemed equally at sea.

'Lor' bless you, sir,' said he, 'I'm all right; don't you bother your head about *me*.'

'But you haven't even got a truncheon!'

'Not likely to want one either. You see, sir, it's early as yet; in a few minutes these here rooms will fill up; and there's safety in numbers, as they say.'

'Oh, it will fill up soon, will it?'

'Any minute now, sir.'

'Ah!'

'It isn't often empty as long as this, sir. It's the Jubilee, I suppose.'

'Meanwhile, what if my friend and I had been professional thieves? Why, we could have overpowered you in an instant, my good fellow!'

'That you couldn't; leastways, not without bringing the whole place about your ears.'

'Well, I shall write to *The Times* all the same. I'm a connoisseur in all this sort of thing, and I won't have unnecessary risks run with the nation's property. You said there was an attendant just outside, but he sounds to me as though he were at the other end of the corridor. I shall write to-day!'

For an instant we all three listened; and Raffles was right. Then I saw two things in one glance. Raffles had stepped a few inches backward, and stood poised upon the ball of each foot, his arms half raised, a light in his eyes. And another kind of light was breaking over the crass features of our friend the constable.

'Then shall I tell you what *I'll* do?' he cried, with a sudden clutch at the whistle-chain on his chest. The whistle flew out, but it never reached his lips. There were a couple of sharp smacks, like double barrels discharged all but simultaneously, and the man reeled against me so that I could not help catching him as he fell.

'Well done, Bunny! I've knocked him out – I've knocked him out! Run you to the door and see if the attendants have heard anything, and take them on if they have.'

Mechanically I did as I was told. There was no time for thought, still less for remonstrance or reproach, though my surprise must have been even more complete than that of the constable before Raffles knocked the sense out of him. Even in my utter bewilderment, however, the instinctive caution of the real criminal did not desert me. I ran to the door, but I sauntered through it, to plant myself before a Pompeian fresco in the corridor; and there were the two attendants still gossiping outside the farther door; nor did they hear the dull crash which I heard even as I watched them out of the corner of each eye.

It was hot weather, as I have said, but the perspiration on my body seemed already to have turned into a skin of ice. Then I caught the faint reflection of my own face in the casing of the fresco, and it frightened me into some semblance of myself as Raffles joined me with his hands in his pockets. But my fear and indignation were redoubled at the sight of him, when a single glance convinced me that his pockets were as empty as his hands, and his mad outrage the most wanton and reckless of his whole career.

'Ah, very interesting, very interesting, but nothing to what they have in the museum at Naples or in Pompeii itself. You must go there some day, Bunny. I've a good mind to take you myself. Meanwhile – slow march! The beggar hasn't moved an eyelid. We may swing for him if you show indecent haste!'

'We!' I whispered. 'We!'

And my knees knocked together as we came up to the chatting attendants. But Raffles must needs interrupt them to ask the way to the Prehistoric Saloon.

'At the top of the stairs.'

'Thank you. Then we'll work round that way to the Egyptian part.'

And we left them resuming their providential chat.

'I believe you're mad,' I said bitterly as we went.

'I believe I *was*,' admitted Raffles; 'but I'm not now, and I'll see you through. A hundred and thirty-nine yards, wasn't it? Then it can't be more than a hundred and twenty now – not as much. Steady, Bunny, for God's sake! It's *slow* march – for our lives.'

There was this much management. The rest was our colossal luck. A hansom was being paid off at the foot of the steps outside, and in we jumped, Raffles shouting 'Charing Cross!' for all Bloomsbury to hear.

We had turned into Bloomsbury Street without exchanging a syllable when he struck the trapdoor with his fist.

'Where the devil are you driving us?'

'Charing Cross, sir.'

'I said King's Cross! Round you spin, and drive like blazes, or we miss our train! There's one to York at 10.35,' added Raffles as the trapdoor slammed; 'we'll book there, Bunny, and then we'll slope through the subway to the Metropolitan, and so to ground *via* Baker Street and Earl's Court.'

And actually in half an hour he was seated once more in the hired carrying-chair. Then, and not until then, when we were alone at last, did I tell Raffles, in the most nervous English at my command, frankly and exactly what I thought of him and of his latest deed. Once started, moreover, I spoke as I have seldom spoken to living man; and Raffles, of all men, stood my abuse without a murmur, or rather he sat it out, too astounded even to take off his hat, though I thought his eyebrows would have lifted it from his head.

'But it always was your infernal way,' I was savagely concluding. 'You make one plan, and you tell me another – –'

'Not to-day, Bunny, I swear!'

'You mean to tell me you really did start with the bare idea of finding a place to hide in for a night?'

'Of course I did.'

'It was to be the mere reconnoitre you pretended?'

'There was no pretence about it, Bunny.'

'Then why on earth go and do what you did?'

'The reason would be obvious to any one but you,' said Raffles, still with no unkindly scorn. 'It was the temptation of a minute – the final impulse of the fraction of a second, when Roberto saw that I was tempted, and let me see that he saw it. It's not a thing I care to do, and I shan't be happy till the papers tell me the poor devil is alive. But a knock-out shot was the only chance for us then.'

'Why? You don't get run in for being tempted, nor yet for showing that you are!'

'But I should have deserved running in if I hadn't yielded

173

to such a temptation as that, Bunny. It was a chance in a hundred thousand! We might go there every day of our lives, and never again be the only outsiders in the room, with the billiard-marking Johnnie practically out of earshot at one and the same time. It was a gift from the gods; not to have taken it would have been flying in the face of Providence.'

'But you didn't take it,' said I. 'You went and left it behind.'

I wish I had had a Kodak for the little smile with which Raffles shook his head, for it was one that he kept for those great moments of which our vocation is not devoid. All this time he had been wearing his hat, tilted a little over eyebrows no longer raised. And now at last I knew where the gold cup was.

It stood for days upon his chimney-piece, this costly trophy whose ancient history and final fate filled newspaper columns even in these days of Jubilee, and for which the flower of Scotland Yard was said to be seeking high and low. Our constable, we learnt, had been stunned only, and, from the moment that I brought him an evening paper with the news, Raffles's spirits rose to a height inconsistent with his equable temperament, and as unusual in him as the sudden impulse upon which he had acted with such effect. The cup itself appealed to me no more than it had done before. Exquisite it might be, handsome it was, but so light in the hand that the mere gold of it would scarcely have poured three figures out of the melting-pot. And what said Raffles but that he would never melt it at all!

'Taking it was an offence against the laws of the land, Bunny. That is nothing. But destroying it would be a crime against God and Art, and may I be spitted on the vane of St. Mary Abbots if I commit it!'

Talk such as this was unanswerable; indeed, the whole affair had passed the pale of useful comment; and the one course left to a practical person was to shrug his shoulders and enjoy the joke. This was not a little enhanced by the newspaper reports, which described Raffles as a handsome youth, and his unwilling accomplice as an older man of blackguardly appearance and low type.

'Hits us both off rather neatly, Bunny,' said he. 'But what they none of them do justice to is my dear cup. Look at it; only look at it, man! Was ever anything so rich and yet so chaste? St Agnes must have had a pretty bad time, but it would be almost worth it to go down to posterity in such enamel upon such gold. And then the history of the thing. Do you realise that it's five hundred years old and has belonged to Henry the Eighth and to Elizabeth among others? Bunny, when you have me cremated, you can put my ashes in yonder cup, and lay us in the deep-delvèd earth together!'

'And meanwhile?'

'It is the joy of my heart, the light of my life, the delight of mine eye.'

'And suppose other eyes catch sight of it?'

'They never must; they never shall.'

Raffles would have been too absurd had he not been thoroughly alive to his own absurdity; there was, nevertheless, an underlying sincerity in his appreciation of any and every form of beauty, which all his nonsense could not conceal. And his infatuation for the cup was, as he declared, a very pure passion, since the circumstances debarred him from the chief joy of the average collector, that of showing his treasure to his friends. At last, however, and at the height of his craze, Raffles and reason seemed to come together again as suddenly as they had parted company in the Room of Gold.

'Bunny,' he cried, flinging his newspaper across the room, 'I've got an idea after your own heart. I know where I can place it after all!'

'Do you mean the cup?'

'I do.'

'Then I congratulate you.'

'Thanks.'

'Upon the recovery of your senses.'

'Thanks galore. But you've been confoundedly unsympathetic about this thing, Bunny, and I don't think I shall tell you my scheme till I've carried it out.'

'Quite time enough,' said I.

'It will mean your letting me loose for an hour or two under cloud of this very night. To-morrow's Sunday, the Jubilee's on Tuesday, and old Theobald's coming back for it.'

'It doesn't much matter whether he's back or not if you go late enough.'

'I mustn't be late. They don't keep open. No, it's no use your asking any questions. Go out and buy me a big box of Huntley & Palmer's biscuits; any sort you like, only they must be theirs, and absolutely the biggest box they sell.'

'My dear man!'

'No questions, Bunny; you do your part and I'll do mine.'

Subtlety and success were in his face. It was enough for me, and I had done his extraordinary bidding within a quarter of an hour. In another minute Raffles had opened the box and tumbled all the biscuits into the nearest chair.

'Now newspapers!'

I fetched a pile. He bid the cup of gold a ridiculous farewell, wrapped it up in newspaper after newspaper, and finally packed it in the empty biscuit-box.

'Now some brown paper. I don't want to be taken for the grocer's young man.'

A neat enough parcel it made, when the string had been tied and the ends cut close; what was more difficult was to wrap up Raffles himself in such a way that even the porter should not recognise him if they came face to face at the corner. And the sun was still up. But Raffles would go, and when he did I should not have known him myself.

He may have been an hour away. It was barely dusk when he returned, and my first question referred to our dangerous ally, the porter. Raffles had passed him unsuspected in going, but had managed to avoid him altogether on the return journey, which he had completed by way of the other entrance and of the roof. I breathed again.

'And what have you done with the cup?'

'Placed it!'

'How much for? How much for?'

'Let me think. I had a couple of cabs, and the postage was a tanner, with another twopence for registration. Yes, it cost me exactly five-and-eight.'

'*It* cost *you*? But what did you *get* for it, Raffles?'

'Nothing, my boy.'

'Nothing!'

'Not a crimson cent.'

'I am not surprised. I never thought it had a market value. I told you so in the beginning,' I said irritably. 'But what on earth have you done with the thing?'

'Sent it to the Queen.'

'You haven't!'

Rogue is a word with various meanings, and Raffles had been one sort of rogue ever since I had known him; but now, for once, he was the innocent variety, a great grey-haired child, running over with merriment and mischief.

'Well, I've sent it to Sir Arthur Bigge, to present to Her Majesty, with the loyal respects of the thief, if that will do for you,' said Raffles. 'I thought they might take too much stock of me at the G.P.O. if I addressed it to the Sovereign herself. Yes, I drove over to St. Martin's-le-Grand with it, and I registered the box into the bargain. Do a thing properly if you do it at all.'

'But why on earth,' I groaned, 'do such a thing at all?'

'My dear Bunny, we have been reigned over for sixty years by infinitely the finest monarch the world has ever seen. The world is taking the present opportunity of signifying the fact for all it is worth. Every nation is laying of its best at her royal feet; every class in the community is doing its little level – except ours. All I have done is to remove one reproach from our fraternity.'

At this I came round, was infected with his spirit, called him the sportsman he always was and would be, and shook his dare-devil hand in mine; but, at the same time, I still had my qualms.

'Supposing they trace it to us?' said I.

'There's not much to catch hold of in a biscuit-box by Huntley & Palmer,' replied Raffles; 'that was why I sent you for one. And I didn't write a word upon a sheet of paper which could possibly be traced. I simply printed two or three on a virginal post card – another halfpenny to the bad – which might have been bought at any post office in the kingdom. No, old chap, the G.P.O. was the one real danger; there was one detective I spotted for myself; and the sight of him has left me with a thirst. Whisky and Sullivans for two, Bunny, if you please.'

Raffles was soon clinking his glass against mine.

'The Queen,' said he. 'God bless her!'

THE FATE OF FAUSTINA

"Mar – ga – rì,
    e perzo a Salvatore!
Mar – ga – rì,
        Ma l'ommo è cacciatore!
Mar – ga – rì,
        Nun ce aje corpa tu!
Chello ch' è fatto, è fatto, un ne parlammo cchieù!"

A PIANO-ORGAN was pouring the metallic music through our open windows, while a voice of brass brayed the words, which I have since obtained, and print above for identification by such as know their Italy better than I. They will not thank me for reminding them of a tune so lately epidemic in that land of aloes and blue skies; but at least it is unlikely to run in their heads as the ribald accompaniment to a tragedy; and it does in mine.

It was in the early heat of August, and the hour that of the lawful and necessary siesta for such as turn night into day. I was therefore shutting my window in a rage, and wondering whether I should not do the same for Raffles, when he appeared in the silk pyjamas to which the chronic solicitude of Dr Theobald confined him from morning to night.

'Don't do that, Bunny,' said he. 'I rather like that thing, and want to listen. What sort of fellows are they to look at, by the way?'

I put my head out to see, it being a primary rule of our quaint establishment that Raffles must never show himself at any of the windows. I remember now how hot the sill was to my elbows, as I leant upon it and looked down, in order to satisfy a curiosity in which I could see no point.

'Dirty-looking beggars,' said I over my shoulder: 'dark as dark; blue chins, oleaginous curls and earrings; ragged as they make them, but nothing picturesque in their rags.'

'Neapolitans all over,' murmured Raffles behind me; 'and

that's a characteristic touch, the one fellow singing while the other grinds; they always have that out there.'

'He's rather a fine chap, the singer,' said I, as the song ended. 'My hat, what teeth! He's looking up here, and grinning all round his head; shall I chuck them anything?'

'Well, I have no reason to love the Neapolitans; but it takes me back – it takes me back! Yes, here you are, one each.'

It was a couple of half-crowns that Raffles put into my hand, but I had thrown them into the street for pennies before I saw what they were. Thereupon I left the Italians bowing to the mud, as well they might, and I turned to protest against such wanton waste. But Raffles was walking up and down, his head bent, his eyes troubled; and his one excuse disarmed remonstrance.

'They took me back,' he repeated. 'My God, how they took me back!'

Suddenly he stopped in his stride.

'You don't understand, Bunny, old chap; but if you like you shall. I always meant to tell you some day, but never felt worked up to it before, and it's not the kind of thing one talks about for talking's sake. It isn't a nursery story, Bunny, and there isn't a laugh in it from start to finish; on the contrary, you have often asked me what turned my hair grey, and now you are going to hear.'

This was promising, but Raffles's manner was something more. It was unique in my memory of the man. His fine face softened and set hard by turns. I never knew it so hard. I never knew it so soft. And the same might be said of his voice, now tender as any woman's, now flying to the other extreme of equally unwonted ferocity. But this was toward the end of his tale; the beginning he treated characteristically enough, though I could have wished for a less cavalier account of the Island of Elba, where, upon his own showing, he had met with much humanity.

'Deadly, my dear Bunny, is not the word for that glorified snag, or for the molluscs its inhabitants. But they started by wounding my vanity, so perhaps I am prejudiced after all. I sprung myself upon them as a shipwrecked sailor – a sole survivor – stripped in the sea and landed without a stitch – yet they took no more interest in me than you do in Italian organ-grinders. They were decent enough. I didn't have to pick and steal for a square meal and a pair of trousers – it would have been more exciting if I had. But what a place! Napoleon couldn't stand it, you remember, but he held on longer than I did. I put in a few weeks in their infernal mines, simply to pick up a smattering of Italian; then got across to the mainland in a little wooden timber-tramp; and ungratefully glad I was to leave Elba blazing in just such another sunset as the one you won't forget.

'The tramp was bound for Naples, but first it touched at Baiæ, where I carefully deserted in the night. There are too many English in Naples itself, though I thought it would make a first happy hunting-ground when I knew the language better and had altered myself a bit more. Meanwhile I got a billet of several sorts on one of the loveliest spots that ever I struck on all my travels. The place was a vineyard, but it overhung the sea, and I got taken on as tame sailor-man and emergency bottle-washer. The wages were the noble figure of a lira and a half, which is just over a bob, a day, but there were lashings of sound wine for one and all, and better wine to bathe in. And for eight whole months, my boy, I was an absolutely honest man. The luxury of it, Bunny! I outheroded Herod, wouldn't touch a grape, and went in the most delicious danger of being knifed for my principles by the thieving crew I had joined.

'It was the kind of place where every prospect pleases – and all the rest of it – especially all the rest. But may I see it in my dreams till I die – as it was in the beginning – before anything began to happen. It was a wedge of rock sticking out into the bay, thatched with vines, and with the rummiest old house on the very edge of all, a devil of a height above the sea; you might have sat at the windows and dropped your Sullivan-ends plumb into blue water a hundred and fifty feet below.

'From the garden behind the house – such a garden, Bunny – oleanders and mimosa, myrtles, rosemary, and red tangles of fiery untamed flowers – in a corner of this garden was the top of a subterranean stair down to the sea; at least, there were nearly two hundred steps tunnelled through the solid rock; then an iron gate, and another eighty steps in the open air; and last

of all a cave fit for pirates a-penny-plain-and-twopence-col-
oured. This cave gave upon the sweetest little thing in coves,
all deep blue water and honest rocks; and here I looked after
the vineyard shipping, a pot-bellied tub with a brown sail, and
a sort of dinghy. The tub took the wine to Naples, and the
dinghy was the tub's tender.

'The house above was said to be on the identical site of a
suburban retreat of the admirable Tiberius; there was the old
sinner's private theatre with the tiers cut clean to this day,
the well where he used to fatten his lampreys on his slaves
and a ruined temple of those ripping old Roman bricks, shallow as dominoes and ruddier than the cherry. I never was much
of an antiquary, but I could have become one there if I'd had
nothing else to do; but I had lots. When I wasn't busy with the
boats I had to trim the vines, or gather the grapes, or even
help make the wine itself in a cool, dark, musty vault underneath the temple, that I can see and smell as I jaw. And can't
I hear it and feel it too! Squish, squash, bubble; squash,
squish, guggle; and your feet as though you had been wading
through slaughter to a throne. Yes, Bunny, you mightn't think
it, but this good right foot, that never was on the wrong side
of the crease when the ball left my hand, has also been known
to

> ... crush the lees of pleasure
> From sanguine grapes of pain.'

He made a sudden pause, as though he had stumbled on a
truth in jest. His face filled with lines. We were sitting in the
room that had been bare when first I saw it; there were basket-
chairs and a table in it now, all meant ostensibly for me; and
hence Raffles would slip to his bed, with schoolboy relish, at
every tinkle of the bell. This afternoon we felt fairly safe, for
Dr. Theobald had called in the morning, and Mrs Theobald
still took up much of his time. Through the open window we
could hear the piano-organ and 'Mar – ga – rì' a few hundred
yards farther on. I fancied Raffles was listening to it while he
paused. He shook his head abstractedly when I handed him
the cigarettes; and his tone hereafter was never just what it
had been.

'I don't know, Bunny, whether you're a believer in transmigration of souls. I have often thought it easier to believe than lots of other things, and I have been pretty near believing in it myself since I had my being on that villa of Tiberius. The brute who had it in my day, if he isn't still running it with a whole skin, was or is as cold-blooded a blackguard as the worst of the emperors, but I have often thought he had a lot in common with Tiberius. He had the great high sensual Roman nose, eyes that were sinks of iniquity in themselves, and that swelled with fatness, like the rest of him, so that he wheezed if he walked a yard; otherwise rather a fine beast to look at, with a huge grey moustache, like a flying gull, and the most courteous manners even to his men; but one of the worst, Bunny, one of the worst that ever was. It was said that the vineyard was only his hobby; if so, he did his best to make his hobby pay. He used to come out from Naples for the weekends – in the tub when it wasn't too rough for his nerves – and he didn't always come alone. His very name sounded unhealthy – Corbucci. I suppose I ought to add that he was a Count, though Counts are two-a-penny in Naples, and in season all the year round.

'He had a little English, and liked to air it upon me, much to my disgust; if I could not hope to conceal my nationality as yet, I at least did not want to have it advertised; and the swine had English friends. When he heard that I was bathing in November, when the bay is still as warm as new milk, he would shake his wicked old head, and say, "You are very audashuss – you are very audashuss!" and put on no end of side before his Italians. By God, he had pitched upon the right word unawares, and I let him know it in the end!

'But that bathing, Bunny; it was absolutely the best I ever had anywhere. I said just now the water was like wine; in my own mind I used to call it blue champagne, and was rather annoyed that I had no one to admire the phrase. Otherwise I assure you that I missed my own particular kind very little indeed, though I often wished that *you* were there, old chap; particularly when I went for my lonesome swim; first thing in the morning, when the bay was all rose-leaves, and last thing at night, when your body caught phosphorescent fire!

Ah, yes, it was a good enough life for a change; a perfect paradise to lie low in; another Eden until –

'My poor Eve!'

And he fetched a sigh that took away his words; then his jaws snapped together, and his eyes spoke terribly while he conquered his emotion. I pen the last word advisedly. I fancy it is one which I have never used before in writing of A. J. Raffles, for I cannot at the moment recall any other occasion upon which its use would have been justified. On resuming, however, he was not only calm, but cold; and this flying for safety to the other extreme is the single instance of self-distrust which the present Achates can record to the credit of his impious Æneas.

'I called the girl Eve,' said he. 'Her real name was Faustina, and she was one of a vast family who hung out in a hovel on the inland border of the vineyard. And Aphrodite rising from the sea was less wonderful and not more beautiful than Aphrodite emerging from that hole!

'It was the most exquisite face I ever saw or shall see in this life. Absolutely perfect features; a skin that reminded you of old gold, so delicate was its bronze; magnificent hair, not black but nearly; and such eyes and teeth as would have made the fortune of a face without another point. I tell you, Bunny, London would go mad about a girl like that. But I don't believe there's such another in the world. And there she was wasting her sweetness upon that lovely but desolate little corner of it! Well, she did not waste it upon me. I would have married her, and lived happily ever after in such a hovel as her people's – with her. Only to look at her – only to look at her for the rest of my days – I could have lain low and remained dead even to you! And that's all I'm going to tell you about that, Bunny; cursed be he who tells more! Yet don't you run away with the idea that this poor Faustina was the only woman I ever cared about. I don't believe in all that "only" rot; nevertheless, I tell you that she *was* the one being who ever entirely satisfied my sense of beauty; and I honestly believe I could have chucked the world and been true to Faustina for that alone.

'We met sometimes in the little temple I told you about,

sometimes among the vines; now by honest accident, now by flagrant design; and found a ready-made rendezvous, romantic as one could wish, in the cave down all those subterranean steps. Then the sea would call us – my blue champagne – my sparkling cobalt – and there was the dinghy ready to our hand. Oh, those nights! I never knew which I liked best, the moonlit ones when you sculled through silver and could see for miles, or the dark nights when the fisherman's torches stood for the sea, and a red zigzag in the sky for old Vesuvius. We were happy. I don't mind owning it. We seemed not to have a care between us. My mates took no interest in my affairs, and Faustina's family did not appear to bother about her. The Count was in Naples five nights of the seven; the other two we sighed apart.

'At first it was the oldest story in literature – Eden *plus* Eve. The place had been a heaven on earth before, but now it was heaven itself. So for a little; then one night, a Monday night, Faustina burst out crying in the boat; and sobbed her story as we drifted without mishap by the mercy of the Lord. And that was almost as old a story as the other.

'She was engaged – what! Had I never heard of it? Did I mean to upset the boat? What was her engagement beside our love? 'Niente, niente,' crooned Faustina, sighing yet smiling through her tears. No, but what did matter was that the man had threatened to stab her to the heart – and would do it as soon as look at her – that I knew

'I knew it merely from my knowledge of the Neapolitans, for I had no idea who the man might be. I knew it, and yet I took this detail better than the fact of the engagement, though now I began to laugh at both. As if I were going to let her marry anybody else! As if a hair of her lovely head should be touched while I lived to protect her! I had a great mind to row away to blazes with her that very night, and never go near the vineyard again, or let her either. But we had not a lira between us at the time, and only the rags in which we sat barefoot in the boat. Besides, I had to know the name of the animal who had threatened a woman, and such a woman as this.

'For a long time she refused to tell me, with splendid obduracy; but I was as determined as she; so at last she made conditions. I was not to go and get put in prison for sticking a knife into him – he wasn't worth it – and I did promise not to stab him in the back. Faustina seemed quite satisfied, though a little puzzled by my manner, having herself the racial tolerance for cold steel; and next moment she had taken away my breath. 'It is Stefano,' she whispered, and hung her head.

'And well she might, poor thing! Stefano, of all creatures on God's earth – for her!

'Bunny, he was a miserable little undersized wretch – ill-favoured – servile – surely – and second only to his master in bestial cunning and hypocrisy. His face was enough for me; that was what I read in it, and I don't often make mistakes. He was Corbucci's own confidential body-servant, and that alone was enough to damn him in decent eyes; always came out first on the Saturday with the *spese,* to have all ready for his master and current mistress, and stayed behind on the Monday to clear and lock up. Stefano! That worm! I could well understand *his* threatening a woman with a knife; what beat me was how any woman could ever have listened to him; above all, that Faustina should be the one! It passed my comprehension. But I questioned her as gently as I could; and her explanation was largely the threadbare one you would expect. Her parents were so poor. They were so many in family. Some of them begged – would I promise never to tell? Then some of them stole – sometimes – and all knew the pains of actual want. She looked after the cows, but there were only two of them, and brought the milk to the vineyard and elsewhere; but that was not employment for more than one; and there were countless sisters waiting to take her place. Then he was so rich, Stefano.

' "Rich?" I echoed. "Stefano?"

' "Si, Arturo mio."

'Yes, I played the game on that vineyard, Bunny, even to going by my own first name.

' "And how comes he to be rich?" I asked suspiciously.

'She did not know; but he had given her such beautiful jewels; the family had lived on them for months, she pretending an *avocat* had taken charge of them for her against her marriage. But I cared nothing about all that.

' "Jewels! Stefano!" I could only mutter.

' "Perhaps the Count has paid for some of them. He is very kind."

' "To you, is he?"

' "Oh yes, very kind."

' "And you would live in his house afterwards?"

' "Not now, cara mia – not now!"

' "No, by God you don't!" said I in English. "But you would have done so, eh?"

' "Of course. That was arranged. The Count is really very kind."

' "Do you see anything of him when he comes here?"

'Yes, he had sometimes brought her little presents, sweetmeats, ribbons, and the like; but the offering had always been made through this toad of a Stefano. Knowing the men, I now knew all. But Faustina, she had the pure and simple heart, and the white soul, by the God who made it, and for all her kindness to a tattered scapegrace who made love to her in broken Italian between the ripples and the stars. She was not to know what I was, remember; and beside Corbucci and his henchmen I was the Archangel Gabriel come down to earth.

'Well, as I lay awake that night, two more lines of Swinburne came into my head, and came to stay:

> God said, "Let him who wins her take
> And keep Faustine."

'On that couplet I slept at last, and it was my text and watchword when I awoke in the morning. I forget how well you know your Swinburne, Bunny; but don't you run away with the idea that there was anything else in common between his Faustine and mine. For the last time let me tell you that poor Faustina was the whitest and the best I ever knew.

'Well, I was strung up for trouble when the next Saturday came, and I'll tell you what I had done. I had broken the pledge and burgled Corbucci's villa in my best manner during his absence in Naples. Not that it gave me the slightest trouble; but no human being could have told that I had been in, when I came out. And I had stolen nothing, mark you, but only borrowed a revolver from a drawer in the Count's desk, with one or two trifling accessories; for by this time I had the measure of these damned Neapolitans. They were spry enough with a knife, but you show them the business end of a shooting-iron, and they'll streak like rabbits for the nearest hole. But the revolver wasn't for my own use. It was for Faustina, and I taught her how to use it in the cave down there by the sea, shooting at candles stuck upon the rock. The noise in the cave was something frightful, but high up above it couldn't be heard at all, as we proved to each other's satisfaction pretty early in the proceedings. So now Faustina was armed with munitions of self-defence; and I knew enough of her character to entertain no doubt as to their spirited use upon occasion. Between the two of us, in fact, our friend Stefano seemed tolerably certain of a warm week-end.

'But the Saturday brought word that the Count was not coming this week, being in Rome on business, and unable to return in time; so for a whole Sunday we were promised peace; and made bold plans accordingly. There was no further merit in hushing this thing up. "Let him who wins her take and keep Faustine." Yes, but let him win her openly, or lose her and be damned to him! So on the Sunday I was going to have it out with her people – with the Count and Stefano as soon as they showed their noses. I had no inducement, remember, ever to return to surreptitious life within a cab-fare of Wormwood Scrubs. Faustina and the Bay of Naples were quite good enough for me. And the prehistoric man in me rather exulted in the idea of fighting for my desire.

'On the Saturday, however, we were to meet for the last time as heretofore – just once more in secret – down there in the cave – as soon as might be after dark. Neither of us minded if we were kept for hours; each knew that in the end the other would come; and there was a charm of its own even in waiting with such knowledge. But that night I did lose patience; not in the cave but up above, where first on one pretext and then on another the *direttore* kept me going until I smelt a rat. He was not given to exacting overtime, this *direttore*, whose only fault was his servile subjection to our common boss. It seemed pretty obvious, therefore, that he was acting upon some secret instructions from Corbucci himself, and, the moment I suspected this, I asked him to his face if it were not the case. And it was; he admitted it with many shrugs, being a conveniently weak person, whom one felt almost ashamed of bullying as the occasion demanded.

'The fact was, however, that the Count had sent for him on finding he had to go to Rome, and had said he was very sorry to go just then, as among other things he intended to speak to me about Faustina. Stefano had told him all about his row with her, and moreover that it was on my account, which Faustina had never told me, though I had guessed as much for myself. Well, the Count was going to take his jackal's part for all he was worth, which was just exactly what I expected him to do. He intended going for me on his return, but meanwhile I was not to make hay in his absence, and so this tool of a *direttore* had orders to keep me at it night and day. I undertook not to give the poor beast away, but at the same time told him I had not the faintest intention of doing another stroke of work that night.

'It was very dark, and I remember knocking my head against the oranges as I ran up the long, shallow steps which ended the journey between the *direttore's* lodge and the villa itself. But at the back of the villa was the garden I spoke about, and also a bare chunk of the cliff where it was bored by that subterranean stair. So I saw the stars close overhead, and the fisherman's torches far below, the coastwise lights and the crimson hieroglyph that spelt Vesuvius, before I plunged into the darkness of the shaft. And that was the last time I appreciated the unique and peaceful charm of this outlandish spot.

'The stair was in two long flights, with an airhole or two at the top of the upper one, but not another pinprick till you came to the iron gate at the bottom of the lower. As you may read of an infinitely lighter place, in a finer work of fiction than you are ever likely to write, Bunny, it was "gloomy at noon, dark as midnight at dusk, and black as the ninth plague of Egypt at midnight." I won't swear to my quotation, but I will to those stairs. They were as black that night as the inside of the safest safe in the strongest strong-room in the Chancery Lane Deposit. Yet I had not got far down them with my bare feet before I heard somebody else coming up in boots. You may imagine what a turn that gave me! It could not be Faustina, who went barefoot three seasons of the four, and yet there was Faustina waiting for me down below. What a fright she must have had! And all at once my own blood ran cold; for the man sang like a kettle as he plodded up and up. It was, it must be, the short-winded Count himself, whom we all supposed to be in Rome!

'Higher he came and nearer, nearer, slowly yet hurriedly, now stopping to cough and gasp, now taking a few steps by elephantine assault. I should have enjoyed the situation if it had not been for poor Faustina in the cave; as it was, I was filled with nameless fears. But I could not resist giving that grampus Corbucci one bad moment on account. A crazy handrail ran up one wall, so I carefully flattened myself against the other, and he passed within six inches of me, puffing and wheezing like a brass band. I let him go a few steps higher, and then I let him have it with both lungs.

' "Buona sera, eccellente signore!" I roared after him. And a scream came down in answer – such a scream! A dozen different terrors were in it; and the wheezing had stopped, with the old scoundrel's heart.

' "Chi sta la?' he squeaked at last, gibbering and whimpering like a whipped monkey, so that I could not bear to miss his face, and got a match all ready to strike.

' "Arturo, signore."

'He didn't repeat my name, nor did he damn me in heaps. He did nothing but wheeze for a good minute, and when he spoke it was with insinuating civility, in his best English.

' "Come nearer, Arturo. You are in the lower regions down there. I want to speak with you."

' "No thanks. I'm in a hurry," I said, and dropped that match back into my pocket. He might be armed, and I was not.

' "So you are in a 'urry!' and he wheezed amusement. 'And you thought I was still in Rome, no doubt; and so I was until this afternoon, when I caught train at the eleventh moment and then another train from Naples to Pozzuoli. I have been rowed here now by a fisherman of Pozzuoli. I had not time to stop anywhere in Naples, but only to drive from station to station. So I am without Stefano, Arturo, I am without Stefano."

'His sly voice sounded preternaturally sly in the absolute darkness, but even through that impenetrable veil I knew it for a sham. I had laid hold of the hand-rail. It shook violently in my hand; he also was holding it where he stood. And these suppressed tremors, or rather their detection in this way, struck a strange chill to my heart, just as I was beginning to pluck it up.

' "It is lucky for Stefano," said I, grim as death.

' "Ah, but you must not be too 'ard on 'im," remonstrated the Count. "You have stole his girl, he speak with me about it, and I wish to speak with you. It is very audashuss, Arturo, very audashuss! Perhaps you are even going to meet her now, eh?'

'I told him straight that I was.

' "Then there is no 'urry, for she is not there."

' "You didn't see her in the cave?" I cried, too delighted at the thought to keep it to myself.

' "I had no such fortune," the old devil said.

' "She is there, all the same."

' "I only wish I 'ad known "

' "And I've kept her long enough!"

In fact, I threw this over my shoulder as I turned and went running down.

' "I 'ope you will find her!" his malicious voice came croaking after me. "I 'ope you will – I 'ope so."

'And find her I did.'

Raffles had been on his feet some time, unable to sit still or to stand, moving excitedly about the room. But now he stood still enough, his elbows on the cast-iron mantelpiece, his head between his hands.

'Dead?' I whispered.

And he nodded to the wall.

'There was not a sound in the cave. There was no answer to my voice. Then I went in, and my foot touched hers, and it was colder than the rock ... Bunny, they had stabbed her to the heart. She had fought them, and they stabbed her to the heart!'

'You say "they",' I said gently, as he stood in heavy silence, his back still turned. 'I thought Stefano had been left behind?'

Raffles was round in a flash, his face white-hot, his eyes dancing death.

'He was in the cave!' he shouted. 'I saw him – I spotted him – it was broad twilight after those stairs – and I went for him with my bare hands. Not fists, Bunny; not fists for a thing like that; I meant getting my fingers into his vile little heart and tearing it out by the roots. I was stark mad. But he had the revolver – hers. He blazed it at arm's length, and missed. And that steadied me. I had smashed his funny-bone against the rock before he could blaze again; the revolver fell with a rattle, but without going off; in an instant I had it tight, and the little swine at my mercy at last.'

'You didn't show him any?'

'Mercy? With Faustina dead at my feet? I should have deserved none in the next world if I had shown him any in this! No, I just stood over him, with the revolver in both hands, feeling the chambers with my thumb; and as I stood he stabbed at me; but I stepped back to that one, and brought him down with a bullet in his guts.

' "And I can spare you two or three more," I said, for my poor girl could not have fired a shot. "Take that one to hell with you – and that – and that!"

'Then I started coughing and wheezing like the Count himself, for the place was full of smoke. When it cleared my man was very dead, and I tipped him into the sea, to defile that rather than Faustina's cave. And then – and then – we were alone for the last time, she and I, in our own pet haunt; and I could scarcely see her, yet I would not strike a match, for I knew she would not have me see her as she was. I could say good-bye to her without that. I said it; and I left her like a man, and up the first open-air steps with my head in the air and the stars all sharp in the sky; then suddenly they swam, and back I went like a lunatic, to see if she were really dead, to bring her back to life ... Bunny, I can't tell you any more.'

'Not of the Count?' I murmured at last.

'Not even of the Count,' said Raffles, turning round with a sigh. 'I left him pretty sorry for himself; but what was the good

192

of that? I had taken blood for blood, and it was not Corbucci who had killed Faustina. No, the plan was his, but that was not part of the plan. They had found out about our meetings in the cave: nothing simpler than to have me kept hard at it overhead and to carry off Faustina by brute force in the boat. It was their only chance, for she had said more to Stefano than she had admitted to me, and more than I am going to repeat about myself. No persuasion would have induced her to listen to him again; so they tried force; and she drew Corbucci's revolver on them, but they had taken her by surprise, and Stefano stabbed her before she could fire.'

'But how do you know all that?' I asked Raffles, for his tale was going to pieces in the telling, and the tragic end of poor Faustina was no ending for me.

'Oh,' said he, 'I had it from Corbucci at his own revolver's point. He was waiting at his window, and I could have potted him at my ease where he stood against the light listening hard enough but not seeing a thing. So he asked whether it was Stefano, and I whispered, "Si, signore"; and then whether he had finished Arturo, and I brought the same shot off again. He had let me in before he knew who was finished and who was not.'

'And did you finish him?'

'No; that was too good for Corbucci. But I bound and gagged him about as tight as man was ever gagged or bound, and I left him in his room with the shutters shut and the house locked up. The shutters of that old place were six inches thick, and the walls nearly six feet; that was on the Saturday night, and the Count wasn't expected at the vineyard before the following Saturday. Meanwhile he was supposed to be in Rome. But the dead would doubtless be discovered next day, and I am afraid this would lead to his own discovery with the life still in him. I believe he figured on that himself, for he sat threatening me gamely till the last. You never saw such a sight as he was, with his head split in two by a ruler tied at the back of it, and his great moustache pushed up into his bulging eyes. But I locked him up in the dark without a qualm, and I wished and still wish him every torment of the damned.'

'And then?'

'The night was still young, and within ten miles there was the best of ports in a storm, and hundreds of holds for the humble stowaway to choose from. But I didn't want to go farther than Genoa, for by this time my Italian would wash, so I chose the old Norddeutscher Lloyd, and had an excellent voyage in one of the boats slung inboard over the bridge. That's better than any hold, Bunny, and I did splendidly on oranges brought from the vineyard.'

'And at Genoa?'

'At Genoa I took to my wits once more, and have been living on nothing else ever since. But there I had to begin all over again, and at the very bottom of the ladder. I slept in the streets. I begged. I did all manner of terrible things, rather hoping for a bad end, but never coming to one. Then one day I saw a white-headed old chap looking at me through a shop window – a window I had designs upon – and when I stared at him he stared at me – and we wore the same rags. So I had come to that! But one reflection makes many. I had not recognised myself; who on earth would recognise me? London called me – and here I am. Italy had broken my heart – and there it stays.'

Flippant as a schoolboy one moment, playful even in the bitterness of the next, and now no longer giving way to the feeling which had spoilt the climax of his tale, Raffles needed knowing as I alone knew him for a right appreciation of those last words. That they were no mere words I know full well. That, but for the tragedy of his Italian life, that life would have sufficed him for years, if not for ever, I did and do still believe. But I alone see him as I saw him then, the lines upon his face, and the pain behind the lines; how they came to disappear, and what removed them, you will never guess. It was the one thing you would have expected to have the opposite effect, the thing indeed that had forced his confidence, the organ and the voice once more beneath our very windows:

'Margarita de Parete,
    era a' sarta d' e' signore;
    se pugneva sempe e ddete
    pe penzare a Salvatore!

Mar – ga – rì,
  e perzo a Salvatore!
Mar – ga – rì,
  Ma l' ommo è cacciatore!
Mar – ga – rì,
  Nun ce aje corpa tu!
Chello ch' è fatto, è fatto, un ne parlammo cchieù!'

I simply stared at Raffles. Instead of deepening, his lines
had vanished. He looked years younger, mischievous, and
merry and alert as I remembered him of old in the breathless
crisis of some madcap escapade. He was holding up his finger;
he was stealing to the window; he was peeping through the
blind as though our side street were Scotland Yard itself; he
was stealing back again, all revelry, excitement, and suspense.

'I half thought they were after me before,' said he. 'That was
why I made you look. I daren't take a proper look myself, but
what a jest if they were! What a jest!'

'Do you mean the police?' said I.

'The police! Bunny, do you know them and me so little that
you can look me in the face and ask such a question? My boy,
I'm dead to them – off their books – a good deal deader than
being off the hooks! Why, if I went to Scotland Yard this
minute, to give myself up, they'd chuck me out for a harmless
lunatic. No, I fear an enemy nowadays, and I go in terror of
the sometime friend; but I have the utmost confidence in the
dear police.'

'Then whom do you mean?'

'The Camorra!'

I repeated the word with a different intonation. Not that I
had never heard of that most powerful and sinister of secret
societies; but I failed to see on what grounds Raffles should
jump to the conclusion that these everyday organ-grinders belonged to it.

'It was one of Corbucci's threats,' said he. 'If I killed him the
Camorra would certainly kill me; he kept on telling me so; it
was like his cunning not to say that he would put them on my
tracks whether or no.'

'He is probably a member himself!'

195

'Obviously, from what he said.'

'But why on earth should you think that these fellows are?' I demanded, as that brazen voice came rasping through a second verse.

'I don't think. It was only an idea. That this is so thoroughly Neapolitan, and I never heard it on a London organ before. Then, again, what should bring them back here?'

I peeped through the blind in my turn; and, to be sure, there was the fellow with the blue chin and the white teeth watching our windows, and ours only, as he bawled.

'And why?' cried Raffles, his eyes dancing when I told him. 'Why should they come sneaking back to *us*? Doesn't that look suspicious, Bunny; doesn't that promise a lark?'

'Not to me,' I said, having the smile for once. 'How many people, should you imagine, toss them five shillings for as many minutes of their infernal row? You seem to forget that that's what you did an hour ago!'

Raffles had forgotten. His blank face confessed the fact. Then suddenly he burst out laughing at himself.

'Bunny,' said he, 'you've no imagination, and I never knew I had so much! Of course you're right. I only wish you were not, for there's nothing I should enjoy more than taking on another Neapolitan or two. You see, I owe them something still! I didn't settle in full. I owe them more than ever I shall pay them on this side Styx!'

He had hardened even as he spoke: the lines and the years had come again, and his eyes were flint and steel, with an honest grief behind the glitter.

THE LAST LAUGH

As I have had occasion to remark elsewhere, the pick of our exploits from a frankly criminal point of view are of least use for the comparatively pure purposes of these papers. They might be appreciated in a trade journal (if only that want could be supplied) by skilled manipulators of the jemmy and the large light bunch; but, as records of unbroken yet insignificant success, they would be found at once too trivial and too technical, if not sordid and unprofitable into the bargain. The latter epithets, and worse, have indeed already been applied, if not to Raffles and all his works, at least to mine upon Raffles, by more than one worthy wielder of a virtuous pen. I need not say how heartily I disagree with that truly pious opinion. So far from admitting a single word of it, I maintain it is the liveliest warning that I am giving to the world. Raffles was a genius, and he could not make it pay! Raffles had invention, resource, incomparable audacity, and a nerve in ten thousand. He was both strategist and tactician, and we all now know the difference between the two. Yet for months he had been hiding like a rat in a hole, unable to show even his altered face by night or day without risk, unless another risk were courted by three inches of conspicuous crape. Then thus far our rewards had oftener than not been no reward at all. Altogether it was a very different story from the old festive, unsuspected, club and cricket days, with their *noctes ambrosianæ* at the Albany.

And now, in addition to the eternal peril of recognition, there was yet another menace of which I knew nothing. I thought no more of our Neapolitan organ-grinders, though I did often think of the moving page that they had torn for me out of my friend's strange life in Italy. Raffles never alluded to the subject again, and for my part I had entirely forgotten his wild ideas connecting the organ-grinders with the Camorra, and imagining them upon his own tracks. I heard no more of it, and thought as little, as I say. Then one night in the autumn – I shrink from shocking the susceptible for nothing – but there was a certain house in Palace Gardens, and when we got there Raffles would pass on. I could see no soul in sight, no glimmer in the windows. But Raffles had my arm, and on we went without talking about it. Sharp to the left on the Notting Hill side, sharper still up Silver Street, a little tacking west and south, a plunge across High Street, and presently we were home.

'Pyjamas first,' said Raffles, with as much authority as though it mattered. It was a warm night, however, though September, and I did not mind until I came in clad as he commanded to find the autocrat himself still booted and capped. He was peeping through the blind and the gas was still turned down. But he said that I could turn it up, as he helped himself to a cigarette and nothing with it.

'May I mix you one?' said I.

'No, thanks.'

'What's the trouble?'

'We were followed.'

'Never!'

'You never saw it.'

'But *you* never looked round.'

'I have an eye at the back of each ear, Bunny.'

I helped myself, and I feared with less moderation than might have been the case a minute before.

'So that was why – –'

'That was why,' said Raffles, nodding; but he did not smile, and I put down my glass untouched.

'They were following us then!'

'All up Palace Gardens.'

'I thought you wound about coming back over the hill.'

'Nevertheless, one of them's in the street below at this moment.'

No, he was not fooling me. He was very grim. And he had not taken off a thing; perhaps he did not think it worth while.

'Plain clothes?' I sighed, following the sartorial train of thought, even to the loathly arrows that had decorated my person once already for a little æon. Next time they would give me double. The skilly was in my stomach when I saw Raffles's face.

'Who said it was the police, Bunny?' said he. 'It's the Italians. They're only after me; they won't hurt a hair of *your* head, let alone cropping it! Have a drink, and don't mind me. I shall score them off before I'm done.'

'And I'll help you!'

'No, old chap, you won't. This is my own little show. I've known about it for weeks. I first tumbled to it the day those Neapolitans came back with their organs, though I didn't seriously suspect things then; they never came again, those two, they had done their part. That's the Camorra all over, from all accounts. The Count I told you about is pretty high up in it, by the way he spoke, but there will be grades and grades between him and the organ-grinders. I shouldn't be surprised if he had every low-down Neapolitan ice-creamer in the town upon my tracks! The organisation's incredible. Then do you remember the superior foreigner who came to the door a few days afterwards? You said he had velvet eyes.'

'I never connected him with those two!'

'Of course you didn't, Bunny, so you threatened to kick the fellow downstairs, and only made them keener on the scent. It was too late to say anything when you told me. But the very next time I showed my nose outside I heard a camera click as I passed, and the fiend was a person with velvet eyes. Then there was a lull – that happened weeks ago. They had sent me to Italy for identification by Count Corbucci.'

'But this is all theory,' I exclaimed. 'How on earth can you know?'

'I don't know,' said Raffles, 'but I should like to bet. Our friend the bloodhound is hanging about the corner near the pillar-box; look through my window, it's dark in there, and tell me who he is.'

The man was too far away for me to swear to his face, but he wore a covert-coat of un-English length, and the lamp across the road played steadily on his boots; they were very yellow, and they made no noise when he took a turn. I strained my eyes, and all at once I remembered the thin-soled, low-heeled, splay yellow boots of the insidious foreigner, with the soft eyes and the brown-paper face, whom I had turned from the door as a palpable fraud. The ring at the bell was the first I had heard of him, there had been no warning step upon the stairs, and my suspicious eye had searched his feet for rubber soles.

'It's the fellow,' I said, returning to Raffles, and I described his boots.

Raffles was delighted.

'Well done, Bunny; you're coming on,' said he. 'Now I wonder if he's been over here all the time, or if they sent him over expressly? You did better than you think in spotting those boots, for they can only have been made in Italy, and that looks like the special envoy. But it's no use speculating. I must find out.'

'How can you?'

'He won't stay there all night.'

'Well?'

'When he gets tired of it I shall return the compliment and follow *him*.'

'Not alone,' said I firmly.

'Well, we'll see. We'll see at once,' said Raffles, rising. 'Out with the gas, Bunny, while I take a look. Thank you. Now wait a bit ... yes! He's chucked it; he's off already; and so am I!'

But I slipped to our outer door, and held the passage.

'I don't let you go alone, you know.'

'You can't come with me in pyjamas.'

'Now I see why you made me put them on!'

'Bunny, if you don't shift I shall have to shift you. This is my very own private one-man show. But I'll be back in an hour – there!'

'You swear?'

'By all my gods.'

I gave in. How could I help giving in? He did not look the man that he had been, but you never knew with Raffles, and I could not have him lay a hand on me. I let him go with a shrug and my blessing, then ran into his room to see the last of him from the window.

The creature in the coat and boots had reached the end of our little street, where he appeared to have hesitated, so that Raffles was just in time to see which way he turned. And Raffles was after him at an easy pace, and had himself almost reached the corner when my attention was distracted from the alert nonchalance of his gait. I was marvelling that it alone had not long ago betrayed him, for nothing about him was so unconsciously characteristic, when suddenly I realised that Raffles was not the only person in the little lonely street. Another pedestrian had entered from the other end, a man heavily built and clad, with an astrakhan collar to his coat on this warm night, and a black slouch hat that hid his features from my bird's-eye view. His steps were the short and shuffling ones of a man advanced in years and in fatty degeneration, but of a sudden they stopped beneath my very eyes. I could have dropped a marble into the dinted crown of the black felt hat. Then, at the same moment, Raffles turned the corner without looking round, and the big man below raised both his hands and his face. Of the latter I saw only the huge white moustache, like a flying gull, as Raffles had described it; for at a glance I divined that this was his arch-enemy, the Count Corbucci himself.

I did not stop to consider the subtleties of the system by which the real hunter lagged behind while his subordinate pointed the quarry like a sporting dog. I left the Count shuffling onwards faster than before, and I jumped into some clothes as though the flats were on fire. If the Count was going to follow Raffles in his turn, then I would follow the Count in mine, and there would be a midnight procession of us through the town. But I found no sign of him in the empty street, and no sign in the Earl's Court Road, that looked as empty for all its length, save for a natural enemy standing like a waxwork with a glimmer at his belt.

'Officer,' I gasped, 'have you seen anything of an old gentleman with a big white moustache?'

The unlicked cub of a common constable seemed to eye me the more suspiciously for the flattering form of my address.

'Took a hansom,' said he at length.

A hansom! Then he was not following the others on foot; there was no guessing his game. But something must be said or done.

'He's a friend of mine,' I explained, 'and I want to overtake him. Did you hear where he told the fellow to drive?'

A curt negative was the policeman's reply to that; and if

ever I take part in a night assault-at-arms, revolver *versus* baton in the back kitchen, I know which member of the Metropolitan Police Force I should like for my opponent.

If there was no overtaking the Count, however, it should be a comparatively simple matter in the case of the couple on foot, and I wildly hailed the first hansom that crawled into my ken. I must tell Raffles who it was that I had seen; the Earl's Court Road was long, and the time since he vanished in it but a few short minutes. I drove down the length of that useful thoroughfare, with an eye apiece on either pavement, sweeping each as with a brush, but never a Raffles came into the pan. Then I tried the Fulham Road, first to the west, then to the east, and in the end drove home to the flat as bold as brass. I did not realise my indiscretion until I had paid the man and was on the stairs. Raffles never dreamt of driving all the way back; but I was hoping now to find him waiting up above. He had said an hour. I had remembered it suddenly. And now the hour was more than up. But the flat was as empty as I had left it; the very light that had encouraged me, pale though it was, as I turned the corner in my hansom, was but the light that I myself had left burning in the desolate passage.

I can give you no conception of the night that I spent. Most of it I hung across the sill, throwing a wide net with my ears, catching every footstep afar off, every hansom bell farther still, only to gather in some alien whom I seldom even landed in our street. Then I would listen at the door. He might come over the roof; and eventually someone did; but now it was broad daylight, and I flung the door open in the milkman's face, which whitened at the shock as though I had ducked him in his own pail.

'You're late,' I thundered as the first excuse for my excitement.

'Beg your pardon,' said he indignantly, 'but I'm half an hour before my usual time.'

'Then I beg yours,' said I; 'but the fact is, Mr. Maturin has had one of his bad nights, and I seem to have been waiting hours for milk to make him a cup of tea.'

This little fib (ready enough for a Raffles, though I say it) earned me not only forgiveness but that obliging sympathy which is a branch of the business of the man at the door. The good fellow said that he could see I had been sitting up all night, and he left me pluming myself upon the accidental art with which I had told my very necessary tarradiddle. On reflection I gave the credit to instinct, not accident, and then sighed afresh as I realised how the influence of the master was sinking into me, and he Heaven knew where. But my punishment was swift to follow, for within the hour the bell rang imperiously twice, and there was Dr Theobald on our mat, in a yellow Jaeger suit, with a chin as yellow jutting over the flaps that he had turned up to hide his pyjamas.

'What's this about a bad night?' said he.

'He couldn't sleep, and he wouldn't let me,' I whispered, never loosening my grasp of the door, and standing tight against the outer wall. 'But he's sleeping like a baby now.'

'I must see him.'

'He gave strict orders that you should not.'

'I'm his medical man, and I – –'

'You know what he is,' I said, shrugging; 'the least thing wakes him, and you will if you insist on seeing him now. It will be the last time, I warn you! I know what he said, and you don't.'

The doctor cursed me under his fiery moustache.

'I shall come up during the course of the morning,' he snarled.

'And I shall tie up the bell,' I said, 'and if it doesn't ring he'll be sleeping still, but I will not risk waking him by coming to the door again.'

And with that I shut it in his face. I was improving, as Raffles had said; but what would it profit me if some evil had befallen him? And now I was prepared for the worst. A boy came up whistling and leaving papers on the mats; it was getting on for eight o'clock, and the whisky and soda of half-past twelve stood untouched and stagnant in the tumbler. If the worst had happened to Raffles, I felt that I would either never drink again, or else seldom do anything else.

Meanwhile I could not even break my fast, but roamed the flat in a misery not to be described, my very linen still unchanged, my cheeks and chin now tawny from the unwhole-

203

some night. How long would it go on? I wondered for a time. Then I changed my tune: how long could I endure it?

It went on actually until the forenoon only, but my endurance cannot be measured by the time, for to me every hour of it was an arctic night. Yet it cannot have been much after eleven when the ring came at the bell, which I had forgotten to tie up after all. But this was not the doctor; neither, too well I knew, was it the wanderer returned. Our bell was the pneumatic one that tells you if the touch be light or heavy; the hand upon it now was tentative and shy.

The owner of the hand I had never seen before. He was young and ragged, with one eye blank, but the other ablaze with some fell excitement. And straightway he burst into a low torrent of words, of which all I knew was that they were Italian, and therefore news of Raffles, if only I had known the language! But dumb-show might help us somewhat, and in I dragged him, though against his will, a new alarm in his one wild eye.

'Non capite?' he cried when I had him inside and had withstood the torrent.

'No, I'm bothered if I do!' I answered, guessing his question from his tone.

'Vostro amico,' he repeated over and over again; and then, 'Poco tempo, poco tempo, poco tempo!'

For once in my life the classical education of my public-school days was of real value. 'My pal, my pal, and no time to be lost!' I translated freely, and flew for my hat.

'Ecco, signore!' cried the fellow, snatching the watch from my waistcoat pocket, and putting one black thumb-nail on the long hand, the other on the numeral twelve. 'Mezzogiorno – poco tempo – poco tempo!' And again I seized his meaning, that it was twenty past eleven, and we must be there by twelve. But where, but where? It was maddening to be summoned like this, and not to know what had happened, or to have any means of finding out. But my presence of mind stood by me still, I was improving by seven-league strides, and I crammed my handkerchief between the drum and hammer of the bell before leaving. The doctor could ring now till he was black in the face, but I was not coming, and he need not think it.

I half expected to find a hansom waiting, but there was none, and we had gone some distance down the Earl's Court Road before we got one; in fact, we had to run to the stand. Opposite is the church with the clock upon it as everybody knows, and at the sight of the dial my companion had wrung his hands; it was close upon the half-hour.

'Poco tempo – pochissimo!' he wailed. 'Bloomburee Ske-warr,' he then cried to the cabman – 'numero trentotto!'

'Bloomsbury Square,' I roared on my own account. 'I'll show you the house when we get there, only drive like be-damned!'

My companion lay back gasping in his corner. The small glass told me that my own face was pretty red.

'A nice show!' I cried; 'and not a word can you tell me. Didn't you bring me a note?'

I might have known by this time that he had not, still I went through the pantomime of writing with my finger on my cuff. But he shrugged and shook his head.

'Niente,' said he. 'Una questione di vita, di vita!'

'What's that?' I snapped, my early training coming in again. 'Say it slowly – andante – rallentando.'

Thank Italy for the stage instructions in the songs one used to murder! The fellow actually understood!

'Una – questione – di – vita.'

'Or mors, eh?' I shouted, and up went the trapdoor over our heads.

'Avanti, avanti, avanti!' cried the Italian, turning up his one-eyed face.

'Hell-for-leather,' I translated, 'and double fare if you do it by twelve o'clock.'

But in the streets of London how is one to know the time? In the Earl's Court Road it had not been half-past, and at Barker's in High Street it was but a minute later. A long half-mile a minute, that was going like the wind, and indeed we had done much of it at a gallop. But the next hundred yards took us five minutes by the next clock, and which was one to believe? I fell back upon my own old watch (it was my own), which made it eighteen minutes to the hour as we swung across the Serpentine bridge, and by the quarter we were in the Bays-water Road – not up for once.

'Presto, presto,' my pale guide murmured. 'Affrettatevi — avanti!'

'Ten bob if you do it,' I cried through the trap, without the slightest notion of what we were to do. But it was 'una questione di vita', and 'vostro amico' must and could only be my miserable Raffles.

What a very godsend is the perfect hansom to the man or woman in a hurry! It had been our great good fortune to jump into a perfect hansom; there was no choice, we had to take the first upon the rank, but it must have deserved its place, with the rest nowhere. New tyres, superb springs, a horse in a thousand, and a driver up to every trick of his trade! In and out we went like a fast half-back at the Rugby game, yet where the traffic was thinnest, there were we. And how he knew his way! At the Marble Arch he slipped out of the main stream, and so into Wigmore Street, then up and in and out and on until I saw the gold tips of the Museum palisade gleaming between the horses' ears in the sun. Plop, plop, plop; ting, ling, ling; bell and horseshoes, horseshoes and bell, until the colossal figure of C. J. Fox in a grimy toga spelt Bloomsbury Square, with my watch still wanting three minutes to the hour.

'What number?' cried the good fellow overhead.

'Trentotto, trentotto,' said my guide, but he was looking to the right, and I bundled him out to show the house on foot. I had not half a sovereign after all, but I flung our dear driver a whole one instead, and only wished that it had been a hundred.

Already the Italian had his latchkey in the door of 38, and in another moment we were rushing up the narrow stairs of as dingy a London House as prejudiced countryman can conceive. It was panelled, but it was dark and evil-smelling, and how we should have found our way even to the stairs but for an unwholesome jet of yellow gas in the hall, I cannot myself imagine. However, up we went pell-mell, to the right-out on the half-landing, and so like a whirlwind into the drawing-room a few steps higher. There the gas was also burning behind closed shutters, and the scene is photographed upon my brain, though I cannot have looked upon it for a whole instant as I sprang in at my leader's heels.

This room also was panelled, and in the middle of the wall on our left, his hands lashed to a ring-bolt high above his head, his toes barely touching the floor, his neck pinioned by a strap passing through smaller ring-bolts under either ear, and every inch of him secured on the same principle, stood, or rather hung, all that was left of Raffles, for at the first glance I believed him dead. A black ruler gagged him, the ends lashed behind his neck, the blood upon it caked to bronze in the gaslight. And in front of him, ticking like a sledge-hammer, its only hand upon the stroke of twelve, stood a simple, old-fashioned, grandfathers' clock – but not for half an instant longer – only until my guide could hurl himself upon it and send the whole thing crashing into the corner. An ear-splitting report accompanied the crash, a white cloud lifted from the fallen clock, and I saw a revolver smoking in a vice screwed below the dial, an arrangement of wires sprouting from the dial itself, and the single hand at once at its zenith and in contact with these

ιumble to it, Bunny?'

He was alive; these were his first words; the Italian had the blood-caked ruler in his hand, and with his knife was reaching up to cut the thongs that lashed the hands. He was not tall enough. I seized him and lifted him up, then fell to work with my own knife upon the straps. And Raffles smiled faintly upon us through his bloodstains.

'I want you to tumble to it,' he whispered; 'the neatest thing in revenge I ever knew, and another minute would have fixed it. I've been waiting for it twelve hours, watching the clock round, death at the end of the lap! Electric connection. Simple enough. Hour-hand only – O Lord!'

We had cut the last strap. He could not stand. We supported him between us to a horse-hair sofa, for the room was furnished, and I begged him not to speak, while his one-eyed deliverer was at the door before Raffles recalled him with a sharp word in Italian.

'He wants to get me a drink, but that can wait,' said he in a firmer voice; 'I shall enjoy it the more when I've told you what happened. Don't let him go, Bunny; put your back against the door. He's a decent soul, and it's lucky for me I got word with him before they trussed me up. I've promised to set him up in life, and I will, but I don't want him out of my sight for the moment.'

'If you squared him last night,' I exclaimed, 'why the blazes didn't he come to me till the eleventh hour?'

'Ah, I knew he'd have cut it fine, though I hoped not quite so fine as all that. But all's well that ends well, and I declare I don't feel so much the worse. I shall be sore about the gills for a bit – and what do you think?'

He pointed to the long black ruler with the bronze stain; it lay upon the floor; he held out his hand for it, and I gave it to him.

'The same one I gagged him with,' said Raffles, with his still ghastly smile; 'he was a bit of an artist, old Corbucci, after all!'

'Now let's hear how you fell into his clutches,' said I briskly, for I was as anxious to hear as he seemed to tell me, only for my part I could have waited until we were safe in the flat.

'I do want to get it off my chest, Bunny,' old Raffles admitted, 'and yet I hardly can tell you after all. I followed your friend with the velvet eyes. I followed him all the way here. Of course I came up to have a good look at the house when he'd let himself in, and damme if he hadn't left the door ajar! Who could resist that? I had pushed it half open and had just one foot on the mat when I got such a crack on the head as I hope never to get again. When I came to my wits they were hauling me up to that ring-bolt by the hands, and old Corbucci himself was bowing to me, but how *he* got there I don't know yet.'

'I can tell you that,' said I, and told how I had seen the Count for myself on the pavement underneath our windows. 'Moreover,' I continued, 'I saw him spot you, and five minutes after in Earl's Court Road I was told he'd driven off in a cab. He would see you following his man, drive home ahead, and catch you by having the door left open in the way you describe.'

'Well,' said Raffles, 'he deserved to catch me somehow, for he'd come from Naples on purpose, ruler and all, and the ringbolts were ready fixed, and even this house taken furnished for nothing else! He meant catching me before he'd done, and scoring off me in exactly the same way that I scored off him,

only going one better of course. He told me so himself, sitting
where I am sitting now, at three o'clock this morning, and
smoking a most abominable cigar that I've smelt ever since. It
appears he sat twenty-four hours when I left *him* trussed up,
but he said twelve would content him in my case, as there was
certain death at the end of them, and I mightn't have life
enough left to appreciate my end if he made it longer. But I
wouldn't have trusted him if he could have got the clock to go
twice round without firing off the pistol. He explained the
whole mechanism of that to me; he had thought it all out in
the vineyard I told you about; and then he asked if I remembered what he had promised me in the name of the Camorra.
I only remembered some vague threats, but he was good
enough to give me so many particulars of that institution that
I could make a European reputation by exposing the whole
show if it wasn't for my unfortunate resemblance to that infernal rascal Raffles. Do you think they would know me at the
Yard, Bunny, after all this time? Upon my soul I've a good
mind to risk it!'

I offered no opinion on the point. How could it interest me
then? But interested I was in Raffles, never more so in my life.
He had been tortured all night and half a day, yet he could sit
and talk like this the moment we cut him down; he had been
within a minute of his death, yet he was as full of life as ever;
ill-treated and defeated at the best, he could still smile through
his blood as though the boot were on the other leg. I had
imagined that I knew my Raffles at last. I was not likely so to
flatter myself again.

'But what has happened to these villains?' I burst out, and
my indignation was not only against them for their cruelty,
but also against their victim for his phlegmatic attitude towards
them. It was difficult to believe that this was Raffles.

'Oh,' said he, 'they were to go off to Italy *instanter*; they
should be crossing now. But do listen to what I am telling you;
it's interesting, my dear man. This old sinner Corbucci turns
out to have been no end of a boss in the Camorra – says so
himself. One of the *capi paranze*, my boy, no less; and the
velvety Johnny a *giovane onorato*, Anglicé, fresher. This fellow
here was also in it, and I've sworn to protect him from them

ever more; and it's just as I said, half the organ-grinders in London belong, and the whole lot of them were put on my tracks by secret instructions. This excellent youth manufactures iced poison on Saffron Hill when he's at home.'

'And why on earth didn't he come to me quicker?'

'Because he couldn't talk to you, he could only fetch you, and it was as much as his life was worth to do that before our friends had departed. They were going by the eleven o'clock from Victoria, and that didn't leave much chance, but he certainly oughtn't to have run it as fine as he did. Still you must remember that I had to fix things up with him in the fewest possible words, in a single minute that the other two were indiscreet enough to leave us alone together.'

The ragamuffin in question was watching us with all his solitary eye, as though he knew that we were discussing him. Suddenly he broke out in agonised accents, his hands clasped, and a face so full of fear that every moment I expected to see him on his knees. But Raffles answered kindly, reassuringly, I could tell from his tone, and then turned to me with a compassionate shrug.

'He says he couldn't find the mansions, Bunny, and really it's not to be wondered at. I had only time to tell him to hunt you up and bring you here by hook or crook before twelve to-day, and after all he has done that. But now the poor devil thinks you're riled with him, and that we'll give him away to the Camorra.'

'Oh, it's not with him I'm riled,' I said frankly, 'but with those other blackguards, and – and with you, old chap, for taking it all as you do, while such infamous scoundrels have the last laugh, and are safely on their way to France!'

Raffles looked up at me with a curiously open eye, an eye that I never saw when he was not in earnest. I fancied he did not like my last expression but one. After all, it was no laughing matter to him.

'But are they?' said he. 'I'm not so sure.'

'You said they were!'

'I said they should be.'

'Didn't you hear them go?'

'I heard nothing but the clock all night. It was like Big Ben striking at the last – striking nine to the fellow on the drop.'

And in that open eye I saw at last a deep glimmer of the ordeal through which he had passed.

'But, my dear old Raffles, if they're still on the premises – '

The thought was too thrilling for a finished sentence.

'I hope they are,' he said grimly, going to the door. 'There's a gas on! Was that burning when you came in?'

Now that I thought of it, yes, it had been.

'And there's a frightfully foul smell,' I added, as I followed Raffles down the stairs. He turned to me gravely with his hand upon the front-room door and at the same moment I saw a coat with an astrakhan collar hanging on the pegs.

'They are in here, Bunny,' he said, and turned the handle.

The door would only open a few inches. But a detestable odour came out, with a broad bar of yellow gas-light. Raffles put his handkerchief to his nose. I followed his example, signing to our ally to do the same, and in another minute we had all three squeezed into the room.

The man with the yellow boots was lying against the door, the Count's great carcase sprawled upon the table, and at a glance it was evident that both men had been dead some hours. The old Camorrist had the stem of a liqueur-glass between his swollen blue fingers, one of which had been cut in the breakage, and the livid flesh was brown with the last blood that it would ever shed. His face was on the table, the huge moustache projecting from under either leaden cheek, yet looking itself strangely alive. Broken bread and scraps of frozen macaroni lay upon the cloth and at the bottom of two soup-plates and a tureen; the macaroni had a tinge of tomato; and there was a crimson dram left in the tumblers, with an empty *fiasco* to show whence it came. But near the great grey head upon the table another liqueur-glass stood, unbroken, and still full of some white and stinking liquid; and near that a tiny silver flask, which made me recoil from Raffles as I had not from the dead; for I knew it to be his.

'Come out of this poisonous air,' he said sternly, 'and I will tell you how it has happened.'

So we all three gathered together in the hall. But it was Raffles who stood nearest the street-door, his back to it, his eyes upon us two. And though it was to me only that he spoke at first, he would pause from point to point, and translate into Italian for the benefit of the one-eyed alien to whom he owed his life.

'You probably don't even know the name, Bunny,' he began, 'of the deadliest poison yet known to science. It is cyanide of cacodyl, and I have carried that small flask of it about with me for months. Where I got it matters nothing; the whole point is that a mere sniff reduces flesh to clay. I have never had any opinion of suicide, as you know, but I always felt it worth while to be forearmed against the very worst. Well, a bottle of this stuff is calculated to stiffen an ordinary roomful of ordinary people within five minutes; and I remembered my flask when they had me as good as crucified in the small hours of this morning. I asked them to take it out of my pocket. I begged them to give me a drink before they left me. And what do you suppose they did?'

I thought of many things but suggested none, while Raffles turned this much of his statement into sufficiently fluent Italian. But when he faced me again his face was still flaming.

'That beast Corbucci!' said he – 'how can I pity him? He took the flask; he would give me none; he flicked me in the face instead. My idea was that he, at least, should go with me – to sell my life as dearly as that – and a sniff would have settled us both. But no, he must tantalise and torment me; he thought it brandy; he must take it downstairs to drink to my destruction! Can you have any pity for a hound like that?'

'Let us go,' I at last said hoarsely, as Raffles finished speaking in Italian, and his second listener stood open-mouthed.

'We will go,' said Raffles, 'and we will chance being seen; if the worst comes to the worst this good chap will prove that I have been tied up since one o'clock this morning, and the medical evidence will decide how long those dogs have been dead.'

But the worst did not come to the worst, more power to my unforgotten friend the cabman, who never came forward to say what manner of men he had driven to Bloomsbury Square at top speed on the very day upon which the tragedy was discovered there, or whence he had driven them. To be sure, they had not behaved like murderers, whereas the evidence at the inquest all went to show that the defunct Corbucci was little better. His reputation, which transpired with his identity, was that of a libertine and a renegade, while the infernal apparatus upstairs revealed the fiendish arts of the anarchist to boot. The inquiry resulted eventually in an open verdict, and was chiefly instrumental in killing such compassion as is usually felt for the dead who die in their sins.

But Raffles would not have passed this title for this tale.

TO CATCH A THIEF

I

SOCIETY persons are not likely to have forgotten the series of audacious robberies by which so many of themselves suffered in turn during the brief course of a recent season. Raid after raid was made upon the smartest houses in town, and within a few weeks more than one exalted head had been shorn of its priceless tiara. The Duke and Duchess of Dorchester lost half the portable pieces of their historic plate on the very night of their Graces' almost equally historic costume ball. The Kenworthy diamonds were taken in broad daylight, during the excitement of a charitable meeting on the ground floor, and the gifts of her belted bridegroom to Lady May Paulton while the outer air was thick with a prismatic shower of confetti. It was obvious that all this was the work of no ordinary thief, and perhaps inevitable that the name of Raffles should have been dragged from oblivion by callous disrespecters of the departed and unreasoning apologists for the police. These wiseacres did not hesitate to bring a dead man back to life because they knew of no one living capable of such feats; it is their heedless and inconsequent calumnies that the present paper is partly intended to refute. As a matter of fact, our joint innocence in this matter was only exceeded by our common envy, and for a long time, like the rest of the world, neither of us had the slightest clue to the identity of the person who was following in our steps with such irritating results.

'I should mind less,' said Raffles, 'if the fellow were really playing the game. But abuse of hospitality was never one of my strokes, and it seems to be the only shot he's got. When we took old Lady Melrose's necklace, Bunny, we were not staying with the Melroses if you recollect.'

We were discussing the robberies for the hundredth time, but for once under conditions more favourable to animated conversation than our unique circumstances permitted in the

214

flat. We did not often dine out. Dr Theobald was one impediment, the risk of recognition was another. But there were exceptions, when the doctor was away or the patient defiant, and on these rare occasions we frequented a certain unpretentious restaurant in the Fulham quarter, where the cooking was plain but excellent, and the cellar a surprise. Our bottle of '89 champagne was empty to the label when the subject arose, to be touched by Raffles in the reminiscent manner indicated above. I can see his clear eye upon me now, reading me, weighing me. But I was not so sensitive to his scrutiny at the time. His tone was deliberate, calculating, preparatory; not as I heard it then, through a head full of wine, but as it floats back to me across the gulf between that moment and this.

'Excellent fillet!' said I grossly. 'So you think this chap is as much in society as we were, do you?'

I preferred not to think so myself. We had cause enough for jealousy without that. But Raffles raised his eyebrows an eloquent half-inch.

'As much, my dear Bunny? He is not only in it, but of it; there's no comparison between us there. Society is in rings like a target, and we never were in the bull's-eye, however thick you may lay on the ink! I was asked for my cricket. I haven't forgotten it yet. But this fellow's one of themselves, with the right of *entrée* into houses which we could only "enter" in a professional sense. That's obvious unless all these little exploits are the work of different hands, which they as obviously are not. And it's why I'd give five hundred pounds to put salt on him to-night!'

'Not you,' said I, as I drained my glass in festive incredulity.

'But I would, my dear Bunny. Waiter! another half-bottle of this,' and Raffles leant across the table as the empty one was taken away. 'I never was more serious in my life,' he continued below his breath. 'Whatever else our successor may be, he's not a dead man like me, or a marked man like you. If there's any truth in my theory he's one of the last people upon whom suspicion is ever likely to rest; and oh, Bunny, what a partner he would make for you and me.'

Under less genial influences the very idea of a third partner would have filled my soul with offence; but Raffles had chosen his moment unerringly, and his arguments lost nothing by the flowing accompaniment of the extra pint. They were, however, quite strong in themselves. The gist of them was that thus far we had remarkably little to show for what Raffles would call 'our second innings'. This even I could not deny. We had scored a few 'long singles', but our 'best shots' had gone 'straight to hand', and we were 'playing a deuced slow game'. Therefore we needed a new partner – and the metaphor failed Raffles. It had served its turn. I already agreed with him. In truth I was tired of my false position as hireling attendant, and had long fancied myself an object of suspicion to that other impostor the doctor. A fresh, untrammelled start was a fascinating idea to me, though two were company, and three in our case might be worse than none. But I did not see how we could hope, with our respective handicaps, to solve a problem which was already the despair of Scotland Yard.

'Suppose I have solved it,' observed Raffles, cracking a walnut in his palm.

'How could you?' I asked, without believing for an instant that he had.

'I have been taking the *Morning Post* for some time now.'

'Well?'

'You have got me a good many odd numbers of the less base society papers.'

'I can't for the life of me see what you're driving at.'

Raffles smiled indulgently as he cracked another nut.

'That's because you've neither observation nor imagination, Bunny – and yet you try to write! Well, you wouldn't think it, but I have a fairly complete list of the people who were at the various functions under cover of which these different little *coups* were brought off.'

I said very stolidly that I did not see how that could help him. It was the only answer to his good-humoured but self-satisfied contempt; it happened also to be true.

'Think,' said Raffles, in a patient voice.

'When thieves break in and steal,' said I, 'upstairs, I don't see much point in discovering who was downstairs at the time.'

'Quite,' said Raffles – 'when they do break in.'

'But that's what they have done in all these cases. An upstairs door found screwed up, when things were at their height below; thief gone and jewels with him before alarm could be raised. Why, the trick's so old that I never knew you condescend to play it.'

'Not so old as it looks,' said Raffles, choosing the cigars and handing me mine. 'Cognac or Benedictine, Bunny?'

'Brandy,' I said coarsely.

'Besides,' he went on, 'the rooms were not screwed up; at Dorchester House, at any rate, the door was only locked; and the key missing, so that it might have been done on either side.'

'But that was where he left his rope-ladder behind him!' I exclaimed in trimph; but Raffles only shook his head.

'I don't believe in that rope-ladder, Bunny, except as a blind.'

'Then what on earth do you believe?'

'That every one of these so-called burglaries has been done from the inside, by one of the guests; and what's more, I'm very much mistaken if I haven't spotted the right sportsman.'

I began to believe that he really had, there was such a wicked gravity in the eyes that twinkled faintly into mine. I raised my glass in convivial congratulation, and still remember the somewhat anxious eye with which Raffles saw it emptied.

'I can only find one likely name,' he continued, 'that figures in all these lists, and it is anything but a likely one at first sight. Lord Ernest Belville was at all those functions. Know anything about him, Bunny?'

'Not the Rational Drink fanatic?'

'Yes.'

'That's all I want to know.'

'Quite,' said Raffles; 'and yet what could be more promising? A man whose views are so broad and moderate, and so widely held already (saving your presence, Bunny), does not bore the world with them without ulterior motives. So far so good. What are this chap's motives? Does he want to advertise himself? No, he's somebody already. But is he rich? On the contrary, he's as poor as a rat for his position, and apparently without the least ambition to be anything else; certainly he won't enrich himself by making a public fad of what all sensible people are agreed upon as it is. Then suddenly one gets one's own old idea

217

– the alternative profession! My cricket – his Rational Drink! But it is no use jumping to conclusions. I must know more than the newspapers can tell me. Our aristocratic friend is forty, and unmarried. What has he been doing all these years? How the devil was I to find out?'

'How did you?' I asked, declining to spoil my digestion with a conundrum, as it was his evident intention that I should.

'Interviewed him!' said Raffles, smiling slowly on my amazement.

'You – interviewed him?' I echoed. 'When – and where?'

'Last Thursday night, when, if you remember, we kept early hours, because I felt done. What was the use of telling you what I had up my sleeve, Bunny? It might have ended in fizzle, as it still may. But Lord Ernest Belville was addressing the meeting at Exeter Hall; I waited for him when the show was over, dogged him home to King John's Mansions, and interviewed him in his own rooms there before he turned in.'

My journalistic jealousy was piqued to the quick. Affecting a scepticism I did not feel (for no outrage was beyond the pale of his impudence), I inquired dryly which journal Raffles had pretended to represent. It is unnecessary to report his answer. I could not believe him without further explanation.

'I should have thought,' he said, 'that even you would have spotted a practice I never omit upon certain occasions. I always pay a visit to the drawing-room and fill my waistcoat pocket from the card-tray. It is an immense help in any little temporary impersonation. On Thursday night I sent up the card of a powerful writer connected with a powerful paper; if Lord Ernest had known him in the flesh I should have been obliged to confess to a journalistic ruse; luckily he didn't – and I had been sent by my editor to get the interview for next morning. What could be better for the alternative profession?'

I inquired what the interview had brought forth.

'Everything,' said Raffles. 'Lord Ernest has been a wanderer these twenty years. Texas, Fiji, Australia. I suspect him of wives and families in all three. But his manners are a liberal education. He gave me some beautiful whisky, and forgot all about his fad. He is strong and subtle, but I talked him off his guard. He is going to the Kirkleathams' to-night – I saw the card stuck up. I stuck some wax into his keyhole as he was switching off the lights.'

And, with an eye upon the waiters, Raffles showed me a skeleton key, newly twisted and filed; but my share of the extra pint (I am afraid no fair share) had made me dense. I looked from the key to Raffles with puckered forehead – for I happened to catch sight of it in the mirror behind him.

'The Dowager Lady Kirkleatham,' he whispered, 'has diamonds as big as beans, and likes to have 'em all on – and goes to bed early – and happens to be in town!'

And now I saw.

'The villain means to get them from her!'

'And I mean to get them from the villain,' said Raffles; 'or, rather, your share and mine.'

'Will he consent to a partnership?'

'We shall have him at our mercy. He daren't refuse.'

Raffles's plan was to gain access to Lord Ernest's rooms before midnight; there we were to lie in wait for the aristocratic rascal, and if I left all details to Raffles, and simply stood by in case of a rumpus, I should be playing my part and earning my share. It was a part that I had played before, not always with a good grace, though there had never been any question about the share. But to-night I was nothing loath. I had had just champagne enough – how Raffles knew my measure! – and I was ready and eager for anything. Indeed, I did not wish to wait for the coffee, which was to be specially strong by order of Raffles. But on that he insisted, and it was between ten and eleven when at last we were in our cab.

'It would be fatal to be too early,' he said as we drove; 'on the other hand, it would be dangerous to leave it too late. One must risk something. How I should love to drive down Piccadilly and see the lights! But unnecessary risks are another story.'

II

King John's Mansions, as everybody knows, are the oldest, the ugliest, and the tallest block of flats in all London. But they are built upon a more generous scale than has since become the rule, and with a less studious regard for the economy of space.

We were about to drive into the spacious courtyard when the gatekeeper checked us in order to let another hansom drive out. It contained a middle-aged man of the military type, like ourselves in evening dress. That much I saw as his hansom crossed our bows, because I could not help seeing it, but I should not have given the incident a second thought if it had not been for its extraordinary effect upon Raffles. In an instant he was out upon the kerb, paying the cabby, and in another he was leading me across the street, away from the mansions.

'Where on earth are you going?' I naturally exclaimed.

'Into the park,' said he. 'We are too early.'

His voice told me more than his words. It was strangely stern.

'Was that him – in the hansom?'

'It was.'

'Well, then, the coast's clear,' said I comfortably. I was for turning back then and there, but Raffles forced me on with a hand that hardened on my arm.

'It was a nearer thing than I care about,' said he. 'This seat will do; no, the next one's farther from a lamp-post. We will give him a good half-hour, and I don't want to talk.'

We had been seated some minutes when Big Ben sent a languid chime over our heads to the stars. It was half-past ten, and a sultry night. Eleven had struck before Raffles awoke from his sullen reverie, and recalled me from mine with a slap on the back. In a couple of minutes we were in the lightest vestibule at the inner end of the courtyard of King John's Mansions.

'Just left Lord Ernest at Lady Kirkleatham's,' said Raffles. 'Gave me his key and asked us to wait for him in his rooms. Will you send us up in the lift?'

In a small way, I never knew old Raffles do anything better. There was not an instant's demur. Lord Ernest Belville's rooms were at the top of the building, but we were in them as quickly as lift could carry and page-boy conduct us. And there was no need for the skeleton key after all; the boy opened the outer door with one of his own, and switched on the lights before leaving us.

'Now that's interesting,' said Raffles, as soon as we were alone; 'they can come in and clean when he is out. What if he keeps his swag at the bank? By Jove, that's an idea for him! I don't believe he's getting rid of it; it's all lying low somewhere, if I'm not mistaken, and he's not a fool.'

While he spoke he was moving about the sitting-room, which was charmingly furnished in the antique style, and making as many remarks as though he were an auctioneer's clerk with an inventory to prepare and a day to do it in, instead of a cracksman who might be surprised in his crib at any moment.

'Chippendale of sorts, eh, Bunny? Not genuine, of course; but where can you get genuine Chippendale now, and who knows it when they see it? There's no merit in mere antiquity. Yet the way people pose on the subject! If a thing's handsome and useful, and good cabinet-making, it's good enough for me.'

'Hadn't we better explore the whole place?' I suggested nervously. He had not even bolted the outer door. Nor would he when I called his attention to the omission.

'If Lord Ernest finds his rooms locked up he'll raise Cain,' said Raffles. 'We must let him come in and lock up for himself before we corner him. But he won't come yet; if he did it might be awkward, for they'll tell him down below what I told them. A new staff comes on at midnight. I discovered that the other night.'

'Supposing he does come in before?'

'Well, he can't have us turned out without first seeing who we are, and he won't try it on when I've had one word with him. Unless my suspicions are unfounded, I mean.'

'Isn't it about time to test them?'

'My good Bunny, what do you suppose I've been doing all this while? He keeps nothing in here. There isn't a lock to the Chippendale that you couldn't pick with a penknife, and not a loose board in the floor, for I was treading for one before the boy left us. Chimneys no use in a place like this where they keep them swept for you. Yes, I'm quite ready to try his bedroom.'

There was but a bathroom besides; no kitchen, no servant's room; neither is necessary in King John's Mansions. I thought it as well to put my head inside the bathroom while Raffles went into the bedroom, for I was tormented by the horrible idea that the man might all this time be concealed somewhere in the flat. But the bathroom blazed void in the electric light. I found Raffles hanging out of the starry square which was the bedroom window, for the room was still in darkness. I felt for the switch at the door.

'Put it out again!' said Raffles fiercely. He rose from the sill, drew blinds and curtains carefully, then switched on the light himself. It fell upon a face creased more in pity than in anger, and Raffles only shook his head as I hung mine.

'It's all right, old boy,' said he; 'but corridors have windows too, and servants have eyes; and you and I are supposed to be in the other room, not in this. But cheer up, Bunny! This is *the* room; look at the extra bolt on the door; he's had that put on, and there's an iron ladder to his window in case of fire! Way of escape ready against the hour of need; he's a better man than I thought him, Bunny, after all. But you may bet your bottom dollar that if there's any boodle in the flat it's in this room.'

Yet the room was very lightly furnished; and nothing was locked. We looked everywhere, but we looked in vain. The wardrobe was filled with hanging coats and trousers in a press, the drawers with the softest silk and finest linen. There was a camp bedstead that would not have unsettled an anchorite; there was no place for treasure there. I looked up the chimney, but Raffles told me not to be a fool, and asked if I ever listened to what he said. There was no question about his temper now. I never knew him in a worse.

'Then he's got it in the bank,' he growled. 'I'll swear I'm not mistaken in my man!'

I had the tact not to differ with him there. But I could not help suggesting that now was our time to remedy any mistake we might have made. We were on the right side of midnight still.

'Then we'll stultify ourselves downstairs,' said Raffles. 'No, I'll be shot if I do! He may come in with the Kirkleatham diamonds! You do what you like, Bunny, but I don't budge.'

'I certainly shan't leave you,' I retorted, 'to be knocked into the middle of next week by a better man than yourself.'

I had borrowed his own tone, and he did not like it. They never do. I thought for a moment that Raffles was going to strike me – for the first and last time in his life. He could if he liked. My blood was up. I was ready to send him to the devil. And I emphasised my offence by nodding and shrugging towards a pair of very large Indian clubs that stood in the fender, on either side of the chimney up which I had presumed to glance.

In an instant Raffles had seized the clubs, and was whirling them about his grey head in a mixture of childish pique and puerile bravado which I should have thought him altogether above. And suddenly as I watched him his face changed, softened, lit up, and he swung the clubs gently down upon the bed.

'They're not heavy enough for their size,' said he rapidly; 'and I'll take my oath they're not the same weight!'

He shook one club after the other, with both hands, close to his ear; then he examined their butt-ends under the electric light. I saw what he suspected now, and caught the contagion of his suppressed excitement. Neither of us spoke. But Raffles had taken out the portable tool-box that he called a knife, and always carried, and as he opened the gimlet he handed me the club he held. Instinctively I tucked the small end under my arm, and presented the other to Raffles.

'Hold him tight,' he whispered, smiling. 'He's not only a better man than I thought him, Bunny, he's hit upon a better dodge than ever I did, of its kind. Only I should have weighted them evenly – to a hair.'

He had screwed the gimlet into the circular butt, close to the edge, and now we were wrenching in opposite directions. For a moment or more nothing happened. Then all at once something gave, and Raffles swore an oath as soft as any prayer. And for the minute after that his hand went round and round with the gimlet, as though he were grinding a piano-organ, while the end wormed slowly out on its delicate thread of fine hard wood.

The clubs were as hollow as drinking-horns, the pair of them, for we went from one to the other without pausing to undo the padded packets that poured out upon the bed. These were deliciously heavy to the hand, yet thickly swathed in cotton-wool, so that some stuck together, retaining the shape of the cavity, as though they had been run out of a mould. And when we did open them – but let Raffles speak.

He had deputed me to screw in the ends of the clubs and to replace the latter in the fender where we had found them. When I had done, the counterpane was glittering with diamonds where it was not shimmering with pearls.

'If this isn't the tiara that Lady Mary was married in,' said Raffles, 'and that disappeared out of the room she changed in, while it rained confetti on the steps, I'll present it to her instead of the one she lost ... It was stupid to keep these old gold spoons, valuable as they are; they made the difference in the weight. ... Here we have probably the Kenworthy diamonds ... I don't know the history of these pearls ... This looks like one family of rings – left on the basin-stand, perhaps – alas! poor lady! And that's the lot.'

Our eyes met across the bed.

'What's it all worth?' I asked hoarsely.

'Impossible to say. But more than all we ever took in all our lives. That I'll swear to.'

'More than all – –'

My tongue swelled with the thought.

'But it'll take some turning into cash, old chap!'

'And – must it be a partnership?' I asked, finding a lugubrious voice at length.

'Partnership be damned!' cried Raffles heartily. 'Let's get out quicker than we came in.'

We pocketed the things between us, cotton-wool and all, not because we wanted the latter, but to remove all immediate traces of our really meritorious deed.

'The sinner won't dare to say a word when he does find out,' remarked Raffles of Lord Ernest; 'but that's no reason why he should find out before he must. Everything's straight in here, I think; no, better leave the window open as it was, and the blind up. Now out with the light. One peep at the other room. That's all right, too. Out with the passage light, Bunny, while I open – –'

His words died away in a whisper. A key was fumbling at the lock outside.

'Out with it – out with it!' whispered Raffles in an agony; and as I obeyed he picked me off my feet and swung me bodily but silently into the bedroom, just as the outer door opened, and a masterful step strode in.

The next five were horrible minutes. We heard the apostle of Rational Drink unlock one of the deep drawers in his antique sideboard, and sounds followed suspiciously like the splash of spirits and the steady stream from a siphon. Never before or since did I experience such a thirst as assailed me at that moment, nor do I believe that many tropical explorers have known its equal. But I had Raffles with me, and his hand was as steady and as cool as the hand of a trained nurse. That I know because he turned up the collar of my overcoat for me, for some reason, and buttoned it at the throat. I afterwards found that he had done the same to his own, but I did not hear him doing it. The one thing I heard in the bedroom was a tiny metallic click, muffled and deadened in his overcoat pocket, and it not only removed my last tremor, but strung me to a higher pitch of excitement than ever. Yet I had then no conception of the game that Raffles was deciding to play, and that I was to play with him in another minute.

It cannot have been longer before Lord Ernest came into his bedroom. Heavens, but my heart had not forgotten how to thump! We were standing near the door, and I could swear he touched me; then his boots creaked, there was a rattle in the fender – and Raffles switched on the light.

Lord Ernest Belville crouched in its glare with one Indian club held by the end, like a footman with a stolen bottle. A good-looking, well-built, iron-grey, iron-jawed man; but a fool and a weakling at that moment, if he had never been either before.

'Lord Ernest Belville,' said Raffles, 'it's no use. This is a loaded revolver, and if you force me I shall use it on you as I would on any other desperate criminal. I am here to arrest you for a series of robberies at the Duke of Dorchester's, Sir John Kenworthy's, and other noblemen's and gentlemen's houses during the present season. You'd better drop what you've got in your hand. It's empty.'

Lord Ernest lifted the club an inch or two, and with it his eyebrows – and after it his stalwart frame as the club crashed back into the fender. And as he stood at his full height, a courteous but ironic smile under the cropped moustache, he looked what he was, criminal or not.

'Scotland Yard?' said he.

'That's our affair, my lord.'

'I didn't think they'd got it in them,' said Lord Ernest. 'Now I recognise you. You're my interviewer. No, I didn't think any of you fellows had got all that in you. Come into the other room, and I'll show you something else. Oh, keep me covered by all means. But look at this!'

On the antique sideboard, their size doubled by reflection in the polished mahogany, lay a coruscating cluster of precious stones, that fell in festoons about Lord Ernest's fingers as he handed them to Raffles with scarcely a shrug.

'The Kirkleatham diamonds,' said he. 'Better add 'em to the bag.'

Raffles did so without a smile; with his overcoat buttoned up to the chin, his tall hat pressed down to his eyes, and between the two his incisive features and his keen, stern glance, he looked the ideal detective of fiction and the stage. What *I* looked God knows, but I did my best to glower and show my teeth at his side. I had thrown myself into the game, and it was obviously a winning one.

'Wouldn't take a share, I suppose?' Lord Ernest said casually.

Raffles did not condescend to reply. I rolled back my lips like a bull-pup.

'Then a drink, at least!'

My mouth watered, but Raffles shook his head impatiently.

'We must be going, my lord, and you will have to come with us.'

I wondered what in the world we should do with him when we had got him.

'Give me time to put some things together? Pair of pyjamas and toothbrush, don't you know?'

'I cannot give you many minutes, my lord, but I don't want to cause a disturbance here, so I'll tell them to call a cab if you like. But I shall be back in a minute, and you must be ready in five. Here, Inspector, you'd better keep this while I am gone.'

And I was left alone with that dangerous criminal! Raffles

nipped my arm as he handed me the revolver, but I got small comfort out of that.

' "Sea-green Incorruptible?" ' inquired Lord Ernest, as we stood face to face.

'You don't corrupt me,' I replied through naked teeth.

'Then come into my room. I'll lead the way. Think you can hit me if I misbehave?'

I put the bed between us without a second's delay. My prisoner flung a suit-case upon it, and tossed things into it with a dejected air; suddenly, as he was fitting them in, without raising his head (which I was watching), his right hand closed over the barrel with which I covered him.

'You'd better not shoot,' he said, a knee upon his side of the bed; 'if you do it may be as bad for you as it will be for me!'

I tried to wrest the revolver from him.

'I will if you force me,' I hissed.

'You'd better not,' he repeated, smiling; and now I saw that if I did I should only shoot into either the bed or my own legs. His hand was on the top of mine, bending it down, and the revolver with it. The strength of it was as the strength of ten of mine; and now both his knees were on the bed; and suddenly I saw his other hand, doubled into a fist, coming up slowly over the suit-case.

'Help!' I called feebly.

'Help, forsooth! I begin to believe *you are* from the Yard,' he said – and his upper-cut came with the 'Yard'. It caught me under the chin. It lifted me off my legs. I have a dim recollection of the crash that I made in falling.

III

Raffles was standing over me when I recovered consciousness. I lay stretched upon the bed across which the blackguard Belville had struck his knavish blow. The suit-case was on the floor, but its dastardly owner had disappeared.

'Is he gone?' was my first faint question.

'Thank God you're not, anyway!' replied Raffles, with what struck me then as mere flippancy. I managed to raise myself upon one elbow.

'I meant Lord Ernest Belville,' said I with dignity. 'Are you quite sure that he's cleared out?'

Raffles waved a hand towards the window, which stood wide open to the summer stars.

'Of course,' said he, 'and by the route I intended him to take; he's gone by the iron ladder, as I hoped he would. What on earth should we have done with him? My poor dear Bunny, I thought you'd take a bribe! But it's really more convincing as it is, and just as well for Lord Ernest to be convinced for the time being.'

'Are you sure he is?' I questioned, as I found a rather shaky pair of legs.

'Of course!' cried Raffles again, in the tone to make one blush for the least misgiving on the point. 'Not that it matters one bit,' he added airily, 'for we have him either way; and when he does tumble to it, as he may any minute, he won't dare to open his mouth.'

'Then the sooner we clear out the better,' said I, but I looked askance at the open window, for my head was spinning still.

'When you feel up to it,' returned Raffles, 'we shall *stroll* out, and I shall do myself the honour of ringing for the lift. The force of habit is too strong in you, Bunny. I shall shut the window and leave everything exactly as we found it. Lord Ernest will probably tumble before he is badly missed; and then he may come back to put salt on us; but I should like to know what he can do even if he succeeds! Come, Bunny, pull yourself together, and you'll be a different man when you're in the open air.'

And for a while I felt one, such was my relief at getting out of those infernal mansions with unfettered wrists; this we managed easily enough; but once more Raffles's performance of a small part was no less perfect than his more ambitious work upstairs, and something of the successful artist's elation possessed him as we walked arm in arm across St. James's Park. It was long since I had known him so pleased with himself, and only too long since he had had such reason.

'I don't think I ever had a brighter idea in my life,' he said; 'never thought of it till he was in the next room; never dreamt

228

of its coming off so ideally even then, and didn't much care, because we had him all ways up. I'm only sorry you let him knock you out. I was waiting outside the door all the time, and it made me sick to hear it. But I once broke my own head, Bunny, if you remember, and not in half such an excellent cause!'

Raffles touched all his pockets in his turn, the pockets that contained a small fortune apiece, and he smiled in my face as we crossed the lighted avenues of the Mall. Next moment he was hailing a cab – for I suppose I was still pretty pale – and not a word would he let me speak until we had alighted as near as was prudent to the flat.

'What a brute I've been, Bunny!' he whispered then; 'but you take half the swag, old boy, and right well you've earned it. No, we'll go in by the wrong door and over the roof; it's too late for old Theobald to be still at the play, and too early for him to be safely in his cups.'

So we climbed the many stairs with cat-like stealth, and like cats crept out upon the grimy leads. But to-night they were no blacker than their canopy of sky; not a chimney-stack stood out against the starless night; one had to feel one's way in order to avoid tipping over the low parapets of the L-shaped wells that ran from roof to basement to light the inner rooms. One of these walls was spanned by a flimsy bridge with iron hand-rails that felt warm to the touch as Raffles led the way across, a hotter and a closer night I have ever known.

'The flat will be like an oven,' I grumbled, at the head of our own staircase.

'Then we won't go down,' said Raffles promptly; 'we'll slack it up here for a bit instead. No, Bunny, you stay where you are! I'll fetch you a drink and a deck-chair, and you shan't come down till you feel more fit.'

And I let him have his way, I will not say as usual, for I had even less than my normal power of resistance that night. That villainous upper-cut! My head still sang and throbbed, as I seated myself on one of the aforesaid parapets, and buried it in my hot hands. Nor was the night one to dispel a headache; there was distinct thunder in the air. Thus I sat in a heap, and brooded over my misadventure, a pretty figure of a subordinate villain, until the step came for which I waited; and it never struck me that it came from the wrong direction.

'You have been quick,' said I simply.

'Yes,' hissed a voice I recognised; 'and you've got to be quicker still! Here, out with your wrists; no, one at a time; and if you utter a syllable you're a dead man.'

It was Lord Ernest Belville; his close-cropped, iron-grey moustache gleamed through the darkness, drawn up over his set teeth. In his hand glittered a pair of handcuffs, and before I knew it one had snapped its jaws about my wrist.

'Now come this way,' said Lord Ernest, showing me a revolver also, 'and wait for your friend. And, recollect, a single syllable of warning will be your death!'

With that the ruffian led me to the very bridge I had just crossed at Raffles's heels, and handcuffed me to the iron rail midway across the chasm. It no longer felt warm to my touch, but icy as the blood in all my veins.

So this high-born hypocrite had beaten us at our game and his, and Raffles had met his match at last! That was the most intolerable thought, that Raffles should be down in the flat on my account, and that I could not warn him of his impending fate; for how was it possible without making such an outcry as should bring the mansions about our ears? And there I shivered on that wretched plank, chained like Andromeda to the rock, with a black infinity above and below; and before my eyes, now grown familiar with the peculiar darkness, stood Lord Ernest Belville, waiting for Raffles to emerge with full hands and unsuspecting heart! Taken so horribly unawares, even Raffles must fall an easy prey to a desperado in resource and courage scarcely second to himself, but one whom he had fatally underrated from the beginning. Not that I paused to think how the thing had happened; my one concern was for what was to happen next.

And what did happen was worse than my worst foreboding, for first a light came flickering into the sort of companion-hatch at the head of the stairs, and finally Raffles — in his shirt-sleeves! He was not only carrying a candle to put the finishing touch to him as a target; he had dispensed with coat and waist-coat downstairs, and was at once full-handed and unarmed.

'Where are you, old chap?' he cried softly, himself blinded by the light he carried; and he advanced a couple of steps towards Belville. 'This isn't you, is it?'

And Raffles stopped, his candle held on high, a folding-chair under the other arm.

'No, I am not your friend,' replied Lord Ernest easily; 'but kindly remain standing exactly where you are, and don't lower that candle an inch, unless you want your brains blown into the street.'

Raffles said never a word, but for a moment did as he was bid; and the unshaken flame of the candle was testimony alike to the stillness of the night and to the finest set of nerves in Europe. Then, to my horror, he coolly stooped, placing candle and chair on the leads, and his hands in his pockets, as though it were but a pop-gun that covered him.

'Why didn't you shoot?' he asked insolently as he rose. 'Frightened of the noise? I should be, too, with an old-pattern machine like that. All very well for service in the field – but on the housetops at dead of night!'

'I shall shoot, however,' replied Lord Ernest, as quietly in his turn, and with less insolence, 'and chance the noise, unless you instantly restore my property. I am glad you don't dispute the last word,' he continued after a slight pause. 'There is no keener honour than that which subsists, or ought to subsist, among thieves; and I need hardly say that I soon spotted you as one of the fraternity. Not in the beginning, mind you! For the moment I did think you were one of these smart detectives jumped to life from some sixpenny magazine; but to preserve the illusion you ought to provide yourself with a worthier lieutenant. It was he who gave your show away,' chuckled the wretch, dropping for a moment the affected style of speech which seemed intended to enhance our humiliation; 'smart detectives don't go about with little innocents to assist them. You needn't be anxious about him, by the way; it wasn't necessary to pitch him into the street; he is to be seen though not heard, if you look in the right direction. Nor must you put all the blame upon your friend; it was not he, but you, who made so sure that I had got out by the window. You see, I was in my bathroom all the time – with the door open.'

'The bathroom, eh?' Raffles echoed with professional interest. 'And you followed us on foot across the park?'

'Of course.'

'And then in a cab?'

'And afterwards on foot once more.'

'The simplest skeleton would let you in down below.'

I saw the lower half of Lord Ernest's face grinning in the light of the candle set between them on the ground.

'You follow every move,' said he; 'there can be no doubt you are one of the fraternity; and I shouldn't wonder if we had formed our style upon the same model. Ever know A. J. Raffles?'

The abrupt question took my breath away; but Raffles himself did not lose an instant over his answer.

'Intimately,' said he.

'That accounts for you, then,' laughed Lord Ernest, 'as it does for me, though I never had the honour of the master's acquaintance. Nor is it for me to say which is the worthier disciple. Perhaps, however, now that your friend is handcuffed in mid-air, and you yourself are at my mercy, you will concede me some little temporary advantage?'

And his face split in another grin from the cropped moustache downward, as I saw no longer by candlelight, but by a flash of lightning which tore the sky in two before Raffles could reply.

'You have the bulge at present,' admitted Raffles; 'but you have still to lay hands upon your, or our, ill-gotten goods. To shoot me is not necessarily to do so; to bring either one of us to a violent end is only to court a yet more violent and infinitely more disgraceful one for yourself. Family considerations alone should rule that risk out of your game. Now, an hour or two ago, when the exact opposite – –'

The remainder of Raffles's speech was drowned from my ears by the belated crash of thunder which the lightning had foretold. So loud, however, was the crash when it came, that the storm was evidently approaching us at a high velocity; yet as the last echo rumbled away, I heard Raffles talking as though he had never stopped.

'You offered us a share,' he was saying; 'unless you mean to murder us both in cold blood, it will be worth your while to repeat that offer. We should be dangerous enemies; you had far better make the best of us as friends.'

'Lead the way down to your flat,' said Lord Ernest, with a flourish of his service revolver, 'and perhaps we may talk about it. It is for me to make the terms, I imagine, and in the first place I am not going to get wet to the skin up here.'

The rain was beginning in great drops, even as he spoke, and by a second flash of lightning I saw Raffles pointing to me.

'But what about my friend?' said he.

And then came the second peal.

'Oh, *he's* all right,' the great brute replied; 'do him good! You don't catch me letting myself in for two to one!'

'You will find it equally difficult,' rejoined Raffles, 'to induce me to leave my friend to the mercy of a night like this. He has not recovered from the blow you struck him in your own rooms. I am not such a fool as to blame you for that, but you are a worse sportsman than I take you for if you think of leaving him where he is. If he stays, however, so do I.'

And, just as it ceased, Raffles's voice seemed distinctly nearer me; but in the darkness and the rain, which was now as heavy as hail, I could see nothing clearly. The rain had already extinguished the candle I heard an oath from Belville, a laugh from Raffles, and for a second that was all. Raffles was coming to me, and the other could not even see to fire; that was all I knew in the pitchy interval of invisible rain before the next crash and the next flash.

And then!

This time they came together, and not till my dying hour shall I forget the sight that the lightning lit and the thunder applauded. Raffles was on one of the parapets of the gulf that my footbridge spanned, and in the sudden illumination he stepped across it as one might across a garden path. The width was scarcely greater, but the depth! In the sudden flare I saw to the concrete bottom of the well, and it looked no larger than the hollow of my hand. Raffles was laughing in my ear; he had the iron railing fast; it was between us, but his foothold was as secure as mine. Lord Ernest Belville, on the contrary, was the fifth of a second late for the light, and half a foot short in his spring. Something struck our plank bridge so hard as to set it quivering like a harp-string; there was half a gasp and half a sob in mid-air beneath our feet; and then a sound far below that I prefer not to describe. I am not sure that I could hit upon the perfect simile; it is more than enough for me that I can hear it still. And with that sickening sound came the loudest clap of thunder yet, and a great white glare that showed us our enemy's body far below, with one white hand spread like a starfish, but the head of him mercifully twisted underneath.

'It was his own fault, Bunny. Poor devil! May he and all of us be forgiven; but pull yourself together for your own sake. Well, you can't fall; stay where you are a minute.'

I remember the uproar of the elements while Raffles was gone; no other sound mingled with it; not the opening of a single window, not the uplifting of a single voice. Then came Raffles with soap and water and gyve was wheedled from one wrist, as you withdraw a ring for which the finger has grown too large. Of the rest, I only remember shivering till morning in a pitch-dark flat, whose invalid occupier was for once the nurse, and I his patient.

And that is the true ending of the episode in which we two set ourselves to catch one of our own kidney, albeit in another place I have shirked the whole truth. It is not a grateful task to show Raffles as completely at fault as he really was on that occasion; nor do I derive any subtle satisfaction from recounting my own twofold humiliation, or from having assisted never so indirectly in the death of a not uncongenial sinner. The truth, however, has after all a merit of its own, and the great kinsfolk of poor Lord Ernest have but little to lose by its divulgence. It would seem that they knew more of the real character of the apostle of Rational Drink than was known at Exeter Hall. The tragedy was indeed hushed up, as tragedies only are when they occur in such circles. But the rumour that did get abroad, as to the class of enterprise which the poor scamp was pursuing when he met his death, cannot be too soon exploded, since it breathed upon the fair fame of some of the most respectable flats in Kensington.

AN OLD FLAME

I

THE square shall be nameless, but if you drive due west from
Piccadilly the cabman will eventually find it on his left, and he
ought to thank you for half a crown. It is not a fashionable
square, but there are few with a finer garden, while the studios
on the south side lend distinction of another sort. The houses,
however, are small and dingy and about the last to attract the
expert practitioner in search of a crib. Heaven knows it was
with no such thought I trailed Raffles thither, one unlucky
evening at the latter end of that same season when Dr. Theobald had at last insisted upon the bath-chair which I had foreseen in the beginning. Trees whispered in the green garden
aforesaid, and the cool smooth lawns looked so inviting that I
wondered whether some philanthropic resident could not be
induced to lend us the key. But Raffles would not listen to the
suggestion, when I stopped to make it, and what was worse, I
found him looking wistfully at the little houses instead.

'Such balconies, Bunny! A leg up, and there you would be!'

I expressed a conviction that there would be nothing worth
taking in the square, but took care to have him under way
again as I spoke.

'I dare say you're right,' sighed Raffles. 'Rings and watches,
I suppose, but it would be hard luck to take them from people
who live in houses like these. I don't know, though. Here's one
with an extra story. Stop, Bunny; if you don't stop I'll hold on
to the railings! This is a good house; look at the knocker and
the electric bell. They've had that put in. There's some money
here, my rabbit! I dare bet there's a silver-table in the drawing-
room; and the windows are wide open. Electric light, too, by
Jove!'

Since stop I must, I had done so on the other side of the
road, in the shadow of the leafy palings, and as Raffles spoke
the ground-floor windows opposite had shown a light, show-

ing as pretty a little dinner-table as one could wish to see with
a man at his wine at the far end, and the back of a lady in
evening dress towards us. It was like a lantern-picture thrown
upon a screen. There was only the pair of them, but the table
was brilliant with silver and gay with flowers, and the maid
waited with the indefinable air of a good servant. It certainly
seemed a good house.

'She's going to let down the blind!' whispered Raffles, in
high excitement. 'No, confound them, they've told her not to.
Mark down her necklace, Bunny, and invoice his stud. What
a brute he looks! But I like the table, and that's her show. She
has the taste; but he must have money. See the festive picture
over the sideboard? Looks to me like a Jacques Saillard. But
that silver-table would be good enough for me.'

'Get on,' said I. 'You're in a bath-chair.'

'But the whole square's at dinner! We should have the ball
at our feet. It wouldn't take two twos!'

'With those blinds up, and the cook in the kitchen underneath?'

He nodded, leaning forward in the chair, his hands upon
the wraps about his legs.

'You must be mad,' said I, and got back to my handles with
the word, but when I tugged the chair ran light.

'Keep an eye on the rug,' came in a whisper from the middle
of the road; and there stood my invalid, his pale face in a
quiver of pure mischief, yet set with his insane resolve. 'I'm
only going to see whether that woman has a silver-table – –'

'We don't want it – –'

'It won't take a minute – –'

'It's madness, madness – –'

'Then don't you wait!'

It was like him to leave me with that, and this time I had
taken him at his last word, had not my own given me an idea.
Mad I had called him, and mad I could declare him upon oath
if necessary. It was not as though the thing had happened far
from home. They could learn all about us at the nearest mansions. I referred them to Dr Theobald; this was a Mr Maturin,
one of his patients, and I was his keeper, and he had never
given me the slip before. I heard myself making these explana-

tions on the doorstep, and pointing to the deserted bath-chair as the proof, while the pretty parlourmaid ran for the police. It would be a more serious matter for me than for my charge. I should lose my place. No, he had never done such a thing before, and I would answer for it that he never should again.

I saw myself conducting Raffles back to his chair, with a firm hand and a stern tongue. I heard him thanking me in whispers on the way home. It would be the first tight place I had ever got him out of, and I was quite anxious for him to get into it, so sure was I of every move. My whole position had altered in the few seconds that it took me to follow this illuminating train of ideas; it was now so strong that I could watch Raffles without much anxiety. And he was worth watching.

He had stepped boldly but softly to the front door, and there he was still waiting, ready to ring if the door opened or a face appeared in the area, and doubtless to pretend that he had rung already. But he had not to ring at all; and suddenly I saw his foot in the letter-box, his left hand on the lintel overhead. It was thrilling even to a hardened accomplice with an explanation up his sleeve! A tight grip with that left hand of his, as he leant backward with all his weight upon those five fingers; a right arm stretched outward and upward to its last inch; and the base of the low, projecting balcony was safely caught.

I looked down and took breath. The maid was removing the crumbs in the lighted room, and the square was empty as before. What a blessing it was the end of the season! Many of the houses remained in darkness. I looked up again, and Raffles was drawing his left leg over the balcony railing. In another moment he had disappeared through one of the french windows which opened upon the balcony, and in yet another he had switched on the electric light within. This was bad enough; but the crowning folly was still to come. There was no point in it; the mad thing was done for my benefit, as I knew at once and he afterwards confessed; but the lunatic reappeared on the balcony bowing like a mountebank – in his crape mask!

I set off with the empty chair, but I came back. *I* could not desert old Raffles, even when I would, but must try to explain away his mask as well, if he had not the sense to take it off in time. It would be difficult, but burglaries are not usually committed from a bath-chair, and for the rest I put my faith in Dr. Theobald. Meanwhile Raffles had at least withdrawn from the balcony, and now I could see his head as he peered into a cabinet at the other side of the room. It was like the opera of *Aïda*, in which two scenes are enacted simultaneously, one in the dungeon below, the other in the temple above. In the same fashion my attention now became divided between the picture of Raffles moving stealthily about the upper room and that of the husband and wife at table underneath. And all at once, as the man replenished his glass with a shrug of the shoulders, the woman pushed back her chair and sailed to the door.

Raffles was standing before the fireplace upstairs. He had taken one of the framed photographs from the chimney-piece, and was scanning it at suicidal length through the eye-holes in the hideous mask which he still wore. He would need it after all. The lady had left the room below, opening and shutting the door for herself; the man was filling his glass once more. I would have shrieked my warning to Raffles, so fatally engrossed overhead, but at this moment (of all others) a constable (of all men) was marching sedately down our side of the square. There was nothing for it but to turn a melancholy eye upon the bath-chair, and to ask the constable the time. I was evidently to be kept there all night, I remarked, and only realised with the words that they disposed of my other explanations before they were uttered. It was a horrible moment for such a discovery. Fortunately the enemy was on the pavement, from which he could scarcely have seen more than the drawing-room ceiling, had he looked; but he was not many houses distant when a door opened and a woman gasped so that I heard both across the road. And never shall I forget the subsequent tableaux in the lighted room behind the low balcony and the french windows.

Raffles stood confronted by a dark and handsome woman whose profile, as I saw it first in the electric light, is cut like a cameo in my memory. It had the undeviating line of brow and nose, the short upper lip, the perfect chin, that are united in marble oftener than in the flesh; and like marble she stood, or rather like some beautiful pale bronze; for that was her colouring, and she lost none of it that I could see, neither trembled; but her bosom rose and fell, and that was all. So she stood without flinching before a masked ruffian, who, I felt, would be the first to appreciate her courage! To me it was so superb that I could think of it in this way even then, and marvel how Raffles himself could stand unabashed before so brave a figure. He had not to do so long. The woman scorned him, and he stood unmoved, a framed photograph still in his hand. Then, with a quick, determined movement she turned, not to the door or to the bell, but to the open window by which Raffles had entered; and this with that accursed policeman still in view. So far no word had passed between the pair. But at this point Raffles said something, I could not hear what, but at the sound of his voice the woman wheeled. And Raffles was looking humbly in her face, the crape mask snatched from his own.

'Arthur!' she cried; and that might have been heard in the middle of the square garden.

Then they stood gazing at each other, neither unmoved any more, and while they stood the street-door opened and banged. It was the husband leaving the house, a fine figure of a man, but a dissipated face, and a step even now distinguished by the extreme caution which precedes unsteadiness. He broke the spell. His wife came to the balcony, then looked back into the room, and yet again along the road, and this time I saw her face. It was the face of one glancing indeed from Hyperion to a satyr. And then I saw the rings flash, as her hand fell gently upon Raffles's arm.

They disappeared from that window. Their heads showed for an instant in the next. Then they dipped out of sight, and an inner ceiling flashed out under a new light; they had gone into the back drawing-room beyond my ken. The maid came up with coffee, her mistress hastily met her at the door, and once more disappeared. The square was as quiet as ever. I remained some minutes where I was. Now and then I thought I heard voices in the back drawing-room. I was seldom sure.

My state of mind may be imagined by those readers who take an interest in my personal psychology. It does not amuse me to put myself in Raffles's place. He had been recognised at last, he had come to life. Only one person knew as yet, but that person was a woman, and a woman who had once been fond of him, if the human face could speak. Would she keep his secret? Would he tell her where he lived? It was terrible to think we were such neighbours, and with the thought that it was terrible came a little enlightenment as to what could still be done for the best. He would not tell her where he lived. I knew him too well for that. He would run for it when he could, and the bath-chair and I must not be there to give him away. I dragged the infernal vehicle round the nearer corner. Then I waited – there could be no harm in that – and at last he came.

He was walking briskly, so I was right, and he had not played the invalid to her; yet I heard him cry out with pleasure as he turned the corner, and he flung himself into the chair with a long-drawn sigh that did me good.

'Well done, Bunny – well done! I am on my way to Earl's Court; she's capable of following me, but she won't look for me in a bath-chair. Home, home, home, and not another word till we get there!'

Capable of following him? She overtook us before we were past the studios on the south side of the square, the woman herself, in a hooded opera-cloak. But she never gave us a glance, and we saw her turn safely in the right direction for Earl's Court, and the wrong one for our humble mansions. Raffles thanked his gods in a voice that trembled, and five minutes later we were in the flat. Then for once it was Raffles who filled the tumblers and found the cigarettes, and for once (and once only in all my knowledge of him) did he drain his glass at a draught.

'You didn't see the balcony scene?' he asked at length; and they were his first words since the woman passed us on his track.

'Do you mean when she came in?'

'No, when I came down.'

'I didn't.'

'I hope nobody else saw it,' said Raffles devoutly. 'I don't say that Romeo and Juliet were brother and sister to us. But you might have said so, Bunny!'

He was staring at the carpet with as wry a face as lover ever wore.

'An old flame?' said I gently.

'A married woman,' he groaned.

'So I gathered.'

'But she always was one, Bunny,' said he ruefully. 'That's the trouble. It makes all the difference in the world!'

I saw the difference, but said I did not see how it could make any now. He had eluded the lady, after all; had we not seen her off upon a scent as false as scent could be? There was occasion for redoubled caution in the future, but none for immediate anxiety. I quoted the bedside Theobald, but Raffles did not smile. His eyes had been downcast all this time, and now, when he raised them, I perceived that my comfort had been administered to deaf ears.

'Do you know who she is?' said he.

'Not from Eve.'

'Jacques Saillard,' he said, as though now I must know.

But the name left me cold and stolid. I had heard it, but that was all. It was lamentable ignorance, I am aware, but I had specialised in Letters at the expense of Art.

'You must know her pictures,' said Raffles patiently; 'but I suppose you thought she was a man. They would appeal to you, Bunny; that festive piece over the sideboard was her work. Sometimes they risk her at the Academy, sometimes they fight shy. She has one of those studios in the same square; they used to live up near Lord's.'

My mind was busy brightening a dim memory of nymphs reflected in woody pools. 'Of course!' I exclaimed, and added something about 'a clever woman.' Raffles rose at the phrase.

'A clever woman!' echoed he scornfully; 'if she were only that I should feel safe as houses. Clever women can't forget their cleverness, they carry it as badly as a boy does his wine, and are about as dangerous. I don't call Jacques Saillard clever outside her art, but neither do I call her a woman at all. She does man's work over a man's name, has the will of any ten men I ever knew, and I don't mind telling you that I fear her more than any person on God's earth. I broke with her once,' said Raffles grimly, 'but I know her. If I had been asked to

241

name the one person in London by whom I was keenest *not* to be bowled out, I should have named Jacques Saillard.'

That he had never before named her to me was as characteristic as the reticence with which Raffles spoke of their past relations, and even of their conversation in the back drawing-room that evening; it was a question of principle with him, and one that I like to remember. 'Never give a woman away, Bunny,' he used to say; and he said it again to-night, but with a heavy cloud upon him, as though his chivalry was sorely tried.

'That's all right,' said I, 'if you're not going to be given away yourself.'

'That's just it, Bunny! That's just – –'

The words were out of him, it was too late to recall them. I had hit the nail upon the head.

'So she threatened you,' I said, 'did she?'

'I didn't say so,' he replied coldly.

'And she is mated with a clown!' I pursued.

'How she ever married him,' he admitted, 'is a mystery to me.'

'It always is,' said I, the wise man for once, and rather enjoying the *rôle*. 'Southern blood?'

'Spanish.'

'She'll be pestering you to run off with her, old chap,' said I.

Raffles was pacing the room. He stopped in his stride for half a second. So she had begun pestering him already! It is wonderful how acute any fool can be in the affairs of his friend. But Raffles resumed his walk without a syllable, and I retreated to safer ground.

'So you sent her to Earl's Court,' I mused aloud; and at last he smiled.

'You'll be interested to hear, Bunny,' said he, 'that I'm now living in Seven Dials, and Bill Sikes couldn't hold a farthing dip to me. Bless you, she had my old police record at her fingers' ends, but it was fit to frame compared with the one I gave her. I had sunk as low as they dig. I divided my nights between the open parks and a thieves' kitchen in Seven Dials. If I were decently dressed it was because I had stolen the suit down the Thames Valley beat the night before last. I was on my way back when first that sleepy square and then her open window proved too much for me. You should have heard me beg her to let me push on to the devil in my own way; there I spread myself, for I meant every word; but I swore the final stage would be a six-foot drop.'

'You did lay it on,' said I.

'It was necessary, and that had its effect. She let me go. But at the last moment she said she didn't believe I was so black as I painted myself, and then there was the balcony scene you missed.'

So that was all. I could not help telling him that he had got out of it better than he deserved for ever getting in. Next moment I regretted the remark.

'If I have got out of it,' said Raffles doubtfully. 'We are dreadfully near neighbours, and I can't move in a minute, with old Theobald taking a grave view of my case. I suppose I had better lie low, and thank the gods again for putting her off the scent for the time being.'

No doubt our conversation was carried beyond this point, but it certainly was not many minutes later, nor had we left the subject, when the electric bell thrilled us both to a sudden silence.

'The doctor?' I queried, hope fighting with my horror.

'It was a single ring.'

'The last post?'

'You know he knocks, and it's long past his time.'

The electric bell rang again, but now as though it never would stop.

'You go, Bunny,' said Raffles, with decision. His eyes were sparkling. His smile was firm.

'What am I to say?'

'If it's the lady let her in.'

It was the lady, still in her evening cloak, with her fine dark head half hidden by the hood, and an engaging contempt of appearances upon her angry face. She was even handsomer than I had thought, and her beauty of a bolder type, but she was also angrier than I had anticipated when I came so readily to the door. The passage into which it opened was an exceedingly narrow one, as I have often said, but I never dreamt of barring this woman's way, though not a word did she stoop to say to me. I was only too glad to flatten myself against the wall, as the rustling fury strode past me into the lighted room with the open door.

'So this is your thieves' kitchen!' she cried, in high-pitched scorn.

I was on the threshold myself, and Raffles glanced towards me with raised eyebrows.

'I have certainly had better quarters in my day,' said he, 'but you need not call them absurd names before my man.'

'Then send your "man" about his business,' said Jacques Saillard, with an unpleasant stress upon the word indicated.

But when the door was shut I heard Raffles assuring her that I knew nothing, that he was a real invalid overcome by a sudden mad temptation, and all he had told her of his life a lie to hide his whereabouts, but all he was telling her now she could prove for herself without leaving that building. It seemed, however, that she had proved it already by going first to the porter below stairs. Yet I do not think she cared one atom which story was the truth.

'So you thought I could pass you in your chair,' she said, 'or ever in this world again, without hearing from my heart that it was you!'

II

'Bunny,' said Raffles, 'I'm awfully sorry, old chap, but you've got to go.'

It was some weeks since the first untimely visitation of Jacques Saillard, but there had been many others at all hours of the day, while Raffles had been induced to pay at least one to her studio in the neighbouring square. These intrusions he had endured at first with an air of humorous resignation which imposed upon me less than he imagined. The woman meant well, he said, after all, and could be trusted to keep his secret loyally. It was plain to me, however, that Raffles did not trust her, and that his pretence upon the point was a deliberate pose to conceal the extent to which she had him in her power. Otherwise there would have been little point in hiding anything from the one person in possession of the cardinal secret of his identity. But Raffles thought it worth his while to hoodwink Jacques Saillard in the subsidiary matter of his health, in which Dr Theobald lent him unwitting assistance, and, as we have seen, to impress upon her that I was actually his attendant, and as ignorant of his past as the doctor himself. 'So you're all right, Bunny,' he had assured me; 'she thinks you knew nothing the other night. I told you she wasn't a clever woman outside her work. But hasn't she a will!' I told Raffles it was very considerate of him to keep me out of it, but that it seemed to me like tying up the bag when the cat had escaped. His reply was an admission that one must be on the defensive with such a woman and in such a case. Soon after this, Raffles, looking far from well, fell back upon his own last line of defence, namely, his bed; and now, as always in the end, I could see some sense in his subtleties, since it was comparatively easy for me to turn even Jacques Saillard from the door, with Dr Theobald's explicit injunctions, and with my own honesty unquestioned. So for a day we had peace once more. Then came letters, then the doctor again and again, and finally my dismissal in the incredible words which have necessitated these explanations.

'Go?' I echoed. 'Go where?'

'It's that ass Theobald,' said Raffles. 'He insists.'

'On my going altogether?'

He nodded.

'And you mean to let him have his way?'

I had no language for my mortification and disgust, though neither was as yet quite so great as my surprise. I had foreseen almost every conceivable consequence of the mad act which brought all this trouble to pass, but a voluntary division between Raffles and me had certainly never entered my calculations. Nor could I think that it had occurred to him before our egregious doctor's last visit this very morning. Raffles had looked irritated as he broke the news to me from his pillow, and now there was some sympathy in the way he sat up in bed, as though he felt the thing himself.

'I am obliged to give in to the fellow,' said he. 'He's saving me from my friend, and I'm bound to humour him. But I can tell you that we've been arguing about you for the last half-hour, Bunny. It was no use; the idiot has had his knife in you from the first; and he wouldn't see me through on any other conditions.'

'So he is going to see you through, is he?'

'It tots up to that,' said Raffles, looking at me rather hard. 'At all events he has come to my rescue for the time being, and it's for me to manage the rest. You don't know what it has been, Bunny, these last few weeks; and gallantry forbids that I should tell you even now. But would you rather elope against your will, or have your continued existence made known to the world in general and the police in particular? That is practically the problem which I have had to solve, and the temporary solution was to fall ill. As a matter of fact I am ill; and now what do you think? I owe it to you to tell you, Bunny, though it goes against the grain. She would take me "to the dear, warm underworld, where the sun really shines," and she would "nurse me back to life and love!' The artistic temperament is a fearsome thing. Bunny, in a woman with the devil's own will!'

Raffles tore up the letter from which he had read these piquant extracts, and lay back on the pillow, with the tired air of the veritable invalid which he seemed able to assume at will. But for once he did look as though bed were the best place for him; and I used the fact as an argument for my own retention in defiance of Dr Theobald. The town was full of typhoid, I said, and certainly that autumnal scourge was in the air. Did he want me to leave him at the very moment when he might be sickening for a serious illness?

'You know I don't, my good fellow,' said Raffles wearily; 'but Theobald does, and I can't afford to go against him now. Not that I really care what happens to me now that that woman knows I'm in the land of the living; she'll let it out, to a dead certainty, and at the best there'll be a hue and cry, which is the very thing I have escaped all these years. Now, what I want you to do is to go and take some quiet place somewhere, and then let me know, so that I may have a port in the storm when it breaks.'

'Now you're talking!' I cried, recovering my spirits. 'I thought you meant to go and drop a fellow altogether.'

'Exactly the sort of thing you would think,' rejoined Raffles, with a contempt that was welcome enough after my late alarm. 'No, my dear rabbit, what you've got to do is to make a new burrow for us both. Try down the Thames, in some quiet nook that a literary man would naturally select. I've often thought that more use might be made of a boat, while the family are at dinner, than there ever has been yet. If Raffles is to come to life, old chap, he shall go a-Raffling for all he's worth! There's something to be done with a bicycle, too. Try Ham Common or Roehampton, or some such sleepy hollow a trifle off the line; and say you're expecting your brother from the Colonies.'

Into this arrangement I entered without the slightest hesitation, for we had funds enough to carry it out on a comfortable scale, and Raffles placed a sufficient share at my disposal for the nonce. Moreover, I for one was only too glad to seek fresh fields and pastures new – a phrase which I determined to interpret literally in my choice of fresh surroundings. I was tired of our submerged life in the poky little flat, especially now that we had money enough for better things. I myself had of late had dark dealings with the receivers, with the result that poor Lord Ernest Belville's successes were now indeed ours. Subsequent complications had been the more galling on that account, while the wanton way in which they had been created was the most irritating reflection of all. But it had brought its own punishment upon Raffles, and I fancied the lesson would prove salutary when we again settled down.

'If ever we do, Bunny!' said he, as I took his hand and told him how I was already looking forward to the time.

'But of course we will,' I cried, concealing the resentment at leaving him which his tone and appearance renewed in my breast.

'I'm not so sure of it,' he said gloomily. 'I'm in somebody's clutches, and I've got to get out of them first.'

'I'll sit tight until you do.'

'Well,' he said, 'if you don't see me in ten days you never will.'

'Only ten days?' I echoed. 'That's nothing at all.'

'A lot may happen in ten days,' replied Raffles, in the same depressing tone, so very depressing in him; and with that he held out his hand a second time, and dropped mine suddenly after as sudden a pressure for farewell.

I left the flat in considerable dejection after all, unable to decide whether Raffles was really ill, or only worried as I knew him to be. And at the foot of the stairs the author of my dismissal, that confounded Theobald, flung open his door and waylaid me.

'Are you going?' he demanded.

The traps in my hands proclaimed that I was, but I dropped them at his feet to have it out with him then and there.

'Yes,' I answered fiercely, 'thanks to you!'

'Well, my good fellow,' he said, his full-blooded face lightening and softening at the same time as though a load were off his mind, 'it's no pleasure to me to deprive any man of his billet, but you never were a nurse, and you know that as well as I do.'

I began to wonder what he meant, and how much he did know, and my speculations kept me silent. 'But come in here a moment,' he continued, just as I decided that he knew nothing at all. And leading me into his minute consulting-room, Dr Theobald solemnly presented me with a sovereign by way of compensation which I pocketed as solemnly, and with as much gratitude as if I had not fifty of them distributed over my person as it was. The good fellow had quite forgotten my social status, about which he himself had been so particular at our earliest interview; but he had never accustomed himself to treat me as a gentleman, and I do not suppose he had been improving his memory by the tall tumbler which I saw him poke behind a photograph-frame as we entered.

'There's one thing I should like to know before I go,' said I, turning suddenly on the doctor's mat, 'and that is whether Mr Maturin is really ill or not!'

I meant, of course, at the present moment, but Dr Theobald braced himself like a recruit at the drill-sergeant's voice.

'Of course he is,' he snapped – 'so ill as to need a nurse who can nurse, by way of a change.'

With that his door shut in my face, and I had to go my way, in the dark as to whether he had mistaken my meaning, and was telling me a lie, or not.

But for my misgivings upon this point I might have extracted some very genuine enjoyment out of the next few days. I had decent clothes to my back, with money, as I say, in most of the pockets, and more freedom to spend it than was possible in the constant society of a man whose personal liberty depended on a universal supposition that he was dead. Raffles was as bold as ever, and I as fond of him, but whereas he would run any risk in a professional exploit, there were many innocent recreations still open to me which would have been sheer madness in him. He could not even watch a match, from the sixpenny seats, at Lord's Cricket-ground, where the Gentlemen were every year in a worse way without him. He never travelled by train, and dining out was a risk only to be run with some ulterior object in view. In fact, much as it had changed, Raffles could no longer show his face with perfect impunity in any quarter or at any hour. Moreover, after the lesson he had now learnt, I foresaw increased caution on his part in this respect. But I myself was under no such perpetual disadvantage, and, while what was good enough for Raffles was quite good enough for me, so long as we were together, I saw no harm in profiting by the present opportunity of 'doing myself well'.

Such were my reflections on the way to Richmond in a hansom cab. Richmond had struck us both as the best centre of operations in search of the suburban retreat which Raffles wanted, and by road, in a well-appointed, well-selected hansom, was certainly the most agreeable way of getting there. In a week or ten days Raffles was to write to me at the Richmond post office, but for at least a week I should be 'on my own'.

It was not an unpleasant sensation as I leant back in the comfortable hansom, and rather to one side, in order to have a good look at myself in the bevelled mirror that is almost as great an improvement in these vehicles as the rubber tyres. Really I was not an ill-looking youth, if one may call oneself such at the age of thirty. I could lay no claim either to the striking cast of countenance or to the peculiar charm of expression which made the face of Raffles like no other in the world. But this very distinction was in itself a danger, for its impression was indelible, whereas I might still have been mistaken for a hundred other young fellows at large in London. Incredible as it may appear to the moralists, I had sustained no external hall-mark by my term of imprisonment, and I am vain enough to believe that the evil which I did had not a separate existence in my face. This afternoon, indeed, I was struck by the purity of my fresh complexion and rather depressed by the general innocence of the visage which peered into mine from the little mirror. My straw-coloured moustache, grown in the flat after a protracted holiday, preserved the most disappointing dimensions, and was still invisible in certain lights without wax. So far from discerning the desperate criminal who has 'done time' once, and deserved it over and over again, the superior but superficial observer might have imagined that he detected a certain element of folly in my face.

At all events, it was not the face to shut the doors of a first-class hotel against me, without accidental evidence of a more explicit kind, and it was with no little satisfaction that I directed the man to drive to the Star and Garter. I also told him to go through Richmond Park, though he warned me that it would add considerably to the distance and to his fare. It was autumn, and it struck me that the tints would be fine. And I had learnt from Raffles to appreciate such things, even amid the excitement of an audacious enterprise.

If I dwell upon my appreciation of this occasion it is because, like most pleasures, it was exceedingly short-lived. I was very comfortable at the Star and Garter, which was so empty that I had a room worthy of a prince, where I could enjoy the finest of all views (in patriotic opinion) every morning while I shaved. I walked many miles through the noble park, over the commons of Ham and Wimbledon, and one day as far as that of Esher, where I was forcibly reminded of a service we once rendered to a distinguished resident in this delightful locality. But it was on Ham Common, one of the places which Raffles had mentioned as especially desirable, that I actually found an almost ideal retreat. This was a cottage where I heard, on inquiry, that rooms were to be let in the summer. The landlady, a motherly body, of visible excellence, was surprised indeed at receiving an application for the winter months; but I have generally found that the title of 'author', claimed with an air, explains every little innocent irregularity of conduct or appearance, and even requires something of the kind to carry conviction to the lay intelligence. The present case was one in point, and when I said that I could only write in a room facing north, on mutton chops and milk, with a cold ham in the wardrobe in case of nocturnal inspiration to which I was liable, my literary character was established beyond dispute. I secured the rooms, paid a month's rent in advance at my own request, and moped in them dreadfully until the week was up and Raffles due any day. I explained that the inspiration would not come, and asked abruptly if the mutton was New Zealand.

Thrice had I made fruitless inquiries at the Richmond post office; but on the tenth day I was in and out almost every hour. Not a word was there for me up to the last post at night. Home I trudged to Ham with horrible forebodings, and back again to Richmond after breakfast next morning. Still there was nothing. I could bear it no more. At ten minutes to eleven I was climbing the station stairs at Earl's Court.

It was a wretched morning there, a weeping mist shrouding the long straight street, and clinging to one's face in clammy caresses. I felt how much better it was down at Ham, as I turned into our side street, and saw the flats looming like mountains, the chimney-pots hidden in the mist. At our entrance stood a nebulous conveyance that I took at first for a tradesman's van; to my horror it proved to be a hearse; and all at once the white breath ceased upon my lips.

I had looked up at our windows and the blinds were down!

I rushed within. The doctor's door stood open. I neither knocked nor rang, but found him in his consulting-room with red eyes and a blotchy face. Otherwise he was in solemn black from head to heel.

'Who is dead?' I burst out. 'Who is dead?'

The red eyes looked redder than ever as Dr Theobald opened them at the unwarrantable sight of me; and he was terribly slow in answering. But in the end he did answer, and did not kick me out as he evidently had a mind.

'Mr Maturin,' he said, and sighed like a beaten man.

I said nothing. It was no surprise to me. I had known it all these minutes. Nay, I had dreaded this from the first, had divined it at the last, though to the last also I had refused to entertain my own conviction. Raffles dead! A real invalid after all! Raffles dead, and on the point of burial!

'What did he die of?' I asked, unconsciously drawing on that fund of grim self-control which the weakest of us seem to hold in reserve for real calamity.

'Typhoid,' he answered. 'Kensington is full of it.'

'He was sickening for it when I left, and you knew it, and could get rid of me then!'

'My good fellow, I was obliged to have a more experienced nurse for that very reason.'

The doctor's tone was so conciliatory that I remembered in an instant what a humbug the man was, and became suddenly possessed with the vague conviction that he was imposing upon me now.

'Are you sure it was typhoid at all?' I cried fiercely to his face. 'Are you sure it wasn't suicide – or murder?'

I confess that I can see little point in this speech as I write it down, but it was what I said in a burst of grief and of wild suspicion; nor was it without effect upon Dr Theobald, who turned bright scarlet from his well-brushed hair to his immaculate collar.

'Do you want me to throw you out into the street?' he cried; and all at once I remembered that I had come to Raffles as a perfect stranger, and for his sake might as well preserve that character to the last.

'I beg your pardon,' I said brokenly. 'He was so good to me – I became so attached to him. You forget I am originally of his class.'

'I did forget it,' replied Theobald, looking relieved at my new tone, 'and I beg *your* pardon for doing so. Hush! They are bringing him down. I must have a drink before we start, and you'd better join me.'

There was no pretence about his drink this time, and a pretty stiff one it was, but I fancy my own must have run it hard. In my case it cast a merciful haze over much of the next hour, which I can truthfully describe as one of the most painful of my whole existence. I can have known very little of what I was doing. I only remember finding myself in a hansom, suddenly wondering why it was going so slowly, and once more awaking to the truth. But it was to the truth itself more than to the liquor that I must have owed my dazed condition. My next recollection is of looking down into the open grave, in a sudden passionate anxiety to see the name for myself. It was not the name of my friend, of course, but it was the one under which he had passed for many months.

I was still stupefied by a sense of inconceivable loss, and had not raised my eyes from that which was slowly forcing me to realise what had happened, when there was a rustle at my elbow, and a shower of hothouse flowers passed before me, falling like huge snowflakes where my gaze had rested. I looked up, and at my side stood a majestic figure in deep mourning. The face was carefully veiled, but I was too close not to recognise the masterful beauty whom the world knew as Jacques Saillard. I had no sympathy with her; on the contrary, my blood boiled with the vague conviction that in some way she was responsible for this death. Yet she was the only woman present – there were not half a dozen of us altogether – and her flowers were the only flowers.

The melancholy ceremony was over, and Jacques Saillard had departed in a funeral brougham, evidently hired for the occasion. I had watched her drive away, and the sight of my own cabman, making signs to me through the fog, had suddenly reminded me that I had bidden him to wait. I was the last to leave, and had turned my back upon the grave-diggers already at their final task, when a hand fell lightly but firmly upon my shoulder.

'I don't want to make a scene in a cemetery," said a voice, in a not unkindly, almost confidential whisper. 'Will you get into your own cab and come quietly?'

'Who on earth are you?' I exclaimed.

I now remembered having seen the fellow hovering about during the funeral, and subconsciously taking him for the undertaker's head man. He had certainly that appearance, and even now I could scarcely believe that he was anything else.

'My name won't help you,' he said pityingly. 'But you will guess where I come from when I tell you I have a warrant for your arrest.'

My sensations at this announcement may not be believed,

but I solemnly declare that I have seldom experienced so fierce a satisfaction. Here was a new excitement in which to drown my grief; here was something to think about; and I should be spared the intolerable experience of a solitary return to the little place at Ham. It was as though I had lost a limb and someone had struck me so hard in the face that the greater agony was forgotten. I got into the hansom without a word, my captor following at my heels, and giving his own directions to the cabman before taking his seat. The word 'station' was the only one I caught, and I wondered whether it was to be Bow Street again. My companion's next words, however, or rather the tone in which he uttered them, destroyed my capacity for idle speculation.

'Mr Maturin!' said he. 'Mr Maturin, indeed!'

'Well,' said I, 'what about him?'

'Do you think we don't know who he was?'

'Who was he?' I asked defiantly.

'You ought to know,' said he. 'You got locked up through him the other time, too. His favourite name was Raffles, then.'

'It was his real name,' I said indignantly. 'And he has been dead for years.'

My captor simply chuckled.

'He's at the bottom of the sea, I tell you!'

But I do not know why I should have told him with such spirit, for what could it matter to Raffles now? I did not think; instinct was still stronger than reason, and, fresh from his funeral, I had taken up the cudgels for my dead friend as though he were still alive. Next moment I saw this for myself, and my tears came nearer the surface than they had been yet; but the fellow at my side laughed outright.

'Shall I tell you something else?' said he.

'As you like.'

'He's not even at the bottom of that grave! He's no more dead than you or I, and a sham burial is his latest piece of villainy!'

I doubt whether I could have spoken if I had tried. I did not try. I had no use for speech. I did not even ask him if he were sure, I was so sure myself. It was all as plain to me as riddles usually are when one has the answer. The doctor's alarms, his unscrupulous venality, the simulated illness, my own dismissal, each fitted in its obvious place, and not even the last had power as yet to mar my joy in the one central fact to which all the rest were as tapers to the sun.

'He is alive!' I cried. 'Nothing else matters – he is alive!'

At last I did ask whether they had got him too; but thankful as I was for the greater knowledge, I confess that I did not much care what answer I received. Already I was figuring out how much we might each get, and how old we should be when we came out. But my companion tilted his hat to the back of his head, at the same time putting his face close to mine, and compelling my scrutiny. And my answer, as you have already guessed, was the face of Raffles himself, superbly disguised (but less superbly than his voice), and yet so thinly that I should have known him in a trice had I not been too miserable in the beginning to give him a second glance.

Jacques Saillard had made his life impossible, and this was the one escape. Raffles had bought the doctor for a thousand pounds, and the doctor had bought a 'nurse' of his own kidney, on his own account; me, for some reason, he would not trust; he had insisted upon my dismissal as an essential preliminary to his part in the conspiracy. Here the details were half humorous, half gruesome, each in turn as Raffles told me the story. At one period he had been very daringly drugged indeed, and, in his own words, 'as dead as a man need be'; but he had left strict instructions that nobody but the nurse and 'my devoted physician' should 'lay a finger on me' afterwards; and by virtue of this proviso a library of books (largely acquired for the occasion) had been impiously interred at Kensal Green. Raffles had definitely undertaken not to trust me with the secret, and, but for my untoward appearance at the funeral (which he had attended for his own final satisfaction), I was assured and am convinced that he would have kept his promise to the letter. In explaining this he gave me the one explanation I desired, and in another moment we turned into Praed Street, Paddington.

'And I thought you said Bow Street!' said I. 'Are you coming straight down to Richmond with me?'

'I may as well,' said Raffles, 'though I did mean to get my kit first, so as to start in fair and square as the long-lost brother from the bush. That's why I hadn't written. The function was a day later than I calculated. I was going to write to-night.'

'But what are we to do?' said I, hesitating when he had paid the cab. 'I have been playing the Colonies for all they are worth!'

'Oh, I've lost my luggage,' said he, 'or a wave came into my cabin and spoilt every stitch, or I had nothing fit to bring ashore. We'll settle that in the train.'